Liam F...

BLIZZARD KIN

a novel

INDELIBLE

PUBLISHING

Published in Canada by
Indelible Publishing
A division of Indelible Moving Images Inc.
www.indelible.ca
Toronto, Ontario, Canada
© 1994, 2003, Liam Kiernan

Cover rendering: Nicolas Préault   Concept: Séamus O'Doyle

All Rights Reserved

The contents of this novel are completely fictitious. Any similarity of names or characterizations to actual persons living or dead; or of any place, locale, incident or setting is purely coincidental. This work is solely a product of the writer's imagination. The author has asserted his moral rights.

Based on the screenplay 'Northwest Terrorstories' © 1991, Liam Kiernan

National Library of Canada Cataloguing in Publication

Kiernan, Liam, 1960–
Blizzard Kin

Freshly revised, this novel was previously only released in Canada as a limited edition 1994 MMP pressing entitled "Northwest Terrorstories; a novel"

ISBN 0-9697061-2-X

I. Title.

PS8571.I376N6 2003   C813'.54   C2002-906073-7
PR9199.3.K4289N6 2003

Manufactured and bound in Canada
First Canadian printing– MMP, March 2003

cover art: Akpaliapik, Manasie   Canadian; Inuit   1955–   Arctic Bay
"Respecting the Circle" ©1989 (adaptation & detail) whalebone
ART GALLERY OF ONTARIO, TORONTO
Gift of Samuel and Esther Sarick, Toronto, 1996

For Gretta & Willie

comments on
Blizzard Kin (pka Northwest Terrorstories);

"Every now and then a book comes along, like James Joyce's *Ulysses*, which leaves the unprepared reader in shock. Let me see if I can do justice to Kiernan's novel by illustrating the depths and shallows of this incredible work, destined to become a cult classic."

Mick Mallon—the Arctic Reader, *Above and Beyond*, NWT

"... incorporates a strong setting and story premise ... the novel warrants keen reading."

Canadian Book Review Annual

"... beautifully weaves a story combining the spiritual beliefs of the Inuit people with the cold and calculating bureaucrats of Canada. Kiernan effectively blends a mosaic of people and events ... an intricate tale of deception and self revelation."

Directors Guild of Canada National News

" ... looks, sounds and smells like a thriller, ... plenty of ingenuity and inventiveness."

Books in Canada

Innumerable thanks and appreciation go out to a gracious freelance editing staff, my technical advisors, associates and friends, who helped me get this novel into fit shape—mostly by throwing it across a spectrum of rooms to get it to bounce—it eventually did.

They are:

John and Jill for their technical expertise in mining engineering and geology. M. I. Tookalukangleent, John and Mary, Claudette, Nicolas, Kelly, Gloria, Faye, Elizabeth, Felicia, Sean, Carlo, Alan, Gina, Howard, Melody, Gretta and Willie, Luch, Donna, Julio, for their tremendous moral support, insightful editing tips and suggestions,—*and good pitching arms*.

Hats-off especially to my great friend, John Hopperton, who over several weeks, drained himself and many a pen with his generous commentaries. Another special thanks goes to Manasiah Akpaliapik who in 1989 carved into form, images and intentions which I coincidentally attempted to sculpt with words in 1993. I was thrilled to come across his marvellous and compelling sculpture known as "Respecting the Circle" at the AGO in 1998 and after a few moments of bewilderment, imagined the possibility of a delicate kinship between the purity in the natural elements of his creation and the alloy in the steel-wheels of my story. *Perhaps they would get along*, I thought.

Cheers, y'all

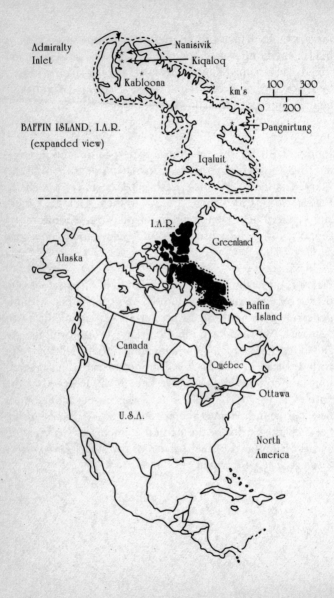

Admiralty
Inlet

Nanisivik

Kiqaloq

Kabloona

km's

100   300

0   200

BAFFIN ISLAND, I.A.R.
(expanded view)

Pangnirtung

Iqaluit

I.A.R.

Greenland

Alaska

Baffin
Island

Canada

Québec

Ottawa

U.S.A.

North
America

BLIZZARD
KIN

one

'PERLERORNEQ,' HE MUMBLED to himself in Inuktitut, his Inuit tongue.

Jag sorted through some antique photographs which he'd spread across the top of his old wooden desk. His weathered hands foraged through the fanned-out photos under the orange tinted light of the whale-oil lamp which was perched on the corner of his desk.

'The weight of life,' he repeated in English. His coal-black eyes surveyed the deteriorated collection of memories.

The cold late-October air crept into the mobile trailer office from a hole in the floor which Jag had refused to have repaired. The hole was inadequately covered by a small square of plywood, draped over with a fox pelt.

It was his connection with the *spirit of the wind* he'd say, to any nosy white engineers there at the mining camp. The whites all thought he was off his rocker, given the biting cold of the high arctic. He was given the courtesy of privacy as he *was* the superintendent, and if he preferred to freeze his ass off with his spirit friends—so be it, they'd say.

He looked down at the two dead engineers on the floor of his narrow hallway. He stared blankly at the harpoon sticking out of the engineer's chest and the bloodied seal club which laid beside the head of the other white.

As the crow flies he thought to himself.

It was going on his second year as superintendent of Kabloona. This was the name of the refurbished gold mine, coined by Jag himself. It meant *white dog*. The mining camp was a pilot program arranged between the Independent Aboriginal Republic and the Government of Canada. It was brokered and managed by Roblaw Inc, an Ottawa-based natural resource management company.

The operation practically ran itself. Jag's posting there (which he petitioned adamantly to have) was to keep an eye on ... *things*. It was a prison boot-camp outfit, and now things were getting out of hand. The I.A.R., as the Republic was commonly called, generated much needed revenue from the boot-camp venture. It fed the slowly evolving self-reliant economy.

Jag looked longingly at the photographs, chanting away to an unusual melody. A breeze crept into his office and the oil-lamp flickered. His graying hair rippled subtly with the fleeting wisp of air. His leathered face puckered slightly, acknowledging the presence which he'd called.

Without breaking the stride of his concentration, he reached out over his desk and picked up a small cup, lifting it to his mouth and swallowing back the dregs of his elixir.

Jag's zeal for the resurgence of the bygone traditions of his Inuit ancestors had become a daily rite. An intoxication in which he'd indulge for many hours of the day.

By rote, he lifted his curved whalebone, semi-circular sunglasses to his temples and slid them on. The carved eye-slits afforded him a pinpointed view. This view, bolstered his meditative focus, allowing him to ponder on points of interest as he scoped them.

Things he had seen hundreds, even thousands of times, came into fresh perspective in his rapture. The hand crafted harpoon—which only minutes ago had hung on the wall; the feathered masks, the horn of the whale known as a narwhal, and the seal club. All of these vestiges spoke to him with secret whispers of astonishing feats, of incredible journeys, of successful hunts and ample prey.

He looked at the sinew stitching of his caribou parka, which had been sewn together by his mother long ago, and which was worn by his deceased father on many hunting expeditions.

In this trance, visions and sounds of the past reveled in his mind. Swirling round and round in his head, were images of carefree living, of prey offering itself to the hunters' bow, inexhaustible laughter and family peace. Self reliance, with no concern for the future—no Inuit word for the future.

A frown slowly crept over his lined face. The bliss subsided, giving way to apprehension, which smothered his glee like frost. Each affirmation of traditional Inuit strengths of the blood and spirit, salted the wounds of the modern Inuit's addictions and weaknesses. A plight of the innocent, the Inuit people were wronged from the start. Several generations had fallen prey to family fragmentation, spiritual erosion and lies. Big, fat, *white* lies.

To Jag, the trickling resurgence of *tradition* wafting through the I.A.R., was just an ointment for a cancer which, to him, required amputation and a tourniquet. The proof was in the hallway.

An Eastern Arctic Nunavut land claim in '92, cemented their quest for self government. In '99 they controlled their own affairs and were no longer a part of Canada's Northwest Territories. In 2005, the Qikiqtaaluk region cleaved itself from Nunavut. Even now in 2007, after two years as the I.A.R.—an internationally recognized country, the leaches still threatened to drain their blood and spirit. He looked over at the bodies. The odour of their blood repulsed him.

There was a knock at the door. He had sent an urgent

message requesting his nephew Perq to come to the trailer. There was a duty to be done, requiring skill, dedication, and a tight lip. The door opened ...

§

Only hours before the whole mess had begun, Jag was sitting at his desk and day-dreaming through his photo collection, when the clattering of the snow bus tractor in the distance, hastened a sobering return to reality. As the bus neared, its bright headlights obliquely shone through his office windows. The rattling diesel motor idled, and the swatch of light held tight with the varied surfaces on which it shone. The audible signature idle he had come to recognize as the harbinger of wretchedness, grated on his nerves.

Lifting his hand, he pressed his index finger into his forehead almost as though to plug the hole which had punctured the musings he entertained. Even in light of separation, the Republic's independence proved no potent inoculation against foreign influence which was manifesting itself at Kabloona.

He pressed harder to thwart the deflation of his spirit. The rumblings got louder, and he pressed harder. With a scowl, he jerked his finger from his forehead.

The racket of the snow bus brought home the painful reality. It stuck in his brain. He hated the residue of the white curse! This loathing pulsed like a light in his mind. With each new inmate, came a twist of the dagger. The growing problem eclipsed an elusive solution. He looked at the harpoon on the wall.

In a fit of intolerance, Jag pulled himself from the desk.

He stood up, removed the whalebone glasses, and turned in the direction of the clamor.

He walked to the west window of his compartmentalized trailer office, in amongst the shadowed communications cubby which hosted an array of neglected technological toys. These instruments, according to company policy, remained powered up at all times, regardless of use. It was as though this foreign electronic connection boasted diplomatic immunity.

The L.E.D.-lit cubby seemed a surreal, miniature airport. The surrounding rows and pockets of multi-coloured instrument-panel lighting seemed to simulate control towers and runways—they were in a way, such.

Jag positioned himself at the window allowing his head to rest against his well defined muscular forearm, which he stretched across the window's frame. Sitting back against a computer stand, he eased himself down, nestling his backside on a protruding shelf which was braced and solid.

Inadvertently, his posterior leaned on the keyboard, depressing a cluster of keys, and instigating a chain reaction of repeated letters on the screen.

Outside in the twilight at the main gate, Jag could see the snow bus filled with its belligerent load. He detected their disdain as the transferee's had their blindfolds promptly withdrawn by his nephew Perquanoak. He had met the prison transfer plane five hours prior at the air-strip in Nanisivik, a town of nine-hundred, located at the northern tip of Baffin Island.

Jag was oblivious to the beeping which filled the room. The computer attempted to draw attention to itself, as the screen was drowning with letters. Jag however, had conditioned himself to ignore the frippery of the electronic tenants, since they whirred into action independently, and at the oddest times.

The satellite computer link was a circle unto itself, the

short-wave radio talked to itself, and the FAX machine received itself. Layer upon layer of FAXED materials littered the catch basin. All these gadgets were scorned by Jag to be left alone to change their own diapers, as he saw it.

Jag's breath climbed the half frosted window. Each breath like the same wave cresting over and over itself, across the glass pane. He gazed in a state of anoesis towards the snow bus, and his nephew, both delayed at the main gate.

Perquanoak had been taken under Jag's wing, after the boy's trying bout of alcohol and substance abuse, mixed with over-nights at the Yellowknife jail.

At eighteen, he had habitually terrorized his parents and family, taken up the life of a gasoline-sniffing thief, and had attempted suicide five times. Jag, rather than seeing his for-lorn nephew subjected to futile therapy and un-enforceable probation, asked that the young man be sent to him at Kabloona for an apprenticeship in shamanism.

Now twenty, Perq, as he was called, was enthused at the suggestion, since he, as a young boy, had remembered his uncle Jag, and his mystical bag of tricks. Perq knew his uncle was a rebel with a cause. This burned inside his own belly, but was frowned upon as reckless in his case.

This opportunity was like a heavenly door prize to him. A game show with a guaranteed outcome. An open door through which he would enter as a rabble-rouser, and emerge as a firebrand with wisdom which would garner him power—power, respect, and all its trappings.

All this could be his for no money down, and no payments ever. No judges, no juries, no pressure. The one and only expenditure required, was from his will. His will to sacrifice one thing for another. His free will to change. It was a glam-orous offer.

Jag had somewhat of a local hero celebrity status in the I.A.R. He was chaos with structure to Perq. An upstart, who immersed himself in local and regional government affairs, and who held sway during the separation process. Jag was regarded far and wide as a powerful shaman, whose insights thwarted outside influences. He was a viable check on foreign interference. He resented the greed of foreign interests, especially if it was represented by a native son, the ilk of Gaar Injugarjuk, a foreign national who made good in the competitive white-world of the south. Gaar was the lawyer who acted as a go-between, representing Roblaw Inc in the negotiations setting up the camp. To Jag, he was nothing but a quick-change artist.

Jag was a back-benching pariah, who accused some I.A.R. politicians of posturing to foreign interests and industrial conglomerates. A true reactionary with considerable support, he was designated the IAR's Chief Superintendent over the Kabloona pilot mining program. Jag was front, right, and center in the off-kilter operation, and a hero worth emulating. Here was the chance to ride the coat-tails of this god, from whom one day, the coat would be passed down. If not, he would take it.

After weeks of regimented and intensely sickening detox, Perq proved a willing and worthy apprentice to Jag. In time, he had learned to develop and harness his hidden talents, and had soon begun to demonstrate leadership abilities.

Perq became eager to learn the ins-and-outs of everyone's job at Kabloona. He garnered an understanding of the basics of mining, elevator and shaft maintenance, but mostly, he focused on blasting. The blasting technician's job was by far the most exciting.

Eight months had gone by and Jag decided to get Perq on the Roblaw Industries payroll. He nominated Perq for a position in administration. As would be expected shortly after, Jag designated Perq as the Assistant Superintendent of the Kabloona prison mining camp. The assignment was a compliment to the personable youth.

He would tie his hair back in a pony-tail when he was engaged in company business, exposing his well defined jaw, his full lips with the hint of a mustache, and slim yet lively, dark-pooled eyes. Well liked, and seldom slandered, he bore his responsibility proudly, winking slyly after giving work orders to the inner circle of camp personnel, as though there were a secret agenda afoot, or some mischief in the making.

The snow bus vibrated incessantly. Jag had seen little of Perq lately, thinking that perhaps his disciplined lessons had been a bit too harsh for the impressionable young man.

He touched the cold window with the palm of his free hand, and withdrew it, leaving a small clear patch in the shape of his palm. He peered through, looking on at his nephew in the bus at the gate.

It saddened Jag that his nephew decided to insulate himself more and more from his mentor, choosing to deliver and fetch the inmates to and from the plane, rather than pursuing his studies, which had been his passion. If he were home-sick or depressed, surely by now he would have made his feelings known to his own uncle!

Perq's reticence annoyed Jag slightly, but had not yet driven him to confront the situation.

From the window, Jag viewed Perq moving up and down the bus with a clipboard in his gloved hand. It perplexed him to see Perquanoak spending so much time on banal errands. With a spring in his step, he appeared amenable with the job at hand.

Perq chatted with the bus driver, then opened a window and called out to a guard at the gate, who, after taking a head count of the new inmates, was eagerly changing the population number on the large sign standing independent of the gate. It was erected for government visitors and V.I.P. guests. The inmates were usually referred to as "trog", an un-official term which caught on and stuck. It stemmed from "troglodyte" or *brute*, and alluded to the villains and hoodlums in the prison population. No one could remember who coined the term, but most liked the ring of it.

Perquanoak stepped down from the warm bus, and the driver shut the door. He approached Nick Kuujjarviq, the gate guard, who was fumbling with the numbers to be hung on the sign. It was an innocent enough trifle, which excited the guard no end, and which brought pity to Perq's heart. Nick begged patience from Perq, who obliged him. The unfortunate sot managed, after much ado, to hang only the zero on the end of two hundred and ten.

Perq waited, patiently amused behind the guard, who suddenly stepped back from the sign to check his work under the illumination of the lamps of the bus. He collided with Perq and sent them both falling to the icy ground. The playing-card sized numbers were strewn in all directions. A trace of a smile emerged from Jag's lips as he looked on.

Perq sat up, and burst out laughing. He laughed so hard that his gut forced him down flat on his back in the snow. It was evident to Jag, that his nephew was holding something back from him. Perq had been confiding less and less with Jag. He thought about the subtle mood swings he began to detect in his nephew.

The fallen guard staggered to his feet, rubbing his head. He looked at Perq, then to the sign, over at the bus, and then around at all the scattered numbers. The sign read, *population "0"*. The guard began to laugh with Perq. They both pointed at the sign and joined together in a contagious round of laughter.

The new inmates were annoyed at the display, looking on from the bus' windows. An inmate pointed at a small sign fastened to the fence which read:

"*DO NOT FEED THE ANIMALS!*"

Jag recognized the inmates' confusion. It was common for

fresh prisoners to get the feeling that by *animals*, the sign painter was alluding to them. The new trogs investigated further, crowding the left side of the snow bus, and gawking out. The larger sign read:

"Roblaw Natural Resource Management Industries
in cooperation with the Independent Aboriginal Republic
and the Government of Canada
welcomes you to Kabloona,
the 3R Capital Works Barter Agreement's pilot program.
Our mandate:
Rehabilitate, Re-educate, and Release,
instated and opened November 1, 2005
Designation: Kabloona Prison Mining camp
Superintendent: Najagneq
Population: .. 0"

Nick fumbled with the numbers as he gathered them from the ground with Perq's help. The guard fixed the mistake, by adding the *two* and *one* to the sign, making the population including the new trogs, total two hundred and ten.

Large snow flurries had begun to drop from the sky and were swept along by a biting wind. This was a precursor to the blizzard which was coming. Jag was grateful to the kindred spirits and his familiars, who ensured Perq's safe return to Kabloona. He would chant a song later, in gratitude.

Perq slapped Nick heartily on the back, walked over to the doors of the bus and re-boarded it. Nick slid back the gate, and the bus proceeded through with a clatter and a moan.

Jag remained at the window, and looked longingly at the Aurora Borealis, which twinkled and waved about in the sky. Like a gauze curtain, the diffusing effect of the falling snow softened his outlook. The sky and the arctic landscape were glorious. Both had a soothing analgesic effect on him. It was primordial. Past the gate of this circus, time stood still.

In the high Arctic, at 72° 22' north, and 81° 30' west, the crisp dry air offered a range of vision relatively un-obscured by dust particles or haze. It was a splendid October twilight to behold. The transitional twilight would soon give way to total darkness, remaining so, for the next six months. The shadow of the gold mine's head frame ominously loomed across the icy ground, stretching over the fence and beyond.

'Kabloona,' Jag uttered to himself. Kabloona was an economic boon to the IAR and Canada, but was no benediction to Jag, or his followers.

Jag rose from the corner of the desk, and detected the computer screen movement with the corner of his eye. He couldn't fathom the screen, which was filled with rows upon rows of jumbled letters, hyphenated with the occasional spasmodic cluster of mixed letters. He reached up, and grasped a feathered mask which hung on the darkened wall. Jag suspended the mask over the nonsensical screen, and left the cubby.

He proceeded through the dimly lit kitchenette en route to his desk. The encoutrements of the kitchen were as they were when Jag arrived at his posting at Kabloona, two years prior. The kitchenette was unused, the communications cubby, ignored; his bed, un-slept in. The mine was over forty years old, having been drained of water and refurbished for the boot-camp program. The whites often thought that Jag was more antiquated than the mine.

He never wore a watch, or hung a wall calendar. He wrote no reports, never lifted the radio to his lips, nor had he ever required supplies for the modern toilet outfitted in his trailer. No one could ever remember having seen Jag eat or drink. He was a loner. No one had ever gotten familiar with Jag, except for his nephew apprentice, Perq.

Jag inherently wielded the respect of the Inuit contingent

at Kabloona, who took his word as law, and his will as their command.

Jag reinstated himself at his desk, and slowly slid his glasses back on. No sooner had he picked up where he had left off, a muffled knock at his trailer door disturbed him. Jag's demeanor lightened, expecting Perq to walk through the door.

The door opened with a creak. Jag's spirit sunk. The door opened full swing, ushering in a stocky engineer named Gordon Frobisham. The engineer peeled back his parka hood with his gloved left hand. A biting gust of cold air quickly burst through the open doorway, pulling the door handle from his grasp.

A photo from Jag's desk took flight in the gust of wind. Frobisham fumbled with the door, finally closing it. It was snowing in Jag's office.

With contempt, Jag looked on at the man, who by all appearances, was a good-natured sort, with short blond hair and glasses which were set against his round face.

Jag began to growl at the untimely intrusion, and awkward display. He acrimoniously began to look around for the photograph.

'Your nephew asked me to drop this in,' Frobisham said, with a Newfoundland accent. 'Perq's a good kid. Y'know, he'd make a good engineer. Likes to talk about physics and things.'

Jag followed Frobisham with his masked eyes, as the man meandered to the far wall to hang the clipboard with some other clipboards on the pegged wall.

Frobisham paused at the wall, looking over the information on the hanging clipboard.

'Is it ever *dark* in here. What a sour bunch, those nine new trogs,' Frobisham offered with indifference.

Jag sat aloof.

'An Islamic terrorist, two first degree murderers, a child molester, kidnapper-extortionist, arsonist, counterfeiter, a pimp, and an armoured car robber! Perq tells me he won't ante-up where the booty is,' Frobisham chuckled, shaking his head. 'He'll make a lot of friends here. I'm sure he'll blab eventually or someone'll pry it out of him.'

There was a deadpan look on Jag's face, which was a response worth heeding.

Jag stood up and looked around his desk for the photo which had blown from the desk. Frobisham looked around the floor and found what Jag was looking for. The large photo was pinned under the heel of his large snow boot. He peeled the photo from the underside of his boot and sheepishly looked up to meet Jag's spurious glare.

Jag reached for the photo from the engineer, who expressed his embarrassment and remorse by shrugging his shoulders, twisting his neck, and raising his eyebrows in rapid succession, as he handed over the sixty year-old relic.

Jag's face dropped at first, then turned to stone while inspecting the damage. Frobisham's boot tread had been indelibly pressed deep into the surface of the photo.

'Sorry,' Frobisham said timidly.

Jag slowly leaned back in his chair, took in a long deep breath of air, and exhaled slowly as he studied the photograph in a charged silence. His eyes darted back and forth across the picture, from behind the eerie slits of the carved glasses.

'I can bring it with me to Yellowknife, and have it airbrushed or ironed, or something. Make it as good as new ... or old—whaddya say?'

Jag scoffed at his offer, bluntly exhaling and sucking his teeth, which were in very good shape considering he'd never seen a dentist in his life.

'You don't say,' Frobisham said, floundering in the cruel silence, rolling his eyes upward, in contempt of Jag's childish behavior. It irked him, that Jag wore the sunglasses through all of this.

As the moment lingered, Frobisham half-entertained the thought of snatching the photo from Jag's hands, tearing the picture into tiny little pieces, taking Jag by the scruff and giving him a swift kick out the door.

Jag darted his eyes up at Frobisham. The fantasy was all too short-lived, as Jag placed the photograph carefully into the drawer, ending the ordeal.

Frobisham kept a stiff upper lip, knowing he had but a couple of short days left in his trimester contract with the turnstile operation, and it's voodoo-king superintendent.

'Their orientation is complete, and they've been put in their barracks?' asked Jag, stiffly.

'Yes—' Frobisham squeaked, managing the curt response to his question, which was a shoehorn intended to wedge him from the office.

'Fine—' Jag replied, as he stood up from his chair, and rudely turned his back on Frobisham, feigning to inspect his numerous medicine jars, spread along the shelves encircling the office.

'Until next time,' Frobisham muttered, as he saluted Jag's back. He donned his gloves, draped the parka hood back over his head, and exited the trailer office.

Stepping outside and down from the stair into the crisp hard packed snow, with its fresh sugar–like frosting, Frobisham paused.

One small step for man he thought, as he pondered his surroundings and his situation on the whole.

He slightly pivoted his body toward the trailer, allowing his head to turn further in his hood, and looked back surreptitiously at the trailer. His sneaking feeling was confirmed.

There stood Jag, the curmudgeon, at his window looking down at this white trash, giving Frobisham a self denigrating feeling as though he were a bolting dog, having been chided for nipping at the heels of his master.

Frobisham was annoyed at himself for having looked back. He became more so, thinking out the scenario. He comforted himself with the thought that if indeed he were a dog, he would have taken him off at the knees. Jag was simply a seal's butt hole. *And*, if Jag the shaman, not by noble blood inheritance—but only by practice, could read minds—*he should go kiss the ass of a whale!*

Frobisham exhaled a plume of steam, and walked on satisfied.

The snow under foot, emitted sounds much like snaredrum rolls, heralding the way for a man en route to the firing squad. The bad taste Jag had left in his mouth, had invaded his mind. Fear, anger, humility, and vengeful thoughts, haunted Frobisham as he walked on his way to the engineers' residence which was several hundred yards away. He walked to the rolls of the ominous snare-drums. *Maybe he can read minds*, he thought to himself.

two

'GREETINGS, PARKA DWELLER!' hailed Frobisham, through the fluttering snow, as he found himself on a welcome convergence with Matawi, a bright and friendly half-Inuit engineer, whom Frobisham was aware had recently returned to Kabloona. She had been on a compulsory trimester respite of sixteen weeks, in her hometown of Tuktoyaktuk.

Frobisham had always been enamored with Matawi. She possessed the most exquisite and unusual good looks; a lithe body, and a wistful voice, which complimented her charismatic nature. Those qualities stoked his ardent desire.

As much as he enticed her to cross the line of friendship, with such feeble tools as subtle lechery, romantic allusions, guilt, and displays of physical and mental prowess; she just would not allow their friendship to evolve into sex. *Why*, he did not know. He *did* know that the longer they remained friends, the further away any hope of sex was.

He enjoyed her company and their candid bantering though, and so, he was unwilling to give up the chase, which was an integral part of his repartee and a release for his frustrations.

There was a noticeable difference in their strides, as they plowed along their oblique paths through the snow, which funnelled into a wide well-packed trail towards the rear of the camp. They reached the apex of the path and Matawi swayed her body towards Frobisham, paralleling her steps with his.

She reached out and took his billowy waist with her right arm. He reciprocated, and gathered her up in her cumbersome parka, drawing her slightly off step as he hugged her.

'Good to see you, Gordon,' she said, squeezing him. 'You'll be a free man soon, yeah?'

'Not soon enough.'

'The remoteness has got you down. It's the air—arctic delirium.'

'That explains Jag, then.'

'Jag has his own rhyme and reason.'

'Jag has what?' He asked, cupping his hand beside his parka hood, and bowing slightly.

'His own rhyme and reason. He's an anomaly!' She said, beefing up her projection, to avoid having to continue twisting her parka hood in his direction to talk.

Frobisham pulled his hood back, so that it cradled his head, rather than having it snorkeled beyond his face.

'I've been here thirty-two weeks almost, and not once has Jag said "Hello", "See ya later", "Nice day for a picnic", nothing—squat. Can you slow down a bit? I'm not three hundred years old, but you'd think *he* was, with all that luggage.'

'All that *what*?' Matawi asked loudly as she too drew back her hood, as they made their way.

'Can you slow down just a smidgen? See, the words leave my mouth and get swept behind in your wake. They're back there. *And*, we're over here. Together, alone, walking the path—don't you ever wonder if I snore, or hog the covers, or talk in my sleep?'

'No,' she replied coyly, but with affection.

'Well, I often wonder if *you do*.'

'I thought you were wondering if Jag was three hundred years old?'

'Okay, tell me he's not.'

'He's not,' she answered with a giggle, and a quick acceleration in her step.

'I know he's *snot*. He's a *snot-rag*. But he isn't three hundred.'

'You're incorrigible, Gordon.'

'Well? Listen, his ancestors—and your ancestors too, well, fifty percent of them,' he stammered, feeling bad that he'd unnecessarily noted her half-Inuit status, 'um, they would have welcomed me with open arms, asked me to sleep with their wives, offered me food and furs, for very little in return. No suspicions, no expectations.'

'And, you would have availed yourself of all these offerings?'

'I don't know. I wouldn't take advantage,' he said, while betraying false airs.

'Don't lie, you rascal,' she said, brushing snow from her hair, 'you know it would have been an insult not to accept their hospitality—that goes for today, too.'

'Alright, I would have lavished!'

'Then you understand why Jag isn't so hospitable?'

'That was then, and—'

'This is now?' she interjected, 'no, that was then, and *this* is then. Once burned, *you* know,' she said, clapping her mittened hands together, and picking up the pace. Frobisham hustled to keep up with her. 'If *you'd* thrown a party, say when your parents went away, and your guests not only ate you out of house and home, but *trashed* the joint, after getting you and your little brother high on some great drugs, and then their vulture friends show up with more great drugs, and decide to stay and form a commune, and you're too high to realize what's going on, and too good natured to toss them out on their asses tout d'suite ... well, it's a poor analogy, but you get the point.'

'Sorry,' he said, 'I'm a bit jaded I guess.'

'Let's just say he's a square peg,'

'Don't say it,' he piped, 'there ain't any square holes around here. *Shit*, maybe there is,' he said, thinking about Kabloona. 'One big round square. No, that's physically impossible. I'm an engineer, so I should know,' he joked, lifting his gloved left wrist into the air, and slapping it with his right.

'After your sixteen weeks off—*and believe me, you need it*, ask for another camp. Cornwallis, or Ellesmere Island.'

Frobisham began to shake his head, negating her suggestion.

'I know lots of engineers who hop-scotch around the IAR. I may do it myself, it's no big deal.'

'It doesn't look good on paper,' he replied, 'I'll stick it out for my contract term with Roblaw, here. Piss on Jag if he can't take a joke, right?'

'If it makes you feel any better, he doesn't care much for me either,' Matawi admitted, as they weaved around with the path, past the mine's head frame. The engineer's residence was in sight.

'Why doesn't he like you? You're half Inuit.'

'Precisely. If I were whole-blooded Inuit, I'd be the salt of the Earth. But, I'm not, so I'm salt on the wound. I have a half-sister who's whole-blooded Inuit— she's beautiful. Her name's Girly. A teacher.'

'There's *two* of you? Be still, my loins!'

'No, one and a half of me. There's no half measures with Jag though. It's all, or nothing.'

'I guess that makes me *less* than nothing, more than anything.'

'The snow looks funny on your head! You look like a big puff pastry, with sugar coating,' she laughed.

'So, you think I'm sweet. Well, this pastry can't stay on the shelf indefinitely, y'know.'

'I just don't feel like desert right now.'

Frobisham opened his parka slightly, reaching into an inside breast pocket. He pulled out a small silver flask, unscrewed the top, and swigged it back.

'Keeps me fresh!' He exclaimed. 'The embalmed pastry-man. If the Jag-man found out the reason Perq's so eager to meet the plane at Nanisivik, he'd have seals,' he said, slipping the flask back into his parka. 'Could the proud and mighty *Jag* admit failure?'

'*Failure* is a relative term,' she said.

'Yes, it is. I'd never dare mention it, 'cause he'd kill me, and hug half-pint. Besides, I'm fond of Perq, and he's a responsible kid. I think he knows his limitations. An occasional drink never killed anyone.'

'It's *medicinal*,' said Matawi, finishing the cliché. 'Is he the one that's been smuggling booze to the inmates?'

'I'm an engineer, not a guard,' he replied aloofly, 'he gets me mine, and that's all I know. Where would the trogs get the hard cash to pay for it , anyway?'

'Maybe he takes it out in trade—'

'The trogs don't have access to booze or dope. He would-n't be that foolish—what d'ya mean *trade*?'

'You know he's gay—don't you?!'

'Get the hell outta here,' he said, laughing.

'I would, 'cept I have a three-year contract.'

'Well ... I don't care if Perq wears high heels and garters on his days off. He's never bothered me. *Gay* huh? Y'know *I'm not*, and I've got a double bed,' he said, jumping on front of her, and walking backwards.

'Double beds give me a rash,' she replied, pushing him down into a snow pile. 'So stop being an itch.'

Matawi continued on, leaving him in her wake. Frobisham

struggled to his feet and scurried back to her side, brushing the snow from his parka.

'Speaking of *rash*, Jag's a pretty rash guy. In his office before I met up with you, I stepped on an old photograph, on the floor—watch it!!'

Frobisham stopped her from stepping on some iced wolf tracks, which crossed their path.

'*Now* who's superstitious?' She laughed, patting him on the head.

'I don't know how they get in here, but that's one local superstition I abide by,' he said, nervously. 'Especially *frozen* paw marks. I'll walk under a ladder any day, it's inanimate.'

'You're funny; peculiar, not ha-ha'

'So, anyway,' he continued, slightly out of breath, as they leveled out and walked along. 'I stepped on this old photo on the floor, and he went bananas inside. No yelling, just interior bananas. He's a loose cannon, or a splintering bow, or something.'

'Sure, I think he has a few loose screws. But, he pines for the lost innocence. He's a *shaman*. I don't think he's vindictive.'

Matawi paused for a moment, arresting her steps as the icy ground vibrated below their feet; tremors and audible reverberations caused from the intense blasting going on below in the mine.

'*Oooh*,' mocked Frobisham, feigning fright.

'C-shift blasting, *rash-man*,' knowing full well what Frobisham was alluding to. She stomped the ground. 'Turn the music down, or I'll call the cops!' she shouted at the ground.

Frobisham chuckled at her foolery. 'I thought it was Jag's burning ears.'

An armed Inuit guard emerged from behind the corner of the fenced-off power station, and plodded their way. The wind turbines dutifully rotated, almost mockingly, in the presence of the solar panels which now denied of sustenance, lay impotently frozen in a layer of frost, adjacent to them. The few days of twilight would soon give way to a solid six months of darkness. The guard glared in their direction as he passed them.

'They wouldn't take kindly to you slagging Jag like that. Gotta watch your step, they honour him like disciples around here.'

'What kinda rat would coerce his people back into the dark–ages, instead of embracing technology? Evolution moves us forward. Can't put a fish back on its bones.'

'Don't let Jag ever hear that you said that.'

'Yeah, maybe he *can* with his voodoo.'

'It's not *voodoo*, it's shamanism. Don't disparage it.'

'Not *it*, *him*,' he replied apologetically. He stretched his arm and pointed, 'Look past the fence there. See the northern lights? Below that, the distant hills, the glaciers, the water and sky?'

'Are you really *seeing* what you're looking at, Gordon?'

'It's the same as it looked hundreds of years ago. Only the faces have changed. They're free, they're enlightened, they can watch TV, or read a book, or dance a dance—oh, and hunt or fish. "Go to it", I say.'

'Or they can fight, or drink, or indulge in non-traditional pastimes like wallowing in depression with boredom, or emulating bad-ass TV characters,' she said, lifting her hood back up over her head.

'White tutelage didn't enslave them, it enlightened them. I'm sorry if there were abuses, and growing pains or something, as the years went on, but I wasn't there, and I won't bear any of the blame; I can't accept any of the credit either, y'know, for the toys of technology that every one of them clamor for and enjoy.'

'You're foaming at the mouth,' Matawi interjected, 'you just need a razor now, and you can shave.'

'Is there a law against venting of the spleen?'

'As long as I'm not down wind.'

Nearing the residences, they both looked over towards the rear perimeter fence, where the many B-shift trogs tended the mountains of mine-waste rock. There, tons of daily extracted rubble were being dumped from scores of miniature rail carts, onto the large portable conveyor, which was being manipulated by a drove of male and female inmates.

The long reach of the conveyor, deposited the rubble along the crest of the elongated ridge, which formed a rampart against the fury of arctic blizzards.

Mac Tighearnain, the young Irish B-shift engineer, waved at them as they walked along. He left his shift and jogged over to them from the perimeter.

'Hi, Matawi,' he huffed as he reached them. 'Gordon, is the delivery *in* yet?'

'Yup,' Frobisham replied as the three of them stopped to talk.

'If you see Perq, tell 'im I've got his money, will ya?' Mac asked.

'Will do.'

'Otherwise,' Mac continued with a wide grin, 'I might lose it in the card game tomorrow and he'd have to take a cheque.'

'I don't think a cheque on the barrel-head would put a smile on his face. Too many people owe him money 'round here,' Frobisham chuckled. The B-shift trogs at the perimeter caught his attention. 'Don't those stupid trogs of yours know how to operate that conveyor? Look at them.'

Matawi giggled as Mac turned to see his shift scattering away from a rockslide caused by a badly operated conveyor. Mac stomped off to supervise.

'Later!' Mac shouted as he stormed back to his shift crew.

Frobisham and Matawi reached the refurbished residences

from the 1950s. Passing a guard, Frobisham unlocked a door and they entered a shared lobby area. They began to stomp their boots, and shake their parkas. Frobisham heaved a sigh. Matawi took his gloved hand and patted it.

'Poor baby, I think Jag doesn't like you 'cause you stepped on his picture.'

Frobisham blushed, and laughed out, knowing he had been a boor, imposing his opinions on her.

'Yeah, I guess I didn't rape the living Arctic, I molested his inanimate photo.'

'Which is probably the same in his eyes,' she replied.

'When you flux between the real and the unreal, and can't distinguish.'

'You talking about yourself, or Jag?'

'Both. I exhaust myself worrying about stupid things. Why?'

'Because you're a retard,' she retorted.

'Listen,' he began, clearing his throat, and removing his parka. 'There's six of us leaving on the weekend, and we're having a little party in the common room, tomorrow night. No politics, no religion, no frothing at the mouth. Interested?'

Matawi looked at him with a wry smile.

'You just wanna get into my pants.'

'Well, that's a touch political, a might religious, and a bunch o' frothing at the mouth—yes, I guess I want to get into your pants.'

'They won't fit, but you're welcome to them,' she replied, and opened the door which led to the female engineers' residence. Frobisham smiled and called after her.

'Bring your own poison, and oh—no shamans allowed!'

three

Eamonn Müeller nodded at the guard, as he unlocked the door and proceeded through into the inmates dormitory.

In his forties, Eamonn strode along like a spry twenty year old, with a clipboard in his gloved hand. The Inuit guard lagged behind him, making no effort to close the ever widening gap.

He was a hands-on career miner, who was the scourge of all the taverns in both Inuvik and Yellowknife. Never one to back down from a challenge, and always looked up-to after a bar fight, Eamonn was a drill master second to none.

His large parka was adorned with stitching of birds of all sorts, and colours. He had an unbashful penchant for birds, which seemed incongruous with his fiery nature and formidable size. His co-workers were fond of him, and he reciprocated with good natured fellowship at all turns.

A rumour was always circulated amongst rookie engineers about Eamonn. It was said that Eamonn once wrestled a fledgling peregrine falcon from the jaws of a polar bear, which had crept up on the bird while it pecked at the carcass of a snow hare. Eamonn had emerged with the scars on his face and hands, which attested to his bravura, but the bear fared much worse from the skirmish, and now polishes the floor in the private office of Philip Roblaw. Nobody really believed the tale, but its legacy lingered in the back of people's minds when in his presence, as the prominent scars revived the tale.

Eamonn loomed at the entrance of the vacated male inmate's dormitory. Removing and pocketing his mitts, he pulled a cigar stub from his pocket, and lit it with commanding assurance.

A quadrant of the wooden dorm, which housed seventy inmates, bustled with boisterous conversation and spurts of crude laughter.

A couple of the nine new male transferees, wandered amongst the bunk beds and tugged at locked doors at the end of the dorm. Eamonn walked towards the brunt of the group, all donning the prison garb of black jump-suits with bright yellow vertical reflective stripes.

As he approached, he lifted a small tubular whistle which was strung around his neck, and blew into it, causing a chirpy, fluctuating tone, which pierced the air.

The new inmates twisted their attention to the approaching hulk.

'Gather 'round!' Eamonn barked.

The inmates looked around at each other and grinned. Kiratek, the guard, finally came through the door, and stood sentry. Eamonn dismissed Kiratek with a wave of his hand, and the guard obliged by leaving the room and shutting the door behind himself.

The inmates' grins got bigger, and some began to laugh. A few looked-on for a reaction from Eamonn to the derisive laughter targeted at him. Abdul Shellal-ali, the now resident terrorist, stared arrogantly at Eamonn.

'Woof,' he said, in a cocky challenge.

Eamonn centered himself in the aisle, adjacent to the first

bunk, where the child-molester lay with his arms behind his head. He pinched the cigar from the corner of his mouth, grit his teeth and curled his lips, and from between the teeth of his mercenary grin, he spat on the floor on front of him. He stared at Abdul, looked down at his clipboard, and began a slow bullish approach to the man.

The laughter subsided, excepting for the giggles of the fat kidnapper, who sat rocking his head with expectancy of the impending showdown.

Abdul leaned against a bunk-bed with assurance, and stuck his chin up in the air.

'That's the spirit!' Eamonn shouted, as he confidently closed in. 'You're the holy-terror in the bunch, right?'

Abdul began to fidget, rocking his head nervously as Eamonn stalked him.

'You jumped the first hurdle in your rehabilitation. You got two "R"s left. I want to shake your hand,' he said outstretching his hand.

'Don't do it,' said Ketcham, the WASP murderer, who rubbed at his crew-cut, and stood up in the aisle.

'Words to live by, *convict*,' Eamonn replied back, with a quick twist of his head. He popped the stogy back into his mouth and adroitly slipped off his parka, letting it rest to the floor, as he snaked his way towards Abdul.

He flung the clipboard back onto his parka. His face burgeoned with a wide derisive smile.

'Stay in the nest little jail birds, and you'll be safe 'til winter's over,' Eamonn sarcastically quipped, as he moved to within two feet of Abdul, who struggled to maintain his composure. 'Now share with the rest of the class, the correct response to the whistle.'

Abdul raised his clenched hands defensively, his fists swaying in the air like cobras.

'One step closer!' Abdul bellowed.

Eamonn turned his head back to the gawking convicts.

'To *freedom*,' Eamonn added in a humdrum fashion.

Abdul swiftly wound up to sucker-punch his tormenting jailer. The room echoed the impact of Abdul's fist as it collided with Eamonn's large palm, which caught and stopped the punch in mid air. Like a snake swallowing a rat outright, the wavering fist was pushed forward and downward by Eamonn.

The wiry pimp leapt up from the edge of his bunk to join the fracas. As he leaped forward to jump in with both feet, he was thwarted by impaling himself into Eamonn's left fist, which like a battering ram, sent him reeling back into his bunk gasping for air. Eamonn was a pro at brawling with more than one assailant at a time.

A gripping silence seemed to amplify the moans and squeaks of Abdul, whose face grimaced in pain and embarrassment, as he was lowered almost to his knees under the strain of the crushing vise of Eamonn's grip. The audience went glum and silent. Eamonn shoved Abdul backwards onto the floor.

Abdul, now crestfallen, struggled to his feet and began to limber up, as though round two might offer him a chance to redeem himself in the eyes of the other inmates. At the very least, this show of bravado, win or lose, would garner him respect within the population.

Abdul bobbed up and down, engaging Eamonn in a dance of rotation, which brought Abdul half circle to the bunk of Wilkes, the child molester, who reveled in the excitement by vicariously swinging his own fists in the air.

Eamonn hunched himself slightly, and mouthed the cigar back and forth between his lips from one side of his face to the other. The inmates cheered and razzed, but none would dare interfere. Eamonn began to curl his hands and fingers inwards, beckoning his rival's best shot. He pointed to his nose, and Abdul swung wildly. Eamonn adeptly ducked below the swoop of his fist.

Abdul swiftly raised his leg to kick Eamonn, but slipped on the spittle on the floor. He flipped backwards, smashed his face on the bunk-bed's frame, and landed on his side with a resounding thud. The jeering ceased.

Blood flowed from Abdul's lacerated nose, as he curled slowly in pain. Ketcham went over and turned him over. He yelped in agony as Ketcham touched his chest.

'Broken ribs,' Ketcham whispered to the other inmates.

'There are rules around here, and I've broken one now fraternizing with you stinking gobs, so, if any of you want to file a complaint against me, be my guest,' said Eamonn, turning back to business. 'I'm trying my best to be a good host, but maybe my best isn't good enough for you, so I forgive you for not sending me any thank-you cards. No hard feelings. We have an infirmary, which your friend here will be escorted to, and believe me, the food is wretched, and the nurses are uglier than the expression on Abdul's face. That's punishment enough for him. You've had your orientation, and now it's my job to turn you punks into miners. I'm your shift boss, and when I blow this whistle, you better listen up, or you'll have more than a bruised ego to contend with.'

'Is that a threat?' Wilkes, the scrawny child-molester brazenly inquired, as Eamonn picked up his clipboard and hung his parka on the corner of a bunk.

Eamonn leaned down into the inmate's face.

'It's a tip. What're you, little man?' he asked in light of his bold question.

The child molester darted his eyes around to his colleagues, puckered his cheeks and held his tongue.

'I know what you're *in* here for,' Eamonn said, 'but are you *nominating* yourself as the business agent for the Kabloona inmates union?' Eamonn sighed a laugh, and sat in an empty bunk. Puffing on his stogy, he stroked his hair and looked over the roster fact sheet which was fastened to the clipboard. The molester rose, and put his hands on his waist.

'Maybe I should be,' Wilkes saucily remarked, as he looked around, slightly swallowing his breath and hiccuping a nervous laugh.

The other inmates took note of the ailing Abdul, and nodded their heads in approval. With this nominal support, Wilkes began to pace and to use hand gestures to support his words.

'This place is a dump! What is the government *coming to*? I mean, this is an unethical penal colony, right? Right? A fucking frozen boot-camp run by Nazi's and stupid Eskimo's!!'

Eamonn popped the cigar into his mouth, set aside the clipboard, and got up. He walked over to Wilkes, who had been parading up and down the aisle, smacking the frames of the bunks. He stopped Wilkes in his tracks, and stared him closely in his eyes, which fluttered from the smoke of the cigar.

'You're just trying to endear yourself with me,' Eamonn remarked.

There was a chuckle from behind. Eamonn batted his eyes to the extent his sockets would allow in the direction of the comment, and then slowly turned his dog-eared glare back to the child molester.

'I'm half Irish, half German. Hot blood and cold steel, savvy?'

'So yer a potato eatin' Nazi,' Wilkes said, as the room went quiet enough to hear the faint squeaks of the wind turbines outside. 'Gonna hit me now?'

Eamonn looked around at the other inmates who eagerly anticipated his reaction.

'Is this what taxpayers are forking out thirty-grand a year for? For your sweet nothings in my ear?' he said, as he stepped on Wilkes' feet with both of his, and puffed smoke in his face. 'You've been spoiled behind bars. The vacation's over for all you candy asses, except you,' he said, breaking a grin, as the molester struggled beneath the weight of Eamonn's large, booted feet. The man reached out with both hands to each side of the aisle, gripping opposite bunk frames to steady his balance.

'I'm going to the warden!' he protested, with a look that quavered between fear and outrage.

Eamonn took a firm grip atop both the felon's out-stretched hands, pinning him both hand and foot. Wilkes writhed helplessly, pinned tight by his tormentor. Ketcham looked around at the other inmates. Anger and embarrass-ment was felt among the inmates, regardless of the loathe they felt for the child molester.

'I'm too fond of you to allow you to shoot yourself in the foot, yet,' Eamonn said, with a cursory glance around him. '*You're* still on vacation, so I'm sending you to a little resort I know, all expenses paid. It's a chalet. Beyond the gates, far away from this *dump*. Free to molest fluffy polar bears, or grinning wolves, or whatever strolls by. Rub noses with nature! No more Nazis, or stupid Eskimos to taunt you.'

'You're gonna fucking pay for this!' The man screeched.

'No, the taxpayer's pay, I told ya. Your dream vacation. No rules, make snow angels to your hearts content.'

'Cut the fucking games, Müeller,' said Ketcham, 'we're tired of bein' jerked-off, so give us our work details and be on yer way.'

'I'm on my way to making this a trip for two. Maybe *two* faggots, huh? Playing house in the snow? No? Shut your gob then. You're going to have a ball of fun in the winter wonderland, Mr *child-molester*. A Friday night in solitary. Just you, the igloo, your parka, and a candle for light and heat—*if* you can convince the wax to melt! Perfect office for a business agent, in my humble opinion. See you tomorrow, *maybe*.'

Eamonn stepped off the thrashing inmate's feet and released his hands. The man turned his back, grabbed his striped parka, and staggered for the door, cursing under his breath.

'The warden's gonna hear about this!' he roared.

'After you've had a chance to chill out on your vacation, you can warm up to the superintendent,' Eamonn offered to the maddened con. 'Go for coffee and cake, tomorrow. His name's "Najagneq", and it's not true that he's a white-hating, venom-spitting, berserk 'skimo with black-magic up his ass. He's *Inuit*, and he'd *love* to chew the fat with you. With any of you,' he said, looking around at some faces in the contingent.

The inmate wrestled with the locked door. Eamonn walked over to the man and grabbed him by the collar, throwing him off balance.

'We have door-to-door valet service,' he said, keying open the locked door, and calling the guard over, who approached as Eamonn held out the prisoner.

'Igloo,' he said to Kiratek, the guard, who grinned and began to prod the molester with his semi-automatic rifle, for him to start moving.

Eamonn tapped the guard on the shoulder and pointed back to Abdul.

'Send Agaluq in to get *that* one to the infirmary. He's got hurt feelings, and I need him patched up for the next shift.'

Kiratek nodded and shoved Wilkes. As he turned to walk, Wilkes reached out and plucked the cigar from Eamonn's mouth, popping the stub into his own mouth. He proudly puffed away.

Kiratek quickly thrust the butt of his rifle into Wilkes' gut, causing the stub to be ejected, and folding the con over in pain. Eamonn's eyes flared. He took a slow breath, then waved them off.

He shut the door and turned to the rest of the convicts,

who were now engaged in a heated conversation. Irritated, he drew out his whistle and blew it loudly for four seconds. He stomped over to the cons, with a look of disdain on his face.

'Well?'

The inmates looked at each other, knowing what was coming.

'Well!?' Eamonn barked with annoyance.

He blew the whistle again. There was a pause, and then followed an unenthusiastic round of 'woofs', which dominoed from the group.

'Thank you,' he said, getting down to business, 'there are three twelve-hour shifts, of seventy-person crews. Ten in the mine, one hour maintenance detail outside, tending all that rubble you saw piled up out there which comes up from the mine. One hour cooking, cleaning, or garbage detail. Half hour breakfast, half calisthenics, go to your shift then one hour dinner, two to yourselves, and then lights out for your eight hours sleep. All compulsory, no exceptions. That's your twenty-four hour schedule for the duration of your terms. Don't ask me to repeat that.'

The inmates shook their heads, and rolled their eyes.

'Demerits for being an asshole, late for a shift, fighting, refusing to work or eat. Two demerits gets you the *igloo*, which you may or may not hear about tomorrow. "We cannot be held responsible for lost or stolen inmates while on vacation",' he announced with a peculiar timbre in his voice. 'I'm serious. There's no shift swapping or exchanges allowed. The morning, day, and night shifts alternate twice a year. Call the shaft elevator a *cage*, the lights on your hard-hats *cap-lamps* and for Christ's sake, don't shine your cap-lamp in someone's face while you're talking to them—so there.'

'We already been told dis,' piped the other murderer, who was black, and tough as nails.

'Yeah, no maps, pre-programmed educational TV, pre-historic toilets, and *all* the rest,' remarked the arsonist, 'but, what we really wanna know is do we get to fuck the female inmates?'

'Yeah, or are you gonna cut off our dicks as well?' Asked the robber.

Eamonn stroked his stubbly chin. Dominance created respect. That's all they could relate to. Although he despised them for their natures and their crimes, he began to recognize the typical nuances that most of his plebe trogs exhibited. It usually led to a civilized working relationship, allowing him to turn his back on them in the mine without the fear of being crowned from behind.

It was the germination of some perverted type of mutual respect—the start of the "coach and his team" rapport, which separated the hard-core immoral types, from the crimes-of-passion or victim-of-society sort who adapted, and learned. These were the one's who generally could be relied upon to accept rehabilitation and promote civility, regardless of the unfortunate circumstances of their situations.

'You'll probably cut your *own* dicks off when you see some of those banshees,' he said, in a mischievous way. 'They're a lot tougher than *you* lot. I'll give 'em one thing, they're damn good miners, most of them. Make you look like toddlers on the beach, making sand castles with little spades and buckets—so you greenhorns better pull your weight.'

'I wanna go an a panty raid!' The robber blurted out with childish exuberance. It was the kind of apropos unabashed comment one might expect from a lascivious thief. Chuckles of camaraderie rang out.

'The women's barracks are off limits,' Eamonn said flatly, 'if you try, *they'll* cut your balls off, and *I'll* send you on vacation.' Eamonn nodded his head sarcastically. 'In my opinion, I think you all should take a stab at it, and I can have the choir I always wanted—you assholes better get this through your thick skulls; it's business in the mine, and any carousing or lollygagging down there'll get you killed, or someone else. If I catch any of you blockheads messing around down there with the females, or explosives, or each other, I'll turn your life into a living hell. Play by the rules and your life here will be a moderate agony.'

The ground rumbled beneath their feet.

'There it is again! What the fuck?!' The arsonist belched out.

'The C-shift blasting,' said Eamonn, '*your* shift. They'll be up soon, once "A" goes down. When "C" comes up, you'll work with them outside for an hour, and from then on, you'll follow their schedule. It's *powder day*, today. That means the ANFO or Ammonium Nitrate Fuel Oil—our blasting powder, is being re-stocked into the mine. It requires a detonator to set it off, so don't worry if you're asked to help cart it around. It won't explode if a match is thrown on it.'

Agaluq, an armed Inuit guard, entered the dorm. Eamonn turned and nodded at the man, then pointed at Abdul. The guard waited at the door, as Eamonn walked over to the bloodied and dejected Abdul, who lay silently in his bunk, brooding over his wounds.

'Get your ass to the infirmary,' said Eamonn officiously, '*now*! Ribs, or no ribs, you'll be haulin' ass on your shift, or you'll be joining your bum-buddy in the igloo.'

The black tough-guy murderer helped Abdul to his feet, who grimaced in pain crawling from his bunk. He was helped on with his parka, and then despondently shrugged off any further assistance. He quietly hobbled over to Agaluq, who walked behind him through the door.

'Okay girls, I'll come and fetch you in an hour, to hook you up with C-shift outside. Now, I've got to go and tend to some unfinished business, so take a deep breath and hold it.'

Eamonn donned his parka, picked up his clipboard, and swiftly moved through the door, locking it behind himself.

The inmates looked at each other. Ketcham stood up and stared at the door for a moment.

'Six years with *that* breathing down my neck? I'll cut his heart out tomorrow night, and take my chances slipping out the gate,' Ketcham said.

'It'll take more than his heart to get you 'cross the tundra,' piped the arsonist.

'Well, aren't we chi-chi with the lingo? *Tundra*,' he mocked.

'They said it was over a hundred miles of nothing to the next igloo. Huh? Then, who knows what? Another three hundred to the airport we flew into; or a seaport?'

The thief reclined on to his side in his bunk, and propped his head up with his arm, opening his mouth to add his two cents.

'How fast was that bus traveling? It seemed like forever to get here from the plane.'

'And, with the blindfolds, couldn't spot landmarks,' added the arsonist.

'Yeah, you could go in circles for days out there,' the thief interjected. 'You gonna ride polar bears and surf ice flows?'

Ketcham scowled. 'Don't rain on the parade, asshole. Maybe I'm gonna steal a snow-mobile. No, that tractor bus—shit, too noisy and slow. Look, we'll gather some supplies. Yeah, a rifle, map, and food. Who's with me?!' Ketcham paced up and down the aisle, looking for accomplices. 'C'mon, none of you guys have the guts to waltz outta here with me?'

'I'll run with you,' the fat kidnapper said to Ketcham, who looked back at him with a tepid frown.

'You'd be dead weight, grease-ball. I need someone fit, and resilient to the cold.'

'He's right, you palooka,' said the arsonist, chiding the man for his absurd eagerness. 'Look at you. You're shivering now. What'd you be like three days out, with maybe no food, no shelter or water?'

'I could drink snow! Or suck on icicles,' he pleaded.

'I could just picture you with your lips frozen to a glacier,' laughed the thief.

'If I had to, I'd eat Müeller's heart, liver, and brains to survive!' The kidnapper said in a desperate logic. 'I got twenty to serve, and I can't cope with this kinda discipline,' he paused to catch his breath, 'and I gotta confess, I'm *claustrophobic*. I—I could never survive *down there*,' he said, wrapping his arms around his mid-section, and rocking.

'Well, *I* can't cope with cry-babies. Not out there. Get fucking *real*,' he said, pragmatically.

The tall and slim, black counterfeiter, leaned forward in his bunk, having resigned himself to observing and listening throughout both the journey and their settling-in process. He broke his silence.

'He's right, my friend,' he said with a deep clear voice, as the others took note of his centre-staging. 'The reality is, that it's minus fifty degrees Centigrade out there on a good day—with wind-chill maybe minus seventy-five, know what I'm sayin'? Steel would shatter like glass if you hit it hard. Icicles hang off your face, you get dehydrated worse out there than you would in a desert, so you need gallons of water a day to keep you going, and you couldn't stop to suck on a glacier for a week,' he scoffed, as his dissertation gleaned an eager audience.

'Go on,' Ketcham said, with great interest.

'See, your body tries to keep the core of you warm, so it sacrifices the blood supply to your extremities, like your fingers and toes. Then, you get frostbite, and they go all blue, and scorched, and you get searing blisters— and then they just fall off!'

'That's just for fat fucks and lazy bastards who don't have the grit it takes,' boasted Ketcham, 'you gotta have balls of fire, like me and you guys,' he said, nodding to the others around him.

'He's right fat-man, you'll be safe and warm in the mine,' said the thief, 'you'll see.'

'Please?! I gotta get *outta here*!' The kidnapper bellowed and pleaded.

'Better off alive and diggin' gold, than killin' me with your gold-bricking whines 'cause your dick fell off!' Ketcham replied, with a cruel snap of his fingers. The others laughed at his comment, as he caught the eye of the counterfeiter.

'What about you? You seem to know a lot about this place. Break outta here with me! Samuels, right?'

The counterfeiter nodded and laid back in his bunk, clasping his hands behind his head.

'That's right.'

'You 'n' me, make a go of it—freedom.'

'I don't think so.'

'C'mon, don't be a pussy.'

'I knew I was being transferred here, so I read up on this god-forsaken area. I got too much respect for the Arctic now, to step even one foot outside those gates without planning for *months*, and moving out. And, that's with nothing less than a dog team, map, *hundreds* of pounds of supplies, and a good rifle. Gotta get to know the guards, see if you can bribe 'em; it's an *expedition*, brother.'

'You're a fucking fool, and you ain't my brother, *mofo*,' Ketcham said, lashing out at his logic, which scuttled any iota of interest from the others, in his escape scheme. 'This is a cake-walk for smart guys like me. You're a stinkin', lilly-livered pissed-on blanket!'

'No, I'm a pragmatist,' he said, in a cool and calm fashion, as the others looked on, silently admiring his nerve. 'I've got two years to serve here, and I don't mind making four bucks a day, in this bargain basement boot-camp. I'll leave here with a skill. Make some honest bucks maybe, out there. I'm just tired of looking over my shoulder. Got a wife and kid, and I'd rather play marbles with him, than lose them with you.'

'Mine *this*, jerk-off,' Ketcham said, grabbing his crotch and leering. 'I'd have you looking over your shoulder for the duration, *if* I was stayin', just for being so rude to me.'

'I'll kick your butt from here to hell, asshole, so keep pushing,' warned Samuels.

Ketcham laughed, and grabbed his crotch again, mocking Samuels.

'I'll go it alone! I don't need any stinkin' help from any of you spineless douche-bags! *And*, you know what? I'll even make a pit stop in Ottawa, and visit this "Roblaw" guy, and shove an icicle up his ass for you guys, to repay his hospitality! *Then*, I'll send you a post card from Bolivia, and you know what it'll say? Huh? Two words. *Blow me!*'

'*I'll* blow you, if you take me with you, *please*!?' The fat kidnapper begged.

'You'll blow me, even though I won't, asshole! But, I think I'll pass, and trade you for something a little more satisfying—a pack of smokes for the journey!'

four

THROUGH SPORADICALLY LIT passages, with areas of blinding light, and dark shadow, the C-shift worked incessantly, like ants in a colony. The mine was a labyrinth of railed tunnels, exploration drifts, and cross-cuts. The echoed reverberation of the mingling sounds of compressed-air driven machinery, jack-hammers and tools striking stone, rang out. Steel wheels on rail, and technical conversation, formed the gritty backdrop of life in the mine.

Pockets of inmate trogs picked, lifted, pushed and laboured at the gold mining. Narrow gauge rail lines transversed most of the braced tunnels accommodating the miniature slag cars, which rolled from area to area, transporting rubble to the shaft's elevator cage.

A group of trogs loitered at the archway of an exploration drift, where blasting had been undertaken. Minute particles of dust mingled in the bright work lights, and in the lungs of the miners who hacked and sneezed occasionally from the peppered air. The assistant shift boss, Slater Boweman, was busy conversing with his blasting technicians at the drift wall.

Slater was a seasoned miner, having spent years in mines in both Northern Ontario and Manitoba. Essentially an engineer, but without his papers or formal training, Slater had visited many gold mines on company field trips with Roblaw engineers to various parts of the globe, including South Africa, Siberia, and South America. A sinewy man, with a stray eye, and slightly balding up the sides, Slater was Eamonn's right hand man, and good friend—Eamonn knew which eye to focus on when talking to him.

A grotesque female trog, Brunhilde Hamilton, casually inspected a detonator. One of the blasting technicians, Jason Palmeroy, launched into her for touching the blasting gear.

'Get your fat mitts off that!' Jason yelled.

'Goddammit, you asked me to help you!' she replied with a raspy drone.

'Yeah, to cart my tool box, not to fuck with the detonators,' he said, as she stood away from his instruments and shrugged her bulbous shoulders. 'Go find Peterson, and ask him if he has my spare battery for the unit.'

'Spare battery for the unit.'

'Yeah, and make it fast, we want to blast this before the shift ends.'

'Jason, we going to do this, or what?' Inquired Slater. Jason nodded to Slater and waved at Brunhilde to quickly fetch what he'd asked for.

Eamonn appeared at the drift entrance. Slater winked at Eamonn, and approached him.

'We're going to blast in a couple of minutes.'

'Uh huh. Got nine new sour pusses to join the shift up top for slag duty.'

'Can we have a bit of privacy, please?' Slater said to the loitering trogs, some of whom had removed their hard-hats, revealing a line of untarnished flesh-tone on their foreheads, the strip having been covered by the suspension bands of their helmets.

'Get your hats on, you lot,' said Eamonn, leveling his arm swiftly and pointing at the offenders. The thrust of his arm launched a small object from the cuff of his parka. The object bounced off a wall, and came to rest a couple of feet from Slater. The loitering trogs set their hard-hats back on their heads and moved into the tunnel to gather a comfortable distance from the two men. Slater bent over and picked up the tiny object.

'This a *tooth*?' Slater inquired.

'Well, it's not a fibula.'

'You've been playing paddy-cakes with the inmates again?'

'Smoking can cause tooth decay, nine out of ten dentists say.'

'Why do you waste your time being so chummy with them?'

'Jealous?'

'No, I want you to come and slum with us for a change. We're having a going away party tomorrow night. You know I'm outta here Saturday. Benson's taking my place.'

'Yes, I know, he's good.'

'Join us in our elbow-bending fest.'

'Sure Slater, you can count on me. I'll bring some scotch for a chaser.'

Jason and another technician walked past the two, into the blast site.

'So when's your wife due?' Eamonn inquired of Slater.

'Month and a half.'

'You'll be there. Perfect timing.'

'Couldn't have planned it better myself. Sheila's parents are going to be flying into Toronto to visit us.'

Jason and the other technician emerged from the blast site, and approached them.

'Well, Mr soon-to-be-first-time-dad, and maestro Müeller, I found *another* battery, and we can go ahead. Holes plugged, detonator's ready, site clear, spotters are up. Let's party.'

The four of them walked from the archway, following the blasting technician's lead wires. Eamonn drew his whistle to his mouth and blew it forcefully and lengthily. He let the whistle fall back down his neck, and looked around.

'Okay guys and gals, ear and eye protection, and filter masks! Spotters in your positions, and everyone way back under cover. You know the drill!' Eamonn yelled out with his deep and sonorous voice. 'Fire in the hole!'

They tugged down their ear-protecting head sets from their hard-hats, slipped on their safety glasses, and strapped filter masks over their noses and mouths. Jason hit the remote control button to activate the portable strobing red lights, which warned of the imminent explosion. As they hunched themselves behind a wall fifty-yards from the blast site, Eamonn leaned over to Slater as they were making themselves comfortable and braced.

'What are you going to name him if it's a boy?' Eamonn asked, removing one ear cup from his head.

'*Jag*,' replied Slater, as a wide grin crept out past his filter mask.

They both laughed heartily, and secured their ear protection. Slater looked at Jason, who was the last to take cover. He nodded to Slater, and they gave the "thumbs-up" to each other. Jason looked down at the "T" bar, and gave it a brisk, forceful twist.

There was a silence.

Then, three concussive explosions in a row. The ripping bursts seemed to suck the air from their lungs, and then spit it back at them with a vengeance.

Expelled rock fragments, and clouds of heavy dust and smoke filled the immediate area. There was a loud shriek, which emanated from the general blasting area. Eamonn and Slater furrowed their brows in inquiry to each other. They had only detected a distant muffled scream due to the ear protection. A secondary cloud of lighter dust spewed everywhere, and sparkled against the moving columns of strobing red light.

Eamonn, Slater, and the surrounding technicians looked at each other, eyes ablaze and mouths agape. They quickly removed their protective gear. They detected a moan from a tributary shaft, gaping at each other in a perplexed fashion, as they moved to investigate.

Once the reverse-fans dispersed the lethal gasses known as oxides of nitrogen—produced at detonation from the explosive device, scores of trogs jogged to the blast site. Only a month prior, a trog had drowned from ruptured blisters in the lungs, having breathed the gasses and soon-after developed chemical pneumonia.

Light beams from cap-lamps shook randomly as they approached the drift. It was visual mayhem in the mine, with the strobing red, and the white-light rays cutting across the suspended dust particles.

Eamonn and Slater quick-stepped their way through the debris, moving carefully towards the source of the dire moans.

'Quiet! QUIET!!' Eamonn shouted out, as he attempted to locate the source of the moans.

They searched and found Brunhilde, collapsed at the corner of a secondary tunnel. Her head was bleeding profusely. It was obvious that a spotter had been absent from that particular safety post. Brunhilde had been injured by ricocheting debris. Jason turned off the strobing red lights. Eamonn blew his whistle again.

'Get this woman up top to the infirmary, now! Someone get the first aid kit!'

A guard dispatched two inmates to fetch a stretcher. Slater produced a kerchief from his pocket as Brunhilde regained a shaky consciousness. Slater leaned down and carefully wiped away some blood from her face to find its source.

'You're going to be alright, just relax, there was an accident,' Slater soothingly said to her, as her eyes began to flare.

'Tell Palmeroy here's his *fuckin'* battery, which he couldn't go ahead without—THE ASSHOLE!!' Brunhilde yelled at the top of her lungs.

Slater had covered his ears in time, as her screams reached super-sonic by the last word. Eamonn however hadn't, and he was busy reaming his fingers around in his ears, to spread the nerve-attention from his aching ear drums.

Slater dabbed her head with the kerchief. Brunhilde snatched it from his hand, and held it to where she felt the head wound was located. Drawing the kerchief back, she visually inspected the damp and bloodied linen, then looked around non plussed.

'Get outta my face! I've had worse cuts shaving,' she barked, challenging the faces which ogled her.

The other trogs smiled at her comment, and she attempted to rise. One of the other inmates dared try to help her to her feet, and she managed to stand upright, but her feet were unable to support her. She looked drunk. Other trogs walked past with work lights, heading to the drift's blast site.

'You're a stout hearted woman, Hamilton,' said Eamonn.

'I could go for a *stout*, right about now. You fuck-ups owe me big time!'

'I'm afraid seal broth is about the best the infirmary can do.'

Two trogs arrived with the first-aid kit and a steel-meshed stretcher. They assisted her onto the stretcher and leaving the first-aid kit aside, the inmates lifted her into a small rail car, and pushed the car under escort of a guard, in the direction of the cage. Eamonn and Slater shrugged their shoulders at each other, and walked towards the blast site.

A haphazard cap-lamp approached them through the settling dust. The trog who bore the light bolted past them, stumbling along the shaft as though he'd seen a ghost.

The two rounded the bend, curious now at the unusual silence which engulfed them. They took the corner to find the crowd of trogs motionless and silent. Some had their hands over their mouths, and somewhere from within the group, an hysterical giggle could be detected. Eamonn and Slater pushed their way through the gawking trogs.

'Well? Get with it!' Eamonn shouted, as he came upon the wall they were blasting, challenging the faces of the spellbound inmates.

Slater grabbed Eamonn's arm. Eamonn looked at him, confused by the expression on his face. Eamonn followed his glare. Looking up, he viewed before him, the thickest vein of gold he had ever seen before, or had even heard stories of. It was practically flawless, and wider than a five-ton truck. The "vein" commanded the moment.

Slater's mouth quivered with awe. Eamonn drew a breath to steady himself, and broke the hallowed silence and greedy glares of the men and women around him. He turned his back to the golden wall, and addressed the contingent in a booming voice.

'Welcome home, you prodigal rat-bags!'

Slater burst out laughing, causing some of the trogs to chuckle along, while others remained mesmerized by the find. Eamonn let out a quick blow of his whistle.

'Alright, break it up! Shifts over, and "A" is coming down to clean up your mess,' Eamonn said, waving his hand on front of a few hypnotized faces. 'You'll be here tomorrow, so join the rest of your shift, and let's have an orderly changeover. Go!'

The trogs began to file out, peering back occasionally for

a glimpse of the jackpot. Eamonn approached Slater and shook his hand.

'Congratulations—we're daddy's! Now, let's get Jason to gather some samples to send to the lab for the acetate test— I know, *why bother*, but let's get it done, and go up top and make the production report. Oh, and call Roblaw.'

'I'll get the camera and the ruler, for the file shot—'

'And change your shorts,' Eamonn said, with a dead-pan glance, 'I want to go over the extraction plan with Frank. I'll wait for his shift to file in, and, you know, take-in the sights in the meantime.'

Slater walked to the wall, and slapped it approvingly, as though it were a fine horse.

'It's gotta be twelve feet wide, and look at this second one! There's no telling where this could lead!'

They stood dumbfounded for a few moments, their minds racing and scattered, like little boys at recess on the last day of school. Slater nodded his head and shook Eamonn's hand again, the strong silent glare of pride glowing in his eyes. Eamonn slapped him on the shoulders with both hands.

'I didn't tell you, but *this* is your going away gift. I hope you can fit it in your luggage.'

They shared a laugh, and Slater left to get Jason who had been packing up his tool kit after the explosion. Eamonn looked up and wondered if this were only a minuscule sampling of a leviathan of gold. He shivered, positive it was just the tip of the iceberg, and just stared, enchanted by its overwhelming allure.

The personnel cage gates were drawn back at ground level, as the elevator stopped. Slater bounded from the car which he shared with Brunhilde in the stretcher, the trogs carrying her, and the armed Inuit guard who dawdled behind on their way to the infirmary.

A-shift milled onwards into the elevator, which carried thirty five at a time. The second half flowed forward to fill the waiting space. The gates closed on the wood and metal meshed car, and it went down, heading for the bowels of the mine.

When the entire A-shift contingent of men and women reported to mine level, the C-shift would be brought up to attend slag duty. Hard hats were handed off from shift-to-shift below, in organized transfer lines. The re-charged batteries for their cap-lamps would then be retrieved from the office area.

Up top, Slater maneuvered through the waiting trogs, and bumped into Frobisham, who was waiting to go down with the rest of the shift.

'Gordon,' Slater began, with an enthusiasm which he tried to quell. 'Gordon, come with me, to Jag's office!' Slater asked, hardly able to contain his exuberism.

'*Forget it* !' Frobisham laughed out. 'It's my *last* shift, and I don't have to look at that skunk for *sixteen weeks*. You tryin' to bring me down?'

'Okay, you don't wanna be part of *history*, then, *go* down with your trogs!' Slater said, pushing him aside and moving on.

'Wait ... wait, wait a second!' Frobisham blurted out, not wanting to miss out on anything, and grabbing Slater's parka. 'Whaddya mean, part of history?'

'I'll tell you on the way. You comin'? C'mon, it's happy hour, buddy-boy!'

Frobisham joined Slater. The two walked quickly, towards Jag's office. Frobisham almost tripped a few times walking sideways in his prodding attempt to get the scoop. As they walked across the camp, Slater waved his arms frantically up, down and cross-ways. Frobisham got the news.

Slater and Frobisham danced into Jag's office without

knocking. Oblivious to formalities, their glee was their calling card.

'The streets are paved with gold,' sung Slater to a melodious lilt.

'And no one ever grows mold,' finished Frobisham, as they made a spectacle of themselves before Jag, who was taken aback with the boldness of the intrusion.

'What is the meaning of this!?' Jag demanded, making a swift wave of his hand as he stood up angrily, sending his chair toppling over backwards.

Slater collected himself, and demurely braced himself on the edge of Jag's desk as Frobisham continued his bunny-hop solo dance performance.

'We've just blasted into the biggest vein of gold,' Slater whispered, in his best understated dead-pan cajolery, 'Huge!! Eamonn was awestruck! Eamonn!!' Slater shouted, breaking out into unbridled hysteria, and spinning like a dancer in a circle, to face Jag again. 'I don't need to hear the results of the acetate test! The purity is astonishing! It's just the tip of the iceberg, my friend! I'm sorry, we're not actually friends, but perhaps today we can be!'

Jag's eyes widened with dire apprehension, then quickly closed into little slits, in suspicion. The two hadn't noticed Jag's reticence to partake in the celebrations. Jag lowered his head slightly, and slid on his whale-bone sunglasses.

'You're gonna need those when you see the *wall* of gold,' Slater chirped.

'I've got to let Roblaw know his ship has come in! Jag— oops, *Superintendent Jag, sir*, may I use your short-wave—no, sorry, your FAX. Slater, we should send a FAX, right? It's more dramatic than an e-mail,' boasted Frobisham.

'Mr Jag, you're not reveling with us. It's a momentous occasion,' said Slater, in a considerate fashion.

'Yes, it is,' replied Jag flatly, 'monumental,' he added, almost stunned.

Jag meandered back into the communications cubby, with Frobisham following not far behind. Once into the cubby, Jag surreptitiously disconnected the cables from behind the FAX machine. He pulled the plugs randomly, and desperately.

As Frobisham skipped into the cubby to the FAX machine, Jag moved around to the short-wave, and plucked a handful of cables from the back of it, and from the computer modem and satellite link. As Frobisham prepared his FAX, Jag rejoined Slater in the front of the office, who was preparing his production report.

'Are the trogs up from the shift yet?' Jag inquired mechanically.

' "A" is going down now, and "C" will be up for conveyor duty in about twenty,' replied Slater, who couldn't fathom why Jag was so morose, but wasn't about to allow it to become contagious, even though he obliged Jag's obtuse question with a similar response.

'After Gordon contacts Roblaw, can I call my wife? It's a *special* occasion, you understand.'

Jag nodded diffidently, preoccupied with the problem he had dreaded, and yet welcomed, which now stared him in the face. He had however, committed to his course of action, knowing the cat would be out-of-the-bag momentarily, and that there was no turning back. Someone once told him that *bones would rot on gold*. It was his duty now. It was the right thing—the wish of all the spirits, it was the only way to save his precious land, and his unenlightened people. It was a necessary baptism, and it would be done. It had to be done.

'Have you told anyone else of the find?'

'We're the first two up, but within twenty minutes it's going to spread like wildfire. This feels like a surprise party!'

'The FAX doesn't work!' Frobisham yelled from the back.

'Do the radio then,' replied Slater, looking up from his report.

Jag looked towards the cubby, anticipating each word, observing the "mice" investigating and exhausting their limited avenues in the maze, getting ready for the bottom to fall out.

Frobisham sat at the short-wave and fiddled with the dials, to no avail. He swished over to the computer, to utilize the computer's satellite link. He was taken aback at the slung feathered mask which covered the screen. He grabbed the mask off-handedly, and placed it on the stand beside the keyboard. It teetered on the edge, fell to the floor, and was deflected under the table after hitting the stand's metal leg.

Jag looked on in amazement, as Frobisham kicked the mask around inadvertently, in order to find comfortable footing. Jag felt a pang in his heart, which set him adrift in a world unto himself. There was no more feeling, no more physical or aesthetic concerns. There was only the inevitable.

'What the hell's this crap on the screen?' Frobisham asked, as he cleared the alphabetical cacophony, and began to fervently type in the contents of the FAX he had prepared. Slater looked up from his report, curious as to the source of Frobisham's difficulties. He stood up and began to walk towards the cubby.

'Excuse me, Jag,' Slater said as he neared him, 'I'm a pretty good trouble-shooter.'

Slater brushed by Jag, who rocked subtly, half humming, half singing a chant. Slater reached Frobisham and leaned over his shoulder.

'Jag is at a loss for words,' whispered Slater.

'What else is new.'

Jag's eyes moved from side to side, behind the slits of his glasses. He went over to a shelf and selected some roots and dried herbs from several of the medicine jars. Drawing some sort of liquid from an urn into his bone-cup, he mixed in some additional ingredients, and began to slurp away.

Putting down the small gourd, he picked up a small finger drum, and began to chant and sway. Jag's senses became very acute, and he could hear clearly, the whispers of the two engineers in the cubby. His neck throbbed, and his eyes began to dilate.

'News of this will spread like hoar-frost,' Slater said to Frobisham in a hushed tone.

'Yeah, this region will be smothered by mining companies and prospector's in a staking rush. They *need* more development. Hell, think I'll stake a claim myself —start a company. Don't need a barter deal when you know the motherload's waiting. I *know*, the *contract*. So, I'll get someone else to front for me. Give this lot their dividends, and they'll be happier than pigs in shit.'

'This tundra's *Swiss cheese*,' sighed Slater.

Frobisham hit the "transmit" key on the computer, and nothing happened.

'With rail links cutting through as the crow flies, like a proper outfit—what's *with* this thing?'

Jag became incensed with the boasting in their conversation. They spoke in hushed tones, but he heard every word. He tenderly stroked the artifacts adorning his office. He knew what was in store, and it wasn't pretty. He began to tap his finger drum, and his head rocked in an obscure fashion. His body began to tremble.

Back in the cubby, Slater scratched his head in confusion at the unresponsive equipment.

'Hang on, before we start mucking around, let me just ask Jag if he knows anything—check the back panels for loose connections.'

Slater got up, and moved towards the main office area. He passed through the kitchenette, and along the short, slim hall, into the main office.

'Jag? Jag, is there a problem—?'

WHOOSH! Slater's chest was punctured by a harpoon

which Jag had thrust with tremendous force. Slater's eyes bugged with shock. He stood in the archway wavering for a moment, his mouth beginning to accommodate the well of blood which flooded up from his heaving chest. He meandered backwards, off balance, his knee's barely willing to support him.

'Sonofabitch!! The cables are *disconnected* from the back's of all these instruments,' yelled Frobisham, from the cubby, 'Slater, come help me get this show on the road, will you?'

Slater staggered backwards towards the cubby. He collapsed in Frobisham's lap, gurgling out his last breath.

'SLATER!!' Frobisham screamed in horror, as he looked down at his friend in his lap, the harpoon's shaft protruding from his damp chest. His mouth fell, as he gripped the shaft, the tears of confusion welling up in his anguish filled eyes. He sobbed in distress, peering forward in the direful direction, where Slater met his fate.

Frobisham froze with fear.

Entering the cubby, was a demon, with a feathered face and clawed hairy hands which brandished a spiked seal club. The living daylights passed through Frobisham's bowels posthaste, his being, succumbing to the kismet which chanted and stalked him like the defenseless prey he was. Slater's lifeless body pinned him to the chair, sealing his imminent fate. His mouth opened, emitting almost inaudible pleading squeaks. The squeaks fizzled out, eclipsed by the chanting growls of the beast.

A soul-sharpening wolf howl echoed through the camp.

five

TRIQ ANGAARK, a loyal Inuit cronie of Jag's and senior officer of the guard, dashed across the camp from Jag's office to the head-frame elevators. His short legs carried him clumsily over undulating snow mounds and around clusters of broken machinery and damaged mining gear.

The snowfall had increased and the polar winds had picked up substantially; so much so, that Triq had to struggle to avoid being blown off course from his destination.

Triq arrived at the elevator cage prior to it descending. He called for the attention of the two guards who were about to depart the surface to attend their posts below with the shift. They took serious note of Triq as he gripped the wire meshed door and breathlessly voiced Jag's wishes through the fencing.

'Hold the elevator and open the gates! Jag needs to see you guys right away outside his trailer!'

'Send Jag hugs 'n kisses for us,' a trog blurted from somewhere within the sardined contingent.

The inmates began to laugh and a surge of mock kissing-sounds emerged from the packed elevator.

'It takes a battalion of them to shoo away a stray wolf. Buncha chicken shits,' said a voice from the squashed bunch as the wire meshed gate rose.

'Why don't they just shoot the howling fucker?' said another inmate.

The two Inuit guards departed the elevator and lowered the gate behind them. Triq took a few deep breaths, then bolted for the Inuit engineers' and guards' barracks to gather the five off-duty guards and two resident engineers. The elevator began its descent downwards into the mine. The thirty-five trogs sarcastically waved bye-bye to the guards who monitored their departure, then the middle finger *trog salute* was collectively given.

Once the elevator was beyond their sight, the guards followed Triq's order and made their way along the path to Jag's office.

As the elevator descended, the trogs talked amongst themselves, oblivious to the shrill squeaks which their black and yellow parkas emitted when the nylon outer-linings rubbed against each other. There was a sudden jolt of the cage.

'What the fuck was that?' a deep male voice enquired from the midst of the thirty-five closely packed riders.

'It was a burp,' replied another faceless voice.

The elevator continued uninterrupted, clanking and humming as it lowered.

There came another jolt, this time more heavy. The inmates became quiet, and the majority began to look up and around in a mild state of alarm.

'That was no fuckin *burp*!' yelled another rider.

'Don't worry, there's a safety cable with counterweights if a cable snaps—the cage *can't* fall,' replied someone with an overtone of fear.

'Perq sees to it that maintenance is kept up on these rust buckets,' the man with the deep voice uttered.

A peculiar rapping sound came from the plywood ceiling of the elevator. The strange sound was like a legion of rats scurrying across the roof. It continued and the trogs looked to the ceiling. The sibilant squeaks of their parka's increased in volume with their restlessness. They were no longer oblivious to the by-product of their close quarters.

'I don't fuckin' like this one bit!' cried an inmate, spreading alarm among the group.

'Goddammit, how long before this fucker touches down?' shrieked a woman, as the rapping came to an abrupt end with a very loud "snap".

As they looked around at each other, another very distinct and different sound began above their heads. It was as though an immense zipper were being drawn closed across the plywood.

A trog at the perimeter of the group looked through the meshing and noticed two cables hanging directly in front of him which hadn't been in his line of vision before. He took his glove off and stuck his right index finger between the mesh to touch one of the cables. He discovered that the cable was moving downwards rapidly with gravity. It then began to slow down and appeared to stop. Poking his finger even further, he found he could reach the second cable which was falling tremendously fast. It was possible that this was the descending loop of a single cable. Suddenly, the frayed wire end of the thickly wound metal cable lopped the end of his finger off. He withdrew his finger instantaneously. The man's eyes bulged as he looked at the crude amputation in silent shock.

A tension "crack" reverberated through the elevator, caused by the single end of the cable which was fastened to the roof of the car.

'Shhhhiiitttttt!!!' screamed the injured man, still staring at his mutilated finger. The car jiggled slightly and then began to pick up speed; a lot of it.

'Oh fuck! *Oooh fuuuuuuck*!!' yelled an inmate.

'Sweet Jesus, not this!' called out another in despair, as the elevator began to fall with gravity. The thirty-five passengers were stricken with panic. Some attempted to climb the meshed walls while others ducked low in their spots.

Screams of horror and sobbing pleas to the Almighty interwove but were left behind like sorrowful parachutes, freed from the plummeting descent of the men who uttered them. *Their* freedom was only seconds away; the once deafening chirps of their parkas was now silent. They were like nesting baby birds now, their hearts thumping, paralyzed in the awareness that their was no mercy to be had. Nothing could defy the beastly universal forces which drew them into its gullet. Gravity was their master. There was no pride in their new-found innocence.

Below in the mine, Eamonn and the short and chubby A-shift boss, Frank DeiLagasia emerged from within the milling trogs changing over shifts.

Jason Palmeroy and another engineer excitedly entered the lackluster offices beside the cage elevator banks which held the tool lock-up, communications room, lunchroom and first aid station.

A high pitched whistle from the main shaft caught Eamonn's attention. As he and Frank approached the the elevator shaft, the first dribble of trogs from the dismissed C-shift loitered at the elevator gates. Eamonn's trained eye picked up on the signs. The short bangs of hair on the idling trogs' forehead's were being powerfully swept up by the tremendous gust of wind being forced out at the base of the elevator shaft by the plummeting elevator.

Eamonn and Frank reached the entrance gate. Eamonn grasped the meshed gate and turned his head sideways and upwards, pressing it against the cold and corroded steel netting. He shouted to Frank over the noisy blanket of local mixed conversations and the mine clamor.

'Radio the surface, quick! We've got a run-away!' Eamonn belted out.

Frank rushed into the dilapidated offices beside the shaft. Eamonn attempted to clear some of the trogs from the proximity of the elevator banks. Eamonn's attention was drawn back to the shaft, as the heavy steel cable smacked the base of the elevator pit. The cable began to rapidly coil up on itself as the elevator fed the accumulating mound. Eamonn blew his whistle loudly. He dragged some curious bystanders away with him, his mind all the while with the hapless wretches aboard the car.

In a flash, the runaway crashed with thunderous resonance into the rock base of the shaft. A waft of dust spewed from the wreckage. The other cables rained down on the devastation. Rampant confusion and shouts of enquiry swept into the dusty air.

Eamonn ran to the wreckage with a heavy heart. Reaching the gate, he grasped the fencing, ferociously attempting to lift the jammed gate. Hordes of trogs dashed to the site and were aghast at the occurrence. Faint moans could be detected amidst the wreckage of the car. Several trogs knelt at the foot of the gate trying to peep into the crushed car which had collapsed into the lower pit, five feet below floor level. The trogs called to any survivors.

'Get back, *everybody*!' Eamonn yelled, turning to forcefully push the gawking observers back.

Frank pushed his way through the crowd and grabbed Eamonn's arm. 'No answer up top!'

'Keep 'em back, I'm going to get the hydraulic jaws from the tool cubby—it's ...' Eamonn was flabbergasted. His eyes became slightly glazed and he gripped Frank's shoulder. 'Do what you can for them.' He pointed at two large inmates nearby. 'You two, come with me,' he said, shoving his way through the milling crowd.

Frank made his way to the elevator opening. The trogs had managed to disengage and lift the cage elevator's damaged gate. From above, a bundle of TNT with a lit fuse struck the roof of the car and bounced around within the elevator shaft. The front line of observers registered the harbinger of death. A second and third bundle touched down. The same happened in the adjoining skip-lifts which were for rubble extraction. They immediately turned to run, but were obstructed by the impenetrable wall of oblivious onlookers. Frank leapt onto the roof of the mashed elevator car in a futile attempt to diffuse the bundles of TNT.

On the surface, Agaluq and Kiratek—the guard whom Eamonn had escort the child molester to the "igloo", accompanied Matawi and a male resident engineer named Tutuyea, across the camp. Ambling along through the snow squall, they passed the mine's head-frame on their way towards Jag's office.

Several tremendous explosions from below knocked the group slightly off balance, as a clouds of billowing smoke erupted from the esophagus of the shaft. The group gaped in shock at the evident catastrophe. The kenneled sled dogs began barking wildly from their sheds. The resident engineers immediately ran toward the site. The bewildered guards paused, then followed after the others.

As Matawi and Tutuyea reached the head-frame, they carefully assessed the damages. At the elevator gate, Tutuyea turned to notice the hoist-room door wide open. The absence of cables coming through the holes in the wall, alarmed him. Entering the hoist room, he could smell the amonia-like odour of detonated charges and saw right away that someone had sabotaged the cable pully system. On the floor, he noticed the empty boxes which once held C4 plastique cable-cutting charges. Someone knew what they were doing. He rushed out of the hoist room.

Matawi noticed a small fork-lift bearing a skid of double-decked diesel fuel barrels parked adjacent to a small skid of ANFO at the head-frame. It made no sense. The blustering wind blew the stench of a burning tape-fuse her way. Searching out the source, her eye caught the tell-tale sparkling of a burning fuse behind the fuel drums, and her face filled with alarm. The wick was advanced almost to the point of completion.

Tutuyea ran towards her, and with a sniff of the air, realized what she was staring at.

'IT'S TOO LATE, GET BACK!' she shrieked.

They both began to make a run for it down the hilled roadway, waving back the approaching guards.

'GET BACK!! IT'S GONNA—' she shouted, as the salvo thrust her and the other trainee into the air, engulfing both in a wave of billowing flames, their catapulted bodies landing like sacks of fish on the incline.

The guards were bowled over from the violent concussion, brutally thrust back onto their backs, and left helplessly squirming in the snow. The nearby dogs yelped in fear. Agaluq regained his bearings and peered over towards the engineers' smouldering bodies which had landed only yards in front of the stricken guards.

He dashed over to Matawi who was writhing in agony, his attempts to smother the incessant flame in her parka proving to be in vain as she ceased to struggle. He gave up trying to separate her from the charcoaled parka, as she expired with a choked breath and a frown. The life left her, but her eyes stared upwards at Agaluq. He searched deep into her lovely dark pools and wanted to dive in after her. Slowly, he closed her lids with a gentle stroke.

Agaluq sat back on his heels and sobbed into his singed gloves. He had great respect for this ambitious woman, and had harbored a secret love for her, hoping to get close to her in the coming months.

Kiratek, the other guard, staggered to his feet. He approached Tutuyea's body which lay lifeless in the snow. Turning the body over, he detected neither a breath or a pulse from the hapless victim. He went to his stunned comrade and leaned over him, patting him on the shoulder in condolence. Helping him up, the two sullen guards gathered their wits and traipsed through the biting winds in the direction of Jag's office.

As they despondently departed, a loud creak came from behind. They looked back to see the flaming head-frame collapse with a monstrous groan.

Outside Jag's trailer office, eight Inuit guards, both off-duty and on, had congregated. The remaining two guards and resident engineers were being waited-on in order that an important address by Jag be heard.

Triq was riddled with tension as he spoke with Charlie Tutsweenarluq, a heavy set fellow who incessantly bucked for promotion to management, but who hadn't the skills or background to propel him higher than a position as a guard. He was relieved now that he had no responsibilities other than to follow orders, as the seven other guards present chatted nervously, pointing at the dark trails of smoke which the burning head-frame emitted. They'd all heard the the explosion and were anxiously awaiting guidance. They stood waiting in the squall as the kenneled sled dogs barked and yelped from the far side of camp, adding to the confusion.

Jag emerged from his office with Perq preceding him. Jag closed the door behind himself, and they stepped down from the trailer. Perq appeared somber and slightly dazed. Stepping down into the snow, he stood to the right side of Jag who placed his bare right hand on Perq's shoulder in a paternal gesture, as though there were some secret understanding between them. Jag stood on the first step up from ground level in order to loom over the contingent. The congregation stood respectfully silent, awaiting his words.

Perq drew his parka hood up over his head—noticeably without the customary wink. Jag remained aloof, keeping his hood withdrawn and moving his head slowly from side to side observing those present. The assembly faced forward, their features barely discernable, tucked within their cold-weather gear.

The squall had increased in intensity, yet Jag with his hood cradling his neck and only his whalebone glasses between him and the biting wind, seemed impervious to the elements. He appeared to display a calm which only the serenity of a trance could induce. The men looked on in awe at his temperament.

Jag beckoned Triq over to him with a subtle nod. He obediently approached and withdrew his hood, taking up a position on Jag's left. A lengthy briefing ensued with Jag speaking and Triq attentively nodding his head.

Finally, Jag looked away from Triq, withdrew his hand from Perq's shoulder and proceeded down the step. He made his way through his disciples, patting them on the shoulder as he went. He walked towards the un-manned camp gates. His men watched silently as he reached the gate, slid open the fence panel effortlessly, and walked off into the twilight tundra. Jag disappeared into the fury of the squall.

Agaluq and Kiratek jogged towards the disoriented gathering. 'Matawi was killed!' Agalug cried out as he and Kiratek reached the group.

'What?!' Perq screamed, as he took hold of Agaluq's arm. 'Did you say Matawi was killed? She wasn't in the mine!'

'How?' asked Triq, as he confronted the two of them.

'The explosion at the head-frame!' shouted Kiratek. 'As well as Tutuyea Iyataliknareq! Both of them—*dead*!'

Perq bolted from the group, en route to the smouldering head-frame. Triq raised his arms high in the air and waved them about.

'Listen to me, all of you! There is a saboteur lurking among us!' Triq belted out to the group. They turned to each other in surprise and anxiously listened further with eager ears. 'An inmate or angry white dog of Roblaw's, has turned to terrorism to bring this operation to its knees,' he said, waving the group into a tight huddle. 'All communication systems have been destroyed. Najagneq has called for assistance, and in Jag's own words—"we will squash the saboteur who wants us on our knees!" He has gone out to seek guidance from his familiars and helpful spirits. When he returns, I will tell him of the tragic loss of our brother and sister who have perished at the hands of these desperate men. There may be more than one!'

'There's people trapped in the mine?' asked Nick Kuujjarviq the clownish gate guard. He looked at Triq with innocent concern.

'Two shifts below,' Triq replied, 'and one in their barracks. From what we know, if the headframe has collapsed, the elevator workings have been disabled badly I'd think.'

'There were big explosions,' Kiratek said, 'if it was in the shaft itself, there could be tons of rubble blocking them from climbing the shaft ladder.'

'I don't know, but until we find the madmen, the few of us can't manage a big rescue effort. Help is on the way though. Jag told me himself.'

'What can we do?' asked Nick.

'There's no need to jeopardize the lives of you all, so most of you will be returned to your villages for the time being. The snow bus will drop you off. We think the food supply has been poisoned, so eat nothing—'

'Shit—I had some fish about an hour ago,' said Nick, with grave concern, holding his stomach and frowning. The others followed suit, pressing on their stomachs and wondering if they had been poisoned.

Triq waved his right hand, declining their fears. 'Don't get too alarmed, I said we *think*, so don't eat anything more, and say nothing, 'cause your lives may be in danger! If you disappear, we may be able to flush out the perpetrators if they think we're dead. Jag is sure of your loyalty—so it's *not* one of us.'

The men looked at each other and nodded approval of Triq's wise words.

'Should we gather our things before we go?' asked Agaluq, extending his head from within the huddled circle of heads.

'I—*we* would like you to stay, Agaluq ... to help us apprehend the culprits. Will you stay?' Triq asked.

'Yes,' he said proudly, 'I will stay, to bring the killers to justice.'

Triq nodded his head approvingly. 'A noble gesture.'

'I would like to stay!' announced Kiratek with a vengeful scowl.

'Me too!' Charlie stated with assurance.

'And me!' added Nick.

'I know you would all bravely volunteer to stay, but I will agree only to Agaluq and Kiratek staying behind,' Triq announced to a circle of disappointed faces. 'The rest of you must depart immediately, before the weather worsens. Lock your weapons up in the armoury room before you go. The B-shift boss and engineer will be forced to stay and to help supervise the rescue, after the collaborators are in custody. They, along with their crew are all under suspicion, and are under camp arrest and confined to barracks—we'll be fine here.'

'I wish you luck,' Nick blurted out, starting a round of well-wishing within the huddled circle.

'Thank you all, and may the helpful spirits guide you to your homes!' Triq shouted, then broke from the assembly and made his way through the group shaking hands, heading in the direction of the collapsed head-frame where Perq had gone off to.

Agaluq and Kiratek made a likewise round of farewells, and followed Triq. The gathering disbanded and headed off towards the snow bus. Charlie broke away from the group, and chased off in the direction of the head-frame after the others.

'See you, guys!' he shouted, 'you go ahead—they need me here!'

six

IN THE RANCOROUS depths of the mine, echoey murmurings could be detected. Dim battery operated work lights, made even dimmer by the floating dust, barely illuminated what had become of the main shaft. What was once an intestine, hastening the comings-and-goings of the trogs, was now reduced to a hopelessly blocked artery.

The explosion had smothered the main elevator shaft, bringing down the structural concrete, timbers and steel which had framed the opening for the past forty years. A huge plug had been formed from the collapsed materials, much of it from the lining of the shaft itself. Many had perished and scores of trogs had been severely injured.

There appeared to be about twenty five cap-lamps beaming from hard hats in the vault, half of them moving slowly and haphazardly around in the area. Eamonn's voice emerged from the stale dimness.

'Hang tough, and we'll get around to everyone,' he said, with a fatherly warmth in his voice. The sounds of material being torn was woven through his words, as splints and bandages were being administered by the able.

'It'll be days before they can rescue us!' screamed an irate inmate, 'will we die of thirst, or smother?!' he yelled, his voice echoing around the labyrinth. The wiry man paced nervously.

Eamonn approached the man and swiftly covered his mouth. He twisted his right arm behind his back and drew him far into a shadowed corner, nearly tripping over a corpse as he hustled the man along.

'Shut your face, Thomason, or I'll remove it,' Eamonn whispered into the convict's ear with a threatening tone, his controlled fury building with each stressed word. 'If you alarm this group with your hysterics and panic sets in, I'm gonna tear you limb from limb. Got it? I'm going to free you now, and you're gonna help tend the injured and assist gathering the corpses into the far end of this chamber. Now!'

Eamonn withdrew his hand from over Thomason's mouth, shoving him back into the dimly lit crypt. Thomason turned back and pointed his finger threateningly at Eamonn. 'You wait ...' he said with a vengeance, aiming his hard hat's cap-lamp into Eamonn's face. The man stormed off.

Eamonn understood the man's compulsion in venting his feelings of helplessness. *How long* he wondered to himself. How long could he control this unfortunate bunch who could collectively rise up in hysterics at the drop of a hat. Strange things happen to people in stressful situations. Angers flare, and fists fly. In panicking over the unknown, he could become the whipping post of their frustrations; perhaps even die at the hands of a group of lunatics who would dispute his leadership and conspire against him—the outsider.

Hope and prayer were his strongest allies. These strengths, coupled with an air of authority and his ability to display skills in technical assessment, might placate their fears—he hoped. For now, he was sure they would follow a constructive and pragmatic approach to their common dilemma. Wary of his predicament, he realized he needed human allies, not just strength of character to hedge whatever chances they had in this catacomb. His hope was that they would gravitate to him, to his leadership.

He tread carefully over towards the immense mound of rubble which blocked the main shaft. He inspected, tugged and prodded at the heap. A large black trog appeared at the blockage. The man pulled strenuously at the rubble which gave way in part, collapsing to the rock floor with a loud smack. The falling rocks landed dangerously close to the the inmate's feet. Regardless of the steel-toed working boots, the various sizes and shapes of the debris would break a leg or foot with their enormous weight.

Standing into the cap-lamp beam of Eamonn's hard hat, the man looked a sight. There were streams of dried blood all over his face and parka. His parka was torn and its goose-down feathers dropped now and again to the shadowed floor.

'Whaddya think, Müeller? Do we stand a chance?' asked Williams.

Eamonn looked at the man whose eyes displayed a sincere realism, amidst his bloodied face and dishevelled appearance. Eamonn recognized this down-to-earth demeanor and answered the man with a smile. 'We do, if you believe in it.'

'I believe we're fucked,' Williams replied with a reciprocal grin.

'Y'know Williams, if we keep our heads, we have a fighting chance,' Eamonn said with assurance. 'Can you see if any headway can be made into the office area? The communications room may still be accessible if we can break through—there may even be survivors.'

Williams shook his head. 'I came from that side. Doesn't look promising. I mean ... heh, it's hopeless, man. Yup, downright fuckin' awful,' he admitted, sitting back on a medium sized boulder and removing his hard hat to wipe his brow. 'The powder and fuse magazines are empty. It *would* have to be powder-day *today*, huh? What kinda bad-ass shit happened here?' he added, rubbing some dried blood from his cheek.

'Don't have a clue. The elevator crashed ... and then ... there was an explosion. Can't figure it,' Eamonn admitted, pulling at his large nose. 'They know we're down here, so the rescue team will be down shortly, I hope. I'm going to check the office area. Can you help cart the bodies?'

'I'm on it,' Williams replied, as he got up and put his hard-hat back on.

'Williams?'

'Yeah?' he replied, looking back at Eamonn.

'Before you do that, check the valves along the water pipes. The mains have been ruptured for sure, behind this mound—but there should be some in the piping. See if you can drain it off into something, for drinking water.'

'Gotcha,' Williams replied, and went off.

Eamonn carefully made his way along the rubbled wall, treading randomly up and down with improvised footing over protruding rocks. He took his chances climbing along the unstable mound, boldly inspecting the harum-scarum barrier which threatened to snap down on him like a giant rat trap. This cap-lamp reconnaissance was a necessary risk. The darkness cloaked its perils in secret.

He reached the point where the office entrance once was, and stepped back off the rubble to shed his cap-lamp on the destruction. Williams was right, and his sentiment—*I believe we're fucked*, rang through Eamonn's head. For all intents and purposes, the rubble had homogenized with the scant offices. Apart from some splintered wood from the pulverized door jamb, which projected from crevasses in the heartless stone fragments; the offices, equipment cubby and first-aid room were no more.

Moans and sighs from behind him which echoed around the large main chamber, momentarily disheartened him.

Desperation was springing up like weeds. He could sense it. If he couldn't smother it, it would smother him. Hopelessness was a painful burden which he was not about to bear.

He rubbed a rough slab of stone which jutted out of the colossal adversary, grieving the tragic loss of Frank and his technical team, thinking as well of the unfortunate trogs who were obliterated in the explosion, or crushed in the elevator cage accident.

Eamonn harbored hope in earnest, knowing that Slater was up top, probably supervising the rescue effort and radioing for special equipment and contacting mine collapse experts.

Ribald, a skinny Caucasian murderer, slithered up beside Eamonn. He knew him as an insolent sonofabitch, a mean natured and conniving sort, who always bore a scowl. He had survived the decimating blow with only a cut below one of his deceitful eyes.

'D'ya really believe that a backward bunch of *skimos* have the skill or equipment to support a rescue effort?!' He said, shaking his head indignantly. 'Even with you geeks supervising the fish-faces, it's hopeless!' he added, snapping his fingers boldly in front of Eamonn's face and shining his cap-lamp in his eyes.

Eamonn pushed the man aside and pulled a handkerchief from his pocket to blow his nose, pretending to take Ribald's ranting lightly. When he had finished, he walked away from Ribald.

The man clumsily followed after him, tripping on things both hard and soft. Ribald gave up on his badgering pursuit of Eamonn, and leaned on a boulder to continue his pestering. He removed his hard hat and smugly wagged the cap-lamp rapidly around the catacomb.

'There's a blizzard up there, and it could take *days* before any equipment could be dropped into the camp, or disaster experts for that matter. The engineers here are the bottom of the barrel—fuckin' losers; we're doomed,' he said to Eamonn, knowing well that each wretch in the crypt ate up his words like spaghetti.

'Don't listen to him, he's delirious,' Eamonn said to the group, looking around the cavern at the sullen darkened faces of the trogs moving corpses. He stared at the outlines of huddled bodies against a wall. 'Carry on, and we'll be outta here ... soon.' He moved to within inches of Ribald's face. 'Keep your negative opinions to yourself,' he ordered, in a hushed tone.

'I'll do nothin' of the sort,' he replied with venomous opposition. '*Keep my opinions to myself*!' he mocked, looking around the shadowed room, illuminating the despair with his fading lamp light which pathetically struggled through the dusty air.

'Do us all a favour, and lower your voice, hmm?' asked Eamonn.

'I'll *lower my voice*, when you lower your mask! When *you* give us an honest expert appraisal, and quit jerkin' us off!'

Eamonn refrained from answering. He had to choose his reply carefully, in order to refute Ribald's frustration which they undoubtedly all felt inside. The claustrophobic bellowing of the man could only be countered by a systematic enlistment of those who would support an energetic will for the achievement of survival.

'Go on,' Eamonn offered, glad now for the opportunity to segregate the fatalists. He would allow Ribald to centre-stage for the moment, in order that every bit of doubt be laid on the line.

Williams returned and went over to Eamonn. 'Rotten luck, man.'

'What do you mean?', Eamonn replied, as Ribald cocked an ear their way.

'Pipe burst at a joint and drained off down into the ballast underneath the rail ties. It all filtered down through the gravel—there's not a pool of water anywhere.'

'There ya go!' Ribald shouted, swiping his hand in the dusty air.

'Shut up,' Eamonn said, lowering his head and thinking.

'Yer a smug bastard,' Ribald replied. 'Even if we survive for a couple o' days; what're we gonna drink, eat, keep sane with? Your *words*? A stinkin' wall of *gold*?' Ribald laughed like a madman, scoffing at the dire options.

'Fine. Now, listen to the voice of reason ...,' Eamonn replied.

'No!' Ribald shouted, '*You* listen. Yer a prisoner like the rest of us, here in hell—'

'I've been in a cave-in before, *asshole*, and I've *seen* it all, and *heard* it all before. Yeah, I'm in the same boat, but I'm *still* the boss! Experience delegates! The compressed-air lines are down, so, we can't operate any machines or tools. But, all the same, we're gonna assist the rescuers by digging from the inside out, and we don't stop 'til we drop!'

'With *what*? Our fingers?! Ribald snapped.

'Our fingers to our toes, buddy-boy,' Eamonn replied.

'Yer not our *buddy*, fuckhead.'

'Maybe not, but you're behavin' like a *boy*, and this is a *man's* game—I've got the will, and I know the way!' Eamonn stated with assurance, beginning to search out faces in the dark crypt. 'Who else has the will to survive? Who's with *me*, and who's with the lay-down-and-die salesman? Huh? Who'll exchange their tears for sweat?'

'I'm with ya, Müeller!' Williams shouted energetically. 'Who's with *us*?!'

A lacklustre round of support emanated sporadically from all sides.

'Then, we're halfway there!' Eamonn shouted with confidence. He walked to the shaft plug and felt along the rubbled wall. '*We* are going to move *this*,' he said, climbing up on the stubborn opponent.

'We gonna kiss it outta our way, Müeller?—what the fuck?' asked Williams, as Eamonn lay vertically against the mound, moving his face slowly on front of the rock adversary as though he were listening for a secret whisper from the rock.

'He's outta his fuckin' mind, goddammit!' Ribald shouted.

Eamonn ignored their remarks and kept up his investigation. 'Air!' he shouted gleefully. 'Not much—but a tiny draft seeping through, right here.' He smiled at Williams, who nodded his head in approval at the find. 'Come see,' he said to Williams, who walked to Eamonn and climbed the mound to experience the germ of hope he pointed to. Williams felt the influx of air and reveled with a burst of joyful laughter. Eamonn and Williams leapt from the tiered wall, shaking hands encouragingly.

'So we won't suffocate. We'll starve and dehydrate instead,' stated Ribald, with a scornful counterpoint.

'I'll tell you what we'll drink—if they don't rescue us first,' Eamonn replied, taking a deep breath to make a general announcement. 'Now, let's get down to work, everyone. Two groups; one digs, the other clears this area of bodies and rubble so we can work. There's a job for everyone. Keep the chatter down so we can hear any calls from the rescue team. I want only essential cap-lamps working on a need-to-shine basis. Those who're carting, keep to it. I need ten of you at this wall with us, and I need one person who's worked the infirmary before, to play doctor and keep up with the injured.'

'I can do it,' replied a woman with a French-Canadian accent, whose firm gruff voice stemmed from the dark, as lamps extinguished rapidly around the perimeter of the chamber.

'Who's that?' asked Eamonn.

'Barclay,' replied the woman as she limped from the darkness into the cast of Eamonn's lamp. She was a hearty woman with resolve in her face, her large pretty eyes appearing even more striking against the dirt and grime smudged around her plump face.

'What's wrong with your foot?' asked Eamonn.

'The fucker's sprained,' she bluntly replied, 'so what?'

'I like her crypt-side manner,' laughed Williams.

'Keep it up and I'll have to perform emergency surgery on your balls, Williams,' she said caustically, as Williams' full throttle grin diminished into a insolent pucker on his face. Eamonn chuckled at her repartee.

'That's fine, Barclay. Go to it then, and get us a head-count, will you?' Eamonn asked, as she turned around, switched on her lamp and hobbled into the dank background.

'She should work in Vegas,' said Williams, 'as a geek.'

'Williams, why don't you root around for anything we can use as a prybar, and we'll get started here without tools.'

Williams nodded at Eamonn and walked towards the office area. He turned his head back at Eamonn. 'We should use her—her tits could derail a train.'

'Easy Williams, she'll make you eat your words,' Eamonn replied.

'Well, if it comes down to drinkin' piss ...,' Williams said, leaving his sentiment dangling as he rounded a corner in the cavern.

Thomason, whom Eamonn had the displeasure of dealing with earlier, approached him and spoke from the cover of darkness. 'If it comes down to cannibalism, you'll be the first one I eat.'

Eamonn swung around to illuminate the shadowy threat. There the wiry man stood like a reprehensible gremlin. Eamonn wound up and socked the man square in the mouth, knocking him tumbling back into the shadows.

A woman shrieked, crying in the face of the violence. 'You'll have to suck me through a straw now,' Eamonn said, turning back to the job at hand.

'Müeller!' Barclay called out.

'Yeah?'

'Twenty-eight.'

'Twenty-eight ... so, there's about seventy of us left?'

'No,' her voice echoed, 'twenty-eight of *us* ... and whatever of d'others.'

'Oh—'

seven

JAG TRUDGED THROUGH the blowing squall, pushed
onwards in a deep trance. A distant wolf howl cut through
the frigid air. He could barely make out the hills in the distance, as he carefully stepped alongside some large angular
boulders on the hill he descended. He allowed his body to
fall faster into step down the slope. The Aurora Borealis
vaguely washed back and forth across the twilight sky, like a
watchful entity beyond the veil of snow. Downward he went,
and faster he walked.

A blackbird overhead called out with an oscillating
squawk, sending Jag's mind dancing into the swirling storm.
He turned in circles and looked up, chanting away. The
snow swirled above him, teaming from the heavens, climbing this way and that, coerced by the fickle gusts which
threatened to lift any living thing from its feet.

As the crystalized tears of the heavens fell, the bestial
antithesis arose, ushered in by familiar sacred winds. There,
on the hillside stood a lone black wolf with thick matted fur,
twisted further by the blustering squall. Behind the wolf
leading to where it lingered, were the diminishing footsteps
of a man. Jag's fiery crimson eyes batted back and forth

under a yearning squint, hungering for something below the built up cliff faces which sprang from the sides of the steep bouldered hills.

The blackbird landed in the distance on a cliff face. It crowed out with a screech that permeated the veil of snow. The wolf's ears twisted to the call, drawing the animal forward. It raced along a ridge, then down the hill toward the perched bird.

His eagerness raced ahead of his footing though. Jag was adept at racing through the snow on both two and four legs, but the steep decline, along with the velocity of his momentum and a boost from the sweeping wind, sent him flying. He thrashed and tumbled downwards, erupting the snow as he plowed through it. He cried out with a yelp as he collided with a boulder.

Regaining his footing after rebounding from the obstacle, Jag climbed the dislocated incline to reach the cliff with the roosting crow. The large black bird peeked out occasionally from its small recess in the rock, where it huddled for cover from the elements.

Jag reached the cliff face and hastily clawed his way up around the sides of the small escarpment. He strove to gain access to the ledge above where the blackbird began to walk in circles, crowing out its shrill caterwauls.

Bounding for the precipice where the blackbird loitered, the blackbird took to flight as the wolf trotted intently along the cliff's ledge with his head low and eyes squinting.

Looming at the edge, Jag blinked defensively as the blustering snow flew into his eyes, obscuring his vision. He peered outward at the glow of the distant twilight horizon. The blackbird cawed in the distance, as Jag sniffed at the air. He let out a tremendous howl which reverberated off nearby cliffs.

Suddenly, his attention was captured by something directly below the protruding bluff. He looked straight down and was mesmerized. The end of his nose twitched and his nostrils flared, exhaling plumes of steam. Apart from the driven snow and his dispeled breath, there was nothing to be seen. Nothing moved below at all, yet he was transfixed on a point below, just beyond the base of the cliff adjacent to where a series of hollow fissures lay amongst an outcrop of large rocks.

He turned with a snort of hot vapor and scurried back along the ledge towards its junction with the hillside.

Speeding down the slope with the necessary finesse, he reached the base of the overhang and began sniffing around. Jag moved in seemingly senseless circles, applying a sparse scratch at the snow here and there, until he found a point which held some enigmatic significance. It was there he began to dig energetically at the snow. Jag rooted and clawed away with his large paws. He excavated the site to the point where he had completely disappeared from the surface.

Eventually, Jag's frosted tail and hind legs reappeared at the entrance of the cavity. He was attempting to draw something from below the surface of the thinly mantled glacial ice. He tugged tirelessly at this obsession in the hole. Finally, he reversed himself. He picked another spot and began to anxiously dig another hole at an angle to converge with the first. Soon, he had disappeared again, except for the very tip of his tail which lurched back and forth like a cobra. He hauled and yanked ambitiously at the same object which was reluctant to be freed.

Abandoning the second attempt, he backed up and emerged from the second hole with his fur wet and dotted with ice-burrs. His thick tongue drooped from the side of his fanged gums and his exhaustion vaporized with heaving breaths.

He laid down in the snow, staring at the hole in front of him, coveting its secret bounty with his diabolic crimson eyes. The raging snow crashed heavily into his eyes but melted on contact with his fiery globes, which were lit by the dark passions of some netherworld.

He observed both holes like a sentinel. Back and forth he stared, until he broke with his posture and rolled onto his back and wriggled around in the snow. He squirmed to his feet and shook himself down from head to tail. Looking up to the littered heavens, he let out an extended feverish howl which dwindled to a growl. The manacing wind howled back with a sweeping gust.

Jag flexed his neck, rocking his head within the fur lined hood of his caribou parka. The shaman was back in his human state, his sorcery hidden behind the whalebone glasses which sheltered his icy black eyes. He rotated his wrists and curled his fingers inwards into fists which he clenched fervently, then sprang open with exuberance.

Looking down at the site the spirit-world had guided him to, he slid down feet first into the original and larger hole he had dug. He leaned down into the pit and laboured at the withdrawal of the object. He was determined to extract the stubborn item which appeared reluctant to break loose without a struggle. Finally, Jag lifted out a human-type figure which was petrified and preserved in the icy grave.

The corpse had been reduced to a skeleton in nature, possessing a tight singed leathery covering of skin which held the mummified remains intact. The ice-man was short and lightweight. Jag effortlessly handled the mummy, turning it around carefully and briefly inspecting the mystical benefaction. The ice-man bore the weathered semblances of a ceremonial costume much like the shamans of his ancestors.

Jag brushed the snow and ice from the darkened lanky corpse. Its wiry strands of webbed black hair held particles of ancient dandruff, added to now with freshly falling snowflakes.

Slung around the ice-man's darkened and bony right

hand, was a doll of sorts. It was six inches tall and had a sinewy thong wound around its upper torso. In folklore, the personified talisman was known as the Anknonquatok, *the being of all senses*. It was preserved with the ice-man, grasped in his hand when death met him.

The tiny doll was made of bone and was draped with a small amount of animal skins and fur. It appeared to have a veneer of gold leaf, which foiled its crudely carved features.

Jag maneuvered the scrawny ice-man respectfully across his shoulder, resting it on his back. With his face to the wind, he chanted a verse to his familiars, in gratitude for the guidance.

Jag gained his bearings and set out for his return to Kabloona. As he strove up the hill, the ice-man swayed across his back. Unbeknownst to Jag, the doll necklace was knocked free from the petrified grasp of the corpse, after bumping against a boulder. It drooped precariously by its sinewy thong, from the ice-man's hand.

He retraced the route he had navigated to the finding ground, as best he could. The elements swept up harshly on all sides of him as he paused and turned in a circle, entreating his familiars with a mumble. Then, to his right, he perceived the audible crow of the blackbird. It was that direction he would take.

As Jag ambled forward, the vague but distinct clanking of the camp's snow bus could be detected. He stopped and listened carefully for the direction of travel in which the vehicle motored. It was definitely dispatching away from Kabloona, for as he faced his destination, the muffled clamor moved off behind him.

He moved past the last of the protruding boulders, until he had finally emerged onto the flat plain. He proceeded with an effortless stroll into the face of the squall.

As Jag trekked onwards, the jostling passage from the rocky hillside had caused the doll-necklace to hang feebly from the stiffened fingers of the ice-man. As he moved forward chanting an antiphon in his native dialect, the doll simply dropped from the thread it hung from. It fell to the snow silently. Jag obliviously forged onwards in a trance.

eight

IN OTTAWA, CANADA, the Friday business day was winding down to a close. The milling masses had begun to pack the intersections, eager to bolt ahead in their homebound marathon amid the congestion of the late afternoon rush hour traffic.

There, in the country's capitol, Roblaw Natural Resource Management Inc had its offices contained in the riverside quadrant of the seventeenth floor of a twenty storey concrete office tower, nestled near the Rideau Canal. With its beautifully ornate elevators and exquisitely inlaid lobby ceilings, floors and walls, one was inundated with a graceful and welcoming feeling which was conducive to business. Big business.

Inside the Roblaw corporate offices, a round-table meeting was well underway. A secretary knocked and entered, carrying an elegant decanter of fresh coffee into the boardroom and set it down on the shiney opulent teak meeting table. The suited men took only marginal notice of the incidental interruption and conversation went on unhindered.

The boardroom was resplendent in its tasteful dark hardwood touches. It boasted a refined arrangement of pedestaled Inuit carvings and wall mounted aboriginal prints.

Out of the large windows, with their western exposure running the length of the room, one could get a dazzling view of the canal; in the distance, the fine old parliament buildings gave one the feeling of being close to the pulse of the nation.

Gaar Injugarjuk, wearing a dark suit—in keeping with the other eight well dressed emissaries, tarried at the window sipping his coffee. Setting his cup down into his saucer and cradling it at chest height, Gaar indulged in seeing-off the sun, which cast the last of its now reddish rays through the window and on to the lingering admirer. The tail end of the sunset was one appointment he looked forward to, on a daily basis. On a steady mental diet of tedious fourteen hour days, the invigoration of sunset was a second wind to him. At twenty-eight years old, he was a bright and fastidious corporate lawyer for Roblaw Inc.

Gaar peripherally absorbed the dealings which occurred around the table, while taking-in the vista.

Gaetan Vouillard, a fit, middle-aged bureaucrat with dark gray streaked hair, peered over at Gaar from his seat at the table while waiting for his turn to partake of the fresh coffee. As Quebec's Minister of Indian Affairs and Northern Development, Vouillard was in admiration of Gaar, who was a rising star in the legal profession. Gaar was also commendably modest when it came to accepting the kudos for astonishing feats of negotiations performed in his line of duty.

The young lawyer had proved himself astute and relatively unbiased, playing the role of a mediator in negotiating on behalf of Roblaw Inc. with the IAR's High Council and foreign affairs ministry regarding the 3R program.

A tangible shiver flowed through Gaar's body. He turned from the window to return to his seat at the table, catching Vouillard's eye, recognizing that the man observed the shakes he experienced at the window.

'Just a chill,' Gaar said to Vouillard, as he took his position within the small contingent of government officials who chatted amongst themselves, referring to documents and numerous reports which had been given to each at the onset of the meeting.

'Eskimo tutelage has been a disaster for us in Quebec,' Vouillard said in a nasal French Canadian accent, to Philip Roblaw, who sat at the head of the table stirring his coffee, acknowledging Vouillard's statement with a nod. 'Our aboriginals are represented by knowledgeable natives. They're not all backwards and they wield a tremendous amount of political power. *Lobby*? My God, do they ever!'

Roblaw tapped his teaspoon on the brim of his cup and set it down in its saucer. 'Well,' he began, stroking his thick eyebrows while sitting forward and placing his elbows on the table. 'Let's leave *God* out of this,' he remarked, elevating his hands above his elbows and clasping them together with a small clap. 'This is about *dollars*, not domination. The Aboriginal Republic of the North recognize this and embrace it. They *embrace* it,' he said, waving his hands and looking around the table. 'They covertly fawn over the 3R program, while they outwardly hum-and-haw about ecology and interference from us. It's all a facade—they need us more than we need them.'

Gaar glanced over in Roblaw's direction, expecting just such a hackneyed comment from his father-in-law, whose backward views chipped away at the dwindling amount of respect he had retained for the man. Gaar held his composure for his wife's sake. Although Gaar had brokered the IAR deal for the firm, he wanted in no way to be tarnished along with Roblaw for his typically unsympathetic and mercenary viewpoint. Gaar felt a pang of conflict within himself, for as a corporate lawyer, personal feelings and scruples had no business clouding a high stakes business deal. It was just business, yet Roblaw's sweeping generalizations were patently cruel and unjust.

Roblaw was a lawyer himself—a Queen's Council at that, and was now in his mid sixties with grayed temples, dyed hair and small crescent-framed reading glasses which rested on the end of his nose. He seemed to possess—more so develop, avaricious tendencies as the months and years went on and as the company's profits burst at the seams. It was not to the man's credit as Gaar would mull over to himself on many an occasion. Here was a rich and powerful man, who would have done better to tend to his family, rather than his gorging obsession.

Gaar was painfully aware of how Roblaw had denied his family much love and attention through the years in which he built his empire. But, since Gaar was married to the man's daughter, he was married to the business. He had married Louise, who was at the time an estranged daughter, who unfortunately came around and gravitated back into the grasp of the emperor. The once rebellious woman had come back to the fold, and had dragged Gaar with her. He was reluctantly compressed into the folds of Roblaw's accordion.

Alfred McGregor sat near Gaar. McGregor was a retired Royal Canadian Mounted Police officer and was more of a flunkey than a consultant to Roblaw. He detected Gaar wincing at Roblaw's comment and the disapproving stare that followed. He cleared his throat in a chastising way, by bunching up his fist and pressing it against his mouth while staring across at Gaar. He managed to get Gaar's attention, took a brief moment to stare dryly at him and then turned his head down the length of the table. 'Pass the sugar please,' he asked, as he poured himself a cup of coffee from the decanter.

The sugar was passed up the table from Oliver Tunningham, the lanky Canadian Deputy-Minister of Foreign Affairs, to his assistant who handed the sugar to Gerard Depoissante, the Quebec Minister of Justice. Depoissante delayed the passage by scooping another pinch of sugar for his own coffee, then placed it in McGregor's waiting grasp. 'Thank you,' McGregor said, 'good team-work, by the way,' he added, artificially bolstering the association around the table.

Vouillard lifted his index finger and gestured with a smile. 'The abandoned mines in Quebec and Labrador would be ideal for a program mirroring your 3R Capital Works Barter Agreement.'

McGregor lifted two teaspoons of sugar into his coffee and stirred. He batted his eyes around the table, then fixed his eyes on Roblaw, who removed his small flat top reading glasses and sat back in his chair.

'I'm sure we can broker the deal for you,' Roblaw said with assurance and a nod. 'We can offer our assistance as consultants in an operational capacity—pending of course, the outcome of the bilateral trade talks, and the result of the plebiscite which your aboriginals have undertaken. We can make it happen for you.

'Will your program treaty be renewed?' asked Depoissante.

'No doubt,' replied Roblaw, sitting back in his lavish swivel chair and folding his legs. 'The Inuit are recreational junkies—and there's a big demand for recreation up there. Our operation generates them revenue to support that demand.'

Gaar didn't appreciate Roblaw labeling his people as *junkies*. He'd overheard him speaking with McGregor one time, where they were slagging the Inuit by calling them *skimo*s. That really bugged him and made him wonder what they called *him* behind his back. It was time to act on finding another firm. There had to be some way out, without upsetting Louise.

Roblaw babbled on. 'The Koreans have bottomed out the market for replica Inuit carvings and artificial fur. You're aware of the world wide fish-farming boom, which biology and genetic engineering have helped to prosper. So, what do they have left? Nothing. No exports; well, except for ice. I'm going to make a killing on the fresh-water icebergs from their glaciers for drinking water for the United States—I've got a sweetheart-deal locked and I'm looking at the options of taking on partners, if you're game. We can talk about that later,' he said, sitting forward and leaning on the table again. 'Their biggest obstacle is their proximity—or lack therof, in relation to developed transportation networks. It's an unfortunate geographical setting.'

'The remoteness of their backyard is a valuable commodity,' McGregor added, 'income generating ice prisons.'

'A worthwhile asset when their IMF and World Bank debts are piling up on them,' said the amiable and rotund Depoissante.

Roblaw rose from his chair and casually walked around the table. Gaar had expected him to engage his grand-standing habit, which he found boorish. 'The price of independence!' Roblaw said matter-of-factly.

The ministers glanced around to each other, as their assistants took notes and twisted their heads around to follow Roblaw as he paraded.

'My 3R program *makes* them money!' Roblaw boasted, as he made a full swing around the bottom of the table to circle back up the other side. 'Keeps them in the lifestyle they've been accustomed-to when they were on our welfare system, *without* the guilt. The IMF has been more reluctant to forgive large debts, especially when a province has the gumption to separate and become its own country.'

'The ice prisons are viable,' added McGregor as he sipped

away at his cup of coffee, 'and unlike their traditional means of sustenance, there's never a lean year! With crime on the upswing, we can guarantee the mining workforce will be at capacity.'

Roblaw had completed his full circle of the table and instead of taking his seat at the head, he sauntered over to one of the windows where the city lights could be seen with the advent of the early evening. He unbuttoned his suit jacket and put his hands into his pockets casually staring out at the picturesque city-scape. 'Alleviates the controversy over the death penalty,' Roblaw said nonchalantly, 'hard labour.'

'But it's not a chain-gang?' asked Depoissante. 'I've seen the articles about those lobby groups who protest your concept.'

'That's because two-thirds of our prison population is black. Whites don't give a hoot about white thugs in jail—the few who do, are demented. It's not a racial matter, it's a criminal matter, and we're *open for business*,' he touted, then took a breath and shrugged. 'Who wants to spend one hundred thousand dollars a year for scum to relax, read books, indulging in recreation; where's the *punishment*? The hard working middle class are punished enough! Law abiding citizens who struggle to get by, raising families, going to night school after a hard days work, hmm?—*That's punishment*! It's a slap in the face to victims of crime and to taxpayers to spend five times what most people earn in a year to get rid of the trash.'

Roblaw cleared his throat, acknowledging the approving nods of the men in the room. 'Bleeding-hearts—let them go bleed in a pigs trough! There are no *chain-gangs*, and it isn't a *penal colony*,' Roblaw recited, as he made his way back to the table and leaned over the back of his chair to address the group. 'It's a *rehabilitation* camp, plain and simple. There's no need for chains—where would the inmates run to?

They'd end up snow-angels. And while we're on this positive note, think about the positive economic facets of the program. It costs both our governments, ultimately the *taxpayers*, one hundred thousand dollars a year to keep a criminal in prison here. *Thirty* up there; ten for room and board, clothing and training, and *twenty* directly to the Inuit for the permit. It's *sensible* business. Why spend tax dollars on new prisons? I'm saving the government *millions* and doing our Inuit neighbours a huge favour—*plus*, I'm rehabilitating inmates and giving them a new lease on life with trade skills so they can be productive tax-paying members of society. Check the reports—you'll see. It's all per head, per annum.'

'Keeps 'em all purring,' quipped McGregor.

Gaar sat silently watching and listening to the ring-master of this corporate circus as he worked the presentation like a pro. McGregor acted like the horn-playing seal. Gaar animated the scenario for a fleeting moment in his mind. He felt like an acrobat, but couldn't see himself in a sparkling rhinestone jump-suit. McGregor however, would suit a red bandana (to go with his already shiney nose), and Roblaw would be perfect in a large black top hat, replete with the customary twisted handlebar moustache and a bull whip.

There was a knock at the door. Victoria, Roblaw's young and attractive personal secretary, poked her head through the door and lowered her voice almost to a whisper. 'Mr Roblaw,' she voiced with a glint of apology, 'there's a *gentleman* here to see you—says he can't wait. I'm *sorry*, he almost ... well, he claims to have something very important ...'

'Victoria, I'm in a very *important* meeting,' he replied, slightly annoyed at being interrupted and embarrassed with the triviality, 'no disturbances, *remember*?'

'I'm sorry, sir, I'll let him know,' she replied, slightly crestfallen.

'Gentlemen, I beg your pardon for that disturbance.

Please excuse the interruption,' he remarked, apologizing around the table with a sweeping glance.

As Victoria drew her head back into the hall and proceeded to gently shut the door, Roblaw caught sight of a man whom he recognized. The man looked desperately into the room, catching Roblaw's eye, and waved a small package in the air as the door shut. Roblaw stood up and buttoned his suit jacket. 'I'm afraid nature calls. Gaar, why don't you take our guests through the contract with the IAR, and I'll be back momentarily.'

nine

THE SNOW SQUALL maintained its grasp on Kabloona. The camp appeared deserted, more so than usual. The wreckage of the mine's head-frame remained sadly unattended to, but the bodies of Matawi and Tutuyea had been removed.

The yelps of the sled dogs broke the eerie silence of the abandoned mining camp. Kiratek emerged from the kennel area, piloting a dog sled through the camp towards the main gate. Bundled across the sled were the secured bodies of the Inuit engineers. As Kiratek passed Jag's office trailer, Perq emerged from it. He watched Kiratek reach the main gate and secure the sled with its anchor. Perq stepped down from the trailer and walked for the gate. As he reached the gate, some of the dogs began to lie about in the snow while others nipped at each other. Perq approached Kiratek, shaking his hooded head in dismay.

'A sad day,' said Perq, tugging the bindings which tethered the bodies to the sled. He looked up to find Kiratek standing next to him.

'What d'ya say?' asked Kiratek, staring through his hood into Perq's.

'I said, a sad day!'

'You can say that again. Agaluq is with Triq and Charlie at the barracks, interrogating the inmates. Charlie's gonna take this team to Phoquintok Bay. They were both from there.'

'Yup. Jag will want to sanctify the bodies before they go,' Perq said to him matter-of-factly. 'The team's been fed and they're up for the trip?'

'Shit! I didn't feed them—d'ya think Johnny fed them before he left?'

'I doubt it.'

'I'll bring 'em back to the kennel and feed 'em'

'No,' said Perq adamantly, 'I don't want these bodies to be carted around on such a stupid errand. They must move *forward* only! *Bring* the food to the dogs. Get Charlie to help ya. Meet you back here in half hour. I gotta put out a fire.'

'Gotcha Perq, sorry about the mess up.'

ten

THE CAMP INFIRMARY couldn't even lure fakers wanting a rest from the drudgery of the hard labour. It was a large trailer with eight cots, two of which were occupied. It was sparsely decorated. The infirmary was a foul smelling, stingily outfitted medical treatment room with only the barest of necessities—most of those being of limited supply and of dubious condition. Sterility was a thing of the future.

The pink walls and green tiled floor were apparently conducive to some subconscious healing process. Most visitors only felt grumpy and more ill, being surrounded by the putrid colour scheme which was a shade off the original colour. Maintenance neglect and a couple of years wear and tear worked wonders. The grungy blue-coloured curtains which hung from ceiling track around each cot, were draped back against the wall at each station in the ward.

"the handiwork of a drunken madman" was scratched into the wall near the doorway. "Islam sucks" was etched into the original graffiti. In fact, the infirmary was littered with graffiti, most of it scrawled at cot height running the length of the trailer. The washroom was especially laden with musings, chock-full of bad grammar and free associated thoughts, usually as enlightened editorials of someone else's work.

The inmates had nicknames for the infirmary like "the purgetorium", and "Jag's rib house". A common pastime for the trogs, was to come up with the best catch-phrase TV commercial for visiting the infirmary and act it out in the barracks. They salivated for commercial TV, junk food and visitors. Visitation rights were restricted to twice a year; summer and winter solstice. These two days were set aside for everyone's visitors to come en masse. Few visitors came to Kabloona.

A country western song could barely be heard coming from somewhere in the back of the trailer where the nursing station was located. The incongruous twanging was distorted, almost as though it were being blasted from headphones. There was no doubt its source was a cassette tape or CD, as the atmospheric interference was debilitating for AM/FM radios at the latitude of Kabloona. The sounds of someone plunking away at a typewriter were interspersed with the thin tones of the music.

From within the small enclosed nursing station, Maxwell Dopplestein emerged. Sporting an unsanitary and wrinkled lab coat, the short, balding nurse walked smartly over to the cot of a large sedated man who lay in a deep sleep. Max checked the IV unit, fiddled with its drip valve and checked his watch as a matter of course. To complete the ritual, he went to the foot of the bed and lifted the suspended clipboard, marking something trifle into it.

Laying back with her head bandaged, Brunhilde observed from her cot. Max returned to the top of the man's bed and shook him out of his coma-like sleep into a partially conscious state. The man began to wheeze and cough, mumbling in a daze as Max withdrew a vial of pills from a drawer in the man's bedside table.

To Brunhilde, it wasn't apparent what was ailing the big galoot, but whatever it was—she didn't want it. The conspicuous absence of other patients un-nerved her slightly.

Max shook two pills from the container, poured the man a glass of water from a plain stainless steel decanter and administered the dose to him. He then dabbed the man's perspiring forehead with a cloth. Max then proceeded to dampen the cloth in a fastidious maneuver, pouring a few drops of water from the decanter onto the towelette as though he were a priest at an altar. Folding the cloth neatly into a small square, he resumed dabbing the man's face all around.

Brunhilde waited patiently, yet eagerly observed, anticipating her audience with the runt. His fussiness over such a simple errand was becoming unbearable to her.

'You'll be outta here within the week, Walters,' Max said, opening and refolding the cloth as the man rustled in his cot, 'Look, don't knock the catheter loose, okay? Doc'll be back in a few days. You're coming along just like he said you would. You're looking better—looking strong.'

'Fuck off, Dopplestein—asshole,' Walters mumbled, dozing off into oblivion.

Max sighed. He scratched his head, then proceeded to flip through the pages on the clipboard with tremendous speed and agility.

'Florence Nightingale, you ain't,' Brunhilde said from her adjacent cot.

'Sticks and stones ...,' Max replied abruptly, keeping his head buried in the paperwork.

'Nevermind the poetry—I need you to come look at something,' she said, with building impatience.

Max rose from the side of Walters' bed and engaging the

101

airs of a physician, approached Brunhilde. 'What seems to be the problem?' he asked.

'Can you draw the curtain ... pretty please?'

'There's no one else here—well, there's Walters, but do you really *feel* ...'

'I *feel* you should draw the curtain for Christ's sake! Do it *now*!', she shrieked.

Max was caught off guard by her abrupt command and immediately drew the curtain mechanically around the bed. 'Okay, it's drawn—so, *what's* the problem?'

'There's a dead man under my bed,' she said, calmly.

'Oh, is that all?' Max replied, taking hold of the curtain and walking it back around the track.

Brunhilde snatched Max's rumpled lab coat and pulled him back to her along with the curtain, which proved no anchor for Max. 'I *said*, there's a dead man under the bed,' she threatened, pulling him practically on top of her. The curtain tore away from some of its eyelets as Max grasped it for support.

'Would you like something to help you sleep?' Max replied in earnest.

Brunhilde pulled the sheets back from over herself, revealing the blood spattered underbedding and her soiled gown.

'*Holy*—'

'This ain't mine, it's from the downstairs neighbour,' she said, as she shoved Max from her grip and raised her thick eyebrows, staring at Max with a foreboding expression.

Max apprehensively leaned over and gaped under the cot. With sudden shock, he registered the horror and gravity of her offhanded remark. He swallowed his breath in mortification, fumbling with fear having come to the realization of who it was laying crumpled in a dead heap below the cot. 'Cripes, it's Perq! How— You—?' Max stammered, pointing from Perq's body up to Brunhilde, who grinned deviously.

Brunhilde had gained the audience she desired and effect

she anticipated. She grabbed the timid man, who was now mentally dishevelled and teetering on falling to pieces. Brunhilde's tight strangling grip may have been the only thing which held the hapless nurse together.

'He covered my mouth. Tried to smother me,' she said, in a lucid way, 'has the smell of explosives on his hands. If you weren't blasting that crappy music into your pea brain, you would have heard him come in. He slipped off his parka and tip-toed to my bedside.'

Max was speechless. His eyes bulged from their sockets, and his head trembled uncontrollably. Brunhilde relaxed her grip from his collar, and he stood erect, covering his mouth in an attempt to pull himself together. She took a subtle hold of the bottom of his lab coat and sat up on the edge of her bed.

'Hear what I said?' she asked, 'he *reeked* of explosives! Earth to nurse,' she mocked, waving her hand on front of his stupefied face. Max's eyes batted all around the room, as though he were trying to propel himself out of the situation. 'He was reciting my last rites with his gleaming eyes, but I clipped his wings—with *this*,' she said proudly, swiftly brandishing a scalpel, and gripping Max's wrist violently. 'Maybe he wanted to frame *you* for the job. This knife is from *your* lock-up; brought it to my bed as insurance, and that's when I opened up a jugular policy with him.'

'Let go of my arm!' Max cried out, attempting to flee.

Brunhilde stood quickly and spun Max around with an experienced motion, covering his mouth with one hand and applying the scalpel blade to his neck with the other. 'One *word*, and you'll end up another stiff on the Kabloona meat wagon! Now, if you're finished playing nurse, you're gonna get us outta here. *I'm* going to save both our lives,' she said, speaking tersely into his ear. Max mumbled beneath the tight seal of her hand.

Brunhilde gave Max a stern shake and released him. The

scalpel remained elevated and within easy striking distance. She waved the knife back and forth with the amusing squeaks of the country western music playing in the background.

'I'm not going anywhere—you're crazy!' Max announced with half-baked courage.

'Crazy!? I know what's going on around here, see!? Do ya think the head-frame burnt down by accident?'

'The head-frame burned down? Where are the casualties?'

'In hell, fucker—you're so outta touch, *Florence*, and yer as dumb as a lemming. Fortunately, I'm stupid like a fox. I *heard* the guards talking as they walked by my window—an ANFO explosion at the head-frame ... ANFO needs a *detonator*? ... hello?' she said, shaking her head irritably. 'You and yer bloody headphones!'

'I'm to take your word for it? You're a *murderer*!' Max declared, as though he were a prosecutor in a courtroom, pointing to Perq's body which lay in a pool of blood beneath her cot. 'The ground rumbles around here with explosions like clockwork! I won't be a party to murder!'

'When in Rome ... know what I mean?' Brunhilde growled, then began to stew with frustrated anger. She nimbly took him by the collar and twisted it tight. 'Do I have to spell everything out for ya, you *stupid* fuck?! They found *walls* of gold down there! *Best* thing for Roblaw, *worst* thing for the Eskimos. Figure it out. They need a gold-rush here like they need single malt scotch by the skid load. They wanna keep the cat in the bag—so they're fakin' a catastrophe.'

'Whaddya mean?'

'That lunatic, *Jag*, will say this place is cursed. Christians? They're heathens by nature! Spirits and all that shit. You're *Jew* right?'

'Yes, I'm *Jewish*.'

'Well, think of them as ... as—whaddya call them in Jewish?'

'Gentiles?'

'Naw, that's too ... *gentle*, what else ...'

'Philistines?'

'Too mamby-pamby. Fuckin' *heathens* is what they are, and don't you forget it! Now let's get outta here, before they sacrifice *us*! Let's go!'

Max stood reluctant to her prodding. 'We're protected under a federal umbrella—'

'No, we're protected by "Sidney the scalpel", and "Sidney" wants to know whose side yer on,' she cautioned, waving the knife in front of his face.

'You're out of your mind,' he stated nervously, almost pleading with her.

'For doing the same thing that got me in here to get me out? You're definitely in here for a white-collar crime—ain't ya, *chicken-little*?'

The sled dogs at the gate began to bark. It caught Brunhilde's attention. She shed a peripheral glance out the window towards the gate. She was drawn close to the window and caught site of a vague figure entering from outside the gate. Grabbing Max's arm, she yanked him to the window with her.

There, through the fluttering snow, and passing under a light post, was Jag. As he passed through, the dogs barked at him viciously, some even leaping up at him with whatever leeway their tethers would allow. Jag moved aside, stepping out of range of the anchored team. He walked backwards momentarily, soothing the dogs with an overture of a familiar rapport, then straightened himself to walk forward into the camp.

'It's Jag-off. Did you see that?!' Brunhilde shouted, pulling Max so close that she almost shoved his face through the window. 'Look! What's that on his back?! What the fuck?! He's wearing a corpse!'

'Maybe it's a seal,' Max uttered, refuting Brunhilde's claim.

'It's a *corpse*, asshole! He's got King Tut riding his back. Since when does a seal have arms and legs? No *wonder* you can die from a paper cut around here, *nurse*! So, the voodoo-king is on the prowl, eh? You know yer way around these parts ...'

'No ... I'm afraid I ... don't really,' Max replied, attempting to draw his body away from the window, against the imposition of Brunhilde's manhandling.

Brunhilde angrily grabbed Max by the collar again and shook him violently. 'I've *seen* you outside at the gates before—all chummy with the guards and playing with the dogs, you brown-nosing ass kisser! *You're* our ticket outta here—we might even become friends.'

'You need help—it's arctic delirium! Paranoid delusions—it's not your fault *really*,' Max replied in a patronizing way, yet fearful that his tongue could put him in the same boat as Perq. 'Perq came here simply to fill out an accident report and ... you ...'

'Yeah, what? Killed him in cold blood?'

'By mistake, kinda.'

'It'll be no mistake to cut out yer tongue, motherfucker! I don't have to prove anything to you 'cept that I mean business. Now get me the bootlegger's parka,' she ordered, 'over there, beside the last cot. I've got to change out of this bloody gown. Do it!' she barked, kneeing Max in the crotch.

Max dropped to his knees gasping, not daring to inhale and shying from the glimmer of promised agony waiting to blossom. He instinctually postponed the inevitable surrender imposed by the impact of the surprise blow to the gonad. Max tumbled over and curled up in a fetal position, both hands compressing his crotch. His eyes bulged and his mouth remained gaping, yet nothing could convince him to draw a breath. Suddenly, he emerged from his suspended animation, drawing a deep painful breath as though he had been held under water for ages. The tears dribbled from his eyes and he breathed out a long pathetic groan, his face seeming like a clay mask.

Brunhilde kicked his leg cruelly, adding insult to injury. 'You sure got balls for a *nurse*. Now get the parka, or I'll rack 'em up again.'

Max slowly staggered over onto his hands and knees, attempting to regain his composure. Some perched tears ran down his flushed cheeks and off the end of his nose. The fireworks were not over.

eleven

TRIQ WAS SWEPT along from behind, by a high wind. He caught site of Jag entering his office trailer and sailed himself along in that direction, ushered by the snow-freckled wind. As he reached the trailer, he grasped the railing and guided himself up to the door. He knocked and waited. A muffled "enter", beckoned him in.

Triq entered the office and was immediately cast into a state of awe. He mechanically closed the door behind himself, maintaining his gaze as Jag stood there with his back to him. The man was busily mixing up a concoction of herbs from his medicine jars. The ice-man hung from his back, facing outwards, like a symbiotic tenant. Though its eyes were sealed, the dried sinewy facial features exuded a ghostly living appearance— especially in the dim flickering light of the whale-oil lamp.

Jag had fastened the ice-man's ragged hands together across the top of his chest just below his neck and secured its bound wrists to his parka. The ice-man's costume was not at all threadbare and provided additional support in holding the mummy together.

Triq drew back his hood and took a careful step forward. 'The legend *is true*,' he uttered, 'it was said, "K'kadonts d'nee"—the truth will flash before your eyes ... and now ...,' Triq stammered, extending his hand cautiously toward the draped ice-man, then drew it back reverently.

Jag turned to Triq, tapping the polished bone stirring utensil on the brim of his crude cup, and then turned away, moving past the suspended clipboards on the wall, towards his desk. Sliding the thin stirring implement into the eye-holes of a feathered mask, he slurped at his potion as he lifted Slater's production report from the corner of his desk and perused it.

Behind him, the harpoon was noticeably absent from its brackets on the wall, and there was an addition over the narrow hallway entrance. A large red, black and turquoise detailed blanket was draped over the lintel, blocking the view to the communications cubby. Jag looked up from the report and faced Triq.

'Yes,' Jag said, 'it is true—K'kadonts d'nee,' he whispered like a soothsayer, levelling the small gourd to his lips.

'It's an honour to serve you in the presence of great spirits—and the ancestor who lives in death,' Triq said, keeping a respectable distance.

'We will seek out the unfortunate souls of the underworld, when the sky and wind have finished scolding us,' Jag muttered, speaking practically into the cup which encased his words in reverberation. He drank back his potion and looked suspiciously at Slater's production report, his whalebone glasses giving the impression he had X-ray vision.

'The injury from below—prior to the explosion?' Jag enquired, 'was this *Brunhilde Hamilton* brought to the surface?'

'Yes, the woman surfaced,' Triq replied, as the bad news he had to inform Jag of, jumped into his mind.

'Infirmary?' he asked, putting the report down.

Triq nodded, as he strived to bring his news to light. 'Matawi and Tutuyea are dead,' he said, placing his hand over his mouth and raising his eyes to Jag.

Jag repugnantly pursed his lips and looked at the wall where the harpoon once hung. He slammed his cup down on his desk atop Slater's production report. 'How?!'

'In the explosion that burned the head-frame down—the saboteurs.'

'They will suffer. We will see to it,' Jag replied matter of factly, without the animosity or vengeance which Triq was expecting in his words. 'Perquanoak— where is he?'

'Infirmary. To question the woman in the accident.'

'Yes, of course,' Jag said, swinging around and facing the wall. 'I want everyone in pairs, until we catch the *culprits*.'

'I'll go to him, and let him know you're back,' Triq said, as he turned and walked to the door, pulling his hood over his head. Reaching the door, he paused briefly to turn and have another glimpse of the ice-man, then opened the door with an elated sense of purpose and disappeared into the white.

§

In the infirmary, Brunhilde had already slipped back into her prison jump-suit. She stomped the floor, securing her feet into Perq's fancy expedition boots.

'I've only got six month's left on my sentence! If I leave with you, I'm jeopardizing ...,' Max blurted desperately, as he meekly handed her Perq's dark blue parka which was embroidered with wolf images.

'There's plenty of room under this bed, so watch yer step!

Now, gimme that!' Brunhilde commanded, as she snatched the parka and put it on. 'Get yours!' she ordered, shaking her hand in the air. Max stood there like a dolt, hoping she'd just go away if he ignored her.

She kicked his shin. 'I *said* get yer fuckin' coat! Hey, I think "Sidney" wants to dance!' Brunhilde grasped the scalpel and swiftly lashed out at Max with it.

She nicked Max's forearm and he gaped down in shock to locate a wound. There was nothing to be seen, although he definitely sensed the swipe of the blade. He held his forearm up as though he were looking at his wrist watch. Brunhilde looked on wickedly. 'He likes to dance to tinny country-western music—hey look, *line dancing*!'

'*Shit*!' Max shrieked, as a two-inch gash appeared on his forearm. Little droplets of blood began to form along the fine incision.

'Now fetch yer coat, or I'm going to kill you here and now.' She meant it, and Max knew it.

Max obediently turned around in a terrified state and jogged over to the nurses station. He nervously grabbed a bottle of hydrogen peroxide and applied the contents to his cut, spilling half the bottle on the floor. He hastily tore some gauze from a roll, and pressed it on his wet forearm. Fearing her impatience, he dropped his concern over the wound and quickly slipped into his boots. He grabbed his striped parka and trotted back out to her.

Brunhilde stood beside the bed, rummaging through the pockets in Perq's coat. She withdrew a set of keys in delight. 'Well lookee-here,' she said, dangling the keys from her index finger. 'We're gonna get some supplies and a snow-mobile. I don't care if you guide us to an airport, seaport or bottle of port—just get us there fast, 'cause "Sidney" finds you *very* attractive, and I wouldn't want him jumpin' your bones before you've outlived your usefulness.'

Triq entered the infirmary, startling the two inmates. He

looked down and noticed a body on the floor. He became incensed seeing Brunhilde wearing Perq's parka and swiftly drew a semi-automatic pistol from beneath his coat. 'On the floor!' he yelled, whipping himself into a frenzy. 'On your knees now! Hands behind your heads!!'

Brunhilde obeyed Triq's furious bark, kneeling and sliding the blade secretly along her wrist into the cuff of her parka. Max held up his arms and approached. Triq peered down at the body laying on the blood spattered floor, recognizing Perq. The horror beamed from his eyes.

'Thank God! Just in time ...,' said Max, nearing Triq.

Triq smashed Max in the head with the butt of his pistol sending him reeling back, his hands covering the blow. Triq let out a yell, moving forward and kicking Brunhilde with his short but powerful leg. She teetered over unhurt from the punt. Max obediently knelt beside Brunhilde who was regaining her balance.

'I said on your goddamn knees! Murderers!' Triq roared, as he placed the pistol within inches of Max's face, gripping it so tightly, it shook in his vengeful hands. Sweat began to form on Triq's face. A tiny bead slid down his forehead into his left eye. He winced and the salty bead was squeezed out to flow down his pudgy cheek. He briskly rubbed his eye, cautiously looming back from his prisoners.

Brunhilde twitched anxiously. He abruptly resumed his double fisted grip on the weapon, swinging the barrel in front of her face. She remained tight-lipped, eager for a chance to turn the tide on Triq.

'Najagneq will—want to ... deal with you *personally*,' he slowly hissed, attempting to control his fury. He eased up on his double grip of the pistol and searched inside his parka with his free hand. Withdrawing a pair of handcuffs, he secured Brunhilde's left wrist and motioned sideways with his pistol for Max to suspend his right wrist next to the open dangling wristlet.

'Wait, I had nothing to do—'

Triq crowned Max with the butt of the pistol again. He crumbled and sat on his heels. Max pressed his abused skull, cringing in pain. Triq tugged Brunhilde's cuffed wrist over to Max's levelled right hand and snapped the adjoining wristlet on him. 'Jag has your medicine!' Triq barked.

Brunhilde lunged at Triq, flailing the scalpel like an Amazon with her free hand. Still on her knees and with a tethered dead-weight impeding her, she swiped ferociously at Triq, managing to catch him in the leg, face and finally burying the blade in his pistol hand. He yelped in shock and dropped the gun. He stood there, momentarily disoriented, then quickly dove for the gun which was knocked out of both their reaches.

Brunhilde dropped the scalpel and leapt on top of him, dragging Max unwittingly along. She managed to reach out and grasp the pistol, but was confounded by Triq's overlapping grip which wrestled with her for control. Adrenalin was in the air. She yanked the handcuff chain and drew Max closer. He reluctantly participated as a satellite in the turbulent scuffle.

Brunhilde took a firm grasp of Triq's short black hair with her cuffed hand. She desperately pounded his face into the tiles until he lost interest in the pistol.

Max's strength drained, shattering his spirit. He had turned his face away and detached himself from the repulsive hammerings of his arm which he had sacrificed as rubber.

Emerging from the struggle victorious and holding the pistol proudly in her right hand, Brunhilde sat up and pistol whipped Triq into unconsciousness when he attempted to rise.

'The things I do for you,' she said, standing up and pulling Max up on his feet to face him. 'First you kill Perq, and then you beat the shit outta Triq—there's no stopping you.'

'*You* did it!' Max shrieked with impotence. He began to sob and plead with hysteria. 'I—I was in the back room ... typing! I'm innocent!'

'Oh, yes. Thank you for the *alibi-by-baby*,' she said, dragging Max over to the nurses station and looming over the typewriter. She reached for the roll of gauze Max had torn a piece from earlier and tore away two pieces for herself. 'Nice typing music, *Max*,' she said, forcibly maneuvering him like it was a beginners lesson in barn-dancing. She lifted her left arm over Max's head and cuddled him from behind. Max cringed in helplessness. His hands were sitting atop each other and she smothered his space, controlling him from behind.

'What're you doing?!'

'Let's just say I need some oven mitts.'

'You're insane!'

'No, I'm allergic to typewriters—now move with me, asshole. We *need* this typewriter or things will never work out,' she said, taking hold of the portable manual typewriter with her gauze padded hands and guiding Max back into the ward like a malignant shadow. She forced their way to her blood stained bed, where Perq's body lay on the floor.

'What're you going to do?' Max pleaded, as she loomed over Perq's body. She raised the typewriter in the air, drawing Max's hesitant hand with her as her intention became patently clear to Max. 'Nooooo!!' Max pleaded mournfully, as the typewriter was thrust downwards.

A tiny bell rang out, as Perq's skull was crushed by the blow. 'What're you going *on* about? He's dead already. I'd understand if you were bothered that *your* fingerprints are all over this thing—not as pure as the driven snow now, eh?'

Max collapsed to the floor like a whipped dog. A paranoid hysteria crept over him, compelling him to desperately scavenge over the unconscious body of Triq. He searched rabidly through Triq's many pockets. She stuffed the gauze in her own parka, picked up the scalpel and slid it carefully into another pocket.

'Looking for the keys for the cuffs? Don't bother,' she said, tugging Max away from Triq. 'We don't need 'em. We're *married* until we're safely on board a plane or boat— too much a temptation to carry them with us. Now,' she whispered, catching Max by the collar and yanking him an inch from her face, 'supplies.' Brunhilde pulled the hood over her head and ushered Max to the door. 'Oh,' she said, 'you don't have another typewriter do you—for Triq? Ah, fuck it.'

§

Jag stepped down from his trailer into the raging squall, pausing to survey the desolate camp from behind his whale-bone glasses. Looking towards the infirmary, he walked off in its direction, chanting a song to his familiars. The sled team barked at his figure as Jag moved away from them. Their barking permeated the camp and seemed to syncopate and harmonize with Jag's tuneful chant.

Between himself and the infirmary, stood the fenced-off supplies storage hut, in which Brunhilde and Max covertly busied themselves gathering the items needed for the trek through the wilderness. Jag obliviously passed the unlocked fence gate which had been closed to appear locked.

Jag toddled along in the squall towards the infirmary, aware of a sense of death, but was unconscious of what awaited him. He didn't register the significance of the foot-prints stomped recently in the commonly used path, covered slightly now by a dusting of flakes.

As the two hastily emerged from the shed, Brunhilde stopped short of opening the gate having noticed Jag. She kept this a secret from Max, confirming her comprehension of what Jag piggy-backed. When he faded into the squall, she opened the shed's perimeter gate and hauled Max through with her.

'Let's go before the jig's up!'

'I'm going to lose my grip on this stuff if you don't slow down,' Max pleaded, as Brunhilde set a fast pace towards the main gate.

'Shut yer face!' Brunhilde shouted, increasing the pace. Both cradled chin-high boxes of supplies in their arms.

They neared the main gate but were forced to pause. It was only opened slimly, posing a threat to their balancing act. The dogs began to bark as Brunhilde began to shove the gate with her leg, to widen the opening.

'Kiratek?' Charlie shouted from the team, believing the food had arrived from the kennel to feed the dogs. He approached the two who had not noticed his presence.

'Shit!' Brunhilde belched with hostile angst. 'I'll slit your throat—' she said to Max, as Charlie took hold of the gate and slid it open for Perq as he saw it, who had obviously enlisted the help of an inmate.

Brunhilde slid through the gate with an evasive nod, but Max had looked hood-to-hood with Charlie as he passed. To the left of the gate's opening sat the dog-sled. To her right was a snowmobile with a tow-sled hitched to it. She went for the machinery.

'Whaddya say, Max? Not a good day to be a prisoner huh?'

'Charlie—' Max blurted, cut-off in mid breath, being abruptly hushed by Brunhilde with a terse yank of the tandem handcuff. Max dropped a small carton when she tugged him off balance, which Charlie picked up.

Reaching the snowmobile, she dropped her boxes down

into the sled. Max followed suit, allowing the cartons he held to tumble into the aerodynamic plexi-sled.

'Perq?' Charlie shouted, approaching Brunhilde with the stray carton in his hands. 'Kiratek went to the kennels—said he'd manage it himself 'n' for me to wait here.' Charlie walked up next to Brunhilde, looming next to her after dropping the carton with the rest. 'Don't know what's taking him so long—Perq?' he enquired, nudging Brunhilde's elbow.

Brunhilde swiftly swung herself around to face him directly. She smiled childishly at Charlie, taunting his speechless reaction as she rapidly withdrew the pistol she acquired from Triq. She thrust it skillfully into the midsection of his thick parka, firing twice into his guts.

'*Don't*!!' Max screamed belatedly, as Charlie crumbled to the icy ground with a moan. The dogs went wild with the muffled shots. Brunhilde put her boot on Charlie's shoulder and tumbled him out of the way with a push of her leg. She violently tugged her dumbfounded partner with her as she mounted the seat of the snowmobile and attempted to start the machine. She twisted the ignition key and pushed the starter button. The starter motor jumped into action, but failed to turn the engine over. She repeatedly attempted to start the snowmobile without success.

'C'mon *fucker*!' she whined, scolding the machine in a half-pleading way.

An elongated primal scream rifted through the camp.

'Oh, *God*,' gushed Max, anxiously pacing back and forth beside the obstinate snowmobile—as much as his hinged wrist would allow. Brunhilde sternly yanked him towards her.

'Sit in front of me, asshole!' she shouted, dragging him onto the craft and plopping him in front of her. His cuffed wrist moved in parallel with hers as she poked at the instrument panel. 'Do you see anything wrong in the gauges?!' she yelled in his ear, pulling back the hood from his head with her free hand.

'Maybe it needs to be choked.'

'Where's the switch?!' she shouted.

'I ... I don't know!' he sputtered.

'There's so many fuckin' dials and knobs—y'must know!!'

'I don't know how to prime the engine!!'

'I know how to choke the life outta ya—ya fuck!!'

Max lifted his shoulders in nervous ignorance as she dismounted the craft, lugging Max to the attached tow sled. 'Grab this stuff fast—we're taking the dog sled!' she shouted, as Max sluggishly gathered what Brunhilde hadn't and moved toward the dogs which barked incessantly. 'Hurry, Jag'll be up our ass in a minute!!'

Forsaking the few cartons which had fallen from their grip into the snow, they clumsily hustled to the dog sled and dropped the goods helter-skelter down into a vacant spot on the sled. Brunhilde hastily unfastened the dead weight of the tethered load and began to push the heavily draped items off the sled.

'Help me dump this crap for chrissakes, or I'll cut your heart out and feed it to these mongrels!!' she bellowed, as Max begrudgingly assisted shoving the ballast off the laden sled. Brunhilde threw the tie-down cords into the sled, leaving their supplies unsecured.

'*Six months*,' Max pouted. He wavered for a moment pondering his fate. In a sudden burst of desperate insight, he exploded. 'Help!! Clemency! Helllp!!'

'Goddammit!' Brunhilde blurted, withdrawing the pistol and whacking him violently in the face with it. His lip bled profusely as she carted him like a limp fish on a hook, to the rear of the sled. The closest dogs turned and snapped at Max, lapping at the blood which dripped generously to the snow in their tracks.

Brunhilde plopped her delirious partner into the sled,

unfastened the snow anchor, then availed herself of the handy whip which lay across the hand grips at the navigator's post. Cracking the whip with a loud snap, the team began to tune itself to the job at hand. With a determined "*yah*!", the dogs began to tug, and the sled was in motion. Brunhilde gleefully helped the team along with leg strokes, which assisted in propelling the sled forward.

Max sat taciturn in the sled, dabbing his lip with his free left hand. He sulked despondently, sitting directly in front of Brunhilde with his cuffed right hand raised uncomfortably in the air. He found it easier to turn his back to the wind and face her knees, rather than having to twist his arm over his head in order to accommodate the distorting imposition of the handcuffs; Brunhilde grasped the sled handle with her tethered half of the chained wristlets.

The sled moved quickly into the ceaseless twilight, disappearing into the flustering polar snow-squall.

Mac Tighearnain, the B-shift engineer, stealthily dashed up to the gate like a fugitive, creeping from behind Jag's office trailer. He stepped over and knelt beside Charlie, who lay dying in the snow. Drawing his hood back, he put his ear to Charlie's mouth and listened as Charlie breathed out his last words. Mac donned his hood, peering around like a jackal from his perch at the death scene. He surveyed the tracks of the dog-sled, then eyed the snowmobile.

twelve

JAG WALKED SOLEMNLY along the path from the infirmary with the bootless and bloodied body of Perq slung between his arms. He chanted a somber verse with pent-up rage behind each syllable. His mind fluttered with the snow. Perq had come far and had shown great dedication—perhaps to a fault. He had exhibited much promise, and now the promise had been snuffed out. Kabloona had slaughtered him—the *white dogs*. Thieves and murderers. He trembled with anger.

Destruction seemed to permeate the air—the *fear* of it, and the *want* of it. *Here it is, and here it shall stay*, thought Jag. It was a dismal day, with each unique descending snowflake raining down a dismal message. A fall from grace, death. He paused in his tracks, raised his face to the heavens and opened his mouth, capturing some snowflakes on his tongue. The snow clothed the lifeless body of Perq.

A tear streamed down Jag's cheek from behind his elemental spectacles as he began his procession again, occasionally looking down at his nephew whose limp body slumped within his powerful arms.

The ice-man swayed like an ominous metronome on his back as he proceeded towards his office. He arrested his steps when he came upon the unlocked compound fence which held the supplies hut and equipment sheds. He looked suspiciously at the trampled snow, noting the vague but discernable treads of an inmate's boot and the unmistakable signature of Perq's unique expedition boots.

His breathing became heavy and his anger began to build with each vengeful breath. Infuriated with this residue of the murderers' presence, he burst into the small compound laden with his entourage of death and stormed to the equipment shed adjacent to the supplies hut. He kicked the door open with lightning fury and entered. Moments later, he emerged carrying several bundles of dynamite in his arms rather than his beloved nephew. In his right hand he held a flare which he carefully ignited, casting a bright circular yellow glow around himself.

With a volcanic stride, he exited the compound, proceeding to turn in a circle with his face to the turbulent sky. Pocketing most of the bundles of TNT into his caribou parka, he retained a single bundle in his left hand. He spread his arms and cried out with shrieks of vengeance in Inuktitut, petitioning his familiars and the spirits of the elements for assistance.

To Jag, the white scourge had brought on the debacle. *They* had turned him into a murderer—and now his flesh and blood had perished in the undercurrent of the feud. He fixated on the *white-curse*. From a welcome to an inconvenience, from good intention to cruel invention, from a slight to a grudge and from a grudge to destruction; welcome to *Kabloona*! Jag waved his arms, crying out unintelligibly with gut-wrenching agony. He felt cursed.

His hand was forced in this catastrophe, but he recognized

that it was *his* hand which swung the cruel pendulum. Now he'd play the white-man's game—he would one-up them, and introduce them to their own devices. At their prodding, he had struck out in self preservation, on behalf of his people. In defence of his sacred world, he would now apply the solution like a liniment, to destroy the fungus.

Jag's mind swirled back to when he was a youth. One fateful day, the same relative circumstances had produced a similar outcome. Push went to shove, and shove went to the grave.

Jag had served ten years in a Canadian prison for the second degree murder of a Royal Canadian Mounted Police officer whom he'd caught in the act of raping a young Inuit girl. The young woman had come into the habit of begging scraps of food and supplies from the police outpost at Peary Inlet. One day on a scrimmage for food, the officer's desires overcame him and he took what he wanted by force—in full uniform, on unofficial business. Jag had happened by, and ten years happened along.

The overwhelming memories disheartened him; the recent blood he had spilled for the sake of his land, vindicated him. And now, the repercussions of his actions, saddened him.

If he couldn't plug the leak and silence the story, the very heart, mind and *soul* of the Arctic would perish. The plundering would be disastrous. It would be a snow-balling time bomb and the environment would be decimated beyond healing. The temptation to benefit from the windfall would be too irresistible for his innocent people—especially the youth, not to avail themselves of the debt relieving, empire building benefits.

It was his intention that their empire should be only of a spiritual nature. Any further material trappings would cripple the spirit of the Inuit. Modest living in a humble environment was the quest for his nation—as he saw it. He had to bear with the sacrifice of his nephew, and if he could plug the hole, he would stop the leak and end the tears.

Jag trod carefully over mounds of heaped snow to reach the flagpole in the centre of the camp. The IAR's half-masted flag fluttered and turned with the blustering wind.

'Come, my disciples; be spared the martyrdom of the spirits,' he mumbled, 'as I do the deed I must—without staining your souls!' Jag began to chant as he tolled the horizontally suspended metal triangle which was fixed solidly near the base of the flagpole.

A few moments had passed when Jag caught sight of two figures coming from the direction of the prisoner barracks area. He believed them to be Agaluq and Kiratek. Jag covertly circled around the on-coming men. He set out to reach the barracks.

Stealthily pausing behind a heap of broken machinery just beyond the infirmary, Jag noticed Triq emerging from the infirmary. Triq held his hand to his head, tending the blow he received from Brunhilde. Jag continued along secretly, with the descending snowflakes around him reflecting the bright yellowish light from the flare. He disappeared into the twilight shadows.

Beyond the gates, the camp appeared peacefully nestled in a fresh blanket of snow. It was serene with the flurries angling downwards, pushed by the huffing wind through the camps yellowish sodium lights. The dog-sled tracks were apparent but not well defined now, and the snowmobile had disappeared, its tracks leading off in a direction opposite that of the sled. Charlie's dead body lay unattended—except for the attraction of the snow, which was gently enveloping his body in a white crystalline blanket.

thirteen

'WE HAVEN'T HAD a single problem with the 3R pilot camps,' said Roblaw, picking at his ear. 'No escapes, no riots. Refer to your pie-chart diagrams in the prospectus for the hard-copy back up. And although the workforce is integrated with Inuit trainees, there's no threat of a take-over of the co-op—*ever*. They couldn't lure enough ambition from their ranks, for us to ever worry about that. Gaar? Is there a problem with your sandwich—you look like you just ate a fly.'

There was a chuckle around the table as Gaar looked up, wiping his mouth with a napkin, then covering the remnants of his sandwich with it. 'I beg your pardon gentlemen, I'm afraid a migraine is trying to get the better of me,' Gaar replied, bracing his hand against his face. 'I won't let it interfere with our business agenda. In all fairness, we should be weaning the Inuit off recreation to promote self-sufficiency by adding five percent Inuit mining force per year, to a fifty percent ceiling. There should be no limit on engineer trainees though. In my opinion, we should develop a marketing campaign to promote good will, encouraging youth to apply as paid trainees. Accessibility is important.'

McGregor slowly looked over to Roblaw, who was taking all this in stride. Gaar looked around the table, pleasantly assured with the subtle nods of approval from both Tunningham and the Quebec contingent of emissaries. Gaar initiated his own power play maneuver, rising from the table and slowly walking over to a splendid soapstone Inuit carving. He proudly stood by the art, which was of a hunter clasping a drawn bow with his arrow ready to fly.

Gaar gently stroked the cultural ornament which sat atop a teak-inlaid pedestal, elevating the artwork to chest height. 'Within ten years, the Inuit by rights should *control* and operate the mine one-hundred percent—lock-stock-and-barrel. Let the federal inmates break rocks somewhere else, or switch the program to off-shore oil rigs. Perhaps teach them building trades and get the inmates constructing communities—don't you think?'

'Gaar!' Roblaw interjected with a chuckle, 'There's *nothing* wrong with them relaxing and spending their windfall money.' Roblaw stood up and put his right hand in his pocket. He slipped off his reading spectacles with the other, and began to wave his arm in the air in an attempt to dilute Gaar's philanthropy.

He was slightly annoyed that one of his company's lawyers would have the gumption to weave personal views into the tapestry of the business agenda, regardless of his family-tie as son-in-law. He would hide his animosity as he had always done, chalking his strikes against Gaar internally, until the day of reckoning came. 'Gaar is an optimistic fatalist,' Roblaw said, with forbearance and a touch of condescension, 'mostly when it comes to industrious whites, dealing with the Inuit—you know, he's half Inuit.'

'What are the start-up costs?' asked Depoissante, leafing

through his prospectus, 'including consultation from your firm?'

'Nominal,' Roblaw answered, walking around the table to attend the Quebec Minister of Justice. 'Eight million gets you started. Pumping out abandoned mines and refurbishing them, or initiating new sites through our geology department and your Ministry of Natural Resources,' he said, leaning forward to point out the sub-heading in the prospectus Depoissante held.

As Roblaw straightened up, he caught Gaar's eye and subtly gestured with his face, instructing him to resume his seat. Gaar, feeling that he had made suitable inroads with his pet agenda, obliged the ring-master, leaving his position at the Inuit sculpture to take his seat.

McGregor looked at Roblaw and shared a covert glance which was broken when Victoria knocked at the door, eager retrieve the remains of the sandwich tray and to refresh the coffee. Roblaw nodded to her and she entered.

Vouillard raised his head enquiringly to Roblaw. 'I know you have three mines; Kabloona, Ellesmere and Cornwallis Island, with a total population of fifteen hundred and seventy-two—are they paid for their labour? I'm sure it's here somewhere ... Pierre, would you mind ...?' he asked, handing his prospectus to his demure assistant, who obediently rooted through the paperwork to locate the section.

'Yes,' Roblaw replied, 'they're appropriately paid for their labours—four dollars a day. It's a stipend, to learn the value of money, commensurate with the amount of money it costs to keep them. As I mentioned, paying the IAR twenty thousand dollars a head for the permits, and assigning a room-and-board—and not to mention a clothing maintenance fee of ten thousand per head, *saves* our government one-hundred-and-seven *million* dollars a year from all three camps, compared to what it costs to imprison them in

Canada. What do you think?' he asked, raising his eyebrows in a boastful way while strolling to his seat.

'I wouldn't sneeze at that!' said Vouillard, as he was passed the prospectus by his assistant Pierre, who indicated the appropriate material as he handed it to his boss. Roblaw sat down and slid on his small reading glasses.

'We, as management, get four percent of the net savings amount, for the upgrade of equipment and so forth,' said Roblaw with a grin, 'and I'm afraid I've lied to you,' he added, as the men around the table frowned in surprise at his incongruous confession. 'The total inmate wages over a year add up to just over two million dollars, *so*, our government only saves *around one-hundred and five million a year*! And that's only the beginning!' Roblaw exclaimed, dramatically removing his reading glasses.

The group chuckled at Roblaw's jesting. Gaar sat aloof, choosing not to participate in Roblaw's vulgar haughtiness. 'That's with *our* end and *their* end totally covered—and what's more,' Roblaw continued, 'you *tax* the inmates at thirty percent and give them an extra turn of the screws. They'll never darken my door again—guaranteed!'

Tunningham, the Canadian Deputy Minster for foreign affairs sat up and leaned forward. 'We take the savings and allocate a large portion to subsidize hospitals and schools, instead of building more prisons.'

'I can see how the program would alleviate over-crowding and budget restraints on your penal system,' said Depoissante, nodding his approval and looking down eagerly into his prospectus.

'Yep,' McGregor added, between sips of his coffee, 'no more early releases to make room for new offenders. *Export them* as a commodity.'

'Well, we don't *quite* look at it that way,' Tunningham said, clearing his throat, 'we have a consensus of support as there is actually a downturning trend in crime—we think attributable to the 3R program. Its apparent success whittles away at the naggings of opposed ... lobby groups.'

'"*Socially apropos*" for "bleeding-hearts" eh, Gaar?' blurted McGregor.

Gaar snuffed at McGregor's comment, annoyed that the man would direct the comment at him, as though they had had previous discussions on the topic, or to infer he had a tendency to overuse the phrase "socially apropos" in his speech. Neither was true, and as McGregor grinned, Gaar pondered on the distaste he had for this crude man whom Roblaw favoured. He couldn't figure what he could ever hope to achieve acting like a boor. If McGregor didn't wipe the hyena grin off his face—which was still absurdly directed at him, Gaar thought he might leap up on the table and force-feed him his shoe, perhaps to the applause of the assembly—and surely to the dismay of the man's benefactor.

Depoissante looked up from a discussion with Vouillard. 'We're curious,' he began, 'what is the impact on the cultural identity of the indigenous population? How do they feel about it?' He looked up and around before he focussed on Roblaw, then turned his enquiring glance to Gaar.

'They gave Kabloona its name,' McGregor interjected, 'that's cultural identity for you!'

'What does it mean?' Pierre asked innocently.

'It means "*white faith*",' McGregor responded quickly, before Gaar could pipe up with the straight forward derogatory connotations that could be applied to "Kabloona".

Roblaw leaned forward, took his half-eyed reading glasses off and slid them on the table on front of himself. 'Gaar, why don't you explain the *cultural benefits* to our esteemed colleagues? Gaar played a key role in securing the occupation—or *reciprocal* treaty, I should say. We're very lucky to have him. Gaar?' said Roblaw, nodding at Gaar to pick up on the lead and drive the sale home.

The consulting contract stood to be a lucrative account

for Roblaw Inc. The spotlight was on Gaar now, to nail the contract for Roblaw—it was what he was being paid for, to deliver and tout the company's policies and hype its positive public relations message.

'An important point to stress, gentlemen ... is ...,' Gaar began but faltered, as he succumbed to a peculiar spasm in his mind. He remained at his seat, putting his left hand to his forehead to cloak the temporary incapacitation. Vouillard poured Gaar a glass of water from the serving tray and set it in front of him.

'An important point to stress ...?' Roblaw reiterated with anticipation. 'Gaar, you relax, I'll take the reigns—he'll be fine gentlemen, I believe Gaar donated blood at lunch time. You know how orange juice and chocolate cookies aren't exactly food for thought.' Roblaw chuckled as he stood, lifting his glasses to play with in his hand as he spoke. 'An important point to stress, is that this stable economic base for the Inuit provides *increasing* employment and educational opportunities for them. If it weren't for the program, the prospects would be dire in light of the unstable and harsh economic times they've fallen prey to. Heck, we've *all* fallen prey to—but them especially; their deficit, bleak export market and weak currency *behooves* them to enter into such programs with us.'

Gaar shut his eyes as his mind began to spiral upwards. His body felt very heavy like it was being left behind—it was a peculiar elastic experience of which he could indulge in for the moment as he had been absolved to have a private moment at the table. It was a good thing, since he couldn't move. Should anyone have shaken him, he might've toppled over and shattered to pieces. Nothing could be done now about that concern, but he could still hear the bureaucratic dribble leaking from Roblaw's mouth. Especially slobberish was his use of "behooves"—*Roblaw may have hooves*, he thought to himself, much like the rambling thought of a drunkard. *Roblaw may be the devil himself!* Only a demon would ride the caboose of the word train— *behooves!* Roblaw poked with his feeble trident, stressing *obligation* in his use of it rather than *suitability*. It was such a fine hair to split in such a big world, but, little things count most, sometimes. From the perspective of an ethereal universe, a bad thought was the dreaded virus of the soul.

Gaar travelled on from the echoey jabber of the table, moving with his introspection to experience a thousand visions with his mind's eye. The experiences were mostly of his homeland and his youth, taking the form of intoxicating spectral perceptions and insights. These visions of extrasensory calibre, bombarded his mind.

He saw flashes of his wife Louise and his law school days in Ottawa, traces of his childhood, his deceased mother, boyhood chums, and glimpses of a very old man he couldn't quite place—a peculiar phantom he had known most of his life in and out of dreamstates. It was like an omniscient overseer was guiding him through dimensions and plateaus, swishing him around time and space in an impressionistic vortex of both the familiar and the foreign.

This was by far the most extreme encounter he'd had in a building sequence of occurrences. He knew it was *the calling*. It was his blood inheritance—courtesy of his grandfather, and *his* grandfather before that.

A particularly evoking flash was that of his aging father telling an engrossing story to an eager group of young and old Inuit in a dim room, with shafts of dusty sunlight spilling through the windows like waterfalls. He then experienced the vista of snowy-peaked mountains from high above, subterranean dark caverns— which dissolved into a terrifying plummet into deep dark-blue waters walled by glowingly opaque glacial icebergs. The splendid turquoise colour faded and darkened then, swiftly appearing red; the dark red of blood. He experienced a drowning feeling—the dark red pool was drowning him.

Gaar snapped out of his intuitive episode and was left at the table with a very exposed feeling. Unsure of whether or not he had called out, he was embarrassed for a moment as everyone had looked directly his way, then turned their heads back to Roblaw who was still spouting.

Gaar felt numb with ennui. He was aware of the mission of this banal endeavour at the table, and like a sink full of dirty dishes staring at you after an incredible meal, it was a duty which he couldn't avoid. An elated feeling overcame the fleeting resentment he felt for Roblaw, and as it surged through him, he found himself realizing a hunger. It was more a desire for justice than food; to feed the soul rather than the stomach.

Up to now, he had been feeding the entity which made the company stronger and richer, like a minion supporting the bully which would rule the block. He felt the pangs of a traitor's guilt, but he offset that notion, comforting himself in the thought that he hadn't been cast from the mold as a *token* aboriginal who was "bought", or an opportunist who manipulated his way into the bosses family. He preferred anything but that, but was stuck in a situation which unfortunately evolved into just that scenario.

It wasn't his wife's fault that her father was a Machiavellian industrialist. It was a stroke of fate that he should end up as a lawyer maintaining a keen eye on Inuit events. He had married Louise for love, not in anticipation. Back then, she was a rebel and denounced elitism. Surely love could bear the burden of family interference.

Gaar sat up in his seat, feeling invigorated and game to lock horns or ruffle feathers with the pretense of his being the ambassador for the "alternative consciousness" on a brutish playing field.

Roblaw had just finished throwing some numbers at the

group, when Gaar leaned forward and folded his hands on the table. 'Excuse me gentlemen, I'm sorry for that unfortunate delay, but *as I was saying*; the important thing is that the administration of the facets that Philip mentioned, is in *their* hands. The satellite university program offers them an expansive curriculum from engineering to business administration and cultural identity programs in their native tongue. The youth and young children are the primary concern—*and* their relationship with their elders, especially family circles.'

Philip Roblaw looked around the table, pleased with the reception to Gaar's public relations viewpoint and his obvious bias as a person with Inuit roots. But, he became curious and uncomfortably distracted by something elusive and nondescript in Gaar's face—it was something which was betrayed only by the peculiar lilt in his voice. Roblaw listened on, alert to telltale signs of what he suspected was the burgeoning of a saboteur.

'All this makes it worthwhile,' Gaar continued, 'provided the wildlife and intrinsic beauty of the Arctic is left undisturbed in the face of mining and fossil fuel exploration.'

Roblaw nodded, superficially supporting the declarations of this half-breed Eskimo. He was eager for the government officials to perceive Roblaw Inc as a company that cared. It *did* care about adaptability and non-imposition, with Ottawa. 'If we have to detour migrating caribou, hell, I'll build them a bridge to keep them—keep *us* out of their hair.'

'A snowmobile for every caribou!' Gaar mockingly blurted, as the group turned their heads back and forth like they were watching a tennis match. They looked back at Roblaw with half smiles on their faces.

'It's a known fact that caribou can't drive,' Roblaw replied tongue-in-cheek, 'but if they agree to wear diapers, I'll supply them with home furnishings and satellite TV—that's not tutelage is it?' he said, causing a rumble of laughter over the absurd assertion, which quickly dispelled Gaar's poignant stab and knocked the ball out of play.

'What is the post-secondary student population?' asked Vouillard, turning back to business.

'It fluctuates,' replied Tunningham.

'Is there a figure?'

'I believe two-hundred and fifty in post secondary.'

'What community is that figure from?'

'The community of the IAR.'

'The nation?'

'Gentlemen,' Roblaw interjected, 'that's an internal matter which we cannot interfere with.'

'We should suggest marketing efforts to entice—' Gaar began, but was cut off by Roblaw who raised his hand to shift the topic.

'Yes, yes, we support and encourage—but we can't get involved where we don't belong, especially in their internal administration. On a more *positive* note; knock wood,' said Roblaw, knuckling the table, 'allow me the honour of unveiling our five year expansion program!'

McGregor got up from his chair in a well rehearsed manner and went to a cabinet. When opened, it boasted state of the art video playback equipment. Gaar looked at Roblaw who folded his reading glasses and inserted them into his breast pocket. He beamed with pride awaiting the upcoming presentation. A video screen began to lower from the ceiling at the far end of the room. The welcome change of pace prompted the players to abandon their prospectus materials. McGregor flicked the room lights off, and classical music began to play.

The group began to adjust themselves, some taking a long needed stretch while others immediately settled back into a comfortable slouch to take in the screen's fantastic graphics.

On the screen was formed a colour notated map of the North American continent from Mexico to the Arctic

Circle. A smooth, friendly narrator began to extol the virtues of Roblaw Natural Resource Management Inc. The narrator's low, reassuring voice had a sedative effect and the musical accompaniment embellished the company's humanitarian goals.

McGregor quietly closed the video cabinet doors, handed Roblaw a video remote control device and then resumed his seat. Stock film footage of happy-go-lucky Inuit people going about their daily routine of trapping, fishing, singing in small intimate groups and partaking in diverse community games of skill were mixed with footage of wildlife and pristine natural resources.

Spectacular visual graphics captivated all but Gaar, who felt insulted by the propegandizing of the Inuit and the veneer of the sales pitch. He felt the perspective was wrong, the editing was subliminal, and the intent, fraudulent. The music emotionally swelled at strategic visuals, putting across a feeling of pride and accomplishment of Roblaw's work in the Republic.

The video even went so far as to tout Roblaw's interest and assistance to the region when it was known as the province of the North West Territories, years prior.

Suddenly a foray of miniature mining head-frames, executed in fancy computer graphics, converged on the screen and were speckled onto a map of the IAR. Roblaw muted the sound with his hand held remote control, stood up and moved to the large screen.

'Twenty new mines, in five years!' announced Roblaw, with pride and assurance. 'There'll be no *need* for prisons in Canada, *at all*! It'll save the government three *billion* dollars a year! The Canadian deficit? I'll help reduce it from an ape on the Prime Minister's back to a monkey up his sleeve. Rehabilitate, Re-educate—Release!' he said, tapping the screen and incidentally having the images projected onto himself, causing them to distort and flow around the curves of his suit like a hand disrupting flowing water.

Gaar was vexed by Roblaw's audaciousness. His master plan appeared more an invasion plan from Gaar's perspective. *Hang the deficit—what would the Inuit be reduced to*? he thought to himself. 'Philip,' Gaar began, tempering down his animosity to Roblaw and his grand scheme—in light of present company, 'I wasn't consulted, it's too fast, too soon. They'll never go for it. Half of that in *ten*—perhaps.'

The delegation looked around the table, slightly embarrassed at the apparent breaking of rank. It was more a tiff than a horn-locking, and with the darkness of the room and the busy visual images, it was soon forgotten. McGregor however, surreptitiously peered at Gaar, thrusting daggers in his direction.

'It's said that every man has his price, and every country has its handicap,' said Roblaw, 'well, this company's the fairy-godmother of the IAR's handicap.'

Roblaw surveyed the faces around the shiny teak meeting table which reflected the animation and colourful images dancing from the muted presentation behind him. 'I'm awaiting the results of several exploration drifts from the Kabloona mine. I believe it shows the most promise from all three mines, and if my nose serves me well, there's gold in-them-there-hills! And since they have a stake in any mineral finds, my pay-dirt's going to have those aboriginals happier than pigs in—a blanket!'

Taking extreme offence to Roblaw's ignorant remark, and fed up with the downturning gist of the meeting, Gaar stood up, fetched his briefcase and abruptly walked out.

With eyebrows raised, the emissaries looked to Roblaw for an explanation. Now it appeared more than just a tiff.

'The kid's got a lot to learn. He's letting his personal problems creep into his work,' Roblaw said, 'you could see he's under a great deal of stress. I have an Inuit law student who's articling right now—very bright and ambitious. I've already snatched him up for the firm. What Gaar can't handle, he will.'

'I like Gaar,' said Vouillard, 'I hope he doesn't go to pieces. I think we can work with him. What do you say, Gerard?'

'He shows heart,' said Gerard Depoissante, '*and* he's Inuit. Couldn't ask for a better broker. We need that edge.'

§

Gaar emerged from the office building onto the darkened city avenue. The change of scenery, and freedom from the building itself seemed to dissipate the foul taste in his mouth. The faint siren of what he thought was a fire-engine reverberated between the tightly packed tall buildings. It was just the thing to sidetrack his mood and get his mind off Roblaw. The storming blur of the fire truck passed through an intersection two blocks up and moved off, causing the piercing harmonic tone of the siren to lower a notch. He had once read an explanation of that sound wave event, but had forgotten the reason and slipped back into a comfortable astonishment of how sound is perceived.

In a world where the parameters of physics and a mathematical formula can explain anything, there was definitely no formula which could explain the mind-bending experience he had been immersed in, in the boardroom. Gaar wasn't interested in speculating. He decided to just forget about the experience as one would a dream. The more he made a conscious effort to ignore it though, the more frequently stray flashes of the event would invade his mind. It was like the mysterious buffer which autopilots a person to sleep. There was no controlling it.

Night was approaching. He proceeded north towards his bus stop. Around the four corners of the intersection ahead, pedestrians waited for crossing signals. Some dressed for a Friday night out, dashed across with the flashing amber lights before the command of the red stopped them in their tracks and held them back for another cycle. It was the give and take of the alternating city current.

It was now long after rush hour, and although there were moderate amounts of pedestrians, the vehicular traffic wasn't bursting at the sidewalks. His walk ended when he reached the bus stop. His bus operated until midnight. Gaar was always waiting for the bus at the oddest times, given the irregularity of his work hours. He waited patiently for his ride.

Leaning down to the newspaper box to buy an evening edition paper, as was his bus-stop ritual, he was disappointed to find it sold out. Setting his briefcase down on the sidewalk beside himself, he checked his wrist watch. It was getting close to eight o'clock.

Looking up from his watch, he was dumbfounded at the sight of a specter appearing in the middle of the intersection of the crisscrossing streets. It was a large yellowish–white polar bear! It paused in its ambling stride and stared at Gaar. He looked around to see if anyone else had seen it. Neither pedestrians or car drivers observed the phantom as they both walked and drove past the polar bear. One car even made a left hand turn right through the bear. It *was* there, plain and simple. Everyone else just couldn't see straight. *Tongarsoak*, he thought to himself, citing the devilish apparition from folklorish superstition which he recalled from his early native studies. He didn't have to rub his eyes, for he knew it was his mind that needed the rub.

The bus arrived from out of nowhere and blocked his

view of the figment. Replacing the bear was an animated image of a dancing telephone on a poster ad. He stepped back from the bus and collided with a man who came up from behind him to board.

'Watch it!' the man said, squeezing past him and boarding.

'Are you coming?' the driver asked in a monotone voice.

Although he wanted to board and forget the whole thing, Gaar shook his head and waved the driver on, curious to catch another glimpse of the ghostly image. The doors were shut and the bus departed, leaving a small cloud of black exhaust smoke in its wake. Fanning away the fumes, he peered around for the bear. It was nowhere to be seen. *Pihoqiahoak*, he lamented to himself in a rusty but pin-pointed Inuit tongue, alternately referring to the great bear spirit which had presented itself to him. *It's real, but who can I talk to about it?* he asked himself. *No one*, he thought, feeling out of sorts and anxious with the onslaught of these experiences.

His eyes opened wide as he realized an unconscious recollection. *The bear which tore me to shreds in that dream. It's the sickness*, he thought, *my conscription—the draft of the innocent. How soon before the fox or falcon pick at my guts?* He rubbed his temple. *Who's in charge here? I'm sure an out-of-*spectral-*court settlement would be out of the question. Dammit, there's not enough entrails to go around.*

He stepped into the curb to see if another bus might be in the distance, drawing himself back just in time to avoid being struck by a speeding bicycle courier, decked-out like a grungy super hero. The man zipped past him, dashing for the green light through the intersection. Unfortunately for the courier, his eagerness didn't pay off, as he soon met with a rough and bumpy piece of road which catapulted his walkie-talkie from the back pocket of his ragged pants and into the intersection, where it remained like a Christian amid the lions, the odd pedestrian gawking with baited anticipation of the inevitable—some even broke from their determined strides to loiter impatiently for the moment. It wasn't often one came across such a pedestrian sacrifice, for some it was to make-their-day.

The courier looked back in horror as the east-west traffic took its turn through the intersection. Gaar could hear the broadcasted voice of the radio dispatcher blasting out from the abandoned walkie-talkie, when suddenly, the radio voice was abruptly silenced by a large dump truck which bounced through the intersection. When the lights had alternated for the north–south passage, the lanky courier dashed into the roadway, angrily collecting the bits and pieces of circuit boards and plastic. The courier slunk away into the shadows, cradling the shattered remains of his life-line and deposited the bits into a saddle bag on his bike. He rode off like a thief into the night.

If only a random steamroller could chance through my mind, thought Gaar, as he allowed himself to get lost in the sights and sounds of the street, trying not to dwell on recent mind-bending occurrences.

He was set adrift on a tangent of thought which was both compelling and repelling to him. People probably just like Roblaw, actually *owned* and *controlled* all the stone, steel and glass architecture, the physical buildings and the comings-and-goings of the everyday people who slaved day and night to feed the empire. Gaar was into it up to his neck unfortunately, treading the wheel like a hamster.

It was torture to step back and inspect the seams of this existence. His meager existence within the cloak, magnified the loose threads and broken stitches all around him. He was at fault, and his guilt almost compelled him to pull the thread and tear the garment asunder.

The experiences he'd been having lately only made things harder to cope with. His grandfather had been a notable shaman, and his fears were justified as the calling was passed down from grandfather to grandson, skipping a generation.

This feeble veil is tattered and they're coming through the holes for me, he thought to himself, *the wind is blowing through my ribs, I can feel it—dammit all to be torn in half! I'm gonna stay in one piece*, he said to himself, clenching his jaw, *I borrowed piece of mind and now the loan's being called in. I can outrun it, I must— I've got a child on the way! Its father won't be a madman. I won't be taken in that direction, no way. I can out-maneuver, out-flank and squash this ... calling. I've got enough commitments to deal with!*

fourteen

A TRANSIT BUS pulled up at the top of a dreary street and Gaar got off. He trod along the sidewalk moving in and out of shadowy stretches of the street. Some of the street lamps were either burnt out or broken. The street was generously treed but was in dire need of large scale pruning as the boughs of many trees extended their spindly branches low, almost infringing on pedestrians.

Making his way along the sidewalk, he had to dodge around an abandoned tricycle, which lay overturned in the middle of the path. It was obvious that the stray toy belonged to the house that had a hodge-podge of toys and the like, strewn about the verandah and property. He stepped back to lift the tricycle from the sidewalk, placing the toy on the lawn up towards the porch. He was conditioning himself for fatherhood and this seemed a good starting place.

Further along, he had to step around a folded bed mattress which was torn and stained, and had been set out for special collection. It had been there for three days now, requiring a held breath to pass it comfortably. It was evident that the neighborhood dogs had considered it their pit-stop.

Gaar was used to the street and had no problem calling it home, even with the rough edges.

Reaching his home, he turned off the sidewalk and walked the footpath to his door, with his keys in hand. The house was a semi-detached modest two-storey, with dark brushed-brick and a small front porch featuring a bay window looking out over the street.

He looked briefly at his small lawn which was soggy from the rain which had poured earlier in the day, making it look more disheveled in its Fall decay. The porch light was on. A welcome feeling filtered through him as he walked up the creaky wooden steps and aimed his key for the door lock.

Once inside, he shut the door behind himself, put his briefcase down and removed his dark overcoat in the dimly lit hallway. 'Louise, I'm home!' he called out, draping his coat on a hanger and placing it in the tiny hall closet. 'Hon? Louise?' he said again, messing with the closet door which refused to stay closed. The handle was sticking and the door was off-plumb, causing it to fall wide open.

'Did you pick up the family portraits from the photography place? Louise called out loudly from the kitchen, where she was busy cooking their supper.

Gaar didn't reply straight away. He'd forgotten the portraits. His personal crisis had washed the thought completely from his mind. He cringed at his absence of mind as this forgotten errand had the potential to turn into a federal-case. Similar details of late had become major bones of contention with her. It seemed he could do nothing right for her lately, a fact he couldn't deny. Forgiveness and understanding were hard to come by these days, and if they had had a dog he would definitely be vying for a position in the doghouse.

'Gaar? Well!?' she irritably called again. Her voice was devoid of cheer and laden with tedious exhaustion and a self imposed regimentation. She was miserable and Gaar walked her web. He wedged a shoe against the closet door and proceeded through an open doorway into the living room.

He could see her through the adjacent doorway which opened into the kitchen. She was beautiful. Louise was twenty-seven, tall and slim with auburn hair and a generously proportioned body. Being four months pregnant with their baby, she showed slightly which added to her beauty.

She was a goddess. Gaar often admired her finely sculpted nose with its little bump. She had lustfully thick lips and a strong feminine chin which drove him secretly mad; her eyes were brown and her teeth were aligned like the wintry days of February.

He was especially fond of her piano playing hands and hoped that someday they would have a piano so that their eloquence would be manifest in music—preferably with the serenity and charm of Chopin. They were both fond of the piano-works of Chopin. She had been given lessons as a child but had not pursued it with zeal. Things were to remain a far-off dream.

They had been married for three years now. She had travelled extensively after achieving a bachelor of fine arts degree prior to their marriage. Gaar had graduated with a degree in economics with business administration as his minor. He then studied criminal law and passed the bar exam only to switch over to corporate law after being disillusioned with the former.

They had met on campus and became the greatest of friends, sharing spirited debates which feather-dusted their requisite views on the institutions of religion, politics along with the gamut of art and literature.

One time, on a glorious sunny day under a tree on the campus grounds, they were sharing views on their dissimilar backgrounds and upbringings. Frolicking about, they pondered together and took their individual experiences, amalgamating their views and feelings into a hybrid perspective. There was an unforgettable spark. That was the magic moment for them. It was then that Gaar asked Louise to marry him. Accepting his proposal, they stood and danced slowly under the tree, feeling as one. Their rapture was heightened by the chirpings of the birds in the tree and the scent of the freshly cut Kentucky bluegrass. The dance went on. As they blossomed, they shared a common perspective. They multiplied their joys, and hopes and tears and always felt the same outcome—one. It was the square root of being, and they recognized it as such. They hadn't formulated the hypothesis, they stumbled across it, lucky in love as they were.

They enjoyed a similar inclination for existentialist thinking back then. But now, here in the living room, he had to be pragmatic and honest. He had to confess. It was a direct question demanding a direct response.

He paused at a bookshelf which displayed framed photographs of himself and Louise from happier times. Looking up from his daydream, he felt a pang of guilt over how he had obliviously allowed some kind of virus to infiltrate and impose a gridlock on their marriage.

Although theirs wasn't a completely content and happy road, they had an optimistic relationship—until about two months ago. It was either inattentiveness on his part or just stupidity on both their parts. Whatever it was, he wanted it to stop so they could move on.

His stubborn conscience had everything to do with it. He wouldn't accept any financial help from her very wealthy parents. If resisting to accept anything from Philip Roblaw other than his salary, hindered the oblivious happiness she sought—then she had indeed changed drastically, perhaps much farther back than he had realized. The question was— could she be persuaded to change back, or would he have to swallow his scruples and give-in to the easy road to riches and all its trappings?

Truly, the one thing that hadn't changed from their days of rapture, was their idea that perspective was the square root of being. If a couple didn't share a common frame of reference, they were as good as being on different planets. These days she was Mars, showing both her fire and her ice. He loved her and would burn in her fire or freeze up in her ice, if that's what it ultimately came to.

'No,' he replied, 'I'm sorry darling, I'll pick them up tomorrow. I'm nursing a splitter and I'm not one hundred percent.' He sat down on the couch and looked to her for understanding. Louise turned from the stove and walked to the doorless lintel between the rooms, facing him as she rubbed her hands on her flowery apron.

'*Poor baby*. My head hurts too, mostly from your BS.'

'I'm *sorry*, they're probably closed now, anyhow.'

'Priorities. Is this your way of making up to me? Is it? You don't care about anyone except yourself! You're selfish—*selfish*!' she scoffed, tearing off her apron and throwing it at him.

'Love, what's one more day?—oops,' he whispered to himself, realizing he'd put his foot in his mouth.

'What's one more year—one more lifetime!? I'm tired of being treated second best!' she said, putting her hands on her hips and leaning down to him.

'You're my highest priority—the top of my list!' he said, outstretching his hands. He would take his lumps but had to reach out to her. He did so with her apron clutched in his hand.

'Top o' your list for what? You start at the bottom of the ladder and take your time climbing. I'll be in focus when you reach the top, yes? This is more snakes than ladders! *You* can't see the top. Where you come from there's no word for *future*. You told me that. So why don't you make the future now? The *present*.'

Gaar looked down from her and stared blankly, knowing what was coming. 'Louise ...'

'Daddy is offering you a shorter ladder. We're steps into the twenty-first century and you've got me couped up in a cave because of your stubborn ego. He wants you to be a junior partner and you'd better take the ball and run with it so we can win this game! Please! Get us out of this *sandbox*,' she pleaded, turning and returning to the modest kitchen where she leaned on the worn counter and faced the wall.

'Don't exaggerate ... *sandbox*,' he said, rising from the couch to loom at the door jamb. He raised his right arm high against the jamb, holding the top trim and leaning against the side. He dropped his left hand to his waist, still clutching the apron.

'I knew when I married you, you weren't an opportunist,' she said, 'but it's time to *evolve* and get with the program! Let's not let the idealism of youth drive us to the grave!'

'I think I know what or *who's* killing us, but I won't say because I don't want to start a quarrel. You see, I thought when I married *you*, you were content and supportive of that notion yourself,' he said, breaking from the lintel and walking into the kitchen.

She went to the stove and faced the steaming pots on the burners. He cuddled up behind her and attempted to give her a hug. She struck his arms down and turned to him, shoving him back.

'You're not a drunk, and you've never hit me, and you don't have a *lot* of mental problems,' she laughed, 'and I love you ... but—'

'But—?'

'Well, now I *hate* being married to a pride-sucking *anti*-opportunist! Y'know?! I'm slaving with the cooking, cleaning, laundry and shopping. Playing the good wife! It's full-time slavery. You're optimistic, but I'm *realistic* and we need a maid—or a house-keeper. I need to relax and be pampered—I'm *pregnant*!'

'*I'm* pregnant too—in sympathy.'

'Think you're funny? I don't want sympathy, I want action! If I'm going to nurse this baby—you have to nurse your career and your relationship with daddy!'

'It gives me teething pains just to think about it—look, what's the problem?' he asked, scrunching his face. 'On the weekends you relax and *I* do the cooking and all the housework. Be fair now.'

Louise angrily turned around to face the stove in a fit of frustration. 'I don't want weekends off for good behavior! *Why* didn't you pick up the portraits?'

'Louise, darling ... I forgot. It slipped my mind,' he said, suddenly realizing he'd given her more cannon fodder to sink his reasoning.

He had a flash memory of an absurd game he used to play with himself, when he was a boy of eight at his mother's house in Ottawa. She had plucked him from the Arctic and brought him south, to be schooled. In his recollection, he'd be having a bath in the tub, and there was a little plastic sailboat toy which he projected himself vicariously as being—floating around the Arctic Ocean with the soap bubbles being icebergs. The sirens would be singing but the captain would never heed their song.

Underneath the bubbly icebergs in the tub water, there was a cruel and mischievous hand creature as ugly as a prune and with a neck as long as a forearm. The prehistoric beast would always sink the unsuspecting sailboat, but the captain was very good at holding his breath and would always swim to the bottom of the ocean and pull the plug, saving the life of his crew and himself. The ocean drained and exposed the creature, denying it of its elemental cloak, which invariably meant certain death. It was the end, unless the beast on the other hand with its far reaching neck, could plug the hole—

which it always did; refill the tub—which always happened, raising the sailboat and its spirited crew, and the fun would begin again.

To be a boy again, he thought to himself—to play a game where repetition was intoxicating and lives were make believe.

His memory was a momentary respite and convalescence, which sheltered him from the rubble of his crumbling world. But in keeping with the ways of the beast, the tub was filled again, and the conscious displacement of his being caused the water to swell over the brim of this tub.

'It slipped your mind?!' she said, 'You're a *lawyer* for chrissakes! Things don't *slip* your mind—Mr *detail*?'

'What's happening to us?' he whispered.

'I'll tell you what's happening; you just don't care about the things which are important to me now. Mother told me last week that daddy has forgiven us for eloping. Three years he carried that hurt around with him and he never showed any disfavour. The portraits are the first real *truth* of our family's love! You and my father have never been in the same picture before, and you forgot them—I think it's denial more than procrastination or forgetfulness! By denying my father, you deny me! I want us all to be a big happy family!'

'So, what you're saying is, you've been rich and you've been poor and never the twain shall meet. You want to cut to the epilogue of this play. The last few months have been a wash to me and I think I missed the rinse cycle. So ... maybe you can tell me what the turning point was? What was the spark that reversed your way—*our* way of thinking?'

'I've just come to my senses that's all,' she huffed, then turned to the stove top and checked the saucepan and pots, which cooked away.

'I'm not looking for his forgiveness—okay?' Gaar retaliated. 'I don't need him, I need *you*! Listen, next year I want to start my own law practice, so please have a little faith in me!' he insisted, hugging her supportively from behind. 'Maybe sooner than next year. Don't worry, our standard of living will rise.'

'What about the *family* business?' she said, breaking from his hug and grabbing the wooden spoon to stir at the rice. Placing the lid back down on the pot, she held the spoon and stared down at the stove top. 'You don't love me!'

'Don't be ridiculous!' he countered, talking to her back, as she leaned over the stove. 'I married *you*—not your father! You and our child are what I cherish in this world. I love you more than life itself!'

'*Please!*' she protested, swiftly turning and tossing the wooden spoon in the sink. 'Don't exaggerate! You love me enough to keep me in the manner to which I am *not* accustomed!' She snatched the apron from Gaar's hand. 'Give me that!'

'Patience, Louise! My student loans are almost paid off.'

'You had Inuit status before their independence. You didn't have to pay back your education costs! Your mother—bless her soul, would have agreed with me,' she agonized, mechanically putting the cooking apron on. 'You must have got this from your father—this *pride*. Well, since you haven't spoken to him in twenty-odd years, it could be just in your blood. Is it the word *father* that bugs you? What're *you* going to be like as a father?

'I'm going to be a damn good father!'

'I hope you're better with children than you are with money. You let what—over thirty thousand dollars fly out the window? For the sake of filling out a few pieces of paper and categorizing yourself as Inuit? I thought education was supposed to make people smart,' she jabbed. 'My patience is wearing mighty thin, Gaar. Pass me the keys for the car.'

'For what?'

'Just pass me the keys from the rack, I'll go get the portraits myself,' she said, looking at her watch, 'they're open 'til nine-thirty.'

'Okay, I'll go get them if it means so much to you.'

'*I'm* going, because it doesn't mean so much to *you*.'

'It's late and I'm concerned for you.'

'You're concerned for the dinner—*you* watch it!' she said, taking the apron off and throwing it at him. 'I can take care of myself. The back lane is lit. If we're lucky, maybe someone stole the car—I knew I should've left the keys in it. At least someone would be on a joy-ride.'

Louise walked out of the kitchen and Gaar followed her, fastening the flowery apron to himself. 'Don't burn the carrots, and watch the chicken in the oven. Keep an eye on that rice!' she said, as she went into the hall. 'What's this shoe?' she quizzed, as she pushed it aside, pulling her coat from the tiny hall closet and slipping on her sneakers.

'To hold the stupid door shut.'

'You mean like this? she mocked, closing the door and securing it shut with a simple everyday action.

'Yeah ... like that,' he muttered.

She put her coat on, doing it up as she walked out the door.

'Be careful darling—see you soon,' he whispered, closing up the door behind her. He watched her as she headed for the lane which led behind the houses. The telephone began to ring. Gaar walked to the hall stand and picked up the receiver. Their telephone answering machine had unknowingly been malfunctioning of late, and here again it had engaged at the second ring without giving an out-going message. It silently recorded the conversation. 'Hello?' Gaar breathed into the phone as the closet door popped open. Gaar shook his head.

Sitting alone in the empty Roblaw Inc boardroom, Roblaw's private secretary, Victoria, sat at the teak meeting table with the telephone receiver at her ear and a note pad in front of her. She talked away. The boardroom had been cleaned up and the lighting was dimmed. The faint sounds of a vacuum cleaner could be heard as the cleaning staff worked their way around the Roblaw quadrant of the seventeenth floor.

'... I'm congratulating you because the firm apparently got the Quebec consulting contract ... that's right. But the reason I'm calling is that Mr Roblaw would like to see you here at eight o'clock tomorrow morning. The line sounds strange, I think we have a bad connection. Uh huh, ... I can't answer that right now, Gaar, he's on a conference call with the Minister of Northern Affairs and our Canadian ambassador from the consulate in the IAR. He buzzed me to relay the message but he can't be disturbed. How's Louise? I saw her earlier this week but didn't have a chance to chat.'

Gaar had taken a seat at the small telephone stand in the hall. 'She's perfect. Yes, I'll tell her you said hello. So, 8:00 A.M. and no idea of the agenda, huh? Yeah, I worked last Saturday as well. As it is, I hardly get to have *quality* time with Louise. I'm going to have to start really focussing on my family life—neglect is a many splintered thing and all that ...'

In the kitchen, the carrots had begun to burn on the stove, and the rice was in the process of boiling over. Gaar walked through the living room sniffing at the odour in the air. His perplexed look gave way to a startling realization of what was cooking.

Like a bolt of lightning, Gaar scrambled into the kitchen and hastily removed the pots from the stove-top burners. He clumsily burned his hand on the rice pot as he swung it from the stove towards the sink, suffering from a handle burn as well as from a form-fitting rice glove which oozed onto his hand like molten metal. He didn't manage to get the pot to the sink, but instead jettisoned it to the floor.

He went to the fridge and opened up the freezer door, pulling out some frozen vegetables to put in the microwave oven. In the frenzy to start other items cooking and to clean up the mess he'd made, he inattentively laid the frozen vegetables on the counter and ever-so-efficiently swung over to the microwave, setting the timer and starting the appliance without inserting the food. He went to the sink and ran cold water over his burned hand, cursing the name of Murphy and the law which is attributed to him.

He swiftly grabbed a cloth and began to wipe up the spilled rice, pushing it into the toppled pot and disposing the lot into the sink. Ridding himself of the cloth, he grabbed a mop and applied a couple of hearty swipes to the floor. Throwing the mop down and rushing to put on oven mitts, he flung open the oven door and reached in through the smoke to withdraw the burning chicken. It was extra crispy. He could actually see flames inside the cavity of the chicken. He tossed it into the sink and ran water on it. Turning his head to some crackling noises, he watched a rare event— lightning in the microwave! A tremendous melt-down was taking place inside the appliance. He just stood there and watched mesmerized. It was the smoke detector alarm that snapped him out of the daze, and as he moved forward to turn off the microwave, it turned itself off and blew the fuse for all the power in the lower floor of the house. The battery-operated smoke detector filled the house with shrill beeps, taunting him in the dark and striking terror in his mind with the thought that Louise could arrive home any second.

He felt his way to a utility drawer in the lower kitchen cupboards and rooted around until he came up with a flashlight. He then opened up the back door of the kitchen which led directly outside and propped it open to vent the smoke.

Finding the mop he had thrown down on the floor, he went to the hallway with it and beat the heck out of the ceiling smoke alarm with the handle of the mop. It fell to the floor in pieces. He'd buy another smoke alarm the next day—a body just can't buy the satisfaction of putting one out of commission with the handle of a mop. Lawyers don't get to play with mops that often, and as was proven, they can be a lethal combination.

Having satisfied his frustration, he felt the first order of business would be to immediately make reservations at a restaurant. He would call the one which Louise had hinted-at that she'd like to try. After the call, he would fix the fuse which had darkened the house.

He sat down at the telephone stand next to him and plucked the telephone book from the wire rack which formed part of the telephone stand. The pages fluttered through his fingers with the speed of a card dealer in a shuffle. Under the light of his flashlight, his finger ran down the columns and stopped at the phone number.

He grabbed the radio receiver from the cradle of the phone's base and punched in the numbers on the key pad with determined precision, hoping that the restaurant was open late. As this solution was the only option in light of the circumstances, he squinted his eyes and rocked back and forth in anticipation.

'Hello?' he beamed with deliverance, relieved that someone answered the phone, 'what time does your kitchen close, please? Yes, ... eleven o'clock, *good*. I'd like to make reservations for dinner, please. I'd like a booth—you know, quiet and romantic. Say, for ten? No, no, ... o'clock, ten o'clock. For *Injugarjuk* ... I.N.J.U.G.A.—nothing? How about for ten-thirty, or eleven? *Wait*—I'm making these reservations for the Roblaw party. R.O.—, no, ... his daughter and her husband. Ten's fine? Thank you.' Gaar hung up the phone shaking his head in annoyance over having to cite Roblaw's name in order to get a seat in the restaurant.

He stood up, intent now to inspect the fuse box in the basement, but was distracted by the squeak of brakes and the rattling of a diesel truck outside. He moved to the bay window in the living room and parted the sheers out of curiosity, only to see Louise getting out of a tow truck which idled in the street—with their car hanging from its hoist!

He quick-stepped to the front door and opened it. Louise walked up the steps. Their car was towed away by the truck. Louise nonchalantly brushed by Gaar and entered the dark house.

'Louise—?' he said, shutting the door and turning to her, 'the car! What happened? Are you alright?'

'You burned the carrots—and the chicken?! What a stink! Why are the lights off? And what are the crunchy things I'm stepping on, here on the floor?'

'A fuse blew—so what happened?'

'Well, *fix* the fuse before I blow a fuse of my own! What the—?!' she spouted, as she bumped into the open closet door.

'The door's being weird—are you going to tell me what happened?' he said, pointing the flashlight at her and around her as she hung her coat in the closet and dropped a bag of something on the floor.

'Get that flashlight out of my face! Do we even have any spare fuses? We should have *breakers* like everyone else, but *no*. Gaar, I want these lights on, even if it means using one of your dental fillings to override the fuse box!' she said deridingly, feeling her way into the living room and plopping herself on the couch in frustration.

She held a large envelope in her hands which she placed beside her on the couch. Leading with the funnelled light of his flashlight, Gaar made his way to the basement door which led from the kitchen, and descended. Louise sat on the couch staring at the ceiling as the muffled sounds of Gaar bumping around in the basement seeped up through the floor below her feet.

As cars passed on the street, their headlights cast moving reflections up the wall and across the ceiling of the living room. A moment passed and the house lights came on.

Louise looked through to the kitchen from the couch and put her hand to her forehead. She could see the oven door opened and the pile of pots and cooking dishes in the sink. On the kitchen floor she caught sight of small clumps of cooked rice which had stuck together.

The sounds of Gaar running up the wooden basement stairs crept into the living room and she waited patiently for his arrival. He shut the basement door and walked timidly through the kitchen, entering the living room. He sat next to her on the couch and put his hand on her leg.

'Now, tell me what happened.'

'My very question,' she said, levelling her hand towards the kitchen.

'Ladies first.'

'The car croaked—we need a new car. You take the bus to work, but I *need* a car to get around. So, I made an executive decision. I had to *pay* the tow-guy to take it to the scrap heap. The plates and the glove compartment stuff is in the hall, in a bag. Oh, besides the dinner, you also ruined the family portrait.'

'Darling, relax and don't get upset. Forget about the car. I'll see about getting you a new one,' he said, removing the flowery apron, bunching it up and tossing it to the end of the couch. 'I'm taking you to dinner. To that expensive Italian place you've wanted to go to for so long.'

'Making amends when you've broken something and it needs fixing? I'm into *maintenance* over repairs. You want to do this because you ruined the dinner I prepared for us. You

155

couldn't even simply monitor the dinner—sometimes you're pathetic!'

'How did I ruin the portrait when I had nothing to do with it other than posing for it?'

'I don't know how, but you're screwed up in the photo,' she said, withdrawing the portraits from the envelope and handing him the evidence. He looked at the photo and shrugged his shoulders in wonder. 'Look at those blue and orange splotches around you,' she complained, poking at the family portrait photo which featured her parents, Gaar and herself. 'The photographer couldn't explain it, but it's garbage now—he didn't charge us for it. These other ones turned out fine, but you're not in them! It was the same camera, lens and film stock. He told me so.'

'I'm *sorry* for ruining the portrait. Will you accept my apology?'

'It's not your fault directly, but I blame you anyway. Now we'll have to pose all over again. It was such an ordeal to get us all together for it. Would you *please* shut that back door, I'm catching a draft!'

Gaar stood up and went through the kitchen to shut the back door. The smoke had cleared out now, and as he shut the door he paused to survey what appeared like a battlefield in the kitchen. He would happily get to the chore of cleaning up later, but for now he had to immerse Louise in more cordial surroundings. 'Why don't we get out of here and have a nice candlelight dinner?' he said, walking back into the living room and taking a seat beside her on the couch.

'I'm not in the mood to go out—I feel ill,' she stated, turning her body away from him.

'Please, darling—'

'I'm not hungry, and why should you have the opportunity to feel you've done me a big favour? Don't look to me for absolution and don't use me as a pawn by including me in your penance! Stop *insulting* me with your transparent acts of contrition! Just leave me alone!'

The telephone rang and Louise gladly abandoned the couch, leaving Gaar to sit by himself. She picked up the radio phone and marched down the hall with it, away from the smoke detector debris which she kicked out of the way with her foot. 'Hello? *Daddy, hi*! I'm fine. Listen, tell mom I know who killed Rex at the victory ball on our soap! If she watches Monday she'll figure it out, too. They *always* have cliffhangers on Friday,' she babbled, inspecting the kitchen as she talked.

She approached the microwave like a detective and opened it. 'Oh, my God—,' she announced with disdain, angrily peering through the opening into the living room. Gaar apologized with a gesture. 'Nothing, daddy, I've just discovered my microwave which looks like melted toffee— just a moderate catastrophe in my kitchen. Gaar's destroyed our dinner as well as what used to be our kitchen. There was smoke everywhere, but apart from that, things are as usual— oh, the car died. I sent it to the wreckers. Well, Gaar wants to take me to a late dinner to make up to me, but I've got a splitting migraine.'

Gaar rolled his eyes in disappointment, having been privy to the tongue-lashing which he didn't appreciate, especially knowing who was at the other end of the line. If he was going to be scolded like a child, the least she could have done was to keep it between them.

He rose from the couch and strolled to the doorway leading to the kitchen. He stared at her as she paced with the radio phone. Catching her eye, he smiled at her, endearingly attempting to diffuse the escalating animosity which was springing from her tongue.

'Ah, it's from all this nonsense that's all, nothing new. Yes he is ... you want to confirm the meeting at 8:00 A.M.,— Gaar's nodding his head.'

'Ask him if it's going to be anything like today's meeting,' Gaar said, in a cavalier sort of way.

'What?' she said, covering the phone and looking his way as though he were a passerby on the street who'd said something to her.

'Nevermind,' he replied, 'tell him I'll be there.'

'He knows about it, daddy. Did you pick up your set of portraits? ... Yeah, the group one is ruined. We'll have to arrange to re-do them soon. ... Okay, ... thanks daddy, bye for now.' She collapsed the aerial and hung up the phone, heading through the living room for the hall, to cradle the receiver.

'Louise, I wish you wouldn't be so stubborn, and allow me to take you to dinner. We can cab it,' he said, following her to the hall and then to the stairs where she paused at the bannister post.

'I've got a headache, and *I'm* going to taxi myself to bed. And since you're working tomorrow, I guess I'll see you Sunday—maybe.' She started up the stairs leaving Gaar to hug the bannister post.

He rested his forehead on his hands in frustration atop the wooden ball on the post. Gaar shrugged off the cold shoulder treatment and walked sullenly towards the kitchen.

Gaar emerged from the stairs landing and walked into their bedroom. Louise was busy in her closet hanging up her clothes. Gaar caught a glimpse of her in her underwear as she busied herself with the job at hand.

Their bedroom was a cozy room, painted a light blue with matching curtains on the narrow window which had intricate wood trim. It had suffered with age and eight to ten coats of paint which blurred the definition in the contours of the wood. The ceiling had sustained water damage at some point in the past, which was apparent by the obtrusive plaster repair job which had been executed prior to their ownership.

Gaar realized all these details and understood how these kinds of decorative faults would bother someone if they focussed on the down side. Perhaps prominent to a first-time viewer, the faults of the house had been sunk to the back in his head as they didn't interfere with normal living.

Gaar had only found the time to deal with problems you could trip over, hurt yourself on, bump into or which threatened to collapse on your head. He had willingly suspended his distaste for the striking deficiencies of their home, choosing to obliviously live with the shortcomings. Invariably, her subscription to the home decorating magazine which arrived monthly, had something to do with her discriminating view.

In his spare time, for the last two years, he had been keenly working on a fiction novel, but hadn't gotten very far. His time was fragmented by the intensive workload at Roblaw Inc and his interest in nurturing his domestic life with Louise. Evidently, he had been negligent in this personal area as well.

'Louise,' he said, 'I've cleaned up the mess I made in the kitchen. Tomorrow, I'll get us a new microwave and I'll start looking into a car for us.' There was no reply from her as she walked from the closet to her dressing table, withdrew a padded stool from underneath the unit and sat. She began to apply some night cream to her face. Gaar looked on at her reflection. She caught his glare and returned the stare into the mirror.

'What is it? Take a good long look—Louise in her underwear! This is what it's come down to. You've lost our shirts on that worthless stock ...'

'You're not going to bring *that* up again?'

'Why did I ever allow you to coerce me into letting you go ahead with that?' she said in a regretful tone while applying the cream to her face with mechanical accuracy.

'It showed promise,' he replied, standing behind her.

'So did you! Bad gambles, repaying a pride-debt and keeping me in rags and holed-up in this dive of a house!'

'Louise!' he said, taking hold of her shoulders and kissing the nape of her neck. 'This is our *home*, for now at least. Don't say that about it—home is where the heart is.' She shrugged from beneath his hands, and he walked to the closet. 'This closet is not what I'd call full of *rags* ... this is new—when'd you ...?'

'Daddy bought me some of those outfits as gifts,' she said defensively.

'When?' he asked, inspecting some of them in a curious rummage.

'Doesn't matter,' she said irritably, 'where can I wear them? Around the house to clean and do laundry in? To sympathy dinners with you? Overall, you're stingy—yet you gamble! Sometimes I could just ... what a stupid move. Who sold you that stock? Hmm? Who?' she demanded, turning her head away from the mirror to face him directly.

'I told you—a respected *broker*.'

'What's his name? Daddy will see that he never works the stock exchange again. He'll see that his licence is revoked!'

Gaar sat on the edge of the bed and began unbuttoning his shirt. 'It's all speculation—overall,' he said, taking his shirt off and draping it over a bedside chair. Louise peered scrutinizingly via the mirror, as she continued to primp. 'It's going to gain points,' he continued, 'he said so, and I believe him; he said it'd take some time, but to hang on to it!' Gaar removed his socks and began un-doing his belt. '*Four* years, so ... it'll pick up—I trust his nose.'

'What's the name of this *nose*?'

'Max,' Gaar replied, stretching his arms outwards, revealing a firm lithe body. He leaned back on his outstretched arms, supported by the bed. 'Max Dopplestein, and he worked for *your* father's firm. He was your father's accountant *and* broker! A good man, and honest—Max.'

'Honest!' she laughed out, turning her head briefly towards him and then returning her glare to the dressing mirror. She picked up an emery board and began filing her nails. 'He screwed you! If you don't set him straight tomorrow and get at least some of *our* money back, I'll go in there and give him a piece of my mind, and daddy will send him packing! Four years, and *zip*!'

'Appropriate choice of words. He's in jail ... in your father's Kabloona boot camp, oddly enough. You know, the arctic mines? Special privileges though. He's an orderly in the camp infirmary. No mining labour.'

Louise turned to him swiftly with her face covered in the white cream. 'See?! You can't see people for what they are! *Your* judgement stinks!' she said, standing and walking for the bedroom door. She left the room and went into the bathroom which was next to their bedroom.

Gaar laid back onto the bed, with his trousered legs still hanging over the edges of the bed. He pondered on what she'd said about his judgement. He could hear Louise rooting around in the medicine cabinet. She continued speaking from there in a loud echoey voice. 'He's a crook, and you got fished-in! I'm glad he's in daddy's jail! Appropriate—I feel half vindicated for what he did to us,' she continued, as she re-entered the bedroom and sat down again to resume her primping. 'Let him freeze—the bastard!'

'Louise, you don't know him! *He's* no bastard. I believe he's an innocent man who got stuck between a rock and a hard place. Remember ... remember my first criminal defense case—before I switched to corporate law?'

'Yeah, you *lost*,' she said with smugness.

'Yeah, I know. Well, your father engaged me on that supposed open-and-shut case *for Max*!' he said, rising from the bed and pacing randomly around the bedroom. 'Talk about *baptism by fire*! I was shot down like a fish in a barrel. We weren't playing to the same sheet music.'

'Just like us,' she added.

'I managed to appeal and get his sentence reduced to three years from seven—he was lucky. As a matter of fact, he'll be out soon, I think. Maybe I'll have him over for dinner,' he said, trying to rib Louise.

'Over my dead body,' she said matter-of-factly, not missing a stroke with her emery board.

'Be nice to me then, or I'll have to kill you so that my buddy Max can come over for dinner,' he said, sitting on the corner of the bed and smiling at her. 'Paleface,' he added, referring to the white cream all over her face.

'You're just a *riot*; I hate when you hide behind your idea of humour and mock me. It's a shield that won't stand up to me!' she threatened, leaping up and wiping a dab of the white cream across his mouth. 'There! That'll hide your blemishes!'

Gaar let out a big laugh and grabbed her wrists. They play-wrestled apart. He wiped his mouth. 'Y'know, *Max* was hiding something ..., he was protecting your father,' he said elusively.

She took a small folded towel from the corner of the dresser and angrily wiped the cream from her face.

'Protecting my father from *what*? What're you babbling about? Well?!' she demanded, from behind the flailing towel. She stood and threw the towel on the floor as she brought her fists to her waist. 'Spit it out!'

'I can't prove it, but I think Max took the fall for him,' he plainly stated, earnestly looking to her for an open mind, having broached the *modus operandi* topic. 'I'm sorry to say,' he added.

She stood there in silence for a split second, and then went ballistic. 'How *dare* you—how dare you!! You bastard!' she screamed, slapping his face and beating on him, stopping only to storm from the room. Gaar went after her and turned for the bathroom as she did.

Louise lunged into the bathroom and attempted to slam

the door behind herself. Gaar stuck his foot in the door preventing her from sealing the topic. She shoved and pushed at the door, but Gaar was determined to keep it ajar. 'Do you think rich and powerful men like your father get where they are without bending or breaking the rules?!'

'Get your foot out of the door!' she wailed, 'Everyone tries to cheat on their income taxes—you fool! You're the cruelest man I've ever known! You want to hurt me, and turn me against my family!' she said, almost sobbing. 'You're a monster! Now goddammit, get your foot out of this door!'

'I love you, Louise, and I want you to consider the facts and weigh the truth against fiction!' he yelled, not trying to push the door in, but to keep it from slamming shut. 'Max went down for insider trading; they couldn't touch him on tax-evasion or money-laundering. He was your father's scape-goat, though. I'm tellin' you. I didn't bring this up before, but I think your father's got it in for me, and he's poisoned your mind against me! I have nothing to gain by telling you all this, I can only lose by being honest with you about this, but I won't let him come between you, the baby and myself! I want you to consider it—in the remotest stretch of your imagination.'

'You're despicable!' she cried out from behind the door.

'Your father's no angel, so get up off your knees!' he exclaimed, pulling his foot from the door and letting it slam shut. Gaar stood outside the bathroom door and waited in silence for a moment. 'Why don't you ask him? I'd be really curious to see his reaction!'

Louise sharply pulled the door open. 'You're a liar! You just want to ruin his good name!' she barked, slamming the door in his face and continuing in an echoey muffled tone from behind the door. 'You're contemptible! You're just leading me down the garden path of weeds! Go away!'

Someone in the next house, through the adjoining wall on the landing, started to bang on the wall. Gaar went over and banged back, realizing his anger as he pounded the wall. 'You stay out of it!' he screamed at the wall.

Turning from the distraction, he stomped back to the closed bathroom door and banged against that as well. 'I want us to be free of his influence! It's hurting us—can't you see that? Look at your poor mother!' he said, pleading with her.

Louise yanked the door open and burst out, knocking him over onto the floor as she passed him. She turned around to challenge him as he got up.

'What about my mother?! Say anything against her and I swear ...!' she yelled, making a fist and shaking it at him.

'She's a *wonderful* woman! A model mother from what I know of her. But, she's a pale shadow. Not a *peep* out of her. Hushed and obedient! A good woman who fell under his spell, control, domination—whatever you want to call it! And maybe over the years she allowed herself to lull into a state of denial, fearing the truth!' He stood there with a pointed index finger, which he let drop now, having made his point.

Louise raised *her* finger now, and thrust it forward in the air towards him as she made her counterpoint. 'You're talking about *us*! Denial is the key word here. *Denial.* I must be a fool!' she moaned, putting her hand to her forehead and shaking her head back and forth. 'You're jealous, 'cause *your* father doesn't and hasn't ever answered your letters or telegrams! He didn't even come to your mother's funeral!!'

Gaar felt a pain in his heart so great he turned from Louise in shame, wrestling to control a tempest of emotions which rattled him like an earthquake. He closed his eyes, then fought back the hurt. Opening his eyes quickly, he thought about Max coming to dinner, which diverted the flood and welded the tear in his heart.

'*My* father paid to have her brought back from the Amazon! And all her research and everything!' she yelled.

Gaar turned swiftly back to her, moving slowly towards her. 'Not out of the goodness of his heart, as he'd have you believe!' he stammered. His voice quivered slightly, betraying the residue of the emotions which nearly shattered him moments prior. He cleared his throat quietly and continued to attempt to enlighten her. 'He has a stake in the Amazon! Ask him! It was in *his best interests*! Perspective, remember? I'll try if you will, baby! I *love you*! Please—I don't want to see you lost in the vortex of his influence, God forbid to the point of no return! The power—the *greed*! Wake up!' he pleaded, nearing her closely. 'He's sick!!'

Louise slapped him across the face. Gaar stood there and bore her fury. She slapped him again, and he just stood there—until he broke rank, grabbing her by the waist and the back of her head, and smothering her with a long passionate kiss. Her adamant attempts at shoving him away slowly gave way to her arms moving across his naked shoulders and then up to his short dark hair which she ran her intent fingers through.

His powerful grasp evolved into a reciprocal stroking and kneading fest over her body's stoked desire. Her hands flowed down his neck and then along his strong shoulders to his back where she dug her nails into his back, raising welts as she drew her claws slowly downwards. She suddenly leapt up and mounted him, wrapping her legs around his waist.

Gaar held her by her firm ass which he had come to realize again was the softest smoothest form in the universe. He walked the two of them to the hall table, which he cleared with a swipe of his hand and sat her on it. She deliriously stroked him through his pants. She was on fire.

He kissed her splendid breasts, which his imagination decided shared the distinction of being the grandest shapes and feel known to man. He reached his eager hands around behind her to un-snap the clasp of her pretty white bra so that her splendor could be exposed to his appreciation. She un-zipped his suit pants, freeing them from his waist and reveled in the sound of them collapsing to the floor with a slight jingle. With Louise's eager and acrobatic assistance, Gaar removed her panties with one ungracious draw and they moved into position to fulfil the moment.

Her engine was running, but Gaar seemed to have a spark plug problem. They kept at the enticing, cheering each other on spectacularly, but the spokes of the passion wheel began to appear to be moving backwards. The illusion became apparent to both of them, and clear thought crept up on them like a storm cloud over a parade. He tried not thinking of where they would be stranded if he couldn't start his engine and take them where they wanted to go; full speed down the highway and over lover's leap. Gaar's starter motor was dying with the persistent cranking of the ignition for such a long period. He knew he had plenty of gas—but the mixture was too rich!

In a frustrated but subtle backing down, Gaar took a step back and surrendered to the peculiar reality that men must face on occasion. This was not the occasion where consolation and unselfish sweet-nothings would be readily availed on him—and he knew it.

He turned his head to the side in embarrassment, and looked off in that direction, lifting his shoulders slightly in apology. Louise sat up and slapped him across the face, which he actually was grateful for—realizing the elemental failure at hand. There was no honour in an aborted mission. It was a commitment gone sour.

Louise pushed him out of the way and marched into the bedroom, slamming the door behind her. Gaar looked at the floor in disillusionment—his suit pants seeming like a puddle at his feet.

fifteen

GAAR AWOKE WITH A START, as a car which was missing its muffler drove up his street in a fit of acceleration. Watching the reflections of its headlights, as they zoomed along the contours of the living room, he realized he was on the couch, and sadly enough, why he was sleeping on it. It was Saturday morning. *The damn meeting!* he thought to himself. *My day off, and Louise here without company again! A night on the couch and my day in a stinkin' office!*

He reached from beneath the fuzzy blanket which covered him, grabbing for his wrist watch which he'd set down on the coffee table. With the assistance of some very faint street light which seeped into the living room, he plucked his watch from the table and held it close to his eyes, squinting to read the time on its face. It was almost six AM. He was relieved he hadn't slept-in, and in fact, had ample time before he had to leave the house for his eight o'clock meeting. With that in mind, his eyelids became heavy again and he thought about laying back for another half hour of sleep, but he couldn't give-in to the desire for fear of sleeping-in without an alarm. He laid his head back down.

A minute later, he recoiled into a startled sitting up position and checked his watch again. He stood up with resolve, shaking the temptation of snoozing further, by corralling the mismatched bedding. He began to fold the blankets, pausing only to work the kinks from his back.

Having showered, Gaar emerged from the bathroom, securely tucking a fluffy white towel around his waist as he walked quietly across the second floor landing towards their closed bedroom door. He gripped the handle, and with a conscientious twist, opened the bedroom door slowly to peek in on Louise. As the door swung slowly inwards, he was annoyed by the tiny shrill squeaks of the hinges which seemed amplified by the general silence around the house. Pushing the door forward, the ambient light from the bathroom crept in softly, illuminating a portion of their bedroom. The incremental prying of the light was stopped short by Gaar's need to only pop his head and shoulders through.

Louise lay deep asleep on their bed. He felt a bit like a ghost, looking on at his wife and feeling quite apart from the scene. He was perplexed by the fact that although she had the entire bed to sprawl around in through her sleep, she had remained on her normal side of the bed with his side remaining unruffled. She slept silently, laying on her side with her back facing his side of the bed, almost as though she were giving him the cold shoulder in his absence. It appeared that even in her sleep, perhaps unconsciously, she was showing her resentment. He longed to climb into bed with her, but the thought of her rejecting him dispelled that notion.

Sighing with a melancholy breath, he shut the door and made his way down the stairs. As he entered the living room, he decided that he'd get dressed and leave immediately and would have coffee at a shop downtown.

The front door efficiently clicked locked as he stepped out to face the morning. As Gaar began his customary seven-minute march towards the bus stop, not much stirred in the crisp autumn air save for an erratic chase by two young squirrels. The excitement errupted in a large, virtually leaf-less elm tree which stood proudly on the lawn of a modest house across the way. Gaar squinted as a barrage of conflicting thoughts flooded his mind. He glanced over at the squirrels, each taking turns at instigating a rush of crazy maneuvers, spiraling around the trunk and weaving amidst the forlorn boughs.

As he passed the spasmodic action, the fevered rodents brought their hullabaloo cascading to the ground. The two adventurous pipe-cleaners bolted across the street in Gaar's direction, narrowly avoiding the wheels of a paper-boy's bike which appeared suddenly like a 5am roach in a 6am kitchen. Pedalling madly and mechanically pitching folded newspapers in the general direction of various doorsteps, the perceived predator imposed an every-squirrel-for-himself retreat to the nearest tree. As the din of the ruckus subsided with the paper-boy's swift vanishing act, Gaar strode past a tree and cast a glance at one of the disenfranchised squirrels which peeped around the trunk none too pleased with the likes of him. The tiny dark pearls in the sockets of the grey squirrel's head glistened with an ominous sheen. Guilty by association, innocent by indifference. Gaar shrugged his shoulders in apology to the critter, then glanced at his watch.

§

The elevator door opened on the seventeenth floor. Gaar stepped out of the gilded lift into the foyer, which was lit only marginally by the diffused sunlight from the nearby reception area. As he walked along the marbled floor, he came upon the boardroom where he found Tunningham—the foreign affairs deputy minister, and McGregor. They sat at the table sipping away at coffee and chatting.

Gaar stepped in, and set his briefcase down. He held his take-out coffee in his left hand and stuffed his right into his suit-pants. Both Gaar and Tunningham wore fine suits, but McGregor looked scruffy, and although he wore dress slacks and a jacket with a shirt and tie, they were wrinkled. With further inspection, Gaar noticed he was in need of a shave, and wondered whether the man was hung-over.

'Goodmorning,' Gaar said, with a cordial nod.

'Goodmorning Gaar,' Tunningham replied with a chipper smile, which faded fast as he put his coffee mug to his mouth and stared at its brim as he sipped. McGregor sat quiet, staring blankly at Gaar.

Gaar looked at McGregor. 'Where's Philip?'

'*Mr* Roblaw's on the telephone,' McGregor said coldly, nodding down to the telephone sitting nearby on the table, which had a single extension noticeably lit up. Gaar set his coffee on the table and removed his coat, laying it across the back of one of the boardroom chairs.

'I see,' said Gaar, lifting his coffee and wandering over to the windows overlooking the canal, 'have I missed anything yet?'

'Only the fireworks—'

'Alfred, let's wait 'til Philip's done with his call,' Tunningham whispered to McGregor.

Gaar turned from the window and walked towards the table in curiosity. 'What do you mean—*fireworks*?'

'You'll hear all about it in a few minutes,' Tunningham said, unable to disguise his concern.

'Fine,' Gaar replied, having no interest in prying information out of them. He walked back to the windows, where he looked down at the canal and pondered.

After a lengthy wait, the extension light went off on the telephone display, and Roblaw's voice streamed out over the intercom. 'Gentlemen, could you join me in my office?'

The men looked at each other and began to gather their things to cart into Roblaw's office. Tunningham looked at Gaar. 'There's been some *developments*,' he alluded, patting Gaar lightly on the shoulder as he took hold of his coffee mug and made his way for the door. Gaar left his coat draped over the chair, picked up his briefcase and followed the men out of the boardroom and into the hall.

The three men entered Roblaw's resplendent office. The large L-shaped office boasted a comfortable lounge area opposite Roblaw's magnificent dark teak-wood desk which occupied the apex of the room. The walls were of polished dark wood, and the halogen lighting— which was suspended from ceiling track, illuminated specific areas of the office with pools of light. The room was crisp and clean with sparse touches of elegance. There was a large framed map of the IAR on the wall beside his desk, and throughout the office, occasional Inuit sculptures and prints dotted the walls.

There was a disturbing antique polar bear head on a plaque at the back wall of the lounge area. A second plaque symmetrically opposite the polar bear's head, hung bare, as though awaiting a trophy. Gaar had never liked Roblaw's office, and would spend as little time as professionally possible in it. He always felt a twinge of resentment seeing Louise's prominent picture on the edge of the old man's desk, given that his office seemed like a conquest chamber. It felt like night in his office, regardless of the spotty halogen lighting that competed with the daylight, which streamed through the large windows.

Tunningham placed his coffee mug on a coaster near the corner of the desk, and took a seat in a large black leather chair adjacent to Roblaw. Gaar did likewise, occupying a seat on the opposite side of the desk. McGregor sat back in the lounge area, plopping himself comfortably on a black leather couch.

'Morning,' Gaar said flatly to Roblaw, 'I hear there's been a *development*?'

'Actually a bad morning, Gaar,' he replied, sitting back in his elevated and massive swivel chair and removing his reading glasses, 'we have a problem ... an *immense* problem with a criminal and contractual catastrophe in the IAR—Kabloona, to be precise. Take a gander at this,' he said, lifting a sheet of paper from his desk and handing it to Gaar.

Gaar studied the page for a moment. 'Production report ... gibberish, except for "important development" at the top.' Gaar made a motion to hand the transmission to Tunningham who waved it off.

'I've seen it, thanks,' said Tunningham.

Roblaw leaned back in his chair and stared at the ceiling. 'We received it yesterday via satellite transmission, but figured it was garbled after those words, due to weather or sun-flare activity and related technical problems. This morning we found out otherwise,' he stated, as Gaar swallowed down the last gulp of his coffee and tossed the styrofoam cup into an empty pail at the side of Roblaw's desk. Roblaw looked down at the pail, then raised his head, and met up with Gaar's eyes as he was handed back the transmission paper. Roblaw cleared his throat slightly, then put his reading glasses back on to his face, allowing them to slide to the end of his nose.

'There was a colossal mining accident, or *incident* at Kabloona yesterday,' Tunningham said, folding his legs and facing Gaar. 'Two shifts are trapped in the mine. Unfortunately, there's a snow squall causing practically zero visibility. Rescue teams and search aircraft are grounded at Nanisivik.'

'And everyone has to sit on their hands 'til it clears,' Gaar replied, 'how'd they get trapped—and are there many casualties?'

'The bottom line on our books will be a casualty, if we can't rectify this soon,' added Roblaw, 'this morning, those Inuit hill-billies informed me that it's unlikely that the 3R program will be renewed—some of their own were allegedly murdered by some inmates. So, the Indian-givers don't want to renew the treaty.'

'That's their prerogative—bottom line,' Gaar interjected.

'Well, we're in the business of helping them with their bottom line, and so, we've got to change their minds! They want to dump all the inmates back in our laps. They've been spooked by that sonofabitch, *Jag*!'

'He's a jail-bird from way back,' McGregor grumbled, 'never did trust him.'

'Najagneq's a shaman—a cult hero to them in a way,' Gaar said, turning to McGregor. He turned back around and looked directly at Roblaw. 'In the negotiations, we gave over to their stipulation that Kabloona and the other camps have indigenous supervision.'

'I want that amended when we renew. They're considering this obstacle as an omen. They're being exposed to too much Inuit TV programming—cultural documentaries and the like; what they need is a good dose of game shows and sit-coms.'

Tunningham unfolded his legs and leaned forward in his chair towards Gaar. 'There was a major fire, which likely burned the whole camp down.'

'We're talking heavy casualties then,' replied Gaar.

'It was sabotage!' yelled Roblaw, as he stood from his chair, slid his glasses onto the table and began to pace his office. 'They closed my mine! I wish I knew the results of that exploration drift—dammit! Know who they're using as a scapegoat for this mayhem?'

'Guess who's coming to dinner ...' Gaar recited to himself, looking over at Tunningham, who sipped at his coffee and frowned in confusion at Gaar's reply, 'let me take a wild stab at it. It wouldn't be your very own Max Dopplestein, would it?'

'How'd you guess that?' asked Roblaw, who stopped in his tracks and turned to Gaar.

'That's uncanny,' Tunningham said, with a look of surprise on his face.

'Just something you said that triggered it,' Gaar replied, as Roblaw and McGregor shared a brief glance, 'he was on my mind yesterday, and I guess it's a residue thought. They're holding him for arraignment then?'

'He escaped,' McGregor blurted.

'*He's* not the type, and where would he run to?' Gaar quizzed as McGregor shrugged his shoulders in reply. Gaar turned back to Roblaw. 'Are you following the weather closely to see when the rescue effort can get to Kabloona?'

'McGregor's on top of it,' replied Roblaw, who stepped over to the window and looked out.

'They're saying *they* have the engineers and men to handle the rescue when weather permits,' added Tunningham, 'at the moment, we're not welcome to interfere. Everyone's on edge.'

'My inside–source escaped the carnage and wired me this morning from Nanisivik,' Roblaw stated, 'he didn't have details about the mine, but informed me that Max and a female prisoner escaped by dog-sled after she'd shot the gate guard.'

'*No*,' Gaar exhaled, sitting forward in his chair.

'The official account from the high council as reported by Jag, is that allegedly they also killed Jag's nephew, two Canadian engineers ... and are implicated in the mine collapse. Supposedly, they had started a riot among the prisoners, which is impossible since they made a getaway before the camp burned down— according to my source. Apparently, in concern for the lives of Jag's men, *and* to apprehend Max and company, the camp was abandoned.'

'That's seventy men and women fending for themselves, *if* they survived the barracks fire,' added Tunningham with a regretful shake of his head, as he stood up and looked at the framed map of the IAR on the wall.

'Those inmates may be thick-skinned,' announced McGregor from the couch, 'but they ain't tough enough to fly the coop on foot. The law of survival dictates you stay with the wreckage. If they stray off in the squall, they're doomed. It's minus sixty and there's a blizzard. Add frostbite, dehydration and predators—that's a combination for failure.'

Roblaw turned from the window and looked at McGregor who slouched back in the couch. With the sunlight shining through on him, Roblaw could see that he was looking rough around the edges. He beckoned McGregor over to him with a nod. As the man walked towards him, Roblaw leaned into his ear and spoke to him in confidence. 'Alfie, you look a disgrace. There's disposable razors in the washroom—now go get yourself cleaned up. Don't you *ever* come into my office again looking like this—you told me you're on-the-wagon, ... clean up your act!'

Gaar figured out what was being said in the whispers, and decided to join Tunningham at the map. Glancing over, he could see McGregor nodding his obedience. When Roblaw had finished, he patted McGregor on the back. 'I appreciate all your hard work through the night staying on top of this,' Roblaw said loudly for all to hear, in order to cover for McGregor. Roblaw walked to his desk as McGregor left the office. He opened a drawer in his desk and pulled out a cigar.

'Philip, do you *have* to light that?' Tunningham asked, 'it's illegal in this building—and it offends me.'

'Oliver, it offends me that it's illegal, too,' Roblaw replied, sitting at his desk and lighting the cigar. 'McGregor's been working overtime—and he's right, he knows the landscape. A lot of them will end up dying if they venture out. Our immediate problem though, is finding Max. Jag has fingered him and he's on the hunt. Jag has got everybody's balls in a knot, and Max is innocent!'

'I'd venture a guess that he is as well, but only a court can decide that,' replied Gaar, turning from the map and resuming his seat. Tunningham remained standing, keeping his distance from the stinking cigar.

'Unfortunately, Jag's got influence,' Roblaw said, from behind a hanging cloud of cigar smoke, 'and he's got the high council and the people in a *cultural* uproar. He's walking around preaching gibberish about *spirits of the land*, with a goddamn *corpse* strapped to his back!'

Gaar sat up in his seat. 'What do you mean a *corpse*? Whose corpse?'

'I don't know, some corpse.'

'Like a *mummy*, from what we've heard,' added Tunningham.

'Sounds like big trouble for you. Jag's got clout there as a shaman.'

'He's a shyster!' blurted Roblaw with a cough. 'He's a double-crossing back stabber! This is his *Deus-ex-Machina*.'

'You lawyers are always speaking Latin—what do you mean?' asked Tunningham, clearing his throat and waving some smoke from his face.

'It's a theatrical term,' replied Gaar.

'That's his angle,' Roblaw said, with a wave to move the smoke from over his desk which was wafting towards Tunningham, 'Oliver, I see your grasp of Greek tragedy is slipping; this *corpse* is his "god-from-the-machine", it was an introduced contrivance on stage, to fix a difficult plot—to straighten out the mess and untangle the characters for the audience. This is a *tragedy* for our operations, and Jag's using this and his witchcraft to keep me from what's rightfully due ... the company. It's all smoke and mirrors! The three of us should be able to straighten out this ... *misunderstanding*.'

Tunningham took his seat, seeing that the hanging cigar smoke hovered just above sitting height. The smoke seemed to be drawn to him though, as it followed him down as he sat. He cleared his throat again, and leaned forward to Gaar. 'Our ambassador there, has been asked to attend a high council meeting in Nanisivik, on Monday evening. They will try Max in absentia. He's a fugitive and we've got to play by their rules. His sentence will be the sentence of 3R—*your* baby.'

'How very magnanimous of you to extend me the brunt of credit for 3R, now that it's coming apart at the seams,' Gaar replied mildly, looking from Tunningham to Roblaw. 'Philip, who's your source?'

'That's confidential. He'll reveal himself to you if you can find Max and represent him at the tribunal.'

'Wait a second—'

'Gaar, I'm flying up to Nanisivik this afternoon,' Tunningham said, with a hint of enticement in his voice.

'Hold the phone,' he sighed, raising his hands off his lap.

'Fly into Nanisivik, and then overland to Kabloona when the weather clears a bit,' voiced Roblaw, matter-of-factly.

'I need you to accompany me—consider it a political junket,' Tunningham added.

'Can't, sorry.'

'Our future bilateral relations with your people, and perhaps their economic survival, rests in your hands.'

'Oliver—*please*, no melodrama. This sounds like you're more concerned with the 3R expansion, than with the trapped miners.'

Roblaw began to extinguish his cigar into an ashtray on his desk. 'Of course we're sick to death about those trapped prisoners!' he announced transparently, 'sure, they can be replaced, *but they'll never be forgotten!*' Roblaw stood up vigourously and paraded. 'The survivors will be applauded, and I'll have a plaque erected in honour of any casualties at the mine.'

McGregor stepped back into the office, rubbing at a tiny water spot on his tie. He carried a coffee mug in his left hand. The group took a passing notice of his entry. 'I don't want to interrupt the flow, but I made fresh coffee,' he said, slipping back down onto the black leather couch.

Gaar frowned, still miffed at Roblaw's callous remark about the plaque he would erect. 'That's an insensitive remark,' Gaar said, looking back at Roblaw. McGregor looked up from his coffee with slight confusion. Roblaw noted McGregor's expression.

'He's talking to *me*,' Roblaw said to McGregor, then looked at Gaar, 'can we be pragmatic here? We're *lawyers*, not priests. There's a madman loose up there. He's going to drag *your* people down with him. Your *father* lives in that region, near Nanisivik, right?'

'Leave my father out of this.'

'Your father has influence among the elders of the council,' McGregor stated, adding his two cents to the billion dollar pie.

'What the *hell* do *you* know?'

'Twenty-eight years in the region with the Mounties, says I know a bit—and I listen.'

'Since you're half Inuit, and you speak their language ...' Roblaw said assuredly, as though he knew the errand would be done by his *employee* son-in-law.

'Localizers vary,' Gaar protested, 'there's dozens of three–day dialects in that district. My Inuktitut is rusty.'

McGregor chuckled. Gaar turned and stared at him. 'What's so funny?' Gaar flatly asked McGregor.

'*My Inuktitut is rusty*,' McGregor repeated like a parrot. 'A virile young man like you—'

'What's *that* supposed to mean?! *You*—'

'Alfie, that's enough,' Roblaw interjected, 'pay no heed, Gaar ...'

'It's just a joke, so *keep your pants on*.'

'This assignment will give you a second stab at your first criminal case—in your home arena,' Roblaw offered energetically. 'I want you to defend Max—dead or alive.'

'Please, Gaar,' asked Tunningham, 'if Max and the other prisoner can refute the testimony of Jag, and with Philip's source as a witness, they may renew 3R; without them, we could be rendered impotent.'

Gaar pondered for a moment, distracted mostly with Tunningham's analogy which struck painfully close to home.

'My source will remain a secret witness,' Roblaw announced, 'for protection ... I don't want to place his life in jeopardy. He can't stand alone in testifying against Jag; he's got to be a tandem witness with Max, otherwise it's just his word against—a shaman's? I think we all know how the math works.'

Gaar stood up and stepped away from the desk. He lifted his hands in defiance. 'I can't go. I'm sorry about the trapped miners and this whole travesty. I'm not feeling one hundred percent, so if there's a way to fly down an ambassador from there, or set up a video conference with the satellite link— I'm game. Understand this, I have a wife that needs me right now and a baby on the way. Home—need I say more?'

Tunningham drew a breath intending to jump–in with a few words. 'No, hang on a second,' Gaar said, raising his hand as Tunningham tried to interject, '*I'm* not a bounty hunter, and I can't afford to mess around up there. I don't want to end up a statistic—I've got a bad feeling about all this. I'm *sorry*.'

'Your mother would have wanted you to go,' Roblaw said flatly.

'How would you know what *my* mother would have wanted?!' Gaar growled angrily.

'To visit your father. It's been over twenty years, right? It's a shame, I hear he's not well.'

'You're over-stepping the bounds of business, Philip. I don't want this to turn ugly, so—'

'Temper ...'

'*Gentlemen, please*,' Tunningham interjected, stepping between the sight line of Gaar and Roblaw, 'Gaar, bear with me for a moment. You know how mutually important this is between our countries. I can promise you a Queen's Council at the federal level, and I'll lobby for the Order of Canada for you, if you remedy the situation.'

'That's very tempting, but my wife ...'

'It would look very impressive on a business card,' said Roblaw, attempting to ice the cake, 'especially if you ever decided to start your own law practice.'

Gaar's face went blank for a moment. Roblaw and Tunningham looked on at him with expectation. McGregor sat back and grinned at the proposal on the table.

'We've got two days,' said Tunningham in anticipation, 'this *mission*—I'll call it, is confidential. We don't want any press getting in the way until it's resolved.'

'McGregor's an expert tracker, and you—you're a gifted lawyer and a diplomat,' Roblaw said, sitting down and fiddling with his glasses, 'why don't you run it by Louise?'

'Jag already has a hunting party tracking them, but it's not to bring Max back alive, that's for damn sure,' McGregor muttered, as he slurped his coffee.

Gaar looked at both Roblaw and Tunningham and shook

his head. 'To discredit a shaman is no easy feat. To them, he's a cultural institution.'

Roblaw waved his glasses in the air, brushing off Gaar's concern. '*Culture* doesn't put bread on the table—game shows do.'

'Please help us, Gaar,' Tunningham pleaded, bowing his head slightly and wrinkling his forehead. Gaar sensed a sincerity in Tunningham's voice, realizing that Tunningham's goal in all this went far beyond the mercenary posture that Roblaw typified.

'It's up to my wife,' Gaar replied, removing his staunch defiance to the plan, and submitting to the approval of Louise. 'I'm going to give her the last word, okay? What she says is *final*. I'm going to go and call her from *my* office.'

Gaar stepped out of the office and the remaining group breathed a sigh of relief having hurdled a major stumbling block. Roblaw smiled at Tunningham and nodded to McGregor who bore a wry grin. 'Don't worry, Oliver,' Roblaw said confidently to Tunningham, 'it's in the bag.'

§

The telephone rang twice on the hallway stand in Gaar and Louise's home. The malfunctioning answering machine activated and spun into action without playing back any outgoing message. It was almost ten o'clock, and Louise had always been out of bed by nine on Saturday mornings.

It appeared no one was home, until a woman's gloved hand picked up the receiver and put it to her face. She wore sunglasses, a hat, and an overcoat identical to Louise's mohair coat. 'Hello?' she said, in a convincing impersonation of Louise. 'Gaar?!' the mysterious woman sputtered, raising her voice and getting into the act. 'I know I sound awful! I'm in pieces ... I'll tell you what's the matter!! *You're* the matter! Don't you *honey* me, you bastard!!' she shrieked, pacing at the stand now and fidgeting with a silver house key as she acted. She began to choke up and sob, replete with tearful sniffling. 'It's all your fault—the baby went away! Do I have to *spell* it out for you?! I want *you* to go away. I never want to see or hear from you again! Ever!! You killed our baby!'

Gaar stood up from his desk with a violent burst of shock and fright. 'You had a miscarriage?! Oh no!' Gaar exclaimed with despair, automatically moving to his open office door and slamming it shut. 'Honey, you're in shock! Louise, calm down!! I'm coming home right now! ... What do you mean you're leaving? Louise? Stay where you are—screw the taxi!! Where are you going to stay?!' he asked, leaning forward onto his desk and staring angrily at a blank wall. 'Why not? ... A *friend's* ?! What friend? Give me a name for God's sake! Louise, wait—you need to be examined right away! Where's the baby? ... The *toilet*?! Stop. Don't tell me anymore! Oh no—stop!' he groaned, bowing his head, and shaking it with regret. 'What do you mean?! I don't want a divorce! Neither of us are rational right now so stop torturing yourself! Louise, please—*stay where you are*! Don't go! Louise? Louise?!' he yelled into the receiver, frustrated that she had hung up on him. 'Fuck *me*? Fuck *you*!' he said angrily, holding the receiver in the air and addressing it. 'What am I *saying*? She's not herself.' Gaar put down the receiver in utter disbelief.

He stood silent in his disorientation, then kicked his chair back with rage. An overwhelming feeling of helplessness overcame him and he pulled his chair back and sat down at his desk. He dialed his home number again, then hung-up in frustration after a couple of rings.

With his head now resting in his cupped hands, he began to sob. His shoulders jerked in sympathy to his spasms of despair. His body took a short constricted breath to counter-act the long, complete and silent exhalation which was squeezed from him, and he gave into the sorrow which over-came him. He cried and moaned, allowing the tears to stream down his chin, and onto the floor.

For a minute, he mourned in wretchedness. He attempted to pull himself together, taking a handkerchief from his pocket and wiping his face thoroughly. He looked around his modest but tasteful office where everything was so famil-iar yet now seemed so foreign—especially his framed picture of Louise.

Gaar slammed his fists down on the desk, and swiped at the telephone, knocking it from the top of the desk to the floor with a rattle. He stormed up from his chair and bolted out of his office.

Gaar cupped his hand below the flowing water of the open faucet in the elegant company washroom. He splashed some water on his face and looked up despondently into the mirror. There was a flushing of a toilet from one of the stalls behind him, and he cringed at the sound. Out from a stall walked a security officer, who was making rounds of the building. The man attempted to ignore Gaar who restrained his fury, displaying only an annoyed stare at the porcelain sink. The guard proceeded to wash his hands, darting a glance in the reflection of the mirror to assess the identity of the man who loitered over the basin adjacent to him. Recognizing Gaar, he nodded and grabbed a paper towel, dried his hands and exited the washroom.

The toilet had finished flushing, but the echoed horror of the turbulent flushing resonated in Gaar's mind. His child, his *family*. He began to throw up. He slapped his hand over his mouth and dashed into a stall to hide and retch the emotion from his guts. The reverberant gagging gave way to a primal scream, as Gaar flushed the toilet.

Gaar drunkenly entered Roblaw's office. Roblaw was conspicuously absent. Tunningham and McGregor looked up at Gaar, staring blankly at him as he walked straight past them and idled at the window. On Roblaw's desk, an extension light went out on the telephone, and a moment later, Roblaw emerged from the door which adjoined his office with his secretary's.

'Thanks, Victoria.' Roblaw said, poking his head back through the door, 'see you on Monday.'

As Roblaw approached his desk, he observed Gaar at the window, who turned and stared reproachfully at him as he neared.

'I'd like a few minutes in private,' Gaar flatly said to Roblaw.

'Of course, Gaar. Gentlemen, why don't you have some coffee.'

Tunningham had a concerned look on his face, as Gaar turned back to stare out the window. McGregor mechanically stepped out of the office, with the manner of someone who had an inkling of what was afoot. Roblaw pursed his lips and nodded at Tunningham, conveying a promissory gesture of imminent success. Tunningham looked back at Gaar with curiosity, and then departed the room, closing the door behind himself.

Gaar remained looking out the window, choking back his anger. 'Louise had a miscarriage this morning. She's a mess.'

'I know, she called me,' Roblaw replied in sympathy, 'she's staying with a friend for a while—I don't know who, she wouldn't say.'

'Uh huh,' Gaar uttered, turning and pacing the room

slowly. He put his hands behind his back and slowly walked forward as though looking for something on the dark marbled floor.

Roblaw leaned against the outside edge of his desk, and bowed his head to the floor. 'She'll get over it; tells me her friend knows a good specialist who'll look her over and refer her to a psychologist, to get her over this hump. She's been under a lot of stress lately.'

'*Stress.*' Gaar said with a derisive laugh, 'I'm about an inch away from losing it, myself.' Gaar stopped pacing. 'She's not to blame ...'

'No one's to blame.'

Gaar folded his arms in front of his chest, and chuckled scornfully, as he took a few steps forward past Roblaw, then stopped to turn to him. 'Subtle as always ... you *sonofabitch!*'

'How *dare* you address me—'

Gaar leapt forward, leading with a pointed finger as though it were a spear. 'Daddy to a fault! You poisoned her mind against me, underhandedly twisting and digging— manipulating her mind and emotions!' Gaar blurted with a single breath in a passionate denouncement. 'Feeding her anxiety—*derailing our marriage!*'

'It was a freak accident!' Roblaw retaliated, waving his hands to deflect the upbraiding that was directed at him in spits and bounds. 'I take umbrage to you insinuating I was the cause of the miscarriage!'

'Well, I need an *umbrella* for the bullshit that's going down in this office. You play the devil's advocate like no other. I *know* you—your kind. You hate me with a passion! Well, I've grown to hate you and your vindictive, selfish character! You're despicable, and you've put her through hell! You don't love your daughter and you won't let any other man love her! You want to possess her? Is that the spot for her head?!' Gaar scoffed as he stormed into the lounge area and pointed at the vacant plaque, adjacent to the polar bear head. 'Is it?! I'm not giving up without a fight! And right now I could just put *your* head on that plaque!'

'Get a grip on yourself!' Roblaw protested.

Gaar marched quickly toward the man. 'I should get a grip on you!' he hissed, opening his hands in a strangling gesture and holding them apart in a trembling restraint. Gaar stopped, and veered off to the window, where he reached his arms up and leaned forward, supporting himself by gripping the sides of the window frame.

'Gaar, I'm sorry about the baby,' he said with maudlin overtones, rubbing his forehead, 'Louise will come around.'

'*If* you let go of the strings and keep your nose out of our lives!'

'She needs you, and I need you—'

Gaar stared out the window and shook his head disapprovingly. 'You need *me*, to save your ass! Well, *fuck you*!'

Roblaw nodded slyly as he looked at Gaar staring boldly out the window. 'If you do this one last job for me ...'

Gaar turned angrily towards Roblaw from the window with a scowl of determination on his face. 'Are you deaf? Can you read this?' he asked mockingly, as he held up his middle finger and gestured his feelings.

'I'm afraid I can't accept that,' Roblaw said with a deadpan expression, 'you're still in shock, and you're not being rational ... you both need a little time apart, and if you do this job for me, I'll somehow convince Louise to go back to you.'

Gaar folded his arms on his chest not believing the man's audacity. 'You're flagrantly admitting your puppeteering ways—you are scum to the core! You *don't* love your daughter. She's a pawn—a lever!'

'I'll tear up your contract. You'd be free to immediately open your own practice. You'll have your Q.C. and ... one-hundred thousand dollars. I'll stay out of your lives and sing your praises to her—think about it. Take a couple of minutes. Hell, let's make it five-hundred thousand dollars!'

Gaar glared at him, fuming in a state fit-to-be-tied. He proceeded to the window in a huff, and swiped a row of books off a nearby shelf, in a burst of frustration. Gaar put his hand to his head and pondered his situation. His options were dire, and as much as he wanted to thrash Roblaw within an inch of his life, his obscene proposition offered a glimmer of compromised hope.

Gaar turned and paced from the window with his arms folded across his chest. Propping a fist to his mouth, he pondered, calculating the resolution of his predicament. He stopped and stared at the map of the IAR, and then longingly pined over Louise's picture which called out to him from Roblaw's desk. He swiftly turned to Roblaw who stood waiting for a reply.

'One million,' Gaar said with bitter resolve.

Roblaw paused, thinking about Gaar's counter offer, then opened his arms and caved in to his demand. 'Done,' he said, walking behind his desk and sitting down.

'I want this in writing.'

'Don't be insulting. I can give you the money, but not the tools to pry me from the love of my daughter. I give you *my word*. We'll call this *danger money* for the assignment—Louise wouldn't question that. You *will* accept my word of honour, won't you?'

'Renege, and you'll give me your life. Do we understand each other? Mark my words.'

'Agreed,' Roblaw said, getting up and moving towards his secretary's door. He went through to her office and returned with a small suitcase and walked it back with him to his desk.

'What's that?'

'It's a suitcase. *Your* suitcase, complete with toiletries, a change of clothing—everything a man needs. I had Victoria go shopping, after Louise had called me.'

'You're a calculating sonofabitch—'

'Are you having second thoughts because I showed foresight? You can call it quits right now and go home if you want to.'

'I've got nothing to go home to.'

'I'm sorry to have to concur with you on that one. I figured we could come to some arrangement, and although you drove a hard bargain, I think we'll all be better for it—and this way I've saved you the tribulation of having to dash home and pack some things. You have travel credentials in there, maps, treaty documents and our original contract with the IAR and a copy of their constitution. There's parkas waiting for the group of you in Nanisivik. If you're re-routed to Iqaluit or Pangnirtung, the company credit card and expense account are at your disposal. You can charter a plane or boat or whatever; just get there *fast*, and get the job done. No holds barred, right?'

'Words to live by.'

§

Louise walked through the cosmetics aisle of her local pharmacy, and paused at a perfume testing stand. She dabbed a few samples on the underside of her wrist and sniffed at the selections, wondering which one Gaar might be most fond of. She felt a pang of guilt for flying off the handle with Gaar the way she did. She came across a perfume she had changed away from two years prior, and dabbed some on her wrist. The delightful scent called to mind the good times she and Gaar had spent together, and in retrospection, she cracked a smile. How they had laughed and loved, and how they had been such good friends to each other.

She lifted a bottle of the perfume and headed up the aisle towards the prescription counter to collect her medications. As she reached the wall–length prescription area which was barricaded with shelves of vitamins and personal hygiene items, she approached the small service opening and an elevated pharmacist leaned down to her.

'Can I help you?' he said, looking over his reading glasses.

'Yes, someone called me to say my prescription was ready, finally.'

'Name?' he asked, typing something into a computer terminal.

'Louise Injugarjuk—I.N.J.U. garjuk ... two J's'

The pharmacist typed away and a puzzled look came over his narrow face. He rubbed at his bald head, and then pulled his reading glasses from his face and allowed them to hang on their chain. 'I'm sorry, but I have no record of it having come in. Your request is still here on the terminal. The stock should be arriving Monday. Weren't you notified of this when you filed the prescription?'

'Yes I was, but ... someone called me from here. Blast, I wish I got her name or something. I had to take a cab to come over here to fetch it. Can you please check again? Maybe find out who called?' she petitioned, as the pharmacist stroked away at the keys of his terminal once again, but came up dry. 'I'd really like to have my medication,' she added, 'I'm a bit edgy without it, you see.'

The pharmacist nodded, then abandoned the terminal to check with a couple of co-workers behind the counter. Louise sniffed again at the scent of the perfumes on her wrist. She found great delight in the long-lost scent. The pharmacist returned to attend her.

'I'm sorry, nobody seems to know anything about this

phone call you say you received from here. I apologize for your wasted trip.'

'I guess it wasn't a total waste—can I pay for this here?'

'Certainly. Your medication will be in on Monday,' he said, as he rang up the small bottle of perfume on an adjacent money till. 'It comes to forty-seven twenty.'

As Louise opened her purse and reached for her photo-scan credit card, the pharmacist bagged the perfume and set it ready for her. She handed him the card, which he promptly laser–scanned. She punched in her PIN on the hand-held keypad and the pharmacist tore away the receipt which mechanically emerged from the till. Disappointed with having gone on a wild goose chase, she grabbed her purchase and made her way down the aisle for the exit at the front of the store.

§

Louise pushed open the front door of her house and struggled with the key to extract it from the lock. The cab she took home pulled out from the curb and drove off, as she irritably swung the door shut on the outside world. Heaving a frustrated sigh, she set her purse down, slid off her coat, and opened the closet door, grabbing a hanger to to sling her mohair coat across. Finished now with the ritual mechanics of arriving home, she eagerly reached for her purse and pulled out the perfume, which she began to unwrap.

The telephone rang. She turned her head towards it, as she closed the door securely on the closet which had the annoying tendency of swinging open, then made her way to the stand. The answering machine silently kicked–in once again, and Louise picked up the receiver.

At a long bank of vacant telephones, a short pudgy man in an overcoat held a telephone receiver to his ear, as he checked the time on his watch. The noisy acceleration of buses reverberated through the tiled lounge area, as they pulled out of the station.

'It's Gaar,' the man said, convincingly impersonating Gaar's voice. 'I'm going back to the Arctic—for good. I'm leaving you. You're not happy, and there's no way I can make you happy. Let's call it irreconcilable differences, okay?! ... I'm not in love with you anymore, and I can't see any hope at all—you don't love me anymore,' the man said, as a well dressed woman walked by, and hearing part of the conversation, tarried near him. He tried to wave her off, but the woman tilted her head in sympathy and expressed a pouty look on her face as though she were eager to help. He turned his back to the nosey woman.

'Nevermind *sorry*,' the man said into the receiver, 'it's too late for that! Everybody's got to cope with stress! You don't know the meaning of the word *love*!'

The woman reached into her purse and drew out a business card, which she stepped forward with. She tapped him on the shoulder, and handed her card to him as he turned around with a glare of inconvenience. The man nervously grabbed the card and waved her away. She waved a good-bye and was gone.

He looked briefly at the card and was thrown for a loop. His eyes bulged, seeing the woman was a licensed marriage counselor. He crumpled the card and tossed it on the floor. 'That's not love!' he said defiantly into the phone, catching up with his role. 'No you don't! I'm getting on a bus for the airport right now! Listen, this is *best* for both of us. I'm going back to my roots—to rediscover myself. What? I ...

couldn't get it up ... because ... 'cause I'm not interested in you anymore—you're a *damper* on me. Stop crying, and listen! I'm tired of the city and I'm tired of you, and I'd tell you to your face, but you're not worth it.'

The man stood up straight, and swiveled his body as far as the cord would allow, wary of any other eavesdroppers. 'I don't care about the baby—get an abortion or wallow in the ball-and-chain of single motherhood,' he said, crouching forward between the panels which separated his phone from the next. 'I don't know who'd want you then, but *I* don't want you now!' he yelled, as another bus left the terminal and almost overshadowed his voice with its echoey acceleration from the covered terminal. 'I'm not going to spend the rest of my life fighting with you and your father! ... Burn them. Clothes, pictures, pillow—I don't care!!'

'You're a bastard!' Louise screamed hysterically, pacing the hallway. The line went dead and she stood trembling with fury and despair, then slammed down the receiver. When she realized she was holding the bottle of perfume, she violently threw it from where she stood in the hall, straight through to the far wall in the living room. It burst on contact, showering the living room with both glass and liquid.

Her eyes felt very puffy, and she nervously rubbed her face not realizing she'd been crying so hard. Her mind seemed to explode and fragment in a dozen directions, and she angrily paced in a small circle. She picked up the phone's receiver and dialed her father's private line at the firm—if anyone could console her and help collect her thoughts, it was her father. He could shed light on the situation and would fill her in on what happened at the office, and what drove the sonofabitch to drop her like a hot potato.

sixteen

HAVING BEEN EXPEDITED to the airport, Gaar, McGregor and Tunningham sat separate of each other in the sparsely occupied airborne Boeing 737 jet plane. The airplane was large, but had the majority of seats removed to accommodate the vast amount of cargo supplies which were bound for both Nanisivik at the northwest tip of Baffin Island, and Resolute, which was the better part of an hour's flight north of there.

The Monday evening deadline for the tribunal unnerved Tunningham, as the eight-hour flight would shave valuable hours from their time-limited agenda. Tunningham mulled over some logistics in his mind. It being Saturday, and provided they indulged in some in–flight sleep, there wasn't any particular problem with them getting right to business that evening upon arrival, their ETA being eight-twenty PM.

There were perhaps ten other people on the flight and

most sat alone, enjoying the liberty of spreading themselves over two seats in the relatively empty flight. The three envoys had arranged separate work stations over double seats. All were immersed in maps and documents pertaining to the business at hand, although Gaar was still stewing over Louise's erratic behavior which he felt bordered on insanity. The child was tragically gone now, but Louise's condition upset him.

He tried to comfort himself in the thought that this company business would be over and done with by Tuesday, and that he would attempt to pick up the pieces and start again with Louise on his return. He couldn't fathom how he'd taken the word of the same man who had him by the balls, and entrusted his oppressor to resuscitate his marriage—which he was solely responsible for ruining! He pondered on that for a moment, admitting to himself, his guilt in neglecting his marriage and Louise's needs and wishes.

Perhaps Louise would be proud of his sudden mercenary agenda in negotiating himself a million dollar fee for the risky assignment. If this wasn't escalating up the corporate ladder in turbo mode, then what the hell was? If Louise was to come back to him, he would buy her the dream house of her choice with the danger money, and he would finance his own law practice in Ottawa. He imagined breaking an expensive bottle of champagne on the front door to christen their new life, and how he would carry her over the threshold.

The pipe dream was short lived though, and a frown crept across his face. Roblaw was a master manipulator, and there was a chance that what was in store for him might not be the bed-of-roses scenario that he had entertained. The thought of Louise not coming back to him, and of Roblaw contesting or reneging on their deal if this political assignment was to fall flat on its face, was a disturbing thought. It was a gentlemen's agreement, although Gaar had never considered

Roblaw a gentleman. But, as his options were few, this was the only sensible thing to do to put a little time and space between himself and his problems.

He suddenly felt eager to make sense out of the Kabloona disaster, and to hopefully find Max and uncover a few things. This was also a good impetus to look up his father and find out why he'd never answered his letters. A discomforting feeling inundated Gaar, as he realized he was leaving a problem behind only to face another painful encounter.

Gaar began to perspire slightly, and he took his handkerchief to wipe his face and neck. Something was closing in on him, but he couldn't put his finger on it. At the moment, he was not wanted in Ottawa, and perhaps he'd not be welcome in the IAR. Neither by his father or perhaps by the Inuit—but most certainly by Jag! Gaar couldn't help feeling being caught between two worlds. He felt a bit like a traitor and mercenary *to* and *from* both, and was flustered by the tangled web which he not only helped weave, but which now threatened to ensnare him.

Gaar laid his perspiring head back into his airplane seat, and shut his eyes. A delirium overcame him, and his head moved from side to side in agitation. Although he felt himself still awake in some form, he began to powerlessly hallucinate. He was reluctant at first to let go of his consciousness, but felt that something was welcoming him in a way, and so he gave in to the calling, offering no resistance to the trip on which he was being taken. Tunningham glanced over at Gaar, and believing him to be asleep, stood and turned off the overhead light above Gaar's seat.

Gaar found himself walking through a sunlit grassy meadow in the Arctic. It was a peculiar sensation, as though he were floating, even though his feet carried him along, but it was very different than the last time this sensation had enveloped him at the office.

He now had a physical body and was conscious of it, rather than just experiencing events and places in only a visual sense. He knew he was hallucinating, and turned around several times to test the control he apparently had in this dream. As he felt his arms and hands, he realized he was existing in three dimensions, yet he couldn't help confounding his mind with the fact that in parallel to this reality, he was also on an airplane on his way to a wintry facsimile of this lush dreamland. Regardless of his desire for direction in this dream, it was a respite from the nightmare he'd departed. If there was a purpose for him being there, it would be evident as he moved forward through this beautifully cosmic landscape.

He headed for a large solitary tree in the distance, as it was a focal point and a curious anomaly which sprung high and majestically from the expansive tundra. Long before he could reach the tree though, the sky went pitch black. He became concerned that if he strayed off course he might bypass the tree altogether. If there was a sky here, there were no stars or moon; nor was there a sign of the Aurora Borealis. He felt that the tree was something important to get to, and plodded on, but without a beacon, and with the unsure footing of the rolling tundra, his quest seemed futile.

This dark world felt very oppressive and threatening. Without the visual elements, he felt like a prisoner, powerless and unable to wake up or become conscious. He ambled along slowly with outstretched arms, trying to navigate in a straight line towards the tree. Suddenly, he found the tree with his face. He collided at a slow speed with the trunk, and stumbled backwards stunned but unhurt.

Imagining he was seeing stars from the impact, he came to the conclusion after a few moments, that it wasn't stars he was seeing, but the Aurora Borealis, twisting in and around the branches of the tree. The tree as he had imagined it was from a distance, was now quite different. Its easily accessible leafy branches and thickly barked trunk had crystalized and turned to ice, and he was now standing on a frosted ground. The weaving spectral lights of the Aurora Borealis, now corralled within the numerous branches of the tree, both blinded, and yet, enticed him to climb upwards. He set out to do just that.

He found it was no easy task to scale the ice tree, even with the chest height V-split in its trunk. Managing to finally wriggle up into the split platform, he carefully ascended the tree, making slow but positive progress up and around the branches. He was puzzled at the absence of wind and that the ice of the tree was not cold to the touch, although it was exceedingly slippery.

As he ascended to the third branch of the tree, he was at first shocked and then comforted with his first encounter with another entity, which brushed by him and then disappeared behind some crystalline leaves. It was an apparition of an old woman. The old woman consisted only of a giant head with clawed feet, which jutted out from beneath its chin. From his recollection of folklore, he remembered its name as *Katutajuk*.

His brush with the ghastly apparition hadn't caused him to lose his footing, or his desire to go further. As he climbed further, he detected other mischievous incarnations in the quiet yet restless tree. Although he didn't meet head-on with any of them after Katutajuk, he mused on Inuit mythology, and how very real it was. He caught sight of bits and pieces of various creatures who maneuvered throughout the tree in somewhat uncanny ways—like the giant walrus which he'd partially seen, sliding along a very narrow branch without a worry of falling. The balance of the creatures was as extraordinary as the tree itself.

Reaching the seventh branch, Gaar came across a very old man sitting on the branch, who almost seemed to be waiting patiently for him to arrive. The old man, dressed in various

layers of mixed furs, and having thick and matted grey hair
which framed his incredibly lined and creased face, smiled at
Gaar.

He recognized the old man as the face he'd known for
umpteen years in his dreams, and from the dream episode in
Roblaw's office. He had never known his grandfather, but
somehow felt this spirit–being to be family. Gaar felt the
physical inability to talk, for as he attempted speech, not
even his lips would move. The old man nodded at him in a
paternalistic way which soothed Gaar and made him feel
welcome in this unusual place.

'Gaar, I am your ancestor, Injugarjuk—your father's
father,' the old man gently said with a mid-range wafer–thin
voice. Gaar listened with respect and anticipation to his
grandfather. 'Through dark forces, my earthly shell has been
discovered by a black wolf. A great bear will devour the wolf,
whose boldness has overshadowed the path of enlighten-
ment. He is like a child playing with the work of this tree.
Some perceive him as a liberator, but, he is an enslaver,
abusing the ninth branch of this tree, which in its perfection,
holds the others together as one. The branch will rot and
fall unless you intervene. You are the liberator. Free yourself, and the spirits of the land.'

Gaar listened intently, beginning now to understand the
noble obligation of his blood lineage. This experience was
the mystical transference of ability and understanding—his
initiation as a shaman. He was overwhelmed with the recognition and confirmation being availed on him by his
grandfather.

'Your helping spirits are the bear and the falcon,' his
grandfather whispered, 'the wolf is no match for you,
Pihootek—being as *one* with the bear. Treachery closes in on
you from the north and the south. Your instincts will guide
you from here,' he said, touching Gaar's chest at his heart.
'Your familiars will protect you. You must wear the

Anknonquatok—it is then you will be fulfilled. Others who wear it will perish,' he said, gesturing with both hands and drawing the outline of the doll-necklace with his hands first on his own chest, and then on Gaar's.

The plane had landed, and slowly taxied along the Nanisivik airfield. Gaar awoke as the plane came to a stop. Tunningham looked over at Gaar with a look of friendly concern. 'Are you alright? I think we should get you to a doctor—you're perspiring like crazy.'

'No, I'm fine, really,' Gaar replied, as he found his handkerchief in his lap and wiped his face and neck. He re-oriented himself in the aircraft, and began to pack up his paperwork which was strewn all over the two seats he occupied.

'Are you sure? When we touched down, it was so rough I thought we were going to crash off the runway—and you slept right through it!'

'Amazing, huh? Thanks for not trying to wake me.'

'Well, you had your seat belt on, and I figured, why bring you back to the land of the *living* to face the possibility of *dying*?' he said with a laugh.

'You're a politician through and through,' Gaar replied with a smile.

'Well, we've made very bad time because we had to circle around twice—debris on the airfield or something. It's nine forty-five, and by the time we get settled and meet with the elders, we may as well call it a night and get to it first thing in the morning—that is unless McGregor wants to go tracking through the night.'

'Did he sleep?' Gaar asked.

'Don't know.'

'Well, it's up to him, but if we want help from the locals, it'd be no good to track when they sleep, and sleep when they work.'

'It's going to be peculiar to adjust to the absence of day and night.'

'For the short time you're here—it's not that imposing. Try six months of it—sixty years of it ...'

Outside on the airstrip, where the snow was being driven by the unrelenting wind, cargo vehicles pulled up to the plane to unload supplies from the aircraft.

The trio waited patiently to depart the plane with other passengers, peeking out to survey the airport's out-buildings which were illuminated by the sodium lamps fastened to standards and buildings alike. Gaar paused in the door of the jet to breathe in the crisp arctic air, then proceeded down the steps towards some waiting men who held spare parkas in their arms. These men were the security and customs personnel for the IAR, who would expedite the VIP's through customs, and on to a waiting vehicle which would whisk them to their accommodations at the community centre hostel, in the core of nearby Nanisivik.

§

The three emissaries walked through the large double doors of the community centre hostel, toting their light luggage. Putting down their gear, they undid their parkas and looked for signs of life in the large over-lit lobby area. A wall-clock above their heads read 10:25 PM, and no one was to be found. The reception counter was devoid of personnel, and the lights were off in the adjoining office. All the same, Tunningham peeped through the darkened office windows, while Gaar inspected a bulletin board nearby.

'It's Saturday night. They're whoopin' it up somewhere in this stinkin' building,' McGregor blurted.

They aimlessly checked doors and looked down hallways for assistance. McGregor was getting annoyed. Just as he was going to unleash a barrage of insults at their invisible hosts, a small group of boys burst from a set of doors and headed for the exit at the front. Amid their chatter-filled exodus, the boys took passing note of the three.

A mischievous looking boy, diverted from the pack and double-backed to assist them. He had made the connection between the business-like strangers who looked lost, and the elders who had gathered in the large gymnasium which was often used as an auditorium. Eager to join his friends who had left, the boy quickly opened the door which he and his friends had emerged from, and gestured the turns they'd encounter on their way to the gym. Leaving them to it, he bolted, and was gone in a flash out the front doors. McGregor had already grabbed his stuff and was impatiently through the doors, when Gaar and Tunningham picked up and followed.

McGregor entered the gym hall and was followed in short order by Gaar and Tunningham. There were about sixty people in the gym, some engaged in physical activity while others chatted at tables lining the walls. They paused inside the doorway, and surveyed the bright and noisy two-storey high hall, in search of the elders who were likely amongst the perimeter crowd somewhere at a table.

On a long rectangular wall at the far end of the gym, there was an immense colourful mural of various hunting, fishing and domestic scenes painted directly onto the wall, in vividly bright colours. Gaar spotted the elders sitting at one of the tables at the muralled wall, and relayed his discovery to the others with a nod of his head.

As they crossed the gym towards the elders who by this time had made note of the strangers, they passed some young men playing a skills game. They were jumping up from a standing position, kicking with both feet at a small suspended furry object.

'What're they playing, again?' asked Tunningham, as they walked.

'Double-kick game,' replied Gaar. 'Bad hunt—they kick with both feet at the suspended hare—without falling. If it was a good hunt, they'd do a single scissor-kick. Think you're able to kick with both feet without crashing down on your ass?'

'Maybe if they lowered the string.'

'The challenge is in *raising* the stakes,' McGregor interjected impolitely.

They reached the table of elders, and courteously nodded to the group who were engaged in a friendly conversation. The elders nodded their welcome to the trio who put down their bags and gear around the table. Tunningham stepped forward and held out his hand, eager to shake hands with the man he thought was the highest ranking elder. He smiled, shaking the hand of the most distinguished looking man of the group.

'Hello. I'm a special envoy from the Canadian Government—'

'I'm the janitor, *he's* the chief—chief,' the old man said, as he rose from the table and patted the chief elder on the back. 'I'll see you later.'

The janitor chuckled, instigating a round of smiles and laughter around the table as he walked away. Gaar smiled at Tunningham's embarrassment. McGregor just shook his head slightly, hoping that Tunningham's simple mistake wouldn't give them the impression that they were all bureaucratic blockheads.

'Hi, I'm George Tookaluktassie, and this is Simon, Matthew and Kiloonik,' said the elder, waving around the table as he introduced the other men. 'Now what was it you were selling again?' he said with a smile.

'My apologies. I'm Oliver Tunningham, Canadian deputy minister of Foreign Affairs. This is Alfred McGregor, and you may or may not know Gaar Injugarjuk, both from Roblaw Inc.' he said, as a round of hand shaking and nods ensued.

The elders were genuinely friendly towards the foreign contingent, each bearing a charismatic expression which was harmoniously shared within the group of elders, all of whom were over sixty years old. Although they were dressed simply, with plain shirts and trousers—Kiloonik also sported a baseball hat with a Toronto Blue Jays crest; they sparkled with the charm of the past, and seemed to possess an ancient peace within. Their demeanor transcended their clothes, making their attire almost incongruous with the men beneath the cotton and polyester blends.

'We know your father, Gaar,' Matthew said with an approving shake of his head, '... a good and wise man.'

Gaar politely nodded his head, embarrassed to get into his personal history with his father, in the event that they knew of some animosity his father had for him—the one who worked for *the company*; and for the fact that he had no news of his father for twenty years, and didn't want to appear heartless and out-of-touch.

'Have a seat,' George said, 'I know why you fella's are here, but where's Roblaw? This is a very serious matter at hand.'

'Mr Roblaw was detained in Ottawa,' McGregor replied boldly, 'with pressing business matters that needed his personal attention, but will do his best to be here for the tribunal on Monday evening.'

'He's probably shitting his pants over this, and can't stomach facing Jag,' Kiloonik said with a wry smile.

Although McGregor wasn't amused by Kiloonik's

humour, Gaar and Tunningham bit the bullet and grinned uneasily at each other, as the three joined the seated elders at the table.

'Speak of the devil ...?' Tunningham whispered to Gaar, as he saw Jag enter the gym with two cronies at his side, heading straight for their table. He recognized the tell-tale signs of a quarrelsome highhanded type.

McGregor looked on with contempt, as the gym went quiet in a rippled reaction to the obscure presence of the ice-man strapped to Jag's back. To McGregor, Jag was just a charlatan and a racketeer, and the sooner someone put him in his place, the better.

As the troupe reached the table, Jag proceeded to walk slowly around the table of seated men. Triq and Agaluq waited against the muralled wall adjacent to the table. Triq, looking-the-worse-for-wear with his bruised and cut face, waved his arms in the air at the staring crowd in order to get them to carry on with what they were doing. Some carried on with their games, while others kept staring. The partial resumption of normal activities in the gym-hall was enough for Triq as his intention was mostly to dilute the stares which he thought were directed at him and his beaten and ravaged face.

Jag nodded his respect to the elders as he moved around the table. Gaar realized at once, that the ice-man was the "earthly shell" of his ancestor Injugarjuk. 'Pull up a chair for you and *your friend*,' McGregor said insolently.

'I know who you are,' Jag replied caustically, '*servants* of the white slaver, too cowardly to face his problem. I know the look of him, and the meaning of him. You are here to do his dirty work ... to try and bring more misery to our people—'

'Hello, Mr Najagneq, I'm Tunningham, deputy minister for Canadian foreign affairs—'

'Who poisons the minds and bodies of our youth, stinks of

lies and deceit and who would erode mother earth from beneath our feet,' Jag continued, cutting Tunningham off in mid sentence, and grand-standing to quell any bureaucratic niceties.

'That's very poetic,' announced McGregor, 'but uncalled for.'

'*McGregor*,' Tunningham blurted with a nervous edge, and turning on the political charm for Jag as he attempted to speak again. 'I detect your animosity, sir, but we are here to rectify the situation—to make things *better*.'

'What is better than a clean body, mind and soul?' asked Jag.

'Uh ...' Tunningham uttered, stuck for words and flustered with the question as the entire table of Inuit waited on a sensible answer from the man. Gaar observed Jag closely and decided that although he spoke words which rang true about Roblaw, he was hiding behind a cloak of deceit himself, and that there would be an inevitable locking-of-horns between them.

'The IAR High Council meets here on Monday,' George re-iterated, saving Tunningham the embarrassment of coming up with a snappy reply to Jag's query, 'and I'm afraid, dead-or-alive, we are obliged to hold council and pass judgement on the two criminals who have brought death and destruction to our doorstep. The High Council members from all across the Republic are undertaking this journey with resolve on their minds, and there's no way we can extend you any extra time—in case you're wondering.'

'We see it as a harbinger of what's to come, if we continue on with this relationship—however economically rewarding,' added Simon. 'Although you can't see it, your system has put a frown on the face of this great land.'

Occasional glances at the ice-man came from everyone at the table. No one spoke of the obscure rawboned fixture on Jag's back, as though it were a taboo subject, or similar to an unfortunate grotesque physical impairment that can be observed but not commented on in the presence of the afflicted party. Gaar looked around the table in wonder, observing the clout which Jag seemed to command, and it concerned him.

'Respectfully,' said Gaar, 'we must be given the opportunity to find these men and bring them to Canadian justice. If they are guilty of murder, they will pay.'

'We know you Gaar—you and your *Canadian justice*,' mocked Jag, 'you kiss the ass of Roblaw, and kick the ass of your brothers. *Our* justice is on the murderers' trail. Our people will bring them to face the council— dead or alive. If you interfere with the apprehension of this pair, you will face judgement yourself.'

'We will serve *justice*,' said George Tookaluktassie with an impartial nod, which was echoed back to him by Matthew, Simon and Kiloonik. 'You are on your own to find these men if you can, but they must not leave the IAR until our questions are answered. This must be resolved here first. At that point we will discuss your company's presence here, and extradition of the fugitives if necessary. Until then, please accept our hospitality during your wait for the High Council meeting.'

'Thank you,' replied Gaar, 'and believe me, I empathize with your concerns.'

'We would like to continue our good relations, and build an even stronger partnership by renewing 3R once this misunderstanding has been cleared up,' added Tunningham.

'We'll see about that,' Jag resentfully added.

'I understand. Well, on another note, can you tell us; is there any news of the surviving prisoners?' Tunningham asked around the table, looking for a reply from anyone in the know. 'Has the weather cleared enough to get in there?'

Kiloonik leaned forward and adjusted his baseball hat. 'There were intermittent lulls in the storm, which is supposed to blow over by tomorrow. A brief aerial reconnaissance reported that the barracks and out-buildings were burned to the ground. With the spotlight, he saw some wolves and a bear rummaging through the camp. See,' he said, taking a breath and lifting the brim of his hat, 'a plane can't be landed without advance landing-strip preparation, which Jag is seeing to, along with the arrangements for a rescue team to excavate any miners from the mine.'

'We'd like to assist with that, and bring some experts in from Canada—'

'*We* have everything under control,' countered Jag, with a raised hand, 'are you questioning our capabilities?'

'No, I'm merely—'

'Good.'

McGregor was getting tired of the bullshit, and began to fidget as he listened with a smirk on his face. The two opposing parties verbally danced around the touchy subjects, which polarized each side against the other. There was suspicion in the air, and although it was a relatively civil encounter, the writing seemed to be on the wall.

Jag was gunning for the demise of Roblaw's master plan, and the elders were leaning in his direction. The elders maintained some kind of romanticized vision of their land where shortages of seal and hungry bears reflected the unhappiness of the spirits of the land. McGregor was one to believe that if they were swayed by the right spirits—say, good whiskey, the unhappiness could be transposed into glee. After all, most of these people—including Jag, were intoxicated by something; whether it was the shaman's brew, peculiar breathing songs or just the ecstasy and enchantment of the high altitude and the remote introspection that was part and parcel of being an Eskimo.

McGregor pictured the whole lot of them sucking at nipples on the ends of whiskey bottles to keep them from crying. Now that they had their independence, they were like Greenpeace activists without a door to knock on.

It occurred to him that at least with Roblaw digging up their backyard, they had something to complain about—to keep them busy and finely tuned with the counter-intelligence of satellite TV. It was like they had won the lottery, and decided to keep their ramshackle day-jobs. It was a waste, and they were a waste as he saw it, as he had always seen it in the many years he had worked as a Mountie, when the IAR was the North West Territories.

The sooner he could get this job done, the sooner he could get the hell out of this country of carved dreams and space-cadets. Tunningham had made a poor showing when Jag had challenged him, probably due to the unnerving presence of the mummy-figure he bore like a papoose on his back. To McGregor, Tunningham buckled under the rhetoric of a plain man with a clever ruse.

McGregor looked at Jag and pondered. *This guy is an asshole*, he thought to himself, then pictured Hitler in his mind—with a *hair-lip*, and wondered if it would have made him twice as imposing. *Maybe*, he thought, *to skittish people*.

McGregor saw the corpse as an achilles-heel rather than an Excalibur, and Jag was the architect of nothing except misguided ideals. He had heard Jag call Triq for his attention, and decided he would annoy the corpse-master when an appropriate lull in the table business occurred. Now was the time.

'I thought I recognized you,' McGregor said for all to hear, rising from his seat and approaching Triq with an outstretched hand.

Triq was caught off guard and embarrassed at the overt attention, and took a step back from the approach of McGregor. 'I don't recognize you.'

'Sure you do, you've spent time in Iqaluit, right? Back in ninety-one?'

'No ... eighty-eight, I lived there.'

'Eighty-eight, that's right! Remember we used to kick back a few together at the ... Alooloo Tavern? Remember? And the women?'

'I—' Triq stumbled, taken aback with the flukey accuracy that McGregor managed to chance across, with the common denominator landmarks. He lifted his bruised face and looked helplessly at Jag who became annoyed with the conjecture and base associations. The men at the table listened on with curiosity. Gaar figured out what McGregor was up to, but remained impartial.

'Sure you do, *Triq*—hey, relax man, it's me—Alfie, *your buddy*! So this is the flaky shaman you were telling me about that had murdered the cop—he's come a long way for a jailbird, huh?'

'McGregor!' Tunningham blurted, angered that McGregor would be so rude in the company of elders, regardless of how casual they appeared to be.

'I didn't—' Triq angrily protested, only to be cut off by McGregor again.

'We'll talk later, buddy,' McGregor replied, resuming his seat, and happy with his small victory.

'At any rate,' George began, 'you understand that should we find your people guilty of the crimes, our arrangement will likely be forfeited, since we can't tolerate such occurrences—*be damned, the economic benefits*.'

'Thanks for your hospitality. We'll play by your rules,' Gaar said respectfully. 'McGregor will be setting out in what—seven hours?' he asked McGregor.

'Right, when the business day begins,' McGregor replied, ''cause I know you work on Sundays around here, and I'd like to ask questions of your people as I meet them out there—for leads.'

'I think we could all use a bit of sleep,' George said. 'We'll arrange for someone to show you to your rooms.'

Gaar looked up at Jag, who was staring down at him. Although Gaar recognized Jag as the adversary who he'd be contending with, he kept a low profile. He didn't want Jag to recognize him as the one who could bring him down in *both* worlds.

Gaar felt uneasy with the tight-rope he now had to walk across. His sudden indoctrination, and immersion into the peculiar world of shamanism was unnerving. There'd be a time and a place for their confrontation, and it surely wasn't there in the gym.

The silly stunt that McGregor dragged Triq through, was something that reminded Gaar of the rhetorical nature of opposing sides and word games. Debates and negotiations wouldn't be a part of *their* locking of horns, though. It would be a battle of the titans on a metaphysical playing field, which would demand strategy, coordination, strength of conviction and a down-and-dirty physical encounter. Within the next forty-eight hours, one of them would be dead. Gaar was sure of it, and it scared him.

seventeen

IT WAS EARLY Sunday morning on the tundra, although no one would ever know it with the light being the same from the night before, and every day and night before that. The dog-sled which Brunhilde had commandeered with the reluctant assistance of Max, was turned up on its side and propped against an overhanging rock at the base of a small hill, looking out over the rolling plain of snow and ice.

The dogs were sleeping in the snow while Max and Brunhilde took shelter behind the sled amid an impromptu wall of boxes. The wind had lessened somewhat, and only a light amount of snow was drifting down from the sky.

The light from a hurricane lantern shone from behind the cover of the lean-to. Brunhilde kicked the propped sled over onto its ski tracks. She slowly rose to her feet with Max obliged to emulate her movements. Some of the dogs woke up and sniffed at the air while observing the two moving about at the large rock, as she shoved Max up and along the side of the rock and began to undo her parka at her midsection.

'Just stand right there, *asshole*, and do your business!' she said irritably, as Max obediently stood facing the rock.

'I don't have to go right now,' he replied timidly.

'When I go—you go, see? So go now, or forever forget about holding yer piece, you stupid hork!'

'I'm not good with my left hand—'

'Better get used to being a south-paw. Okay, shut-up now and go, you idiot!'

Max turned his head to the left, giving-in to Brunhilde's tug downwards, until finally he was obliged to kneel in the snow. He gave it his best shot, and found that he indeed was able to manage a south-paw pit-stop. After a couple of very long and embarrassing minutes, Brunhilde decided it was time to get back to the business at hand, and caught Max off guard with *his* business at hand. She dragged Max to the pile of supplies which lay strewn at the base of the rock, while Max tried desperately to do himself up on the run.

Standing over the pile of boxes and a satchel, she found a frozen bun, and placed it on top of the lamp to thaw it out. Sticking her hand in the satchel again, she paused as she felt the handle of a machete. Sneaking a peek at the blade, she slid it back into the satchel when Max turned his head in her direction.

'Let's get this stuff on the sled,' she dictated. They lifted box after box onto the sled with Max huffing away in his effort to keep up with her. 'Leave the satchel there,' she ordered, as they tied down the load of supplies on the sled. Sitting on the edge of the sled, she pulled a map from her parka and lajd it across a space on the sled. Max sat down next to her as she withdrew a compass and tossed it on the map. 'How far before the next coastal port? Godammit, I think we've been going in circles! Haven't we?'

'I don't know ... lets see ...'

Brunhilde grabbed the bun from the lantern, and placed the lamp next to the map. She took a bite of the bun, and chewed away at the carbon-smōked food. 'Show me howda read the map properly, and help me use this compass,' she said with a stuffed mouth.

'The compass is useless here near magnetic north. It'd give false readings due to the polar—nevermind. It's no good. The map is our only tool. See, I think we're here,' he said, poking at the map. 'If you look over there and use land marks, ... like that small mountain and the waters edge, you can get an idea,' he went on, looking back and forth between the map and the landscape. 'It's here on the map. See? It's not cutting edge navigation but—'

'Yeah, I see ...'

'Can I have a bite of that?'

'Here,' she said, breaking a stingy morsel from the bun and handing it to him.

'I need more if I'm going to keep up with you.'

'Uh huh. So, this is the closest port, right? Where's the airport, or should I say *airstrip*?'

'Nanisivik's *there*.'

'Got it. That way, right?' she said, pointing her arm off into the distance.

'Yup. Listen, the dogs need food. They're starving. I don't need much, but they're haulin' a heavy load.'

'Hand me your watch—mine's stopped.'

'I can tell you the time ... it's six-thirty AM. Ask anytime.'

'No, I said *give* me your watch,' she hissed, taking hers off and throwing it over her shoulder.

'But it was a gift from my—'

'I don't give a good goddamn if you gave birth to it— just hand me the fucker, *now*!' she shrieked, as Max swung his left wrist around for her to remove it for him, with her two hands. 'Good, now help me put it on my wrist—I'll be nice and put it on my left, so that you can borrow a glance once in a while.'

Max assisted her on with the watch. 'There, you've got my watch now. We should feed the dogs something, it's cruel to make them work so hard and starve.'

'Let 'em starve. Where are we again?'

'We're *here*. You've ruined my life and you're not even a bit sorry for it. Won't share the food ...'

'I saved your life, asshole. You'll have a divorce from this marriage soon, so clam up.'

'My wrist is sore,' he complained, as a wolf howled in the distance.

'What the fuck—' she said, looking around.

'Wolf. I wish we had the key for these cuffs, there could be one or two days sledding before we get there, and I think I'm getting tennis-elbow in my wrist, or arthritis or something.'

'You're so fuckin' disjointed that if you keep complaining, I'm going to give you such a headache in yer eye!'

'Can I say one thing?'

'What?'

'If you don't feed those dogs they'll get sick, and we'll get nowhere.'

'The load is heavy ain't it? Is dog-meat any good?'

'You wouldn't.'

'Okay, I'll feed 'em,' she said, as she slid her hand into the satchel, and slowly slid out the machete. She looked way up into the sky and sighed. 'Look at those colours. Northern Lights are great, huh? Red, red, red.'

'I don't like red,' said Max, almost in a relaxed conversational tone, as though he felt Brunhilde was trying to be civil. 'It's the colour of blood—and bad balance sheets.'

Brunhilde lifted the machete high with her right hand while Max was still gazing above. Aiming for his cuffed wrist, she struck downwards with a mighty force. At the last second, Max turned towards her and instinctively pulled his hand away from the swiftly descending blade. A moment went by.

Brunhilde went into shock as she lifted her left arm in front of her face, and pulled back the sleeve of her parka. Max shrieked in disgust as he surveyed his handcuffed hand, and discovered her severed hand dangling from the other wristlet. He jumped up trying to get away from the bloody severed hand as it fell to the snow.

Brunhilde dropped the machete, and leaped from the sled in horror, compressing her amputated wrist while the dogs hustled to their feet and sniffed at the air. They picked up the scent and saw the blood and the hand in the snow. Brunhilde roared in pain, and began to turn in circles, contorting her body as the reality struck home.

The dogs went out of control and savagely fought over the severed hand, while others ate up the blood soaked snow. Max stood back in horror, not knowing what to do. A few dogs snapped at Brunhilde's dripping forearm, and she ran away from the attack. The bridled dog team—now whipped into a feeding frenzy and realizing that their food had just run away, turned and chased after her with the sled and supplies in tow.

Max was aghast at what had just happened within thirty seconds of utter chaos. He ran the scene through in his mind, and shook his trembling head in disbelief. He felt helpless that he couldn't help her even if he wanted to, and the thought of chasing after the marauding pack of hungry dogs frightened him. He did however feel a marvellous sensation of freedom, even though he was stranded in the middle of nowhere with no food or transportation.

As he calmed down, he thought to himself how she had actually tried to kill him. He felt stupid not to have picked up on the hints that led to the incident—especially when moments before she had alluded to "a divorce". With that in mind, he felt no guilt over the fate of the barbarian. He surveyed the trampled and churned up snow and spotted his wrist watch. Walking over to it, he leaned down to pick up the blood stained watch, but suddenly changed his mind, as he was repulsed with the horrible memories he'd associate with it if he ever wore it again.

With his foot, he buried the wrist watch in the snow. Thinking the same abhorrent thoughts of the machete, he grabbed only the lantern, and walked off despondently in the direction of the dog-sled tracks.

§

Girly, the twenty-seven year old sister of the ill-fated Matawi—who was killed at the Kabloona mine, was driving her way across the remote tundra on her snowmobile. She was unaware of the travesty at Kabloona, and was making her way to a village named Kiqaloq, which she had lectured in many times. Girly was a specialist in aboriginal history and culture.

On a modest salary from the IAR government, she traversed the Republic, region by region, visiting villages on stop-overs to lecture, teach and research local customs and trends for the ministry of culture.

As she bolted with high speed through the lightly falling snow, she detected a rattling from the snowmobile beneath her. Slowing her speed to around ten kilometers an hour, she leaned over the side of the craft and listened closely to the peculiar rapping. Checking her gauges and finding no warning lights lit up on the panel in front of her, she stopped the snowmobile and dismounted it, leaving the vehicle idling.

Perplexed as to the source of the sound, she withdrew a flashlight from a saddlebag and made a once-over around the craft, and then spotted something unusual in the driving tracks of the machine. Wound around the treads of the track-drive was a doll necklace.

Girly freed the object from the treads, and inspected the curiosity which wasn't damaged. She became thrilled with the find, figuring it was very old and some kind of shaman's talisman and not just a child's toy—it was in fact the *Anknonquatok*. Unaware of the dire consequences of her innocent deed, she draped the Anknonquatok necklace around her neck, mounted her snowmobile and sped off.

§

Kabloona appeared desolate in the twilight darkness. The camp was all but destroyed, with no working floodlights and not one intact building to be seen. There were signs of life rooting about the camp in the form of wildlife. Two large polar bears scavenged the ruins, and a small band of six wolves curiously snooped around the virtually abandoned camp compound.

Huddling cautiously around the remains of the prisoner barracks, were a group of four inmates—one of which was Wilkes, the child molester, whom Eamonn had confined to the *igloo* for insubordination. With him was a woman, and two other men. The wreckage of their barracks was strewn with the corpses of those who perished in both the explosion and fire. Jag had burned the compound to the ground, after being whipped into a rage upon finding Perq murdered in the infirmary.

It was a glorious Sunday morning. Freedom for all, and not a drop to drink.

'We gotta get rid of these bodies, or they'll come sniffin' around here,' the female inmate said to Wilkes. She walked to a barricade of sorts, which was comprised of the remnants of a wall and some toppled bunks that Wilkes rested on, as he looked despondently out over the compound.

'If you don't like it—go somewhere else,' he replied, with a peculiar lisp, which was likely due to the missing front tooth which Eamonn relieved him of, when he paid him a visit at the igloo.

'Fuck you, too,' she hissed back, 'I'm splittin'. Better off takin' my chances out there than freezin' to death in this dump with the likes of you,' she said, climbing over the barricade, and starting her jog through the camp towards the front gates.

'So whaddya think, guys?' Wilkes said to the two other inmates who were huddled together in a nook of rubble. 'Will you wait to face the wolves, or will you jump straight into the belly of a bear? *Damn* our government, for this uncivilized treatment! We have rights! They should be here with helicopters and rescue teams!'

'What're you bitchin' about, you *asshole*?' said one of the huddled inmates, 'there's your freedom!' he shouted, pointing out towards the dark desolation of the camp. '*We* have a choice—*they* didn't!' The irate inmate banged on the icy floor of what remained of the barracks. 'We're as good as dead, anyway.'

'I knew I should have run the other way when that bear attacked the igloo. Now I've run myself down a dead-end street—with dead-end company,' Wilkes complained, as the frightening sound of a woman screaming was overshadowed by the nasty snarls of wolves engaging prey in the distance.

§

Gaar, Tunningham and McGregor, had pryed themselves from their beds early, to confer in a strategy meeting, which they held at the same table in the gym adjacent to the muralled wall. Gaar was busy writing notes on an agenda document which was provided by the elders for the tribunal meeting. McGregor and Tunningham surveyed maps of the region.

'Don't worry, we'll find Max before they slit his throat,' McGregor said.

'How can you be so sure?' asked Tunningham.

'Trust me. I've got a feeling—and a plan. Unfortunately, all they've got around here to spare for us, is an old clunker of a snowmobile—it's a piece of crap.'

'It'll have to do,' Tunningham said, 'I can't get over that mummy that Jag—'

'Can you picture him trying to get a seat in a restaurant? What a jerk! It's a bullshit tactic so thick only the natives would step in it.'

'Well—so when do you expect will be the earliest you'll check in?'

'*We'll* check-in when we can,' McGregor replied, as Gaar raised his head from his writing to meet McGregor's stare.

'Wait a minute,' Tunningham replied with hesitation, 'Gaar stays to ensure we're represented at the meeting.'

'Listen,' McGregor said, leaning back in his chair with

resolve in his face, 'Jag will skin, gut, and fillet them. Max and his traveling companion may be the only hope for 3R, and to clear up this whole mess. Do you want Jag to make fools of us, and of justice? I need Gaar to accompany me. He speaks the lingo and knows the terrain—somewhat. I'm sure news of our arrival has moved along the trap lines. Gaar's father—who I'm told is not well, would be anxious to see him, I'm sure,' he said dryly, as Gaar looked up and glared at McGregor. 'Who knows how many more tales he has left in him. Whaddya say, Gaar? You interested in visiting your ailing father?'

Gaar resented McGregor's prodding, but longed for an excuse to make the journey to his father's village, to confront him. The inevitable seemed especially pressing now. To hear of even a rumour that his father was not well, was more reason to make the trip. 'I'll go with you as far as my father's store in Kiqaloq—do you know it?' he asked of McGregor, who nodded in a wearisome way in reply to his question.

Gaar reassuringly looked at Tunningham in an attempt to placate his concern. 'Trappers may stop in at Kiqaloq, and report any sightings of Max. He's probably wearing his prison parka so there'll be no mistake if they see a stranger lurking about. I'll be back tomorrow and McGregor will search on 'til the eleventh hour.'

'I'm a blood-hound—I'll find him,' replied McGregor.

Tunningham folded his arms across his chest and rocked himself nervously. 'Gaar, we can't risk your absence from the meeting, though!'

'He'll make it back, don't worry!'

'Yes, but will *you*?' Gaar said to McGregor. 'If I have to, I'll go it alone at Max's tribunal. The reality is, that we can't bank on Roblaw's ace in the hole.'

'His secret witness,' added Tunningham.

'That's right,' McGregor said, 'can't put all your trust in

one *acebole*. You worry too much, Oliver. Gaar will leave you with his notes and documents in case anything happens. *You* can represent Roblaw and the Fed's should all else fail. Right, Gaar?'

'Right. Don't worry, my writing's legible. It's very straight forward and there's not a whole lot of legalese to muddle through. But I'll be back, so don't rehearse anything.'

'I'm no lawyer, I'm just a bureaucrat,' Tunningham said.

'Just remember—diplomacy,' Gaar uttered.

'Put 'em together,' added McGregor.

Tunningham was thrown for a loop momentarily, by McGregor's prattle. He stared at McGregor. 'What?'

'Diplomacy and bureaucrat. Put 'em together: ... *dip-o-crap*. It's a foul combination, so watch your step with these people.'

'You'd be fine, Oliver, *don't worry*.'

'Alright. I'll walk the high wire if I have to. I guess it's important that you visit your dad—could it wait 'til after Monday?' Tunningham blurted, in a last ditch attempt to bail out of the possibility of going solo at the tribunal. 'No— of course, he's sick. Go. But I'll see you tomorrow early, right?'

'Tomorrow, early afternoon,' replied Gaar, reassuringly. 'Y'know, we haven't talked in over twenty years, and that's his hobby—talking.'

'If we don't cut the gab, they'll whittle Max into a *hobby-horse*,' McGregor said, as he began to gather the supplies, maps and equipment he would bring along with him on the search mission. 'I'll meet you outside,' he said to Gaar, and made his way to the exit door.

eighteen

KIQALOQ WAS A SMALL peaceful village of around one hundred people. Amongst the twenty-five pre-fab houses which were vestiges of the community building association between the Canadian Government and the province of the North West Territories, there stood a moderator's house which was the residence of the mayor, post-man sheriff, and mediator for local disputes. It was a one man job, and the person usually never excelled in any of the titles the job encompassed.

The IAR had kept this public servant position alive after the move to independence, and the local population would vote each year on who would fill that capacity—if there were any candidates who would run for the multi-faceted post. Most couldn't care less for the responsibility, and the job usually went to someone who had nothing better to do and who desired some sense of importance.

Halfway down the short road, was the supply store which was run by Abraham Injugarjuk, Gaar's father, who was in his early eighties and in poor health, but rich in spirit and loved by all in the village, especially for his story-telling abilities. Abraham—or *Abram*, as he was called, lived in the rear of the large store, and would often be spinning stories at any point in the day or night, for intimate gatherings.

People would sit on counters, boxes, and on the wide-open floor to listen to Abram's tales. Abram was renowned for having over one-hundred stories of traditional origin which many delighted in hearing over and over again.

A captive audience of around twenty people mostly of children, but with a few adults, had gathered in Abram's store for a relaxing bout of tales. This was a change from TV and books, and verged on theatre, as Abram would use his hands and face to animate the tales.

A couple of friends and neighbours, who gathered supplies as customers, listened as they shopped—which was the norm, as the story-telling wasn't considered a performance, but merely a background to a chance gathering or casual shopping. Bulbous glass whale-oil lamps burning inexpensive commercial lamp oil, flickered away throughout the shop, adequately illuminating the charming store which was panelled with old planks of wood from the wrecks of sailing vessels. Over the years, large ships had been trapped and wooden vessels crushed by ice, when a twist of ill-fate locked them solid in frozen bays through a harsh winter, which sometimes reduced their worth to the value of kindling.

Abram cleared his voice, and smiled at the gathering. 'Wolf came upon raven in the tundra,' Gaar's father said, with a thin but expressive voice. He looked about his audience with a charismatic expression which conjured up an eerie ambiance of mystery. It seemed to be an experience he actually lived through.

Below his short grey hair, his long lean face with multi-tudinous wrinkles bore a sincere smile. He flashed his dark sunken eyes to entreat the imagination of his listeners. 'Raven was rolling his eyes out of his sockets, sticking them to an icicle, and then recoiling them back into his head. Wolf told raven to show him how to do it—or he would eat him. Raven replied, "I'll show you how, but you mustn't do it more than three times a day, or your eyes will not return to you." Wolf was shown how, and Raven flew off. Wolf began to expel his eyes from his head. After three times, he said to himself, "That raven is stupid. I could do this all day and my eyes would return." He did it a fourth time, but found he could not recoil them. He blindly searched in vain for his eyes,' Abram said, leaning forward and gesturing accordingly. A little girl laughed uncontrollably at the story and his gestures. 'Raven happened by. "Wolf" said raven, "You didn't take heed." Wolf snarled and raised his lips to reveal his sharp teeth. "Find my eyes for me or I will eat you." Raven replied, "They have been eaten by the fox who mistook them for eggs. Your vision has been hatched, and I am a free bird for all to see."'

§

Max trudged slowly along the flattened snow tracks of the stray sled. Occasional blotches of Brunhilde's blood sickened him as he moved through the lightly falling snow, with the hurricane lamp swinging by his side. He wasn't quite sure why he was following the path which would inevitably lead him to the mauled body of Brunhilde, and perhaps an excruciatingly repulsive scene. He felt desperate though, and gave in to the sensible notion of gaining access to the sled supplies and the transportation which he needed to save his life.

As he warily moved along, he saw a moving headlight in the distance. The direction in which it moved, cut across his path—and of the path of the stray dog-sled ahead of him, which may have only been a few hundred yards further into the snow-scape.

Fearing it was a bounty hunter or the law itself, Max extinguished the lamp's flame and hid, ducking back into a snow drift. Hearing the sound of the racing snowmobile getting closer, he cringed at the thought of how he would be taken into custody—or even worse, to be slain by this possible vigilante who could be kin with the Inuit he would be accused of murdering.

It was Girly who was racing across the snow field in the vicinity of the fugitives. She caught a long-distance glimpse of the dog-sled chasing and terrorizing Brunhilde around snow drifts, and she headed towards the peculiar sight.

Coming up on the scene, she maneuvered her vehicle between Brunhilde and the sled, who staggered defensively amongst the ravenous dogs. Brunhilde slipped at the side of the craft and the dogs moved around to her. As Girly leaned over to assist Brunhilde to her feet, the Anknonquatok necklace swung out from her neck. The dogs sensed the ominous enigmatic power emanating from the doll, and shyed back.

'WHA HAPPENED?!' Girly cried out, seeing the blood and not fully comprehending the violence of the scene.

Brunhilde was exhausted and remained silent in her shock, managing to desperately climb up behind Girly on the snowmobile. In a fit, Brunhilde insanely grasped the leather thong which held the Anknonquatok, and twisted it mercilessly tight against Girly's neck in an attempt to strangle her from behind. Girly gasped for air, and in a frenzy, struggled to get her fingers behind the leather thong which was wound around her neck so tightly, that it was practically imbedded in her skin.

Brunhilde laughed like a mad woman, and used her elbows to force Girly forward, offering her no room to struggle off the craft. The dogs went wild and barked viciously at the struggling two. Brunhilde put her knee against Girly's back, and using her powerful right hand with the thong firm in her grasp, tried to tug the life out of the woman.

Brunhilde strangled her with an intensifying greed, and pulled so forcefully on the thong that it snapped suddenly, casting Brunhilde backwards off the snowmobile and sending the doll necklace flying through the air, beyond the scene.

The dogs went into an absolute frenzy and viciously attacked Brunhilde, who lay defenseless, crying out with shrieks of horror, under their relentless barrage of fangs.

Although the pressure of the thong was released, Girly struggled for air, and desperately tried to remain conscious. She coughed painfully, striving to breathe the life back into her body, distressed by the agonizing screeches of Brunhilde, which surged pathetically from the ripping fury of the marauding dogs, only feet from her.

As Girly came partially to her senses, she reeled with fright at the gruesome scene. The horrific sounds of the furor, and the sight of blood flowing into the snow, filled her with such a tremendous fright, that she hastily grabbed for the throttle on the handlebars of her snowmobile. She accelerated away from the site, leaving the lunatic to the fate she had interrupted.

She sped away, realizing the Anknonquatok doll was left behind somewhere in the snow. She didn't care a bit for it now, as she desperately massaged her injured neck with her left hand.

§

Gaar and McGregor rode tandem on the old snowmobile, provided for them by the Council in Nanisivik. Mechanically, the craft was in good working order. It stunk of gasoline though, and was an uncomfortable ride. As they raced along in the twilight, they passed a series of hills with rock outcrops. Gaar gaped at the landmarks which they should have turned towards, to get to Kiqaloq.

'Alfred! ALFRED!!' Gaar shouted, as they zoomed off past the route they had agreed on taking. Gaar tapped on McGregor's shoulder, which was ignored by McGregor, as he motored on through the light snowfall and across the expansive plain. McGregor looked down at his gauges and decided on stopping to refuel the snowmobile, and to straighten out his companion. He brought the vehicle to a halt and dismounted to fetch a can of gas from the laden tow-sled. Gaar got off the snowmobile and followed McGregor.

'What the hell are you up to?! Why didn't you steer for Kiqaloq, at the landmarks we discussed? You're supposed to drop me at my father's store!'

'I need *two* sets of eyes,' McGregor replied flatly, 'mine for what's on front, and your's for what's behind.'

'This wasn't the plan! We can't risk my absence from the meeting! Roblaw and the Fed's need representation and council from me—I'm going to radio a message to Tunningham.' Gaar reached for the radio set in the sled. McGregor stopped Gaar with his arm, using it like it was an off-limits gate.

'Radio doesn't work. Don't worry about it. Tunningham

has your notes—and in your own words *it's a cake walk*. He's bright.'

'*Bright* may not be good enough to cut it! Take me back now!'

'Are you telling me what to do?' asked McGregor, with a threatening look on his face, as though Gaar had just crossed the line in their professional relationship. 'Well? Are you trying to give me orders?' McGregor snickered at Gaar's silence, and lifted a heavy gas can from an insulated box on the sled. Gaar purposely walked back to the snowmobile, got on, and sped ahead fifteen yards from McGregor, who put the gas can down and stood resolutely where he was left, folding his arms across his chest.

'I'll take myself back! What's the big idea?' Gaar shouted, swiveled in the seat, and creating a stand-off from his idled position ahead of McGregor.

'There's not enough gas in that to take you *two miles*!' laughed McGregor. 'Then what?! Gonna strand me here at the mercy of predators—*two and four footed*? Gonna see me dead—and yourself?!'

'My father could be dying! I've got to see him! We had an arrangement. I want your word!'

'Priority to the *Max*! He takes precedence over your personal business.'

'Then you leave me no choice!' shouted Gaar, as he revved the engine.

McGregor reached inside his parka and pulled out a pistol. 'Then you leave *me* no choice!!' he shouted, levelling the pistol in Gaar's direction.

'Gonna shoot me?' Gaar demanded with a huff.

'If you insist. I'm a crack shot!'

'You're a crack, alright!'

'You're a lawyer! Make your move a prudent one!'

'Sonofabitch!' Gaar blurted with frustration, realizing the futility of the situation. He turned the snowmobile around to circle back. McGregor could see that Gaar was giving-in and coming back, but shot him none-the-less.

Gaar felt the full impact of the bullet near his shoulder, and toppled off the snowmobile, which came to a slow stop. McGregor calmly walked towards Gaar, carrying the gas can with his left hand and the pistol in his right.

'Awful sorry, Gaar. *It was an accident*,' he mocked cruelly. 'I thought you were making the wrong choice. Let me see,' he said flatly, putting the gas can down and pulling Gaar's parka off his shoulder as he painfully sat up in the snow. 'It's just a flesh wound ... well, maybe a little worse than a flesh wound.'

'You asshole! You shot me!'

'Yes ... I guess I did—hmm, no exit wound. Guess you're a dog-eared page in my logbook. Bundle up.'

'BUNDLE UP!? Christ! How're we going to go on with me in this condition? You'll have to get me to a doctor. The village doesn't have one, so that means back to Nanisivik, where they have facilities. You sure FUCKED UP!'

'I wouldn't say so. We don't have the time to go back. I don't think it's life-threatening. Here, use this as a tourni-quet or compress,' he said, leaning over and passing Gaar his bandana. 'You may never *reach* a doctor if you keep bleeding like that! Press on it hard, and hold it. We have to move on.' McGregor stood up straight, and folded his arms across his chest. 'As Tunningham suggested—and I like Oliver, he's a good shit; Tuesday would be a better day for you to attend to your personal agenda. I *think* we have an understanding?'

McGregor proceeded to fill the gas tank as though noth-ing had ever happened. Throwing the empty container into the sled, he helped Gaar to his feet and assisted him in sit-ting facing backwards off the end of the seat, to spy for activity behind them as they drove.

'Keep your eyes peeled,' McGregor ordered, as he shifted the snowmobile into gear.

'Is this how far Roblaw's willing to go?'

'Don't be petty and start any rumours now 'cause you got yourself shot. Let's not burn any bridges 'til we cross them, okay? Y'know, It's getting to the point where I'm feeling I can't trust you.'

'The same thought crossed my mind—isn't that peculiar?' Garr derisively replied.

'Look, no more funny business, alright?' he piped, turning his body towards Gaar, as Gaar looked at McGregor over his shoulder. 'And *you*, ... the *son-in-law* of the boss!' McGregor mocked, as he turned to face forward, and applied a full throttle to the machine.

§

Jag's posse plowed through the snow at break-neck speed. Jag rode with Triq on his snowmobile. Both Kiratek and Agaluq drove their own vehicles. In the distance, Kiratek detected a moving headlight and caught the others' attention with a beep of his horn and a wave. They moved off to converge with the distant snowmobile.

Racing up beside Girly, they convinced her to stop. As the group came to a disconcerting halt, Jag dismounted Triq's craft and approached Girly, who became incoherently nervous in relating the experience she had escaped from.

'Who are you?' Jag asked.

Girly noticed the ice-man slung across his back and became doubly confused and disoriented. 'I ..., a dog team just—she's got to be dead now, blood ... everywhere!'

'You've driven from this attack? Miss ...?'

'Yes!—Girly.'

'Where are you going?'

'Who ... who are you, and—?

'The *law*, Girly. And you're on your way to ...?'

'Kiqaloq, to lecture,' she replied, trying to get more of a glimpse of the ice-man. 'What is that?' she asked nervously, rubbing her neck and vaguely pointing at Jag's unusual vestige.

'*The law*,' Jag replied. 'Did this woman say anything to you? Anything at all?' Jag enquired suspiciously, curious to know if talk of gold or murder crept up in her scrape with Brunhilde.

'No, she—she tried to kill me!' Girly shouted out, rubbing her neck where a bruised line marked the attempted strangulation.

'Was she wearing a *blue* parka embroidered with wolves? Was she *alone*?'

'Yes—yes! If you hurry, you may be able to save her—the four of you! She may not be dead!'

Jag looked back at his men and nodded. 'We will follow her tracks,' he said to the posse, pointing down at Girly's snowmobile tracks in the snow. 'Thank you, Girly,' he said, turning to her and nodding. 'How long will you be in Kiqaloq? The law may require some questions answered.'

'Until Tuesday,' she replied with a painful gulp, concerned now over her involvement in the sordid affair. Her scattered mind focussed back on Brunhilde and the attack. 'You've got to hurry to get to her!' Girly squeaked.

Jag swiftly got on the back of Triq's snowmobile, and the bunch took off in the direction she came from. Girly stared at the group scurrying away, catching a fleeting glimpse of the figure on Jag's back. She engaged her snowmobile into drive, and continued her eager journey to Kiqaloq.

§

At the Nanisivik community centre, Tunningham walked from the communal kitchen with a coffee in his grasp. He strode up the hallway, towards his room in the hostel. Spotting George Tookaluktassie, one of the elders he'd met with the night before, he called to him and waved. Approaching the lobby area where George had paused to wait for him, Tunningham approached the elder and reached out offering George a handshake. George reciprocated the formality.

'Goodmorning,' Tunningham said.

'Let's hope so,' George replied playfully.

'Yes, *let's*. Um, if possible—whenever weather permits, I'd like to get out to Kabloona. Can this be arranged for me, or should I just try to hire someone to take me there on my own?'

'It's a restricted area—a *crime* scene. People know now that they just can't *go there*.'

'Yes, of course. In my official capacity, I'd like to survey Kabloona—with your blessings and an approved escort from your team.'

'I'll get back to you on that. But you know, there was a hunter who was checking his trap lines on his way here early this morning. He happened by Kabloona, and stopped in out of curiosity at the burned out camp. It's not good. Didn't see anyone—if they've abandoned the camp, they'd have perished or were eaten by predators.'

'But I thought bears and wolves were afraid of man,' Tunningham said, with curiosity.

'As a rule of thumb, yes—but thumbs don't rule in the wild, *paws do*. See, there's a decline in seal and lemming this year. So, bears and wolves might attack without provocation.

We want to keep Kabloona off limits, except for our search and rescue crew. They're preparing their gear to move out when the others arrive from Iqaluit and Pond Inlet.'

'I've got to make some kind of report for my government. I need to take some pictures, and I've also got to prepare for the inquiry.'

'Tell you what. I'll find the trapper if he hasn't left, and have him meet with you and give you his full observations. He's wearing a patterned toque.'

Tunningham nodded his head in approval. He looked at George, wanting to ask him something else before he left. George smiled at him, then a puzzled look came over his face. 'Is there anything else?'

'I'm just curious ... what do you think of me? Am I accepted here, or is everyone just shy of *official types*?'

George laughed, and folded his arms across his chest. 'Well, you're *diplomatic*—we can see that. And, you're a *bureaucrat*—you can't help that. What else can I say?'

Tunningham felt slightly crestfallen at the overview. 'I see,' he replied, remembering the derogatory amalgam of the two words. 'Great, alright then ... I'll be in my room— number six, right there,' he said, pointing back down the hall.

'Yup, I think I know where six is,' George replied, with a cheery laugh.

'Oh,' Tunningham blurted, as they were departing company, 'any word from Gaar or McGregor?'

'Not a peep.'

'Say—I'm sorry for keeping you; where can I find Gaar's father the storyteller? I'd like to pay my respects, perhaps this afternoon.'

George pulled a piece of paper from his pocket, and searched for a pen. Tunningham reached into his shirt pocket and pulled out a government pen, which he handed to him.

George accepted the pen, and in trying to expose the writing nib, his eye caught the writing on the stem. 'Government issue ... *extra fine*, huh?'

'You can keep it.'

'It's okay, I'm waiting on a planeload of engraved number five HB soft-head pencils—*with* erasers on the end. I don't like the permanence of pens.'

'That's a joke, right?'

'Are you serious?' asked George, who patted Tunningham on the back and laughed heartily. Tunningham began to chuckle along with George, until he caught on, and then laughed with full breath.

Tunningham walked into his room, folding up the directions George had scrawled on the piece of paper. There was a knock at the door. Tunningham walked over and opened it. Outside his door was an older Inuit man with a toque on his head. Tunningham smiled and opened the door wide for the man to step inside.

'You must be the trapper ... come in, please!' he said, as the man entered and looked around. Tunningham shut the door and walked over to speak with the man. He motioned him to sit down, and he did. The trapper pulled a pack of cigarettes from his pocket and offered a smoke to Tunningham, who declined with a raised hand and a grimace. As the trapper was about to light up, he suddenly noticed a small plaque on the wall which simply said "No Smoking"—without the associated icon which usually depicted a cigarette with a slash through it. The man put his cigarettes away, to Tunningham's relief.

'By the way, I'm Tunningham from the Canadian government. I'm preparing a report for an inquiry into the fatalities at the 3R camp at Kabloona,' he said, to the affirmative nods of the trapper as they shook hands. 'I need to know if you took any pictures, or saw any survivors or talked to anyone who knows about what happened there.' The man sat silent looking at him, but nodded as Tunningham spoke. 'Did you see any animals prowling the site? Or maybe some vehicles—anything at all?'

'Onkta kikoq dinnivikatok ...' the man said, pointing his arm outwards, possibly in the direction where his trap lines were. Tunningham came to the realization that the man didn't speak a word of English. *But how can that be in this day and age*, Tunningham thought to himself, feeling a little foolish, and the brunt of a practical joke. 'Thank you, *thank you very much*,' Tunningham said very slowly, as he stood and shook the man's hand. He got up and was seen to the door. The trapper nodded and smiled as he left. Tunningham shut the door with a disappointed frown.

Another knock came to the door. As Tunningham opened it, George stood there looking in the direction that the trapper had walked off in.

'So, was he any help to you?' asked George, as he turned towards Tunningham standing in the doorway.

'Is this your idea of fun and games?'

'What're you talking about?'

'There's people trapped in a mine for days, and there's been a slaughter, and ... I take umbrage—'

'What's that, a medication? Because, you're acting pretty wacky.'

'That guy didn't speak a *word* of English,' protested Tunningham.

'You poor guy,' George said with a chuckle, 'he played you for a fool—I'm sorry. What happened, did you offer him a pen before you said hello? *He* speaks almost perfect English. You must be wearin' government issue after-shave or something. Okay, let's sit down, and I'll tell you what he reported to us.'

§

McGregor and Gaar sped along the tundra on the old clunker of a snowmobile. Gaar pressed at the gunshot wound which pained him somewhat, but which had managed to stop bleeding. Gaar recognized that McGregor was a loose cannon and up to no good. Not for a moment would he accept that his gunshot wound was an accident. He felt foolish and betrayed for allowing himself to be put in this position.

He realized that without a doubt Roblaw was orchestrating something nefarious through his cronie, McGregor. The scenario didn't make a whole lot of sense, but Gaar believed that his life could be in grave jeopardy. If the opportunity arose, he would make a grab for McGregor's gun.

McGregor slowed the machine down and began to lean over the side, peering into the snow. He made a tight circled turn, almost throwing Gaar off the craft, as he suddenly leaned over and executed the tight arc. He anxiously returned to investigate something he'd thought he detected in the snow. Stopping the snowmobile, he was thrilled to have proved himself right, as some tracks were evident in the snow.

'Dog-sled tracks,' McGregor announced. 'Let's stretch our legs.'

Gaar dismounted at McGregor's insistence, knowing that McGregor feared having Gaar alone on the vehicle. The subtle understanding was in the air, without McGregor having to threaten Gaar off the machine at gunpoint. Gaar didn't want to force McGregor's hand yet in that capacity. Downplaying the obvious was to his advantage for the time being. Gaar walked along with McGregor as the man studied the tracks like an expert. 'Could be anyone,' Gaar said, 'gonna follow?'

'It *was* no one,' McGregor huffed, leaning down close to the sled tracks and paw imprints of the dog team.

'No one?'

'No girth to the paw imprints. Shallow pull—willy-nilly. There was no driver navigating this team I'd say; and little weight on the sled. But, we know from Roblaw's source that Max and the woman took supplies. I can tell from these tracks, that the sled was either supply-*less* with one driver possibly, or packed with supplies, with no driver or passenger. And that's what it was—a rogue sled.'

'You can tell all that—by the depressions in the snow?!'

'Do you know how many fugitives I've tracked in my time? This is textbook. We track *backwards* to the source—and who knows, we may meet 'em along the way.'

'Isn't that something,' Gaar remarked. 'You didn't even use a ruler or an electron microscope to do your calculations and come up with your hypothesis. I'm learning new things about you all the time.'

'Don't get fuckin' smart with me! Let's go. Y'know if I thought I could trust you,' began McGregor, as they walked back to the snowmobile, 'I would suggest a reconnaissance split and rendezvous. It'd be practical under these circumstances, because they may be ducking for cover and hiding when they see or hear a snowmobile. With one of us on foot, we could take the edge right off their chances. *But*, I'm questioning your dedication and loyalty to this operation. You're turning into a real liability. Get on,' he ordered, as he stood at the snowmobile.

Gaar began to feel a bit woozy, and rubbed at his forehead. 'I think *operation* is a pretty tall analogy,' Gaar replied, as he took up his position, facing backwards off the snowmobile, 'but I know I could sure use some medical attention. Why don't you just drop me at *even* an igloo, if we come across one. I don't want to be a liability—I'll find a way back to Nanisivik, and you can go on with your astute search.'

'I won't let you suck-out on me now. Besides, I need you. The bleeding's stopped, right?'

'Yeah, I think so, but the pain's killing me.'

'Bite the bullet,' McGregor taunted, as he settled into his position on the seat, put the snowmobile into gear and launched quickly forward to follow the dog-sled tracks to their source.

nineteen

PHILIP ROBLAW SLID his computer card access key for the seventeenth floor inside his pants pocket. With a confident tug on the hem of his jacket, he proceeded from the elevator banks in the lobby area towards his office at Roblaw Inc.

Although it was Sunday, security never passed any remarks on his presence in the office tower. If he *didn't* show up on a Sunday, on or about his usual time, the security guards would raise their eyebrows and let their bets ride in the kitty until the next Sunday—that is, unless someone bet the long shot on a "no-show" and claimed the weekly wagers which accumulated in a pot, until won.

For most of the security staff, checking the street-level clocked sign-in log on Mondays, was the highlight of the day. Unaware of the lottery, Roblaw would often be curious why guards at the front lobby desk would sometimes split hairs over the exact time when he'd come in on Sundays, overhearing their hushed reverberating voices down the marbled hall after he'd leave the desk and move on towards the elevators.

Someday, when he had nothing better to occupy his mind, he would ask them what their quibbling was about. As he passed through his company's hallway, he cast the notion from his head, with something more pressing in mind.

Unlocking a beautifully polished mahogany door, he entered his unmarked private office and shut the door behind himself. He stood looking at his desk for a moment, and although he was alone, he made sure the blinds were drawn on both walls of his L-shaped corner office.

Sitting down at his large desk, he swung his chair around and unlocked a cabinet door behind him. Leaning down, he twisted the tumbler on a small safe which was at the bottom of the cabinet. Unlocking it, he withdrew a small unmarked padded envelope which he laid on the desk in front of himself. It was the package that the mysterious man had dropped off to him two days prior during the meeting with the Quebec ministers.

He emptied the contents on the table. There were two items; a small, digital video-cassette labeled as "lawn bowling highlights"—having what appeared to be a spot or two of blood smeared across the label, and a computer disc marked only as "shopping list". Turning back to the cabinet behind his desk, he extracted a compact video camera, set it on the desk and inserted the tape. He plugged a set of tiny earphones into the video camera, inserted the ear-pieces and depressed the "play" button.

Pressing his eye against the eye-piece, he smiled menacingly at what he was viewing. He had glanced quickly at the delivered material on Friday, to confirm the contents of the tape and disc. He would now indulge in a few private minutes of sinister delight. He peeped down the barrel of the viewfinder with a squint and a smirk.

He had waited almost three years for this moment, and had paid a total of two hundred and fifty thousand dollars for the intensive search and rescue of the items. It was twenty dollars worth of raw materials and the sole collateral for three-million dollars worth of obligation debts—off his blackmail-burdened mind.

Roblaw watched the tape. It was footage which Max had secretly filmed from a hidden camera in a briefcase. It was damning documentation of a clandestine meeting in which Max and Roblaw met to cook-the-books of the company. In self defence, Max had gone to great lengths to cover his ass by videotaping a meeting which would expose Roblaw for the criminal bully he was, if anything untoward should happen to him.

Over a period, Roblaw had at first enticed, then cajoled and finally persuaded Max into some questionable accounting practices which culminated in a tangled web of insider-trading on the stock exchange, money laundering and fixed tax audits. Over time, from seemingly minor legal infractions, Max had found himself over a barrel, and involved with underworld figures in massive fraudulent activities.

Roblaw smiled. On the recording, the whole scope of activities was brought up cleverly by Max in a subtle way. The captured testaments were *very* revealing. He had to give Max credit for his ingenuity in leading the performance, riling him into incriminating himself with his damaging replies to Max's protests of being an unwilling part in criminal undertakings. 'Oh, Max, Max, Max,' Roblaw whispered to himself as he viewed.

On the video, Max had brought up names of some key players in their operation, some of which were government connections, while others were international criminal contacts. Replying with a stern threat on his life, Roblaw offered Max an incentive deal to take the fall in an up-coming indictment by a sting operation, comprised of several police forces and securities agencies.

Roblaw offered to pay him a million a year into an off-shore account for every year in jail, if the case ever went to trial and there was a conviction. Max very astutely refused his bribe on the tape, and that's when the taped footage ended. In the minutes following the end of the recording, Max had accepted Roblaw's deal, having edited the tape and excluded the acceptance of the bribe.

The case did go to trial. Roblaw indirectly engaged Gaar as a fledgling criminal lawyer, to defend Max. The allegations of impropriety levied against Roblaw Inc, which included tax evasion, money-laundering and stock swindle, were dropped against the company, but subsequently filed against Max. Of the charges set forth against him, he was convicted and sentenced for only one of the charges; insider-trading and securities fraud.

Gaar had worked around the clock on the case, and thanks to a successful plea bargain and an appeal, Max scraped through with only a four-year sentence. Gaar found Max a frustrating client to work with, and knew he was holding something back from him.

Initially, to Gaar's surprise, Roblaw—the man who'd hired him to defend Max through a third party; pushed for embezzlement charges as a public relations measure, knowing full well he'd already disposed of any evidence which would nail Max to the wall on that charge.

Everything unfolded as planned; Max went for the install-ment plan, Gaar had no idea of how he'd been used, and Roblaw got off scot-free.

Roblaw chuckled as he ejected the video tape. The fact that Max would put a blackmail tape together as insurance of payment of the bribe impressed him from a tactical point of view, but heightened his desire to see him burn for this back-stabbing deed.

With the video, and the computer disc—which held the double set of books, coded information about bank accounts and money transactions and names; he had Max exactly where he wanted him; dead-to-rights.

Roblaw's next move was to cancel Max's insurance policy, and he did just that by taking the pint-sized video cassette tape over to a Inuit sculpture on a pedestal. Using the sculpture's heavy base as a hammer and the pedestal as an anvil, he crushed the video tape with a few precise blows. Having cracked open the video cassette, he scraped the remnants into a paper bag and returned to sit at his desk.

Taking a pair of scissors from his desk, he slowly cut through the computer disk. Thinking twice about the tape, he reached into the bag of fragments, pulled out the spool of exposed tape and began to snip at the uncoiling ribbons of the video.

While he was at the house-cleaning, Roblaw swung around his chair and reached into the safe again, pulling a stack of posted letters. All were sealed and unopened. They were the detained correspondence between Gaar and his father, which had been intercepted by Isaac, the mail-sorting moderator at Kiqaloq IAR, who was handsomely paid by Roblaw to impound any communications between the two. He had forwarded the letters unopened, directly to Roblaw, under the cloak of a fresh envelope jacket to accommodate the stolen mail.

Roblaw was very proud of himself, having orchestrated such a tight insulated world around himself. He thought back on his childhood, and how he had no control over his life then, nor of the circumstances which shaped his growing years. His mother would be proud of him now.

He had come from an impoverished family that struggled to make ends meet at every turn, having to move every four to six months due to evictions.

Roblaw rocked himself in his swivel chair and daydreamed

of how his mother would instil ambition into his psyche, insisting that by whatever means possible he must make something of himself. She would always remind him that someday he would be rich and powerful if he didn't follow in the shoes of his father, who drank like a fish and brutalized the family physically and mentally when he was around the home. When he wasn't around, he'd be off drumming up scams, boozing and womanizing. Philip, as a very young boy, wasn't completely aware of this. There were times when he thought the domestic situation was on the mend, and the family had taken the shape of a *real* family—the type the other kids all seemed to have. But, the dream soured each time.

His father actually played baseball-catch with him once around that time, but the pitching was short lived. His father couldn't put up with his wayward throws, and after whipping himself into a tantrum, the man walked off in disgust. Not having had the luxury of remaining in one neighbourhood for very long it seemed, denied Philip the chance of making any close or long term friendships with any of his peers. His only friends were his two older brothers and his sister, who was the oldest.

Pondering on his siblings, he felt their friendship was perhaps more of a superficial "chummy" type of relationship, replete with the pats on the head, and friendly teasing which included "pink-bellies" and "Indian rope-burns". That kind of physical attention pleased him though, given, they were painful—it did none the less make him the centre of attention. Unfortunately, they were all more than ten years older than him, which had made him feel like an outsider a lot of the time.

Family business and domestic turmoil were never discussed in his presence. He was not old enough to *understand* such conversation, and would only be confused by the reality of passionate debates and what he could only imagine now, were sordid details about his father. His mother, sister and brothers would often shoo him away from discussions that were held in the absence of his father.

His father's inability to find long-term gainful employment through his entire childhood, had caused him great embarrassment within his circle of short-term chums. Taunting by local boys had led to fights: His father was accused of many a disagreeable action which had him spending some nights in jail. He had been arrested many times, for many reasons.

Philip's mother would often scold him for fighting, but would always give him a big hug when he'd tell her he'd fought for his honour and that he'd won (even if he hadn't) or that the other boy looked worse (even if they didn't). At his prodding, she would deny any rumours he'd heard about his father. She defended her husband by sugar-coating his frequent absence from the family, and the reasons why he was so volatile and destructive sometimes.

They had struggled by without the finer things in life. Sometimes, on occasion, without even the basic necessities. After he'd turned thirteen, the last of his live-in brothers moved out and stranded him with his demented father, who he'd come to know the truth about as the years passed. This left him no more time for one-on-one chats with his ill-fortuned mother, who nobly suffered in silence.

He now wished he had had more time with the finest thing he could remember from his childhood—his mother. Coming home from school one day when he was fourteen, he found police cars parked in front of the house in which they had a basement apartment. An ambulance pulled away as he arrived. He met some detectives at the door, who gently explained how his mother had been killed falling down the concrete steps to the apartment.

He remembered the emotional sobs which drained him, and his explosive flight out the door and up the harsh concrete steps. The police dashed after him, thwarting his get-away at the top of the steps. They restrained him until he calmed down, then explained that his father had been taken down to the police station, and that he was to wait with them until his older brother, who they had contacted, arrived to pick him up.

To see the neighbours looking on, as he stood at the very top of the steps, and seeing them explain to each other what had happened, sickened him. Someone had re-enacted the scene for a curious bystander, and he cringed at seeing the confirmation of his suspicions. There was a terrible fight, and his mother, in fleeing from the apartment, had been caught by the hair by his father, who'd tugged her back-wards, causing her to fall down the pit of concrete steps to her death.

As his brother hadn't shown up to retrieve him, the police decided to leave a note on the apartment door window, and took him to the police station. He remembered how he was left at the station, and how he'd fooled a desk officer into believing that his brother had come for him. He was deter-mined not to be in the same building as his father.

As far as he knew, or could care, his father had died in prison, and he'd not attempted to contact his brothers or sister since that day. He had resolved to make it on his own, and rushed home to pack a bag and make his way in the world—casting off his father's last name and assuming another, making it legal when he saw fit. It was a struggle, and it hardened him, but *he made it*.

Roblaw sat back in his office chair and looked around at his accomplishments. His mother would have been proud of her "little fighter".

Snapping out of his reminiscence, he took the stack of the letters between Gaar and his father, and walked to the far end of the room and switched on the paper shredder. He inserted the letters one by one, until only ribbons remained.

Gathering up the bag from the shredder's catch basin, he walked to his desk and slid the remnants of the tape and disc into the bag which held the shredded materials. Now that he had finished *cleaning house*, he tied up the bag and sat it on his desk. He reached for the phone and dialed a number.

'Hello, Victoria?' he said, relieved to have reached his secretary at home. 'It's Philip. I'm at the office and I'd like you to do something for me. Can you call our agent and book me on a flight tomorrow to Nanisivik? Baffin Island, IAR. Say, eleven AM. That's right, for the tribunal. Yup, ... and the airline limo, and the accommodations, and can you confirm with me or leave a message today? ... Thanks. Huh? ... I'll be coming back early Tuesday,' he replied, and was careful with his reply to her next question which was whether Gaar, Tunningham and McGregor would be joining him on the return flight, ' ... yes, they'll be coming back with me. Right. Bye.' He hung up the receiver and reached into his pants pocket, pulling out a piece of paper with some written information on it. Perusing the details, he stuffed it back into his pocket and prepared to leave.

He locked the small safe in the bottom of the cabinet, put away the video camera and closed the cabinet doors, locking them securely. He then went around to each window and opened the blinds. When he had completed the rounds, he paused for a moment to look around the office, and then simply grabbed the plastic bag and walked to the door.

The office building's freight elevator doors opened with a clank, in the basement level. Roblaw stepped out with bag in hand. Moving through the off-white cinder-blocked hallways, he passed the loading dock area and pushed through a door where the building's garbage compactor was situated.

The large steel work-horse sat idle and ready. The room stunk with a penetrating stench of chemicals, food waste and rotten wet cardboard. He tossed the bag of evidence in the gaping mouth of the big blue machine, briefly looked over the operating instructions, and then set the machine to work. The plastic bag was shoveled into the machine's belly with two other garbage bags which lay in waiting for service. As Roblaw's bag disappeared out of sight, he turned and left the stinking room.

Moving down the basement hallway, he came across a pay telephone and dug the piece of paper from his pocket again. Drawing a quarter from his pocket, he inserted it and dialed a number from the piece of paper. He winced to find he'd reached an answering machine. Waiting for the out-going message to run through, he pondered about the message he'd leave. 'Hello, Frank; hello, Nancy, it's Jeremy calling, and it's two PM Sunday. I'd like to meet up with you at the club tonight, and um, you both did fine work and everything has come up roses. See you tonight. Thanks! Oh, I'll try reaching you at the club, in case you're there. Bye.'

Digging out another two quarters and setting them on top of the wall-mounted pay-phone, he grabbed one and inserted it, dialing a second number from the note. 'Hello, is Frank or Nancy there, please? Hmm? You know, the comedy team that does all those impersonations and things. No? Well, I left a message at their home number ... oh, I see,' Roblaw coyly replied stroking his chin.

'Yes, of course. Can I leave a message with you, then? It's Jeremy. Um, tell them that their assistance paid off, and that I'd like to meet them at the club at—what time do they go on? ... Alright, I'd like to meet them at seven PM then. Pardon me? ... No, I'm unreachable at the moment, I'm afraid. What's your name? ... *Hal*. Listen, thanks a bunch, Hal, ... bye.'

Roblaw smiled wryly, and put away the note. He reached for the last quarter, deposited it, and dialed a number from memory.

twenty

IN AN OLD TENEMENT apartment building in Hull, Quebec, a middle aged woman with curlers in her hair, carting a small bag of garbage, walked down the dim hallway towards the disposal chute. Moving along in her slippers, she detected an unusual stench which was most powerful when she passed the door of apartment 226. She registered the awful odor with a contorted face, and moved quickly past to reach the disposal unit door.

It seemed almost a pleasure to take a breather in the disposal room, and after throwing her small bag down the chute and emerging into the hallway again, she took a deep breath and prepared to quick step her way back to her apartment.

From behind, Claude, the stalky live-in superintendent of the tenement collided with her. With a slight start, she turned to recognize the man who smiled at her.

'Sorry 'bout that, Mariette,' he said, with a French Canadian accent, holding her by the shoulders to prevent her from falling from the bump.

'Oh, you scared me,' she replied, with a small giggle. 'Claude, ... there's an awful odor coming from I think ... 226?'

'So I hear ... and I *think* I smell.'

'It's definitely not a cooking smell, but it sure stinks, oui?' she said, as they began to walk back towards the apartment. 'Can you spray some de-odorizer, or prop a door?'

'Let's see if Schlomo's home. Do you know him?' he asked.

'No, and I don't think I want to.'

'He's a meat and potatoes kind of guy,' he replied, knocking on the door. 'I don't think he's into weird food. Haven't seen him in over a week—maybe he's gone away.'

The woman scrunched up her nose and waved her hand in front of her face. 'I've got to go. I'm sure you'll work it out sometime soon, I hope.'

'Maybe his drains have backed up. You know we had a sewer problem and the laundry room was flooded. How's your plumbing?' he enquired, with a lecherous smile, as she began to walk along towards her apartment.

She turned and smiled at Claude, whom she knew had a crush on her. 'Fine for now, Claude, but why don't you call in next weekend and see if it's up to snuff?'

Her reply took Claude by surprise, causing him to blush at the invitation and clumsily drop the keys he had withdrawn from his pocket to access Schlomo's apartment. She had called his bluff, and now he was obliged to act on it. 'Sure thing,' he said, as he bent over to pick up the keys from the floor, watching her disappear into her apartment. Using his master key, he unlocked the door marked 226. Suddenly, the stink coming from the apartment hit Claude with full potency. It was definitely a decomposing stench. He squinted with confusion. He thought he also detected rustling—almost like the sound of a handful of small glass marbles rubbing together, but continuous. Most peculiar.

twenty-one

MCGREGOR AND GARR finally came upon the site of the sled-dog attack on Brunhilde. It was a disgusting scene, with the devastated remnants of limbs, and clothing strewn about the blood-stained snow. The two got off the snowmobile and looked around at the nauseating carnage.

'The sled was turned in circles here,' McGregor said, 'and look—polar bear tracks. I think there was two of them.'

'This is horrendous!' exclaimed Gaar, shaking his head.

McGregor scrounged around further, and spotted the Anknonquatok doll-necklace. He squatted down beside it, taking a handful of snow to wash the blood off of it. Having wiped it thoroughly, he stood with the clenched doll, scrutinizing it carefully. Gaar took notice of McGregor's find.

'What's that?' Gaar asked suspiciously.

'Some kinda doll on a leather thong.'

'Can I see that?'

'You interested in this? Some kinda shaman's talisman? Roblaw'd love this for his mantelpiece,' McGregor taunted, as he manipulated the doll, and started to swing it in circles with his hand, holding it by the thong.

'If you value your health ...' Gaar muttered, with a shake of his head.

'What'd you say?' McGregor replied scornfully, 'If you value *your* health, you'll shut your face! Don't you dare try to give me orders or advice, *Mr Eskimo lover.*' McGregor turned his head away from Gaar and surveyed the bloody scene. He walked a few feet further, up past a snow drift as he followed a blood trail. He paused and waited for Gaar.

Gaar begrudgingly trekked up to join McGregor, as the two of them came across a boot—with a foot still in it. 'Lookie here! A boot! It's too big for Max—catch!' McGregor tossed the bloodied boot at Gaar, who caught it as it struck his chest. Gaar reeled in pain as his wounded shoulder twinged from the sudden movement.

McGregor put the Anknonquatok doll in his pocket. He pulled a small camera out from the inside of his parka and took a snapshot. 'Smile for the camera,' he said, as Gaar cast off the repulsive boot in disgust.

'What's the big idea?' Gaar said, holding his sore shoulder.

'Let's go!' McGregor ordered flatly, and began to walk back to the craft. As they walked back past the drift, they collided with Max, sending him with his arms pinwheeling for support to the ground. 'YIKES!' McGregor shrieked, as he drew his pistol, almost pulling the trigger on Max.

Gaar came to the realization of whom it was that crossed their path. 'Max?! Max! It's Gaar, remember me? Look!' Gaar said, pulling back his hood, as Max struggled to his feet, ready to make a desperate run for it. 'Put the gun away, McGregor.'

'You!' Max replied, relieved that it wasn't Jag's lot. 'You nearly had me out of my skin!'

'Your compatriot's beat you to it,' McGregor said, pointing at the evident carnage at the site ahead of them, and putting the gun away.

'Holy cow! I told her not to starve the dogs!'

'Talk about biting the hand that feeds you! So you're saying it was the dogs—then the bears?' McGregor asked.

'She was terribly wounded and bleeding, and this is where her hand used to be ... she kept me prisoner in these,' he said, holding up the dangling bracelet of the handcuffs, 'she went for my wrist with a machete and got her own by accident; and the dogs—they just went nuts from starvation and chased her, biting at her like crazy!'

'And now she's gone to pieces,' McGregor cruelly joked.

'Max,' Gaar interrupted, 'we've got to get you to Nanisivik to iron out a matter with the high council there. They see you as a fugitive. They'll try you in-absentia if we don't make it back on time.'

'They're gunnin' for you,' added McGregor, with a perverted pleasure in his words.

'I'm innocent!' Max shouted. 'That woman—Brunhilde Hamilton! She held me hostage! *She's* the killer!'

McGregor eyed Max, and laughed mockingly. 'A woman held you hostage. I believe it!'

Max sneered at McGregor's derisive comment. 'She was huge! Stronger than an ox—and she had a gun! Wait a minute,' Max said, as he mulled over his situation, 'I can't go back. How can I prove my innocence? I've got to get south—everyone's gone looney!'

'You gonna walk to Canada on those spindly little legs of yours?' McGregor mocked. 'Hitch a ride with a polar bear, maybe?'

'He's right, Max. There's only one snowmobile—we'll

triple up. Don't worry, I'll gather the evidence to exonerate you.'

'With you as my lawyer again? Forget it!'

'We've got a surprise witness who'll testify in our favour if you show up,' Gaar insisted, trying to lift Max's spirits and bolster any glimmer of optimism for the plan.

'I've had enough surprises,' Max replied with reluctance, 'I'm not going to stick around to eat it this time!'

McGregor stepped forward and drew his pistol from his parka. 'You'll come with us or you'll eat lead.'

'Charmed,' Max replied, not having met McGregor before.

Gaar approached Max and put his gloved hand on his shoulder. 'Was it Jag behind the travesty at Kabloona?'

'The mine explosion?' Max asked with a wince.

'That, and the fire?'

'What fire would that be?'

'The fire that burned the camp to the ground.'

Max raised his shoulders, ignorant of the fact that Jag had destroyed the camp after their departure. 'I guess only his hair-dresser knows for sure,' he replied, off-handedly.

'Very funny, asshole,' replied McGregor, 'but what's even *funnier* is that he's blaming it all on you.'

'Listen, I've got nothing to do with this, so I'll just try and catch up with my ride,' Max said, pointing at the dog-sled tracks, 'Roblaw and I have some unfinished business, so I better get on my way—say you wouldn't have any food or water you could spare?'

McGregor chuckled. 'Try that boot over there.'

Max looked over at the bloodied boot, and caught a glimpse of the contents. 'You're a regular barrel of monkeys, mister. Fine.' Max began to walk away.

'ON YOUR KNEES, FUCKER!' McGregor commanded, in a booming voice filled with loathing.

Max stopped and turned around to look at Gaar. 'Y'know, I'm not really taking a shining to your friend, Gaar.'

'He's *not* my friend, believe me.'

McGregor fired two warning shots into the air. Gaar and Max reeled at the earsplitting shots, which plainly spelled out McGregor's point. Backing up his display of intent, McGregor lifted a pair of handcuffs from an inside pocket of his parka, walked sternly over to Max and slapped a bracelet on his right wrist.

'Not the south-paw again!' Max complained, seeing that his wrist was turning into some kind of scrap metal depot.

McGregor dragged Max over to Gaar. 'Gaar, hold this ...' he dictated, lifting Max's cuffed hand towards him.

'Hold *what*?' Gaar asked, seeing nothing but the dangling empty bracelet from the first pair of cuffs Max wore.

'Hold that closed ringlet for a second!' McGregor insisted. 'Take hold of it and take him to the snowmobile.'

Gaar lifted his hand to grasp the dangling bracelet, when McGregor slipped Max's other open bracelet on Gaar's wrist and snapped it shut in a flash. 'What the—?! Uncuff me! NOW!!' Gaar demanded, then pondered with a fright.

'Are you giving me orders?' McGregor asked with curious interest, and a derisive smile. Gaar began his math.

'Let's radio-in, that we've found Max, and that I'll need a doctor to fix my shoulder when we arrive.'

'Bad plan. They'd eavesdrop on any transmission and Jag'd be all over us before we got anywhere *near* Nanisivik.'

'Then what the hell'd we bring it for?!'

'So that they'd think we'd give ourselves away.'

Gaar scowled, barking his opposition to McGregor's methods. 'Just uncuff me, right now!' Gaar realized now that not only was McGregor a crude bastard—he was going to murder them! Gaar's only chance now was to play along and play dumb, until an opportunity arose to get the gun from McGregor.

'Don't worry, this is just *insurance*. Let's go. These tracks are like lit fuses,' he said, as he ushered the two towards the snowmobile. Max hung his head and shook it in disbelief.

'Why don't you handcuff Max to *you* then, and let *me* drive!'

'*You're wounded*,' replied McGregor, 'that'd be cruel. You can't drive with that handicap.'

Max turned his head to Gaar and sucked his lip. 'I hope you have a lucky rabbit's foot, Gaar. Last person who held my hand like this ... well—'

'Shut your face, and get on, before somebody comes!' McGregor snapped, as they reached the snowmobile and began to mount it. McGregor stopped the two. 'You two love-birds gotta face off the end of the seat. Gaar, you know the drill. Show this retard what I mean.'

'Listen,' Gaar said, trying to reason with the man, 'my goddamn arm is killing me. If the two of us faced each other, you'd spare me that much pain, and Max wouldn't have to twist his arm behind his back, hmm?'

'Alright. Just get on fast, and let's go!'

Max got on the end of the seat and faced Gaar, whose back was to McGregor's back. Gaar looked at McGregor as though they still had a common mission. 'We should stop at my father's store at Kiqaloq. We'll be safe there 'til we have to depart for the tribunal.'

McGregor looked at Gaar as though he were the biggest idiot in the world. 'Are you stupid? Jag probably has someone watching the place!' he said, climbing up on the snowmobile.

Gaar *felt* like the biggest idiot in the world for being in the situation he was in. He turned his head over his shoulder and feigned as though he were reasoning with a rational person. He didn't want to alert McGregor, nor did he want to alarm Max, who sat frustrated and aloof. 'There's always lots of guests at the store,' Gaar shouted over his shoulder, as McGregor straddled the long cushioned seat and revved the engine, 'he wouldn't try anything with witnesses around; some would accompany us to Nanisivik for the high council meeting!'

McGregor slipped the snowmobile into gear and took off like a shot. 'Anything you say, Gaar!!' McGregor shouted loudly, smiling devilishly as he steered them into the lightly falling twilight snow.

Gaar's ruse to allow him to face Max, gave them the ability to talk. As they bumped and rocked along the ride, Gaar began to dig at Max for details. Whether McGregor could hear them talking hood to hood, and how soon he would put an end to it was unknown to Gaar. He raised his voice over the drone of the motor and gave Max the third degree.

'I know you took the fall for Roblaw. I don't want to see it happen again!'

'I don't know what you're talking about,' Max replied coldly.

'You know goddamn well what I mean. If you don't admit to me now that you did—I can't help you. If you were killed or something, at least I'd have the goods on that rat. Right?! There are no witnesses here—so tell me! Your future doesn't look very bright at the moment, but I can help you!'

'Okay, *lawyer*. I'm engaging you to defend me, so what I tell you is confidential information.'

'Agreed.'

'Roblaw set up two off-shore accounts for me. Antilles, and Swiss, I believe.'

Gaar shook his head. '*Swiss cheese*, and you've fallen through the holes—and I think I've been just as stupid. I don't think we're gonna make it to this tribunal. I think we're both goners unless we can overpower this asshole!' Gaar warned, indicating McGregor with his thumb.

'I've got insurance!' Max boldly proclaimed.

'What was that?!'

'Insurance,' Max said confidently. 'My brother's holding it for me. Damaging video footage shot from a hidden camera, and an accounting disc with contact names and account numbers that'll nail his ass to the wall if he tries to screw me! My brother will expose the evidence against him, which'll send him to jail for years! If I'm killed or disappear—he's up the creek!'

'What's his name and address? He could be in danger! I think the jig is up!'

'Do I look stupid?'

'Okay, I understand. You think I'm Roblaw's weasel.'

'To make things easier for you; we don't share common last names,' Max confided, 'so don't bother getting out the phone book. He doesn't live in Ottawa either. Bet that tastes sour, huh?'

Gaar shook his head. 'Tell me something. Did you hint at you having the goods on him?'

'Did I threaten Roblaw? Of course I did—when I was sentenced. I'm not dumb. I wanted a cushy job at Kabloona, and I needed to be guaranteed protection. So, I laid the ground rules, and he made sure I stayed alive.'

'I don't understand,' Gaar huffed. 'I know that Roblaw can dish out the *fine print*, but can't take it. Maybe I'm wrong about McGregor—I mean, I'm right about *him*, but perhaps wrong about his intentions for us. We'll see. Still want to get that gun from him—don't want to take any chances.'

The trio motored along a coastal route on the snowmobile. They travelled a corridor which put them between the frozen-over shore and a gradually sloping hill of snow. They moved as swift as the struggling old snowmobile would take them, towing a small sled.

They meandered along the eastern shoreline of the south

end of the vast Admiralty Inlet. Chunky ice flows with the occasional iceberg floating slowly along the peaceful expanse of water, gave one a sense of serenity. Gaar stared longingly at the spectacular vista, which he hadn't been a part of for many years. The snowy peaked mountains in the distance and the crystalline ice encrusted waters in the foreground, heightened his senses. Max stared at Gaar, wondering what all the introspection was about.

'Where'd you get the hole?' Max asked.

'He came along as a tracker, to find you.'

'No—*that* hole,' he said, pointing at the bullet hole in his parka. '—a trapper!' Max announced suddenly, setting aside his interest in Gaar's reply.

McGregor pulled up and stopped beside an Inuit trapper, who bore a load of arctic hare and fox pelts across his shoulders. He smiled, nodding his hello to the trio, holding a seal harpoon and a coil of modest gauge rope in his hand. Gaar couldn't fathom why McGregor would bother stopping, but recognized the opportunity to get a message to Nanisivik via the trapper. Gaar piped up with his best broken Inuit tongue, knowing well that his dialect could be miles off the mark.

'Hello,' Gaar said slowly and carefully in a dialect of Inuktitut. 'please—speak to me in Inuktitut, understand? No English, yes?' The trapper understood him marginally, and nodded. 'I'm Gaar Injugarjuk.'

'I'm Joshua Tuktoqinnuk,' he replied, curiously observing the scene and noticing the handcuffs that tethered Gaar with Max.

'Do you have television where your ... camp is?'

'Yes—but I thought everybody had a television.'

McGregor grinned slyly, and observed in silence, as Gaar fumbled through the conversation in Inuktitut. McGregor's patience was incongruous with his nasty nature, which made Gaar wary as he talked without interference from him.

'Please television Nanisivik, and get a message to the high council that I have found the ... *speech-maker* and hope to be there ... soon with him?'

McGregor reached into his pocket for his pistol, as the trapper tried to understand Gaar's convoluted request.

'And,' Gaar continued, 'it's important to sing them that if me don't return with the man, not take the kisses—no, uh ... word! Word of the ... white tracker of white chief who might ... kill faces?' Gaar shook his head apologetically, knowing he mucked up the grammar terribly. He became frustrated with the futile attempt at relaying a secret message to keep the contents from McGregor's understanding and lifted his face to the sky in submission.

'Could we try it in English?' the trapper said slowly to Gaar, in English. McGregor levelled his pistol towards the man.

'Try this on for size ...' McGregor interrupted, shooting the trapper twice at close range.

Gaar and Max scrambled off the snowmobile, falling to the shore side. 'MURDERER!!' Gaar screamed out in disgust, as McGregor pointed the pistol at them and remained on the snowmobile.

'You *are* stupid, aren't you,' he said to Gaar, '*don't* move,' he added with a sneer, turning his head back down to the trapper who writhed on the icy ground, still alive, and struggling to keep it that way. He braced his pistol hand on his forearm and plugged the trapper in the head, finishing him off.

Gaar lunged at McGregor, but was impeded by Max who wasn't ready for the spontaneous jump, foiling Gaar's attempt at catching McGregor off guard. McGregor turned quickly at the ruckus and jabbed the pistol into Gaar's wounded shoulder. He reared back in pain from the force of the impact of his prod.

'You goddamn cold-blooded bastard!' Gaar barked, holding his shoulder, and wincing with a glare of contempt.

'You need me!' Max cried out in a cowardly half pleading manner, realizing what was afoot, and afraid for his life.

'You know, *you're* right,' McGregor said, reaching into an inside pocket of his parka and pulling out another pistol. 'Take this,' he said, handing Max the pistol, 'cover Gaar. I said *cover* Gaar! That trapper was going to kill us both! Gaar didn't realize I spoke Inuit—that was what they were talking about!'

Max held the pistol and reluctantly raised it towards Gaar. 'Is that true, Gaar?'

'Don't be absurd, Max! Put it down! It's a trick!'

Max turned his head back to McGregor, who snapped a photo of the scene, making sure his own outstretched pistol was in the foreground of the picture, as though it were a stand-off. Max turned his gun on McGregor who chuckled at the display. Max raised the gun in the air and pulled the trigger. Nothing. Another desperate *click* followed.

'You're so gullible—if you watched more TV, you might have figured it out before you fucked yourself,' McGregor taunted, belching out a hiccuped laugh. 'Now, I'll take *that*, sissy-boy.' McGregor stuffed the camera in his pocket, and threatened Max with a jerk of his gun, demanding the empty pistol back. Max looked at Gaar apologetically, but was met with only aloof scorn from him.

'Roblaw's screwed if anything happens to me,' Max replied, as he handed over the dud.

'All Roblaw needs is a cancelled postage stamp—*you*, and this photo is his receipt. I think the stage is set now, except for one small detail,' he said, as he stood on the side-runners of the snowmobile and let out a heinous shout as he shot himself through the fatty under-thigh of his left leg.

'You're insane!' yelled Max.

'No, that bullet just christened me a millionaire,' he

replied through grit teeth, and flaring mercenary eyes. 'So, "Max jumped me and shot the trapper and Gaar in cold blood. I scuffled with him and managed to overcome the fugitive and was forced to shoot the raving lunatic in self defense"—it's plausible.'

'It's ridiculous—no one in their right mind would believe you!' shouted Gaar.

'Those dumb Eskimo fucks'll believe anything we tell 'em to believe!'

'You'll never get away with it!' Max protested, 'and Roblaw's gonna burn if you go through with this—I've got him over a barrel!'

'It'll be easier to bring you back dead than alive, Max. You'll be more help to us that way ... *really*,' he said plainly, then turned his attention to Gaar. 'And *you*—half breed! You don't have a round trip ticket, so you're off this love-train, asshole!' He pointed his pistol at Gaar's head and squeezed the trigger. The firing mechanism clicked but nothing happened. He tried again, then swiftly ejected the clip from the gun, digging into his pocket for a loaded clip.

Gaar instigated a rush at McGregor, and Max intuitively followed Gaar's lead. Gaar violently grappled with the mercenary but was compromised with his injured shoulder and was overcome by McGregor's superior strength and agility. McGregor kicked the uncoordinated pair of opponents away from himself. He produced the fresh clip and began to insert it into the butt of the pistol.

Gaar leaped at McGregor again in a frantic maneuver, shoving the man off the machine. McGregor tipped over into the snow near the dead trapper. They made a run for it down onto the waterway which teetered with ice plates.

McGregor struggled to his feet and limped back onto the snowmobile. He braced his pistol hand on his left forearm and cracked off a few shots at his escaping prey, missing each time due to the pair's helter-skelter movements over the bump-and-slip surface of the inlet. The lightly falling snow crisscrossed through his sights, impeding his aim and fanning a spark of desperation. He was forced to chase them down on his snowmobile to get a better shot at them. He wound the craft down the incline and onto the iced-over water mass.

Max looked back, then slipped on the ice, bringing Gaar down with him. McGregor stopped the snowmobile seeing their disadvantage and his fleeting chance to peg off the sitting ducks. He was determined not to venture out further after them on the ice. Leaping to his feet and standing on the side-runners of the snowmobile, he took aim with great satisfaction.

Suddenly, the snowmobile gave out from under his feet. It began sinking nose-first through a large crack which opened up in front of him. He scrambled to dismount the snowmobile, but caught his wounded leg's boot-bindings on an engine lever and ended up twisting himself over his caught leg as he fell to the side of the machine.

The snowmobile sank fast, but stopped halfway as the sled was caught up on a corner of the small thick plate of ice. It tipped up, leaving him knee deep in the freezing water. McGregor struggled, and with a painful shriek, he untwisted his body over his dislocated leg. He gripped the snowmobile for support with his right hand, still greedily holding the pistol, and reached down below the freezing water to attempt to free his boot, or his foot from the caught boot. He could manage neither.

'Help!!' he shouted desperately.

Gaar and Max looked back with confusion, seeing the tipped-up tail of the snowmobile and McGregor frantically reaching under the water at something. They moved in closer, slowly treading over the semi-solid plates of ice towards him. Max became reluctant, but Gaar tugged him along.

'We can try to help you ... if you throw the gun away!' Gaar yelled.

McGregor aimed the gun at them. 'You better fuckin' help, or I'll shoot you both!' he screeched in agony.

'He's gonna kill us!' Max cried out, falling to his knees to get out of the line of fire. Gaar stood his ground.

'My leg is caught!'

'Toss the gun!' Gaar replied.

'Get that rope from the trapper!!'

'The one you killed in cold-blood?!' Max shouted angrily.

'Get it now, or I'll shoot! I'm a crack shot!'

'You're a *crackpot*!' yelled Max.

'Lose the gun, or we're gone!' Gaar shouted, lowering himself out of the firing line, to join Max.

McGregor stuffed the gun into the tread of the snowmobile and desperately dug into his parka pocket. 'Okay! Here it is!' McGregor yelled, pulling out the empty gun he'd given Max earlier and waving it in the air. As Gaar and Max looked up to observe, McGregor threw the red-herring as far away as he could into what appeared to be a churned up area of slushy water and fragments of ice.

Gaar looked at Max with a gleam in his eye. 'C'mon, let's get the rope, and I'll get him to confess—then we'll save him.'

'I don't trust him—hang on,' Max warned. He looked towards McGregor and shouted. 'Throw us the keys for the handcuffs!'

'After you bastards throw me a line—hurry!'

Gaar and Max trotted off to retrieve the rope.

Along with the rope, Max found a machete in the trapper's belt, and brought it with him as a defensive measure. They stepped down the slope and ventured back out onto the ice. Gaar stopped short of coming around to McGregor's side of the snowmobile.

'Are you having second thoughts?' Max asked, 'Fine with me, 'cept we gotta get the keys from him.'

'Don't worry, we'll get 'em. There's just one small detail. McGregor!' Gaar shouted, 'Throw the gun to us! The *real* one!'

Max cocked his head in realization. 'That sonofabitch! Good thinking, Gaar.'

McGregor begrudgingly ejected the cartridge from the pistol's grip and threw the gun ten yards out from himself. Seeing the gun sliding forward, Gaar led Max out to a safe area, settling for the spot where the gun came to a full stop.

Gaar held an end of the coil of rope, and tossed the coil at McGregor, who managed to grasp a hold of it. 'Max, hand me the machete.'

Max gave Gaar the machete, who thrust it with determination down at the crusty ice, burying the blade several inches into the ice. 'Now throw the keys for the handcuffs,' yelled Max, 'so we can pull you out properly!'

'My hands are freezing!' McGregor replied, helplessly groaning at his predicament.

'The keys!!'

'Max, sit down,' Gaar said. They both sat. Gaar braced his foot against the flat side of the blade of the machete which was secured in the ice. Max put the gun in his pocket.

McGregor awkwardly rooted for the keys as though he were drunk. The freezing water had begun to affect his consciousness. He came across the keys and tossed them forward, but only managed to propel them a couple of yards.

'Blast!' Max said with disappointment, 'Blast and damn!'

'McGregor!' Gaar shouted, 'tie the rope around your waist! Can you slip your foot out of your boot?!' he asked, as he began to tie their end of the rope around *his* own waist. Max tugged back with reluctance, as Gaar used both hands to secure the rope. 'Try pulling your leg from your boot! I'm going to give you some slack!' Gaar wedged the machete out from the ice and moved forward a few feet to slacken the rope. Max resisted.

'What're you doing?!' Max protested. 'Don't tie it around your waist—not with *me* attached to you! If you go—*I go!*'

McGregor lumbered at the rope, and managed to fasten a firm knot around his chest. 'I'm in! Put tension on the rope!' McGregor stammered, as he attempted to pull his foot from the tightly bound boot.

'That's right, Max. We may all end up in the big-drink. So, are you going to tell me your brother's name and address?'

'What?!'

'I've lost everything, Max. My baby is dead, my wife's left me, my father doesn't want anything to do with me,' he admitted, as a slight but noticeable tug forward was felt.

'Untie the rope,' Max stated flatly. 'I've got the gun.'

'It's not loaded—we're all fools, Max. The three of us, ... you can turn the tables though; it's up to you whether we're in the black, *or the red*. I've got nothing to live for, really. There's a bullet lodged in my shoulder—and I'm beginning to feel halfway there, know what I mean? So I'll go down, and *you'll* go with me unless you tell me where the goods are on Roblaw—your brother's name and address. Now! Obviously, I want to help you.'

'*Obviously*,' Max replied. They began to noticeably move forward on their backsides, toward the sinking snowmobile.

'Stop it!' McGregor cried out in despair, 'anchor!'

'Let's go for that drink on me,' Gaar said, turning his head around to Max.

'Twelve-fifty Avenue des Chappe, Hull, Quebec!' Max blurted, 'Apartment 226—Schlomo Getz!'

'Schlomo Getz.'

'Right. Now, untie us!'

'Dig in, *you bastards!*' McGregor screamed out, his desperation saturating the words as he breathed them out.

'Not so fast, Max,' Gaar stated, as they were dragged slowly towards the sinking snowmobile, 'the escape—the murders?'

'It was her—Brunhilde! She killed Jag's nephew—I think she said *he* set the explosives in the head-frame and shaft. They'd struck a monumental gold vein in the drift. Jag's got a corpse *strapped to his back*! Now cut us free, or I'm going to *flip-out*!'

'You're telling me the truth, now?'

'Goddammit—yes!'

'And you'll come back with us and tell the truth to the high council?'

'Yes!!' Max shrieked, '*cut us free*!'

Gaar turned to McGregor who was in a panic to frantically free his leg, as he was slowly being pulled downwards with the sinking snowmobile. 'McGregor! I'm getting a lot of peer pressure to abandon this goodwill mission. Keep trying to free your leg! We'll stick at it, but we need the truth! Does Roblaw want us dead?!'

'Yes! Don't let go!!' he yelped, with a lazy drone in his voice.

'Here!!' Gaar yelled, as he slid the machete several yards to within McGregor's grasp. 'Hack your leg off at the knee! It's your only chance!! We can't hold off much longer! Go on! Your *leg* for your *life*!'

McGregor's eyes bulged out of his head, pondering the horror of the ghastly decision. He raised the machete high in the air to do the unspeakable. A sudden jolt drew him down further, bringing the water up to his waist. He slapped at the water desperately with the machete, more in rage than in practicality, having missed the opportunity and now facing an almost certain death. 'Bastards! Bastards!!' McGregor shrieked, falling into a delirious insanity.

'McGregor!!' Gaar hollered, suddenly recognizing the

dire caution that was cited to him by his grandfather's spirit. 'The doll necklace! Throw it to me! It's bad luck for you!'

'Gaar—!! Untie us now!! —Gaar!'

'Come and get it, *half-breed*!'

The snowmobile started to sink steadily now, pulling McGregor down further. The water was at his chest. He was destitute. The sled which was caught on the edge of the ice plate, began to break free from the immense pressure being exerted. The short-wave radio and a small duffel bag came tumbling out of the belly of the small tow-sled, and bounced along the ice.

'Give me ... my *gun*, ... so I can shoot ... myself!' McGregor pleaded.

'I've got the gun!!' shouted Max in a passionate explosion. 'Give me the knife! Give me the knife!! Knife for the gun! Slide it!!' Max squeaked in a maniacal rage, as Gaar worked frantically at untying the knot around his chest. Max saw the ice-frosted knot that Gaar was fiddling with and recognized the futility of his attempts. If he had the machete, he'd chop the rope in five seconds at the outside. McGregor would take that or more to load up his gun in the debilitating state he was in. He would definitely shoot his tormentors out of spite before he killed himself, though—no question. It was a foolish gamble—but there was no choice, and little time.

'On ... three! THREE!!' McGregor barked. The two swapped weapons in a time-limited quest.

McGregor flung the machete in their direction, and Max honourably slid the gun to him. It was a mistake on a grand scale. Max's face dropped as the machete tumbled only five yards from McGregor, while Max had slid the pistol accurately over ten yards to him. McGregor loaded the cartridge into the grip of the gun and smiled in drunken delight.

'No!!' Max shrieked in despair, shaking his head violently. Gaar focussed intently on the knot, not wasting a second on the thought of being shot point blank in the face.

'By ... the way, Max!' McGregor announced with cruel vengeance, 'we got ... to your brother, and he's ... worm-meat, now! HA!' he laughed, as the sled broke free from its ice-hook, and the snowmobile sank swiftly. McGregor went insane and began to shoot with wild abandon. The volley of bullets zinged by their heads like ballistic mosquitoes until the mad shooter went under, and the last shot was fired into the sky.

Max desperately grasped Gaar's wrist with his one good-hand and attempted to dig his heels into the ice in a futile fashion. At this moment—of this day, determination would avail nothing. Nature, as a stone-faced judge had lowered the gavel and there was no appeal to be had.

As Gaar was yanked forward, Max lost his grip. With a whimper, Max was dragged by his shackled wrist, tethered to the end of Gaar's outstretched arm. Gaar slid on his back, intently focussed and picking at the knot with his free hand, as Max flailed about at the end of the other.

They were pulled most-assuredly forward and towards the fractured opening. With the shattering news of his brother and the reality of his own imminent death, Max lost his composure. He was overcome by a crippling psychosis which drove him to giggling, even as he was poked in the face with chunks of ice. It was as though he were on a theme park rollercoaster nearing the crest of the big dip. On their approach to the end of the line, he began to sing out a theme song from some Broadway musical in a deranged fashion, waving his free hand as though he were in a ticker-tape motorcade. Streaking past the machete which lay on the ice en route to their appointment, Max adeptly grabbed the long blade, but only waved it in the air and blew kisses to an imaginary adoring crowd. Catching a glimpse of the slushy hole not six feet away, he closed his eyes and exhaled fero-ciously, as though he were blowing out a hundred birthday candles.

twenty-two

AN EFFERVESCENT WATERFALL of goldfish scurried from the churning bubbly current to orient themselves in their new environment. One after another, they tumbled into their bright and colourful new aquarium. It was a large clean tank with lots of varied plant life, juxtaposed with the singularity of the predominant dwellers within the tank—miniature piranha. The welcome wagon made short work of the newcomers and soon, only fragments of the unsuspecting guests remained after the aquatic rodeo.

Roblaw looked approvingly at his pet army which reacted with ravenous instinct rather than conscience. He considered his piranha marvels of evolution, and anyone who thought otherwise was regarded as having missed the point. After a few moments of gratifying entertainment—courtesy of his *darlings*, he sauntered across the polar bear rug which stretched wide across the floor, and tossed the goldfish baggie into a nearby garbage pail. He checked his watch and left his study.

Walking out the front door of the magnificent house, he brushed by one of the two small concrete lions which lay in watch at the top of the short steps to the door. He jogged down the steps and walked along the expansive driveway. It was surrounded by tall and sturdy pine trees for privacy. A sprinkling of tardy fall leaves from the neighbour's property had gradually blown over to his side which annoyed him. This made for slippery footing on the cobblestoned drive under his hard-soled dress shoes. The smatterings of maple leaves were often hard to spot in the evening hours due to the shadows produced by the English climbing ivy which partially covered the driveway lights.

The perennial pine trees and evergreen English vines which climbed the vast cut-stone walls of his castle-like house, maintained a consistent year-round ambiance on the large estate. In defiance of change in his physical surroundings, Roblaw felt comfort in the fact that the imminent winter snows would swoop through as a mere transitory frosting in his permanent environment.

As he walked alongside the Rolls, he sniffed at the air, detecting chimney exhausts which perfumed the crisp cool air with the odor of burning cedar logs. Looking up to his roof which was silhouetted against the darkened evening sky and just slightly illuminated by the pale October moon, he observed his own chimney smoking away. His wife was undoubtedly in the parlour reading before dinner, as she'd usually do. He found her there whenever he sought her out.

He slipped up on a maple leaf as he approached his maroon Rolls Royce sedan, cursing under his breath as he unlocked the door, got in and started it up.

On a wide downtown thoroughfare, Roblaw pulled his car up to the curb of the street, and parked the Rolls outside a comedy club called the Hippo-Campus Comedy Emporium. He sat in the car and waited a few minutes until finally, the man who'd secured the blackmail materials for him, pulled up alongside him in a brand new, sporty American-made car.

Acknowledging each other with a nod, Roblaw started his car and drove up the street as the man parallel parked the car in the vacant spot the departed Rolls had made available.

Getting out of the midnight-blue American-made car, the man locked the doors and walked up the street to meet Roblaw. Along a stretch of closed shops, Roblaw walked down the street back towards the comedy club, intending to converge with the man. As they neared each other on the sidewalk, they brushed by each other without stopping. Looking down into his hand, Roblaw held the keys for the American car which had been passed to him by the man when they'd grazed past each other.

Roblaw loomed at the doorway of the club and looked at a marquee picture of the man and woman who had impersonated both Gaar and Louise for him. He turned briefly towards the sporty new car parked at the curb adjacent to the club. He pulled at the neon-lit door of the club and entered.

The comedy stylings of the duo he came to see, boomed over the PA system. He sat down at an empty table at the back of the small, dimly lit club. Roblaw declined service from the waiter as he approached the table. Turning his attention back up at the lit stage, he was noticed by his acquaintances who during some laughter and applause, had taken it upon themselves to shade their eyes and survey the audience as part of their act. They spotted Roblaw from the small stage and waved to him but didn't turn his presence into a noticeable affair, to his great relief.

As they finished up their shtick to a moderate round of applause, another comedian was announced by the host, who quickly leapt up to the stage and launched directly into his routine. Exiting the stage, the performers waved Roblaw over to join them in the dressing room at the back of the club.

After a few minutes, Roblaw rose and made his way unassumingly towards the dressing room area.

In the dressing room, Frank, the short pudgy comedian, chuckled after relaying his experience making the phone call to Louise from the bus station. A young waiter knocked and entered the lamp-lit dressing room, bearing a bottle of champagne which he set in a cooling stand. Frank placed an envelope of money which Roblaw had given him, into his pocket. The waiter placed three glasses on the counter and collected an assortment of dirty glasses and empty beer bottles from the counters of the make-up mirror stations. He opened the door to exit the room.

The dull roar of the performance outside flared up with the opening of the door, as Frank's counterpart, Nancy, squeezed through the door as the waiter left. She put her hands to her cheeks as she looked at Frank with an ecstatic look on her face. The banter from the other comedian on stage was diminished when she finally shut the door behind herself.

She was a pretty woman, with long fire-engine red hair, and a slim build. Just to look at her, with her wry grin and telltale eyes which sparkled with impish animation, one would know she was a clever and amusing woman. She went over and leaned into her partner's face and cutely pinched both his chubby cheeks.

'It's *beautiful*! Frank, wait'll you see it—you great lug,' she squeaked, as she turned to Roblaw and shook her head with a modest and sincere expression. 'We can't accept the car *and* the money—Jeremy, *really*!'

'If you don't, I'll take offence,' Roblaw replied, as he began to open the champagne. 'You like fast cars?'

Frank and Nancy looked at each other and smiled. 'Love 'em,' Frank replied, tapping the pocket which held the envelope of money he'd been given. 'This'll pay for our honeymoon—thanks. But, really, the car was unnecessary.'

'You deserve it ... think of it as a wedding gift,' Roblaw announced to both of them, as he pried the cork of the champagne bottle, and squinted as he persuaded the cork to the point of teetering out the end of the spout. The cork discharged with a *pop*, and ricocheted around the room to land somewhere out of sight. The chilled champagne oozed out the top in a frothy eruption. They all chuckled. Roblaw poured them each a glass. 'Where did you say you were going again?'

'We've booked a king-sized isolation tank in Florida,' Frank replied as they tipped glasses. 'Here's mud in yer eye!' he said, raising his glass and then levelling it to his mouth.

Roblaw grinned and lifted his glass. 'I'll drink to that,' he uttered as he sipped at the champagne.

'Frank—that's like drinking to shin-splints or toe mushrooms! How 'bout something proper?'

'Like to ... vomit in the lungs of that scoundrel, Gaar?'

'Frank! You're disgusting!' she protested with an embarrassed laugh, 'you don't even know the man—he's *dung* ... a cow pie with arms, all the way—I'm sorry Jeremy, sometimes when he starts ...'

'That's alright, Nancy, as much as I'd like to drink to that, I couldn't bring myself to wish *anybody* harm. How about ... to your marriage and a smashing honeymoon!'

'That's more like it ... cheers!' she squeaked as she lifted her bubbly in a toast, prompting a group sip and another round of burying their noses in effervescence.

'So, you're going to isolation-tank it on your honeymoon?' Roblaw asked with a grin.

'Marriage tanks. It's the latest in self deprivation, American style,' Nancy touted, with a straight face.

Frank shook his head. 'Our act's mainstay is impersonations, so I can't fathom why she wants to impersonate dying! I just hope it doesn't give me diaper rash.'

'So, you'll drive the car to Florida, to break her in,' Roblaw egged.

'You bet your life!' he said, as they both nodded with satisfaction over the thought.

'Excellent.'

'Later tonight, when we're free of this dive, we'll be freewheeling our way out of town *in our brand new car*!' he shouted, emulating a game-show prize announcer. 'Honey, cancel our flight, and tell 'em they can keep their mock chicken in-flight meal!'

'Sounds like a dream come true,' replied Roblaw, 'give her five-hundred miles, y'know—to break her in, then *open her up*! It's a sports car, and it needs to be pushed a little.'

'Jeremy,' Nancy interjected sincerely, 'I feel *so bad* for your daughter. I *hate* wife-beaters, though, so I don't feel so bad for what we did for you. We're *helping* her—'

'It was best for all concerned,' added Frank, in a serious tone.

'Frank, for all that is good and holy, *you're so right*,' replied Roblaw.

Nancy took a sip from her champagne glass, then reached for something in her bag. She pulled out a sealed letter, and handed it to Roblaw, who looked at the letter with curiosity. 'I'd feel better if you gave her this letter, say in six months, when she gets over it.'

'Sure thing.'

'Y'know, she'll realize we did it—'

'*For the money*!' Frank blurted with an abrupt laugh, then raised his hands in a defensive posture reacting to Nancy's frown.

'Save your flip innuendo for the stage.'

'Isn't he that black Mexican comedian?' Frank retorted,

and smiled at Roblaw, who didn't make the connection, but smiled back anyhow.

'Frank's making light, Jeremy—and I think the bubbly's making *him* light-headed, but we did it for the benefit of all. Is she seeking counselling?'

'Yes. Yes, she is, thank you. I think she'll make a full mental and physical recovery, thanks to *you* two ... well, thanks *so much* again,' he blurted as he stood and shook their hands. 'Happy motoring!'

'Thank *you*, Jeremy. What's your last name? We'll look you up sometime ... if you don't mind—for a drink, when we're in town again?'

'Why of course!'

'*Wyeofckoarse* ... that's the most peculiar last name I ever ... is it Slavic?' Frank asked.

Roblaw smiled. 'Walsworthe,' he replied.

'Walsworthe ... good, I'll write that down,' she said, 'I guess it was lucky for both of us to have met—and mutually beneficial.'

'It's been a pleasure,' Roblaw replied, 'oh,—for now this is *strictly confidential*, right? The job and the car and all that ... you kept hush-hush about it like I asked?'

'Our word of honour—no worries, Jeremy,' she stressed, looking from him to Frank, and in a coordinated gesture, the two of them zipped their mouths closed.

'Good. Oh, here's the keys for the car—it's been plated and insured by an assistant of mine named Crawford. The documentation's in the glove compartment. You can officially switch it over to your name when you get back, I guess. That'd be most convenient for you, right?'

Frank made a motion which simulated him un-zipping his mouth. 'Still in your name—we won't have to worry about parking tickets then,' he wise-cracked, prompting Nancy to make a fist which she waved at him jokingly.

'Goodbye, and best of luck,' Roblaw offered, reaching for the door handle.

'Thanks so much, Jeremy—bye!'

'Take care,' Frank added, ''bye.'

Roblaw walked through the door, and headed for a side exit from the club. 'Good bye!' he said to himself out loud, as he pushed his way through the exit door to outside.

Making his way upwards along the empty street to where his Rolls was parked, he pulled out a cigar and lit it. Lifting the letter that Nancy had given him for his daughter Louise, he lit it on fire with his lighter, holding it until it was necessary to drop it into the curb, where he watched it burn away to ashes. Using his foot, he brushed the charred remains through a nearby sewer grating. Satisfied with the meeting, but dissatisfied with the aftertaste of the cheap house champagne, he spat into the gutter and fished his car keys out of his pocket.

§

Roblaw pulled the Rolls into his driveway. He noticed another car parked up near the garage as his headlights swept over it. Coming to a stop and getting out, he walked over to the visiting car, looked at the licence plate and then peered into the interior through the passenger window. It was a tidy, modest car. He garnered one thing from his perusal—it was a woman's car, and her birthday was in March. Making his way over the cobblestoned drive, he entered the front door of his house.

He moved through the resplendent main foyer. The maid emerged from the living room area and greeted him. She was an unusually good looking woman in her forties and dressed in a black uniform. 'Good evening Mr Roblaw, would you care for some dinner, sir?' she said with a French-Canadian accent and a subtle glint in her eye. She took his coat from him and proceeded to take it to the hall closet.

'Lola, whose car is that in the drive?' he asked, as she returned to the foyer to attend him. He loosened his tie, and looked in a gilded mirror on the wall.

'A friend of your daughters, sir.'

'Do you know her name?' he enquired, looking at the maid through the reflection.

'I wasn't introduced, but I've a vague recollection of her ... her name escapes me,' she replied, searching out his face, and obediently waiting for further instructions or to be dismissed.

'Where's Mrs Roblaw?'

'She has retired early, sir.'

'My daughter's upstairs then, with her friend?'

'The east-wing, in her ... room, sir,' she replied, careful not to say *former*, or *old*, knowing that Roblaw had her dust and change the sheets regularly on Louise's bed, as though she had never left the house. He was *funny* that way, and in other ways as well—but, to Lola, the extra money was very useful, for servicing his *other ways*.

'I'd like to see you in my office,' he said, undoing his tie, and pulling it knot-free through the collar of his shirt. 'I feel like unwinding. After that, you're dismissed for the evening.'

She pursed her lips, and raised an eyebrow. It was usual for her to lead, when he was in these moods, but she waited for the customary clearing of the throat which was his cue for her to begin the fantasy routine.

He looked her up and down, and she waited. He finally cleared his throat, and she instigated the pre-ordained sequence with a stern face. 'Come with me you dirty bastard, I've got a little score to settle,' she whispered with scorn, as she led the way, with him obediently following.

twenty-three

DEEP IN THE MINE, Eamonn and a score of trogs toiled at the massive wall of rubble. It was slow painstaking work, and their faces were blackened and oily from the sweat and dust which was heavy in the air. There was a heavy silence hanging in the musty atmosphere. Save for the grunts of those labouring away at the wall, only an occasional moan or sickly cough abbreviated the dense blanket of despair which was beginning to clot their ambition.

The overwhelming sense of hopelessness ate away at their spirits twice as fast as any fragmented headway that they appeared to achieve. A few stout hearted men and women in league with Eamonn's faith, fed on the glimmer of hope for the energy to continue the quest. The oppressiveness of the dim cavern was enough to make a grown person weep.

The fading battery operated cap-lamps seemed to be diminishing rapidly. No one talked about their declining reserve of rationed batteries, which would eventually leave them in total darkness. Eamonn feared facing that moment, cringing at the thought.

Shaking the morbid images from his mind, he grasped at the steel pry bar he'd acquired. He steadfastly leaned on the tool, assisting two others who worked at pulling away a large piece of concrete. A large slab blocked their access to some more manageable looking material behind it. With desperately held breath and bulging eyes, the group cleaved the concrete scab from the wall, separating the single most obtrusive hindrance to what they saw as perhaps the weak link in the stubborn mound. Allowing the large slab to crash to the rock floor, they took a quick breather and started in on the rubble behind.

§

Over seventy miles west of Kabloona, sitting on the ice collar just off the shoreline of Admiralty Inlet, Gaar tapped Max's cheek, attempting to wake him up. Max had fainted before Gaar managed to break the knot in the rope. Gaar knelt over Max, next to the slushy hole in the ice which had swallowed McGregor.

'*Max*!' Gaar shouted. He was tired of patting his cheek, and waiting for him to come around.

Leaning over, he slipped his hand into the freezing water and began to impatiently splash water into Max's face. After a few face-fulls, Max began to react.

'Huh ... whaaa?—Alright, already!' Max stammered, as he deliriously came-to with a scowl and a shiver. In a burst of anxiety, his face dropped, sitting bolt upright and taking a firm hold of Gaar. He gaped around with a distressed look on his face until he became woozy for a moment, on the brink of almost fainting again.

'Welcome back,' Gaar said, nodding with a grin. 'I hope you're up for a walk.'

twenty-four

LOUISE SAT ON the corner of her familiar old bed, in her old room, in the expansive Roblaw mansion which boasted no less than twenty-four spacious rooms. Beside her sat her confidante Patricia, who was a friend of many years and an acquaintance of Gaar's from their university days.

Pat held her arm around Louise and comforted her, balancing what was a second box of tissues on her lap. It was apparent from the growing pile of tissues on the bed, and the half-full litter basket, that she had loosened her long-standing ecological concerns. By the looks of the emotional tirade, an unsuspecting tree would perish under such conditions supplying her with soft comfort, given her frequent wiping and blowing.

Pat borrowed one tissue to wipe her eye glasses with, then folded the tissue and held it in her hand.

Louise stood up from the bed, and paced around the

large, expensively furnished room. It was outfitted with a French colonial ensemble suite, decorated to the hilt with attention to exquisite detail in a finely understated way. She swung back and tugged another tissue from the box which Pat held out for her on cue.

'I still can't believe it!' Louise sobbed angrily, 'I drove him away—I must have been a horrible wife!'

'Louise don't—'

'Maybe if I had a *real* career, like you ...'

'If you want to call being a graduate student a career,' Pat replied with a smile, running her hand through her short blond hair.

'If I'd have stayed in school and done my masters, and gone on the way you have—but I didn't have the foresight!'

'If you did, you'd be wearing glasses like me, and faced with the dire job prospects. Does that hind-sight make you feel any better? School is like a shield for me, I get paid for my graduate research, and now I'm faced with the dilemma of a job prospect in Moose Jaw, and my supervisor wants to give me the boot—but I don't want to leave Ottawa! And Peter just can't up and leave!' Pat blurted, waving her arms up in the air in frustration.

Louise wiped her eyes and nose, and looked earnestly at Pat. 'They have science and physical chemistry stuff happening in *Moose Jaw*?'

'Maybe they've got a moose in a vacuum chamber that's in dire need of spectroscopy!' she said to Louise with a deadpan look, which incited Louise to laugh. She sat back down on the bed beside Pat and hugged her.

In a sudden flash flood of despair, Louise began to cry on Pat's shoulder. 'He wants me to abort our child!' she sobbed, which gave into rage, spurring her to catapult herself from the bed. She lashed out into the air with her fists clenched and stuffed with tissues. 'Damn him! Goddammit, *I will*! I want nothing to remind me of him!'

'The child is innocent ... *Louise*,' Pat replied, trying to simmer her down and guide her to rational thinking.

'I've got to start all over again. *Square one*!' Louise announced with a sob of self pity and a hint of ambition. 'I'm not getting any younger! *But*,' she continued with a mercenary edge, '*as a rich bitch*, I've got the deodorant that counts—honey enough for most, right?'

'You're *gorgeous*, Louise—and a wonderful person! Any decent man would see that if you were dressed in *rags*.' Pat got up from the edge of the bed and hugged her.

After a moment, Louise broke the comforting hug, holding Pat by the arms as they came apart. 'Do *you* think I still harbor *any* love for the bastard? Well, I *don't*, and this will *prove* it.'

'Time can heal a lot of things—what do you mean *this will prove it*?'

'That lily-livered sonofabitch has got me *crazy*!'

'Exactly, so you shouldn't do anything rash or make snap decisions.'

'You think I'm acting in haste.'

'Don't do it.'

'How can I *not* do it?!' Louise said, shaking off Pat's grip with annoyance, and turning her back to her. 'I've got to get him out of my head—and *out of my body*!'

Pat moved up close to Louise and hugged her from behind. Louise lifted her hands to her face and dropped her head into her palms, crying.

Pat held her shaking friend tightly, rocking her with a gentle sway. 'Louise, please believe me, *lots* of men would accept your child.'

Louise broke away from Pat's cuddle, revolving from her stance and collapsing into a sitting position on the bed. 'Accept my child?' she said weepily. Pat joined her on the bed and looked intently into her welled-up eyes.

'How can *I* accept it?' Louise retorted. 'How? He's

pushed me over the edge. I'm not perfect, and I'm partially to blame, but there's nothing to hide behind in a marriage! He's left me defenseless. I've been made a fool of, and the *shame* of single motherhood will follow me like a curse in anything I do! I'll never have a moments peace with this— *never*! Tomorrow.'

'What're you saying? Louise? It's too soon!' Pat said, standing up, and now finding *herself* pacing up and down. 'He may come crawling back, and you might have a change of heart!'

'I'll never have him back!' she scowled, 'and all the more reason to act now! I have an appointment early tomorrow morning.'

'What?'

'A special arrangement. Six-thirty AM.'

'Why are you acting on impulse like this? Did you talk it over with your mom?'

'No.'

'Why not?'

'Because, that's why.'

'That's no answer.'

Louise lowered her head. 'Come with me?'

'Louise—'

'Come with me to the clinic tomorrow, please. *Please*?'

Pat paced another few steps before sitting down beside her. Louise had anticipation written all over her face.

'Alright. I'll go with you,' she replied. Louise burst forward with a thankful hug. 'Let's go to my place, I've got a great comfy bed for you. You can sleep on it and we'll see how you feel in the morning, alright?'

'Thank you, thank you, *thank you*,' Louise gushed with a sad smile, sniffling back the tears. Pat reached for the box and offered her another tissue.

'It'll be nice to have you stay with me. Peter's work trips always leave me lonely and a bit scared. It'll be like old times, huh? A little pillow talk—a good stiff drink!' Pat said, as Louise allowed her mind to wander away and lull into a peculiar sense of security. 'Peter's got some great brandy hidden away for special occasions, and I think I need a good belt right about now. Peter won't mind if I crack it open.'

'I hope he chokes on his own tongue!' Louise blurted out, like an aftershock to the spent eruption. Pat was taken by surprise, and leaned away from Louise slightly dazed. 'Not Peter! *Gaar*,' she stammered apologetically.

'You had me for a second,' Pat replied, 'listen, I know you don't want to go back to your place right now, so I can loan you anything you need for tonight, and I'll fetch some stuff for you in the morning. Is that okay?'

Louise nodded her approval. 'I can't drink alcohol or eat anything though,' Louise warned Pat, 'until after the procedure.'

'Yes ... of course you can't—I don't know why I suggested it,' Pat replied.

'I hope he burns in hell.'

twenty-five

GAAR AND MAX TRAIPSED along the waters edge of the vast inlet, which hosted many fjord-like divots from the main icy waterway. It was rough going, being bound together. Gaar held the keys for their handcuffs but kept that fact from Max who was under the belief that the keys had been knocked into the water at the skirmish. Gaar was in no condition to plead with Max, and had to ensure their arrival at Nanisivik *together*.

A light snow was falling. They ascended the side of a hill. Gaar could see down into the tiny little bay below which was faint in the twilight. It was made twice as dim by the shadows of the high rocky slopes which walled it. It was obvious to Gaar that they would have to move much further inland to avoid all the miles they would be faced with if they were to trace the landmass at water's edge. It weaved in and out like the teeth of a saw blade.

Their pace was slow, and their desperate trudging got slower by the mile. The cold, their hunger, and the task of covering great empty distances on tired feet, was a crushing challenge.

They had tried the radio earlier, and gotten nowhere with their attempts to transmit or receive. Something was wrong with it, although a cursory inspection of it revealed nothing. Gaar carried the heavy unit anyway, as a matter of course in the event that the shaking of the journey might jostle it back to order. He was never technically minded, and it seemed a longshot, but it held what was perhaps the only chance they'd have.

'What's that?' Max asked as he looked down towards the tiny bay.

Gaar was abruptly halted by Max's full stop. He peered down the hill, and saw nothing. 'Where?'

'Down there,' Max reiterated, as he uselessly pointed down into the terrain. 'It's a hut!'

Gaar intently stared down to find this *hut* of Max's. Suddenly, his eyes fixed on the object, which indeed appeared to be some kind of shack just up off the shore on a gently graded embankment.

After the long haul down the slope, the two neared the abandoned-looking shack, and sniffed around as they ventured towards the most rewarding sight a cold, tired and virtually lost traveller in the middle of nowhere could imagine—the inviting secrets of an actual structure with a wooden door!

'This must've been a whaling station,' Gaar observed, looking around at small gatherings of long bones which littered the vicinity, jutting out from beneath blankets of snow.

'What's that?' Max said, turning his head to a small ancient-looking and weathered wooden contraption which sat alone just outside the large shack.

'That's a trap for polar bears—they'd set a cocked rifle in it, and when the bear'd take the bait, *blam*! It was cruel; when they'd have meat and blubber all around the place, the bears would scavenge, and this way, they'd keep away the unwelcome guests.'

'Probably skinned them for their hides, as well,' added Max, 'Mmmm, all this talk of meat and blubber—I'm *starving*!'

'Yeah,' Gaar replied, as they entered the shack with a convincing shove on the door.

They slowly walked into the old rickety shack which seemed at least seventy years old. A small breeze wafted through the cracks and fissures between the weathered planks of wood. It seemed almost colder inside than out. Max set the satchel which he carried from the altercation with McGregor, onto a shelf of sorts. He began to root through the satchel for the candle he'd discovered earlier in his futile search for food.

'Damn! The other supplies McGregor went down with, were probably food and a proper lamp,' Max complained, as he drew the candle from the bag and clumsily broke it by catching it on a fold in the satchel. 'It's not my day, today.'

'I hope there'll be a day that is,' Gaar responded, setting the radio down on a counter which was adjacent to the shelf. 'Is there a light for that candle in there?'

'Yup, ... here it is,' Max replied, taking a small insulated bag out and producing a lighter from it. Max sparked the lighter into action and began to try and melt a fluid wax base for the candle to sit on next to the satchel.

'I need the candle here, so we can inspect the radio,' Gaar said, indicating a spot on the counter beside the radio. 'Seeing as the candle's broken, why don't you cut it and we'll have two?'

'I suppose you want the tapered part?'

'Yes, I want the proper-topped part—Max, I'm in no mood, *please*,' Gaar replied, separating the radio from its insulated sheathing and proceeding to remove the covering panel from it. Max cut the broken candle with the machete, and fiddled with it. He set the candle up as a work light, so that Gaar could tinker with the guts of the radio.

After great difficulty and with only one hand at his disposal, Max had set up the second candle. He looked around the meagre shack, casing the sparse interior for lack of anything better to do. He spotted an old crate and a miniature barrel in a corner.

'Gaar, there's a couple of seats for us in the corner—my dogs are killing me. Whaddya say, can you hold the work for a second?'

Gaar tore himself from the radio and they moved to the far corner of the shack to retrieve the items. They both squinted at a faded map which was hand drawn on the panels of a wall. A circle with an "X" indicated the old whaling station which they occupied.

'Look, ... we're *here*,' Gaar said, pointing to the mark, 'and near the top of this large peninsula is Nanisivik,' he indicated, pointing out to Max, the large "N".

'That's a *distance*,' Max replied, with a heavy sigh.

'Here's about where my father's store is, here,' Gaar said, touching the approximate area with his finger which was damp with grease, having mucked around with the interior moving parts of the radio. Gaar looked back towards the radio and instigated the retrieval of their "seats", in order to get back to business. 'We should try and cut those reflective stripes off your parka—know what I mean?'

On their way back over to the counter, Gaar noticed a board nailed above the doorway. It had a scrawled inscription which gave the name "Itoqek" and bore the numerical latitude and longitude "72°02'N, 85°05'W".

'I know our position—there you go!' Gaar said, flinching his head up at the board as they passed it.

Max passed a glance as they made their way to the work station. 'Coordinates of the ghost shack,' Max uttered, as they sat down. 'Think the fall damaged it?'

'Don't know.'

'Too bad we couldn't eat it.'

'If it doesn't work, we may have to,' Gaar replied.

'Long as it's not raw.'

'Japanese radios are meant to be eaten raw,' Gaar mumbled, peering into the guts of the radio. 'Hang on a second ...' he said, having detected the possible reason for the radio's demise.

'What is it? Let's see?'

'Here's a dangling wire. Eureka!'

'*Eureka* is for discovery—this is more like a *duh*!' Max replied, with relief. 'Think McGregor disconnected it?'

'Possibly. What's the emergency channel?' Gaar said to himself, as he powered up the radio and began twisting the shortwave dial. He gripped the handset and keyed the button to transmit. 'Hello! Mayday!'

Max leaned forward with a concerned look on his face. 'Wait!' he warned, 'what about what McGregor said about Jag's trackers hearing your transmission?'

'Max, if we don't risk it—we're dead.'

'Well, what are you waiting for ... find help!'

'Any boats out there? Mayday! Anyone hear me? SOS ... hello, anybody?'

The Akwanaque, a large wooden fishing trawler refurbished with steel plates on its hull to help it break through ice, pushed its way through the slushy ice plates of Admiralty Inlet. The converted whaling vessel was moving north to dock at Adams Sound for repairs through the long winter freeze ahead.

On the bridge, the elderly captain of the old trawler, Moses Nahanequatok, picked up the radio handset at hearing Gaar's voice. Jacob, his helmsman, looked quizzically at hearing the unorthodox transmission. Moses keyed his handset and placed it to his mouth.

'This is Captain Nahanequatok, aboard the Akwanaque. We read you. What are your coordinates? Over. Come in, Mayday. Relay your coordinates—over,' he announced, lifting his eyes to Jacob, who placed a notated map of the region on the incline of the instrument panel on front of them. As Gaar's thin radio voice relayed the coordinates of Itoqek inlet, Jacob quickly pinpointed the position and poked at the map.

Cross referencing their position with Gaar's, Jacob gauged an accurate protracter measurement. 'Twenty point-five,' he said to Moses.

'Copy, Itoqek. We are approximately twenty nautical miles from your position. Do you require medical attention? Over,' he enquired, as Gaar affirmed that need. 'Copy that. We will rendezvous with you ETA, two hours. Copy? Over.'

Gaar replied with his understanding of the rendezvous and the time, and Moses hung up his handset. He picked up some binoculars and looked out into the slushy path ahead in the vast inlet. Jacob entered the occurrence into the log book.

Just looking out on the silence of the twilight and the light snow, offered Moses a respite from the brightly lit cabin bridge and the rumblings of the engine which vibrated throughout the vessel. 'So what do you think, Jacob?' he said, rotating in a slow small arc with the binoculars pressed against his eyes.

'Well, you know *me*, Moses—if it has wings, it's a bird; fins—it's a fish, but, feet ..., there's no telling,' Jacob replied.

'Have you been into Sammy's cooking sherry again?'

'No, I was trying to be a poet.'

'But it didn't rhyme.'

The Akwanaque reverberated with the battering of a thick ice patch. Jacob angled his head sideways, smiling at Moses at the timely cue.

'Nice *ice*?' Saul quipped.

§

Gaar had laid his head onto his folded arms while propped forward in an exhausted heap on the wretched old counter. Max emulated his posture, but was forced to break the pose when Gaar sat back and upright, reacting to the bullet wound in his shoulder.

'What's the matter?' Max asked, 'you're sweating like a pig, and your eyes ... they're *weird*—you okay?'

'It's nothing. Pass me the machete.'

'*Why?*'

'Just hand it to me—I'm not going to decapitate you, don't worry.'

With concern rife on his face, Max handed Gaar the machete. Gaar appeared more than tattered from the long arduous hike, and Max suspected him to be coming down with something.

'That hole in your coat—let me have a look underneath,' Max enquired direly.

'It's nothing. I don't want it to turn into a trend, but I think there'll be more *holes* to go before I sleep ... now turn around.'

'Why?'

'Turn around, so I can remove the reflective stripes from your coat.'

'Oh,' Max said, turning his back to Gaar.

Gaar began to sever the stitching at the tops of the luminous prison stripes. Taking hold of a peeled back section,

Gaar braced himself, then with a sudden ripping tug, tore off a long strip down his back. 'Sit still.'

'That felt good—do you do parties?'

'Yeah, *surprise parties*, and you know who I want to throw one for,' Gaar replied, taking hold of a second luminous strip he had broken the threads from.

'I'm glad you didn't give our names over the radio but, I'm ... I'm worried—*scared shitless* actually, for our necks!'

Gaar intently peeled another strip from Max's coat. 'You work on the front, while I'm doing this side.'

'How much?'

'How much, *what*?'

'How much would it take? I mean, what's your price, to go along with me and help get us down to Canada?'

'*No.*'

'I know you're not a bounty hunter or a money-grubber, but I can make it worth your while to help get me to Ontario—right now, *outta here!*'

'No. There's no key for these cuffs, so there's no way but *my* way.'

'I'm good for it—no *bullshit!*'

'There's no discussion,' Gaar mumbled, as he vigorously shred another reflective stripe from his prison issue.

Max sulked and mindlessly tugged at the stripes on the front of his parka. 'I was coming up for early parole ... and now I'm faced with *early retirement*! I'm too young to die! Being a late bloomer *sucks*—and your attitude sucks! You'd see me die to make your point! If I were a violent man ...'

Max's complaining struck close to home, and Gaar was at once hurt and guilt-ridden in his domestic recollections, but took a deep breath and veered his emotions off into an annoyed but rational frame of mind. 'You'd what? Do to me what Brunhilde tried to do to you? Free yourself?' he huffed, ripping the last stripe down his back, 'that's what I'm going to do for you, so stop with the violins. You're coming with me, and I'm going to get you off.'

Max turned to Gaar, detecting the completion of his companion's task, and revealed that he had only partially separated the stripes from the front of his coat. 'No offence Gaar—nothing personal to you or these *familiars* you've mentioned, but do you really think you stand a ghost of a chance against that psycho and his posse? I mean, he's a shaman with a corpse strapped to his back, and everyone's in *awe* of this *voodoo* king!'

'This isn't about magic, it's about nature,' Gaar drowsily replied, 'gotta get it all off, Max.' Gaar pointed at the unfinished work on the front of his parka. 'Don't worry, Max, we're gonna make it.'

Max rubbed his face, and felt the annoying bumps on his head, from the pistol whippings. 'If we do, promise me one thing.'

'I'll do my best.'

'No, I need you to *promise* me.'

'Alright, *I promise*. What is it?'

'Promise you won't bring up that little goo-goo fainting thing—y'know, *back there*.'

'My lips are sealed. You've been through a lot, what with news of your brother—'

'My brother, my poor brother—*it's all my fault*! I put him in danger!'

'Indirectly,' Gaar assured him, 'I mean, who would have figured?'

'Roblaw! That *animal*! I'll *kill* him when I see him!'

'Get in line. Was Schlomo married?' Gaar asked lethargically.

'Divorced,' he whispered.

'Oh,' Gaar replied, blinking slowly as both candles flickered with a breeze which swept through the shack.

'The funeral arrangements! Ahh,' Max whined, as Gaar raised his hand and gently patted the air.

'Not so fast, I'm not going anywhere ...'

'Not *you*, but you're not looking so good come to think of it. We should break the chain somehow ... I mean, what's the boat crew gonna say if they see us handcuffed? Gaar?' Max felt Gaar's forehead, and took hold of his parka lest he fall over. He was sweating profusely now, and Max feared the worst.

'Gaar, don't leave me now. Let me see your shoulder,' he said, undoing Gaar's parka against his feeble unwillingness to cooperate.

'I'm fine,' he stammered with a sleepy, half breath.

Max pulled Gaar's parka back to reveal a blood soaked shirt. '*Oi* ...' Max uttered, sucking his breath and carefully undoing his shirt. With a worried grimace, he tenderly peeled back the moist material surrounding the wound and reeled back when he saw the bullet wound.

'*Shit*! That's serious! Looks infected ... *yup*,' Max sighed, letting out an abrupt breath. 'You need a doctor—I hope we can get you to one on time. If I built a fire out of this scrap wood and heated the machete in it, I could cauterize the wound—if I burn the shack down, who gives a hoot, huh?'

'Do it,' Gaar mumbled, licking his lips slowly.

After a tiring one-handed quest, Max had gathered and splintered enough old wood mostly by bracing pieces against the counter and using his foot to smash them up for the fire. He had found an old weathered journal, from which he'd torn pages from to use as a starter for the kindling. Within a short while, the blade had heated up to a dull red. The fire had smoked up the shack somewhat, but with the structure riddled with holes and cracks, there was some ventilation.

Max sat on the floor with Gaar, and held his arm around him. 'From what I'm told,' Gaar whispered slowly, 'my mother survived for six days with a gunshot wound in her side—she was left for dead ...'

Max looked comfortingly at Gaar. 'Don't worry, I'll make sure she see's you.'

'I hope not, doctor Max,' he mumbled, 'she died on the journey to hospital.'

'I'm sorry,' Max offered apologetically, '*six days*, without treatment ... was she involved in a war?'

'Kinda ... she was doing her research in the Amazon ... ambushed by poachers,' he said feebly, shaking his head, '... y'know—'

Max looked over at the fire, clearing his throat from the smoke. The tip of the machete blade was red hot. He gulped and began to reach for the blade's grip. Pulling his hand back in reluctance, he teetered in self doubt and cowardice. He wasn't good with his left hand and was concerned he might screw up the aim or something. Many times he'd read about this kind of thing in books, and seen it portrayed in the movies, but could he do it? It could mean Gaar's life, and putting off the inevitable wasn't doing anybody any good.

Gaar reached out and put his hand on Max's suspended and shaking hand. He sucked on his lips and molded his words slowly and with conviction.

'Get me something to bite down on—and get on with it!' Gaar insisted, as Max quickly reached into the satchel and withdrew some spare gloves. He looked at them oddly, not knowing what exactly would suit best.

Gaar tapped him on the arm. 'A piece of that ... bone,' he said, indicating a small array of tiny whale bones which lay strewn on the floor. 'If I pass out, don't panic—I'm in good hands,' Gaar squeaked, with little air behind his voice.

Max stretched himself over, and selected a six inch piece of bone which was reasonably flat and retrieved it for Gaar. He placed it in his mouth, and Gaar firmly bit down. Gaar mumbled, laying flat down on his back to the floor. Max placed the satchel under Gaar's head as a pillow, took a deep breath, and grasped the handle of the machete, lifting the glowing blade from the fire.

Following the glow with his eyes, Max adjusted himself at Gaar's side and slowly lowered the near-molten steel towards Gaar's wound. Max's eyes bulged, and his lips quivered, then he placed the tip exactingly down on the area, and closed his eyes tight for a second as Gaar's flesh was seared.

Max was terrified when Gaar's body jerked upwards against his right arm which held him down. The stink of the singed flesh was sickening to him. After what seemed an eternity of horror, Gaar's muffled shriek finally dwindled down to nothing.

Max opened his eyes, pulling away the cauterizing blade and gazing aghast at what he'd done. Gaar appeared dead. Max quivered in confused silence, not knowing whether he'd held the blade down too long and perhaps killed the man.

He shoved the blade through a low crack in the wall to imbed it into the icy snow, causing it to steam away. Taking Gaar's wrist, he felt for a pulse, and was thrilled to find one. He covered Gaar up and sat back to reflect, allowing Gaar to rest a while.

Emotionally and physically drained, Max coughed at the smoke which had diffused somewhat, yet was evenly dispersed in the shack and weighed heavy in the air. Although the embers of the fire were warm beside him, he shivered and was struck with a sense that the shack was haunted. His stomach's grumblings distracted him momentarily, but he was immediately enveloped in an eerie fear of his surroundings, as the wind seemed to whistle through the shack, and the crackling of the embers accentuated the isolation he felt.

He suddenly became rigid with terror, as he detected movement outside the shack. He remained perfectly still, and only his eyes rolled around seeking out the unwelcome disturbance. He thought he could hear something breathing, and he looked down at Gaar to match the rise and fall of his midsection against the rhythm of what he was sure he was hearing. They didn't coincide. It was far too early for the boat to have arrived. He figured that any friendly approach would have been preceded with hailing shouts and a knock at the door.

Turning his head slowly, he prepared to reach back for the machete in self defense. As his arm moved behind him and his hand touched the planks of the wall, he felt downwards for the blade. With his hand wriggling to grasp at the weapon, his head caught up to his hand. Looking back, he was horrified to see the machete was gone from where he'd left it. Pulling his hand back as though it were almost eaten, he adopted a ruse of nonchalance. He didn't want to alert the stalker of his awareness of the impending defense. He looked around the floor for something he might use in the event of a surprise attack. He thought it could be a hungry polar bear scrounging around the perimeter of the shack, or maybe some wolves, or even Jag and his henchmen. What ever it was, he would put up a fight to kill it before it killed him.

A sharp piece of wood was all he could find. He clenched it tight within his grasp. The candles flickered in the wake of a small draft which swept through, putting him on edge, and setting him ready for an assault. He looked down at Gaar, who still lay unconscious, virtually rendering his right hand useless with the cuffs which tethered them. The peculiar sounds seemed to emanate from all sides of the shack, and he braced himself.

'*Aaargh!*' Max shrieked, caught off-guard as Gaar awoke, yanking at their bridled connection. Gaar mumbled, then deliriously fell back to sleep after rustling in his position.

Max's heart thumped, filling his ears with the throbbing reaction to his startled fear. He took a deep breath —as deep as he could manage, to scale down his laboured breathing. He became still, to listen for the real threat which could burst forth any second. With a keen ear he listened warily— as best he could with his hearing being compromised by the rapid pulsing from his racing heart. Even with that hindrance, he could no longer detect movement or sound beyond the insides of the tiny shack.

The pulsing in his ears diminished. Realizing his left arm ached with stiffness, he slowly dropped his stabbing posture, but kept the pointed wooden stick in his hand in case he was ambushed into action.

After staring mesmerized at the candle for some time and having counted twenty drips of wax as they melted down the shaft, he reckoned he'd only been alerted to a couple of creaks from the fragile hut, and resolved that the threat had gone—for now.

twenty-six

GAAR'S FATHER LEANED back on a counter and smiled mischievously. He looked over the congregation of men, women and children from Kiqaloq who had gathered in his supply store to hear some tales. The oil lamps around the store flickered and imparted an air of homespun comfort to the occasion. As old Abram raised his head to begin, the room gradually fell silent and he began his tale.

'*Bear* came across the carcass of a large seal which had been recklessly killed by a wasteful hunter, who couldn't carry the quarry on his already over-burdened sled. About that time, *Wolf* came upon the scene and looked at the kill, then licked his lips. As Bear was leaving, he noticed Wolf sniffing around the kill. Bear warned Wolf not to eat the meat of the wasted kill. Wolf replied "I am hungry to death and I'll have my fill of this offering." Bear warned him off, saying "the soul of this seal will be quite unpleasant to digest. Your belly shall rumble beyond what your small body will tolerate. If you eat of this carcass, you will surely defecate uncontrollably. Heed me," Bear cautioned him as he walked away. Wolf ate the wasted kill.'

Abram scanned the room and raised his eyebrows. Some of the children giggled and put their hands over their mouths in sincere concern, eagerly awaiting the inevitable outcome of the fable.

'Wolf said to himself,' he continued, with an animated wave of his arms and a spry intonation in his voice, '"I'm happy that that foolish bear went away—now I shall have every last morsel to myself!" Shortly after his greedily swallowed meal, Wolf began to break wind. Wolf snorted, "Hmmm. Even if I do break a little wind, I'm still much more clever than that bear who went-off hungry. I'm the one with a belly full." Very soon, Wolf began to uncontrollably break wind. The force of his farts began to propel him forward with his tail between his legs. His belly began to ache, and he broke wind again and was sent flying in the air. Wolf held onto a nearby shack, but was thrust high into the air, taking the hut with him. He frantically burrowed under a village, thinking the weight of of the houses and ice would hold him down. Suddenly, a tremendous explosion from Wolf's bowels sent the whole village flying. The community cursed Wolf. Wolf then began to shit himself to such an extent, that he had to try very hard to climb above his mess just to breathe. Soon he was swallowed up in his own shit and drowned.'

His audience nodded their heads and the children recounted parts of the story to each other with giggles, dishing out passionate critiques of the characters in the story between themselves. Some of the parents who sat on the wood floor with their children, hugged them tightly, listening enthusiastically as Abram began another. 'On the day when the sun came up for one hour ...'

twenty-seven

THE GANGLY ICE-MAN jiggled from the vibrations of the overland chase on the snowmobiles. The three machines darted along the tracks which Girly laid in her frightening escape from Brunhilde and the sled dogs. The beams from their headlights shook as they sped towards the churned up confrontation site where Brunhilde was mauled and invariably consumed.

Finding a polar bear smack-dab in the midst of the bone spattered patch, they cautiously slowed up and beeped the horns of their vehicles. The bear abandoned its futzing about with the picked-dry bones, and lumbered off. When it appeared safe to inspect the site, the men left their snowmobiles and took their rifles from across their backs. They looked around in confusion.

Jag sniffed at the air, and cast his eyes down at the snow covered tracks of both the dog-sled rails, snowmobile tracks and an array of foot prints. It was a confounding scene with all the various bits of tell-tale information impressed into the snowy ground.

Deciphering the confusing array of prints was difficult, but Jag could see one thing plainly. The northward tracks confirmed the exodus towards Itoqek, as was in keeping with Gaar's transmission over the radio which was intercepted.

'I'm certain that at least one of the fugitives is with Gaar at Itoqek Inlet,' he stated loudly, kicking a femur bone out of his way as he walked towards his gathering men. 'You three go on. Forget about the tracks, now. Get to Itoqek overland, there,' he said, lifting his arm and pointing north-easterly, 'and I shall follow the shoreline trail.'

Triq leapt on his idling snowmobile, and the other two did likewise.

'But ... how's Jag—?' Agaluq enquired, seeing Jag had no mode of transportation.

Triq sat forward on his seat. 'For the uninitiated, this may be hard to accept. I'll explain when we get there—*let's go!*' he shouted, as the three zipped off into the twilight after one another.

Jag stood at the site and looked up into the twilight sky. He adjusted the ice-man which was secured on his back, flipping the outward facing corpse inwards now, so that the mummy and he looked in the same direction. The Aurora Borealis swayed in the sky and he stared upwards, spellbound. He chanted an eerie refrain for a few moments and then let out a bloodthirsty howl.

His eyes went red in his diabolic metamorphosis. He now had two ugly heads with black matted fur and his body was the size of a Shetland pony. With the malevolent transmutation complete, he held his elongated heads low to the ground and bore his frothing fangs with the unwelcome gaze of merciless predator. The ice-man had amalgamated with Jag, and with this, the necromancer of the arctic was incarnate in the immense black wolf.

He trotted onwards, then pounced on a tibia bone from Brunhilde's leg, which had traces of flesh on it. In a frenzy, Jag tore at it and ravenously shaved the remaining flesh from the bone, snarling demonically with one head, but only sniffing with the other. He then rubbed his body all over it, urinated on it, then set out in a dash to follow the shoreline to Itoqek Inlet. He moved with the speed of a cheetah, turning up the snow with his huge paws as he made off into the dusk landscape.

twenty-eight

ON THE AKWANAQUE trawler, a deckhand turned his head swiftly in the direction of a large "thud" which came from the stern of the boat. He looked up to the bridge where he saw Moses and Jacob look at each other in surprise. They emerged from the doorway to investigate the peculiar noise stemming from the aft of their vessel.

'What the *hell* is that racket?' Moses shouted out as he and other crew members moved to check out the jolting. It wasn't the sound of ice banging against their hull.

Moses stood on the bridge walkway and was dumbfounded. There, writhing in the stern of the Akwanaque, was a Narwhal. It was the impossible, staring him right in the face.

Several crew members on deck cautiously approached the anomaly, but were prudent and stayed far back from the wriggling twelve-foot whale, which had a long spiral horn emanating from its head. The men were mesmerized with the apparition and along with Moses, couldn't venture a guess as to why or how the whale got to where it was. There was a low edge at the stern, but for a whale to willingly just leap into a boat was unheard of.

'What do you make of it?' Jacob asked Moses, rubbing his face with incredulous awe.

'Well, if it has fins, ... it's a fish—?' he replied, 'Why don't you write a poem about this.'

'No one would believe it ... but I guess poetry isn't believable anyway,' Jacob replied.

'Believe me, we're going to eat this poem tonight.'

'Who has a camera on board? We gotta get a picture.'

Moses lifted his cap and ran his hand through his hair. 'Y'know, if I was a traditionalist, I'd say it was a gift from a powerful spirit. But I'm *not*—so it *ain't*! Think it could be?'

'Well? Should we gut it?'

'After you get your picture. Get Sammy on it, he'll set out the greatest treat for our dinner. I haven't had Narwhal for years. I gotta taste this one—it's a gift from a powerful spirit.'

Jacob stared at Moses and smiled.

twenty-nine

THE CANDLES HAD DWINDLED down to tiny stumps. Max sat on the floor with Gaar still asleep beside him. In his lap was the rotting old journal, into which he wrote out an affidavit with a pencil. In the document, he described his involvement in the whole 3R fiasco, and the speculation which Brunhilde had filled his head with about the events.

He pondered on the concise wording of his arrangement with Roblaw, to plainly spell out the details of the near fatal and illegal repercussions of the wayward deal. The affidavit would serve in his absence from the tribunal. With the imminent arrival of the boat that was to pick them up, he planned on somehow bribing someone—someway, into breaking the chain and smuggling him down to Canada.

Max looked over as Gaar awoke from his sleep with a deep breath inwards drawn hastily though his nose.

'Back to the land of the living,' Max said to him, as he reached for an old tin can in which he had melted some snow. 'It's water—here.'

Gaar slurped at the water while Max wiped his forehead with a cloth he found in the satchel. 'What time is it?' Gaar asked, as he leaned forward and sat upright to Max's surprise and relief.

'I'm not sure,' Max replied, unable to suppress a shudder in his jaw, 'but as you can see, this *isn't* the boat. You're still not well, but I'm glad to see that you seem better than before my *treatment*.'

'My shoulder feels like it's pinned under a steam roller,' moaned Gaar, carefully touching his covered wound, and flinching as he did.

'Hopefully, you'll be tended by a doctor soon. I hope *and pray* that they come *soon*, so we can get some grub in our guts before I drop dead!'

'Max, listen carefully,' Gaar intejected in a drowsy but coherent way, 'my grandfather was a powerful and respected shaman. He died long before I was born. It's *his* mummified corpse Jag has strapped to his back.'

'*Your grandfather*?! Great. A double-decker shaman is after my ass!' Max complained with serious concern.

'The spirits have spoken to me ... I was welcomed to a very wonderful and mysterious place—while I was out.'

'The spirits have spoken ... I'm sorry, Gaar, but *you're still delirious*. It's your imagination.'

'They're angered by Jag's impulsively destructive actions,' Gaar whispered, not having the strength to put his point across with a full voice, 'I'm to right many wrongs.'

'Where are these *spirits*? The hills, your boots, this pencil?'

'Everywhere. Good spirits.'

'Are you saying you're some kind of *gladiator* for the *good spirit* team?'

'I've tried to run from it, but I can't now. It's my inheritance. My duty. I was never baptized into Christianity.'

'Neither was I ... so what does it make you? A heathen?

Y'know, while you were out of it, I thought I heard noises—and the machete had disappeared. Just ... vanished. *This* machete,' Max said, holding up the blade. 'I found it later. It had melted the snow I buried it in to cool the blade, and the stupid thing had sunk down behind the planks! I thought this place was haunted or something—actually, I think it *is* haunted.'

'Don't worry,' Gaar said with confidence.

'Easy when you're unconscious all the time, and don't have to face it.'

'I've been susceptible ... to the helping spirits.'

'Kinda like a flu bug or something? Are you going to have a showdown with Jag or something? You don't need a corpse on your back ... or—?'

'No. He's a rat in a corner though, and he'll fight tooth and nail to defend his mistakes. I've been entrusted with the power to end it ... I was told to wear the doll, but McGregor—listen, Max.'

'I'm listening,' he replied, as one of the candles fizzled out.

'Try ... not to be glib ... things that you may see will ... shock you. I want you to be brave.'

'*What* will shock me?' Max enquired with a pang of concern and bulging eyes. 'What will? ... Gaar?'

Gaar closed his eyes and pondered for a moment, then opened them again. 'I can't give you details ... just be ready ...'

Max leaned forward and frowned. 'I don't wanna have to be brave—just *free*. *You* can be brave for the both of us.'

'Freedom is earned,' Gaar stressed.

'*Money* is earned, freedom is fringe benefits,' Max countered, causing a frown to wash over Gaar's face. 'Maybe you can get these *spirits* to break this chain, and I'll leave you with *this*,' Max suggested, holding up the journal. He hung it in front of Gaar's eyes.

'What is it?'

'An affidavit I wrote in this journal I found. It explains *everything* about the camp stuff and that sonofabitch, Roblaw. Witness it, and it'll serve in my absence. I want to get out of this with a different shirt on my back.' Max placed the pencil in Gaar's sluggish hand which feebly grasped the implement with disinterest.

Gaar reached out and grasped Max's wrist to steady the document for a cursory glance at the affidavit which he contemplated for a brief moment.

'I'll witness it ... but it's a back-up only. There'll be no absence, Max,' he insisted, wriggling his cuffed wrist as a reminder to him. 'I need you in flesh and blood.'

'There's a peculiar ring to the way you said that.'

'We'll leave it here. If we take it with us and we're apprehended ... it'd be useless having it on us 'cause they'd tear it to shreds.'

'I dunno,' Max replied, thinking that he'd write another on the boat and leave a string of these insurance notes, until the time came when he'd steal off from Gaar.

From a distance, a loud low frequency fog horn sounded. Max looked in the direction of the sound with glee bursting through his chubby face. 'The boat's here! Let's get you up, and go down and meet it!'

A sudden discordant tirade of blood curdling howls permeated the air from afar, almost causing Max to drop Gaar as he struggled to get him to his feet. 'What the?—Let's get outta here, *quick*!'

Max stuffed the machete into the satchel and attempted to bring Gaar to his feet. He struggled off balance as he assisted Gaar who was much taller, and weakened to the point of being a limp and cumbersome load. It was like dealing with a wayward drunk. As Max shuffled Gaar to his feet, he keeled backwards against the counter and knocked the radio from its perch, sending it crashing to the floor with a stubborn thud.

The remaining candle died. It darkened the shack considerably. Not bothering to lug along the heavy radio, Max stumbled for proper footing with Gaar leaning heavy on him for support, accidentally kicking the journal across the floor.

Anxious to get out of the haunted shack, Max found that supporting Gaar for the trek down to the shoreline wasn't going to be easy, especially on Gaar. He was hand-cuffed to Gaar's wounded arm.

They clasped their cuffed hands. Max took Gaar's weight on his leveled arm. He moved jerkily over to the rickety door with Gaar in tow and yanked it open. A gust of freezing wind assaulted his face. He winced at the frigid opposition, tightened both their hoods, and hustled to get them down to the water's edge.

Max could see the lights of the trawler out in the waterway, and could made out a small row boat which had dispatched from the Akwanaque to meet them at the edge of the plated ice-flows. Just as Max turned his snorkeled hood towards Gaar, he detected movement off in the distance. Something big and dark was moving rapidly down a slope and appeared to be heading in their direction.

Someone in the row boat signaled with a flash light. Max hurried himself and Gaar down a slight hill. His anxiety mounted as the thick ice below their feet moved in great sheets. Max was distracted by forboding thoughts of whatever it was that seemed to be racing their way.

'Gaar, c'mon pal—help me out a bit ... something's after us, I think!' Max pleaded, striving to pick up the pace.

'We'll be fine,' Gaar replied drowsily, almost to himself. Forsaking the time-consuming luxury of turning to peer back at what distressed him, Max hastily strove to close the gap between them and safety.

They reached the rowboat, and were assisted by a deckhand who helped the awkward duo aboard. The man then pushed off, to taxi them to the Akwanaque. The deckhand strained at rowing the boat through the slushy ice-chunked water. Max huddled with Gaar who seemed to be oblivious to his surroundings, keeping quietly to himself. Max looked back through the light snowfall towards the shore to see if anything was chasing them. It appeared not to be the case.

They neared the idling trawler. Max turned his attention to the boat and returned a welcoming wave to Moses and a deckhand who stood on deck waiting for their arrival.

Being too late to intervene, Jag stood perfectly still in his human form, looking on from the crest of the hill just above the shack. Lifting his whalebone glasses and sliding them back onto his face, he stared out into Admiralty Inlet as the trawler moved north up the channel.

Jag angrily turned his calculating glare from the moving trawler, and walked towards the shack, scrutinizing the immediate vicinity. Now that his prey were in fixed circumstances and moving predictably north to the logical destination of Nanisivik, they could be stalked with relative certainty along the coast until they could be apprehended when departing the boat.

He entered the decrepit and shadowy shack which offered only traces of twilight creeping through the fissures in the walls. Jag perceived the striking aura of both the past and present there. He had found the ice-man to be a tremendous benefit to his mystical powers, but felt shortchanged with the absence of the Anknonquatok, which he had long discovered missing and was determined to find.

As he mulled around the hut, he heard the commotion of snowmobile engines nearing. Jag felt certain that Max would be quiet about who he was, and voyage under the guise of secrecy. If he did spill the beans to the boat crew, he would deal with them accordingly. Monitoring of radio communications was paramount, and nipping the Kabloona events in the bud was the prime focus, in order to get on to bigger and better things. It would be a resurgence of stability and pride, to bring about peace within themselves. This one obstacle, stood in the way of all that, according to the curse.

Jag felt the dawn of a new beginning, close at hand. By succeeding, he would be certain that the curse which was put upon his head by his mentor thirty-six years prior, would be diffused.

He had suffered the burden of the great weight long enough, the signs all mirroring his master's poison words, the riddle had come to be answered.

In 1963, as a young man of twenty-one, after three years internship with Solomon Arluqinaqoosik, the most revered shaman within a thousand mile radius of Pangnirtung, Jag felt the fallout of alcohol abuse. Solomon was an alcoholic.

As his apprentice, Jag resented his mentor's indulgent behavior, which was eating away at the man steadily. The binges became more frequent, and Jag felt powerless to help after being chastised for intervening on many an occasion. Fits of rage and paranoid delusions plagued the man, but Jag, having lost his parents to tuberculosis, and grown up an orphan, couldn't find the heart to abandon Solomon, who had taken him under his wing after passionate pleas to introduce him to the shaman's life. Regardless of his shortfalls, Solomon was the master and Jag honoured him as such.

Jag had been a keen apprentice and learned a great deal. Soon, people sought Jag out for his abilities. Solomon faded slowly into the background, unintentionally upstaged by Jag, who took the reigns on Solomon's behalf to cover for the man's obligations in the community.

One day, Jag had borrowed a substantial portion of Solomon's revered photo collection, which Solomon had loaned him. The old photos were a joy to ponder, and had been the focus of many long talks between them. Jag was eager to have an artist sculpt some of the two-dimensional treasures, which would be his gift to Solomon, to honour his fiftieth year as a practising shaman.

Upon finding his photo collection pilfered, Solomon confronted Jag in a drunken state, accusing him of thievery. A bitter quarrel ensued, and to Jag's dismay, Solomon was struck with a heart attack. As the man crumbled, he levelled a curse on Jag, his unworthy apprentice.

Jag would never forget Solomon's tragic words, and the pathetic intoxicated mumble in which he delivered them. He uttered: "backlash will follow you in all your days and in all your deeds, until the day of reckoning comes when half becomes whole, and bones rot on gold."

Soon after the old man was laid to rest, Jag began to feel the oppression of Solomon's wrath. He had loved him so, but the alcohol had poisoned Solomon's mind, setting a great rift between them. It was too late to set the record straight. The old man's curse was a riddle, delivered with dramatic flare, but, his theatrics packed a punch, and were not to be made light of.

It was during that time that Jag had tragically killed the RCMP officer whom he caught raping the Inuit girl. It turned out that after Jag spent ten years in prison, charged with second degree murder, Jag found out that the girl had been a prostitute, and was now plying her wares in Iqaluit. He had mixed feelings about the outcome of the whole affair. Less dreadful incidents in the following years, plagued Jag with self-doubt.

The curse was always in the back of Jag's mind. He tirelessly sharpened his shamanistic abilities and sought out circumstances and situations which would answer the riddle and relieve him of the curse. One could never know what is attributable to a curse, and it was driving Jag mad.

Jag looked around the whaling shack and pondered. The IAR was free of Canada and scores of trogs were trapped with the wall of gold at Kabloona. The answer to the riddle. It seemed the end of a long journey to him.

As the beams of the nearing snowmobile headlights began to shake on the walls, Jag went to the door to greet his men.

Triq spotted Jag and zoomed over to the shack. Agaluq and Kiratek soon followed, and pulled up near the door where Triq had gone inside with Jag, leading with a flashlight.

Entering the shack, the two joined Triq and Jag who had just noticed the old hand-drawn map scrawled on the wall and were perusing it. As the two neared, Jag was pointing at the grease finger mark.

'It's fresh,' Triq stated, touching the mark and rubbing it between his fingers.

'Kiqaloq,' Jag replied with certainty.

'And then *overland* to Nanisivik.'

'They are on a boat going north on the channel,' Jag announced. 'You men,' he continued with authority and looking at all three, 'get to Kiqaloq and wait. Two of you at the nearest bay, and one in town. I will follow the coast line. *Monitor* the radio at *all times*. When this is *finished* you can sleep,' he scoffed, frowning at Agaluq who attempted to hide a yawn only to be betrayed by a fluttering of his sleepy eyes. He lowered his head in apology for the display of weakness.

Jag walked out of the shack, followed by Triq and his henchmen who were now overwhelmingly in awe of Jag; especially Agaluq and Kiratek ever since Triq had spelled out the scope to which Jag's mystical abilities stretched.

They were dying of curiosity to witness a transformation, but realized that to expect proof was not only an insult to a shaman, but tantamount to a death wish. Triq had warned them that any dealings with Jag's alter-being could prove debilitating to their psyche's and prove ultimately fatal.

Just watching Jag parade around with the ice-man on his back was enough to silence their curious tongues. Sidelined to their vehicles, they shared a quick glance at a map which Kiratek produced, then the three boarded their snowmobiles and took off.

Jag trembled in a furious passion and turned in a circle calling out to his familiars. He reached over his shoulder and gripped the skull of the ice-man chanting out a dissonant tune as he spun. His mouth opened with a slow and tense yearning, and his eyes bulged as he looked to the solar-wind blown Aurora Borealis.

thirty

THE BUZZER ON Pat's alarm screamed out. Louise entered the room and fumbled with the buttons, finally managing to turn it off. It was a minute after six AM. Louise snuggled up beside Pat on the bed, shaking her lightly to wake her from her sleep. 'Pat,' Louise softly whispered, 'Pat?'

'G'morning,' Pat managed from the side of her mouth, still glued to the pillow, with her face buried in it. She reached out blindly and felt for Peter's face in an endearing way, but instead touched Louise's smooth jaw.

'Peter?' she said, quickly rotating her position to turn around. She looked at Louise who smiled at her as she blinked the sleep from her eyes and fell back on the pillow. Pat reached out and took Louise's hand. 'Are you sure, now?' she asked, stroking her hand gently.

'Yes.'

'Alright, you stubborn girl,' she said sitting up, 'You're already dressed!'

'I'm ready when you are—just don't take me on a scenic route.'

'I don't need coffee,' Pat said, waking up completely now and speaking with a full clear voice, 'I'll be ready in ten minutes. If you're eager, you can go and warm up the car. The keys are hanging in the kitchen ... if you want.'

'Sure,' Louise replied, getting up from the bed, 'thanks for helping me, Pat.'

'I'm not helping—you know how I feel. You won't let me help you. I'm *obliging* you, 'cause you shouldn't go through this alone. *But*, if there's a bunch of pro-lifer's picketing outside, we turn back, *right*?'

'They don't show up there 'til nine—so daddy says. He checked into it. If there *were* any, I'd fight my way in, anyhow.'

'You'd fight your way in—you really are rigid in your mind-set. Well, let's get you there on time at least,' Pat murmured, as Louise turned and left the room to fetch the keys for the car. Pat got up out of bed and began her abridged morning routine.

thirty-one

FROM OVER THE CREST of a snow laden hill, a large polar bear emerged and curiously looked on at the Akwanaque, as it slowly moved up Admiralty Inlet. The bear scurried down the hill, and launched into the slushy waters from the ice-plated collar of the shore, and disappeared under the water.

The steady chug of the boat's engines reverberated around the galley. Gaar and Max sat back in the booth-style dining area. There was seating for twelve, but they were alone in the room, except for Sammy, the tall and lanky Inuit cook, who was preparing breakfast for the crew.

Max pushed an empty bowl away from himself, and looked at Gaar who hadn't touched his. Gaar was being very quiet, appearing to be in some sort of trance.

'Thanks for that seal-broth soup,' Max said to the cook, who was busying himself at his cooking. 'How many on board?'

'I was preppin' chow for five, with you guys, seven. It's a skeleton crew, to deliver it up for winter docking for the freeze-over. Maybe they'll renovate the galley!' he laughed, looking through the hanging pots and pans, gazing around at the crumbling state of the galley. Sammy stared at Gaar while he worked away preparing breakfast. 'Your friend looks really sick,' he said frowning at the ailing Gaar, 'is it contagious?'

'No,' Max replied, wiping Gaar's perspiring forehead with his free hand. He felt his head for a fever, and was disheartened to detect one. 'We've been up all night, judging from your clock—say, what's your name again?'

'Sammy.'

'Sammy, do you know of any doctors on the long haul northwards, that might come to tend him if we can radio anybody?'

'There's nothing and *nobody* out this way,' Sammy replied matter-of-factly.

'So nobody with a small plane or anything?'

'Nothing.'

'Oh—'

'So, what brings you to these parts, again? Are you a visiting mineral scientist or something?' Sammy enquired, chopping away at some fish, and finding Max aloof and avoiding his questions by tending to Gaar. 'Did your boat sink or what?'

Max turned his head to Sammy and nodded. 'Yup, my boat is sunk,' he admitted. Suddenly, he stared incredulously at Sammy. '*Where'd* you get *that*?!' Max blurted, seeing the doll necklace slung around Sammy's neck, as the man pulled off his cooking apron.

'This?' he replied, lifting the Anknonquatok and staring down at it. 'We caught a narwhal and this was in its gut! D'ya like whale meat? We're having it for dinner tonight. Unicorn of the sea.'

Max began to nudge Gaar, who was oblivious to the goings-on in the galley. 'I never eat unicorn ... it's not kosher,' Max replied, not wanting to alarm Sammy about the importance of the doll necklace, or of the dire consequences that wearing it could bring to him. 'Gaar, Gaar!' Max practically shouted out, shaking Gaar and tapping him on the cheek to call his attention to the Anknonquatok. 'Can I see that necklace, Sammy?' he asked, stretching out his free hand in a courteous gesture. 'Sorry, I can't really get up to come to you.'

Above on the bridge, Jacob navigated the trawler as solo helmsman at the controls. They were moving through the narrowest portion of the channel, where a hundred-yard wide bottle-neck occurred.

Humming a little ditty to himself, he looked out over the icy waters ahead, and then checked his watch. Looking up from his watch, he squinted his eyes and peered ahead to clarify what he thought he was seeing. Flicking a switch to power up an exterior spotlight, he turned an overhead handle which aimed the small light towards the object in the water.

Reaching over the instrument panel, Jacob grabbed some binoculars and focused on the bear's head which protruded from the icy water. He became mesmerized by the bear, which stared directly back at him.

As the bear slowly stroked its way to the side, Jacob turned his steering and followed, not cognizant of the mystical power the bear had over him, and of the danger he was putting the Akwanaque in.

The boat was now heading directly towards a protruding rock wall which stretched out precariously over the ice. The Akwanaque was on a collision course with the rock face which supported several large boulders sitting unreliably on a ledge. The bear idled in the water at the rock face. Jacob obliviously navigated the trawler directly at it.

Moses emerged from the crew quarters on the lower deck and stared in shock at what was looming ahead. He dashed to a ladder and climbed feverishly up toward the bridge deck, expecting Jacob to have had a heart attack and be laying dead on the floor.

Reaching the door, he crashed through into the bridge only to find Jacob nonchalantly directing the boat towards the rock face. Moses angrily lunged at him, knocked him aside and worked like a crazy man to divert from the imminent collision.

Below in the galley, Max took the doll necklace from Sammy and strung it around Gaar's neck.

'Don't put it around his neck!' Sammy screamed with disappointment, 'I don't want to catch what he's got! His eyes are rolling around in his head for crying out loud!'

'You won't get it, don't worry! He tells me it's a necessary illness. He's a shaman,' Max announced, attempting to make Gaar aware of the Anknonquatok now slung around his neck and resting on his chest, 'the doll is getting *hot*! Feel it!' he shouted, excitedly touching the doll with both hands, and idiotically exposing the handcuffs in his arousal over the supernatural spectacle.

Sammy's face dropped in disdain seeing the handcuffs. In a fit of defence, he pulled open a drawer and produced a gun, which he aimed at the two. He slowly made his way around the island food-prep counter.

'I *hate* when someone tries to pull the wool over my eyes! Where'd you seal-kissers come from?! Who *are* you?!' Sammy screeched.

Suddenly, they were all thrown forward from an immense collision, and a secondary impact of tremendous force which tipped the boat's stern downwards and left it listing sideways at a complete stop.

Gaar and Max were propelled out from the table. A heavy cabinet fell on Gaar as he collided with it. Ice cold water began to seep into the galley. Sammy retrieved the pistol he'd dropped to the floor, and levelled once again on Max, who struggled to lift the heavy cabinet off of Gaar with his untethered arm.

The shuffling of large booted feet could be heard above their heads as the crew scurried to abandon ship with great howls of panic. Sammy anxiously climbed the inclined floor to reach the ladder to the deck. He reached them and turned to the two.

'You're *cursed*!' Sammy screamed, taking a pot shot at Gaar who appeared unconscious and pinned under the cabinet.

Max ducked, as the bullet struck the cabinet, exploding the wood where it made contact. 'Don't shoot!' he cried out.

'That one! The harbinger of death—DIE!' Sammy shouted and aimlessly fired again as he began ascending the cock-eyed stairs of the foundering boat.

'Don't shoot, stupid! Help! Help me get this off him!' Max shouted with futile pleas. 'Hellllp!' he begged, as the water rose rapidly, threatening to swallow Gaar up. He struggled like a cornered rat to push the heavy cabinet off of his companion, which now occurred to him to be wedged on something.

Frantically looking down to Gaar and then over to the stairs, he noticed with great surprise, the tiny silver keys for the handcuffs which had dropped from Gaar's pocket as they both flew through the air from the booth. They were definitely out of reach, and he'd have to find something to extend his reach to them in order to retrieve them.

Max was desperate. He'd have to let go of Gaar's head which he had supported above the rising water, in order to take a chance of reaching them. He had to unlock the cuffs so that he could properly lever the cabinet off of the man. In trying to save Gaar—he could end up drowning him, and possibly himself.

In a stroke of inspiration, he used his foot to prop Gaar's head up above the rising water, and reached for the satchel which had fallen to the floor. Pulling the machete out of the satchel, he desperately reached with it to tap the keys his way. Since they sat higher up on the angled floor, he got ready for them to come sliding down towards him once he jostled them from their position of rest. With a wavering outstretched arm he exhaled slowly and poked at the keys as gingerly as possible. The debilitating cold of the water made the task frustratingly impossible and he clumsily jabbed at the keys with a chattering jaw and fluttering eyes. At once, the stubborn keys broke from their resting position and slid quickly towards him. He reached out, but they went right by him and under the water somewhere. He was freezing now, and frantic, and not sure of what to do.

Suddenly, a wall mounted electrical panel began to submerge and sparked violently, causing all the power to go off on the boat. It became very dark, and as the angle of the sinking trawler increased, he became frightened with the diminishing odds of his survival.

It became physically impossible now to keep Gaar's head above the dark and freezing water, as he was pinned very close to the floor. He sadly relented to the inevitable.

In a last ditch frenzy, he struggled passionately with himself to swing the blade down on Gaar's wrist to free himself, but as with McGregor, the opportunity passed and he would have only been chopping at deep water. He could take himself off at the elbow—and he raised the machete to do just that. That opportunity passed. It was the shoulder or the head now.

Giving himself up for dead, he swept the tortuous

thoughts from his mind, tossed away the machete and took a deep breath, then submerged under the water. Moments later, he appeared at the water's surface to gasp for another deep breath of air, and in doing so, went down again striving to find where the cabinet was wedged in order to free it up. Max emerged once again, choking for air and shivering painfully on borrowed time.

The freezing water was now neck deep. He gave in to his fatal predicament. The numbing cold water began to numb his brain, and he waited patiently in the cock-eyed galley for the water to rise above his anchored body. His eyes bulged in fear, anticipating his imminent drowning.

Without warning, Gaar leapt up like a spooky sea creature from the deep, his eyes ablaze with life. Max laughed in debilitated shock. The cabinet slowly fell back under the dark water. He powerfully ushered Max over to the steps leading to the deck, and dragged him up. Max stiffly giggled away like a madman, all blue and infused with a kooky disposition imposed on him by the tinge of his impending death.

''s it ... you, Gaar? But ... you're ... drowned! How ... breathe water?!' Max slobbered out drunkenly, as they made their way clumsily up the steep stairs.

They climbed along the railings up towards the up-ended stern of the boat, their heavy soaking parkas weighing them down as they struggled. Gaar spotted the five crew members who had long boarded their life boat and made their way to the heavy zone of ice near the shore.

Standing and gawking at the two on the sinking boat, Sammy broke from the ranks of the crew, took aim and began shooting wildly at the two.

'He's the one I told you about!' he screamed, '*that one*! He's *cursed*! And we're cursed unless we see him dead!!' Sammy began taking shots again at the helpless duo.

'Take your clothes off,' Gaar said to Max.

'I ... can't.'

'They're stiff with ice—gotta get out of your shell!'

'Sleepy—,' Max said lightly, as he fell back against the frame of a motorized hoist.

Gaar reached inside his pocket and searched frantically for something, as another shot ricocheted off the hoist frame.

'He's ... getting better—' Max meekly uttered, 'looking ... for the keys?' he grinned, slowly pointing downwards to the water, which had by that time, swallowed half the boat.

'I'm sorry, Max ... I put you through a lot,' Gaar replied, as Sammy's scathing shouts went on like a broken record, denouncing Gaar, and passionately calling for his death.

'My familiars will assist us,' Gaar said as he gripped the Anknonquatok and mumbled out a few words, slightly chanting.

'Hear the ... trumpets, just about—' Max mumbled, blue with cold, and delirious in his hopelessness.

Max blinked, and there stood before him, a statuesque oddity—an eight foot man with a golden face. It had no eyes, only carved features and was covered with furs. The titan slipped its neck under their cuffed wrists and took each of them over a shoulder. The incarnation of the doll, walked straight up and crashed its way through the wooden wall of the stern.

'I—' Max uttered as the creature dropped straight into the water with them, disappearing below, into the dark icy drink.

thirty-two

PAT WALKED ALONGSIDE Louise as she was being wheel-chaired by an orderly along a hallway at the abortion clinic.

'I don't need to be wheelchaired—what's the deal?' Louise complained, as the orderly smiled down at her and kept up the quick pace.

'Don't worry about it,' Pat replied, 'it's protocol or something.'

Louise looked up at her friend with a worried look, but managed a faint smile. Pat held her hand as they moved along.

'They're going to take me in for anesthesia or whatever, shortly, I'm sure,' Louise said despondently, 'so you may as well go and come back in a while? What do you think? Will you come back for me in a few hours? I'll get them to call you—'

'On my cell phone.'

'Perfect. Oh, Pat? Could you please fetch those few things for me? The stuff we talked about ... and my bedside novel? It's—'

'On your bedside table?' Pat interjected, smiling down at her friend.

'Yeah,' Louise admitted, 'in its place where one would expect.'

'Are you sure that stuff can't wait? I'd rather not leave you alone.'

'I could be hours—I don't know. Please ... I don't want you having to hang out here.'

'Alright then, I'll see you in a little bit.'

'I gave you my keys already, right?'

'Yup. Well, I see the off-limits door coming up ... I'll say a little prayer for you ...'

'Oh, uh, *thanks* ... if it's fast I'll get them to try you at my place, and then if not, on your cell phone.'

The orderly stopped at the door, allowing the girls to hug for a moment before they went through. 'Everything will work out fine,' Pat said to her, consoling her as they broke their hug.

'Thanks Pat, for letting me stay at your place for these couple of days—skipping school and all, and being my guardian angel!'

'I can afford the time—and you don't snore! I'll see you soon,' she said, returning a wave to Louise as she was ushered through the doors. Pat stared at the doors for a moment, then turned and walked back down the hallway.

Exiting through the clinic doors, Pat walked down the driveway in the stillness of the early dark morning. Merging with the sidewalk, she ambled along the street towards the parking lot where her car was left.

Observing some kind of street repair ahead, she stepped off the equipment-ridden sidewalk and took to the roadway. Wary of on-coming cars, she walked around a small cordoned-off work area on the street, where deep below the opened manhole, she could hear the echoey prattle of some invisible men who had some task at hand under the street. This piqued her curiosity, and she cast a fleeting glance as she quickly passed the grungy view of the subterranean passageways below.

From out of nowhere, she was almost struck by a carelessly driven car from the adjacent parking lot. It screeched to a halt as she leaned off balance over the hood, mortally shaken, but unhurt.

Realizing she'd almost been killed having been absorbed in the frivolous distraction, she waved off the incident with the apologetic driver. Stepping away from the brush, she bolted to her car in embarrassment.

A similar occurrence had happened when she was a young child. This immediately came to mind. Now, there was no parent to scold her, nor was there anyone to comfort her.

Safe in her car now, she turned the engine over then careened her focus and pondered. Louise's bedside novel ... the house keys ... the errand ... the horror.

Pat entered Gaar and Louise's house, and was immediately struck with the overwhelming whiff of perfume—Louise's old favorite.

Leaving the door open, she reached for a light switch in the hall and flicked on the light. Pat walked back to the door and fiddled with the piston hinge to prop the screen door open to air out the house. As she was doing so, the telephone rang. Abandoning the temperamental screen door, which refused to hold an open position, she started for the phone. It was going on its second ring. Picking up the receiver as she strode to the telephone stand, she was met with a dial tone as she put the receiver to her ear.

Disappointed she missed the call—which seemed rather soon for Louise's pick-up notice, she hung up the receiver and pulled her cellular phone from her coat pocket, ready to receive the back-up call. From the corner of her eye, she caught the movement of the tape turning in the answering machine, and immediately picked up the receiver again.

'Hello? Hello!' Pat called into the receiver, but heard nothing but a dial tone. Looking at the side panel of the machine, she turned up the volume and slammed the receiver down when feed-back occurred. Lifting the cover of the contraption, she saw that it was not the out-going message tape that was turning, but the in-coming tape.

She pushed the stop button on the old machine, then engaged the rewind mechanism which rewound the in-coming tape. It audibly played back the chipmunk-squeaks of backward voices. With innocent curiosity, she stopped the tape and hit the play button.

To her amazement, she heard Louise screaming at Gaar on the other end of the line. As she was about to turn off the spectacle of their private bickering, she heard Louise mention the miscarriage, and pondered a moment as it played on. She was suspicious now. It wasn't like Louise to lie in that fashion.

She stopped the tape and rewound it further back, to get to the bottom of what was said between them. What Louise was saying on the tape was contrary to what *she* was told by Louise. Now she had a personal stake in the goings-on.

Pat felt hurt and betrayed that Louise would lie to her. She stared blankly into the living room as the machine rewound. The paint had peeled off the wall where the perfume bottle had smashed against it. The trails of the spilled perfume were etched into the wall.

Stopping the machine at a gap in the squeaky gibberish, she engaged it to play back. She listened curiously. Her jaw stiffened as the events unfolded on the tape.

There came a call from Gaar. She cocked a curious eye at the tape, hearing Louise going into hysterics, angrily announcing the miscarriage and their marriage break-up. Stunned by the incongruity of her friend, she listened to the next call. It was from Gaar again, this time from a bus station. Now, *he* was irately breaking the news to *her*. This time, *Louise* reacted with shock, by the drastic turn of events and attitude of her husband.

Pat stopped the tape and pondered in confusion. Although the voices were similar for both Gaar and Louise, she detected foul play. She quickly rewound the tape, and set the machine to receive messages. She raised her cellular phone and dialed Louise's telephone number. A second later, when Louise's phone rang, she stood there monitoring the machine, and at the second ring, the machine activated. There was no out-going message. The in-coming tape engaged to record. Evidence of the cruel hoax was on tape— but who else had a key for the house, to take the call *as* Louise?

Pat frantically hung up Louise's telephone. She stopped the machine and nervously fished out the in-coming message tape. She urgently dug into her pocket and pulled out the clinic's telephone number and dialed it on Louise's phone. Shrieking when she only got a busy signal, she immediately dialed the operator, and paced until she got a reply. She made the sign of the cross and closed her eyes in anticipation.

'Hello?! Operator?' she pleaded breathlessly, as the connection was made. 'I'm trying to get through to the Women's Hospital Abortion Clinic! It's busy! Can you cut in on the line for me?! It's an emergency!! ... Why not?!' she screamed, in a fevered frenzy, 'Dammit, it's an emergency! Let me speak to your supervisor, immediately!! Hurry, PLEASE!!'

At the clinic nursing station, a nurse urgently placed the phone receiver down, and dashed down a hallway. She ran for one of the surgical procedure rooms. Skidding on the tiled hallway floor, she came upon the surgical room. She burst through the door, surprising the attending nurse and masked doctor. He jerked his head out from between the stirruped legs of Louise, brandishing a peculiar looking instrument in his hand.

'*Stop*!' the reception nurse blurted desperately.

The doctor angrily faced her. 'What is the *meaning of this*!' he demanded. His mask moved in and out from his mouth, in an exasperated way.

'Abort the abortion!!' she shouted, waving her hand up and down as she caught her breath. 'Is it too late?'

The doctor pulled the mask from his face and stood up from his stool. He angrily placed the dreadful surgical instrument in a tray and fumed out of the room past the nurse.

The attending nurse withdrew her mask and looked blankly at the woman.

thirty-three

MAX CAME TO HIS SENSES—somewhat. He felt very warm and comfortable. The more his groggy eyes took in everything, the more disoriented he became. Turning his head slowly around in an arc, he realized he was in some sort of cave. There was a camp fire burning near him, which animated the dark and jagged rock walls veneered with ice.

Made especially apparent in the dancing light of the fire, were dozens of large pointed icicles above on the ceiling which he was sure would come crashing down if he so much as sneezed. Quickly lowering his eyes down from the threat, he focussed his attention on trying to figure out where he was before he arrived in this peculiar place.

Sitting up, he was immediately distracted by the layers of fresh fur pelts which draped his entire body from head to toe. He could almost feel the life-force energy in the skins which were placed hide to hide, offering him fur on both the inside and out. He pulled at the tight animal sinew bindings which looped around his body and corralled the assembly of fur he bore.

He looked through the shimmering fire and saw Gaar laying comatose an his back, in an identical array of bound white furs. Rubbing his face rigorously with his hands as though he were attempting to erase his face, he almost remembered being on the sinking boat and being shot at, but was definitely uncertain about the events which followed. He recalled a fleeting image of the hulk with the golden face, but wasn't quite sure how or what that dream image had to do with anything that seemed real at the moment.

He clapped his hands together, and then in a sudden panic, covered his head realizing how idiotic such an action was. A cascade of sharp plummeting icicles on his head would prove without a doubt he wasn't dreaming. As he slowly rotated his head to check on Gaar, a drip of ice-cold water from above stung the tip of his nose. Lifting his right hand to wipe at the residue, he had only now noticed that the chain which bound them was gone, and that the wristlets had vanished completely.

His bruised and marked right wrist bore a smudged golden sheen which was only detectable at a certain angle in the wavering fire-light. Dismissing the sheen as grime tinted by the orange flame, he rotated his wrist with great joy, and stood up to experience his long awaited independence, careful not to whoop it up too much lest the stalactites crash his party.

The aroma of the burning wood commandeered his attention and he became aware of the thin blanket of smoke which hung in the air. Looking down, he noticed a mooring tie-down brace made of steel in the charred core of the fire, leading him to believe that the fire was kindled with splintered wood railings from the ill-fortuned Akwanaque trawler.

How long they'd been in this cave was beyond him, and how much of the trawler had been through the fire was a moot but curious point to him. Whoever had dressed him had crossed his mind, but perhaps the most striking and relevant note to himself was the heaping mound of meat, entrails, bones and fins which sat in a pile like a load of laundry, off to the side.

Max went over to Gaar and knelt beside him. 'Gaar? Gaar?!' he urged, nudging his leg, as though it were Christmas morning. He nudged him like a pest until a few grunts came from Gaar's motionless body.

'Max,' Gaar whispered, as he rustled and stretched, finally sitting up to look at his eager companion, and their unusual abode.

'Gaar, is this *Eskimo heaven*? But, *I'm* not an Eskimo.'

Gaar lifted the Anknonquatok which lay at his side, and draped it around his neck. 'Call it what you will— we're safe, and that's all that counts,' Gaar replied, in good form.

'You look ... *normal*. How do you feel?'

'Fine. How do you feel?'

'Free! Look,' he gleefully announced, raising his right wrist and staring in sheer delight. 'I feel like I've got jet-lag, but other than that—'

'Don't expect a stewardess on this flight,' Gaar added with a smile, as he sat up.

'Shaman airlines ... we guarantee you'll wake up with fur in your face, and entrails at your heels ... look.'

Gaar stared at the offerings. 'Good, I'm starved. Don't worry Max, eat the fish, or some of this seal—what's the matter, not hungry?' he asked, as he grabbed some seal meat and began to gnaw on it.

'Uhhh ... the caterer has *got* to go to France and learn the basics of haute cuisine, or something—at the very least, not to run off and leave the carcasses to fend for themselves at coat-check retrieval time.'

'Look, Max, eat or starve. This stuff raw, won't kill you. Don't give me that *it's not kosher* deal, either. I know you, you'd eat a dozen banquet burgers at the drop of a hat, wouldn't you? What'd you eat at Kabloona?'

'Banquet burgers—in season.'

'I rest my case. We've got to go, so there's no time for you to rig up some kind of way to cook any of this on the fire or anything.'

'I'm not feeling so hungry—it's just that I've seen the kitchen ...'

'Fine. But listen, I won't fight with you, Max. So, you can come with me and face the high council *and* nail Roblaw's ass to the wall—or you can go off on your own and die in the wilderness.'

'I'm with you like snow on snow, now,' Max replied, knowing there was no other choice, 'but, can you explain ... how—?'

Gaar stood up and limbered up his body. 'Max, ask me no questions ... and you'll be spared the truth.'

Max took offence and folded his arms across his chest. 'Don't think I'm tough enough?'

'I don't think you're ready—we'll see. Want some of this meat to take with you?'

'I would, 'cept the unknown tailor didn't put pockets in my outfit.'

Gaar began to gather up some meat and stuffed two whole fox carcasses under his arms. 'Max, help me grab some of this. Take a hold of this bear carcass,' he said, standing with both arms full and taking a grip of the bear to drag it out.

'Holy smokes, Gaar. Eat enough for the both of us why don't you. I'm gonna start calling you Gaar the ... *gorman-dizer*!'

'It's not for me, smart guy—it's an offering we're going to spread outside. It's been a lean year y'know—for all.'

'But I'll get blood all over my new white fur ... ahhh,' he complained, pulling up the over-sized flaps of fur from his hand and taking hold of his end of the large bloody carcass. They struggled with great effort to drag the remnants of the beast outside.

'I've got a bad back, y'know,' Max grunted, dropping his

end and rubbing his lower back as they reached the neck of the entrance to the small cave.

'It's all up here,' Gaar said, pointing to his temple, 'you've got to work on your attitude.'

'I'm a *lover*, not a piano mover.'

'Just take an end, *Valentino*.'

'I think—I think I'm going to throw up ...'

'Do it. Then grab your end—'cause we've got to get moving!'

The two emerged huffing and grunting from the ice–mouthed cave at the base of a large hill. As they struggled to a halt and put down the bear carcass, Max ate up a bunch of snow from a nearby ledge, which he shoveled into his mouth. Gaar took a fox carcass and flung it off to one side of the cave. With the other one he did the same, in the other direction.

'Tell me we don't have to lug this to Nanisivik ...' Max groaned, as he wiped his mouth.

'We're going to leave it right there,' Gaar replied, pointing outwards towards the shore area, as he stood waiting for Max to take hold again. When Max grabbed his end again, they dragged the carcass to where Gaar had indicated, and faced the bear north.

'Anything else? Like ... pointing its tongue towards the water?' Max asked impatiently, while catching his breath. 'Y'know, I almost married a woman once who had this weird compulsion to re-arrange her living room every time I came over ...'

'Nice story, Max—let's go,' Gaar said, as he began to walk towards what looked like an easy climb up to a level plateau which would offer them a more direct route towards Nanisivik. Max stood wiping at some blood on his front, only to look up and see Gaar had gone.

With the twilight, and the white furs which covered them

now blending with the background of practically everything in sight, Max couldn't make out where his companion had disappeared to. He listened intently for any sounds, and swiveled in his position to look about for Gaar.

Max nearly leapt out of his skin when he turned and walked right into Gaar.

'I found something,' Gaar said, appearing out of nowhere, 'follow me.'

Max was vexed with Gaar for sneaking up on him like that after having disappeared, but bit his tongue, and followed his companion. They walked a little ways north along the shore's edge.

'So what did you find—or am I *not ready* for that?' Max called out to Gaar who was setting a quick pace.

'See it ahead?!' Gaar announced loudly, and pointed his finger straight out in front of himself.

Max saw what Gaar was referring to. It was the Akwanaque life boat, abandoned and pulled up on the buffer ice near the shore.

'I hope they're out of bullets!' Max moaned.

They reached the row boat. Gaar looked inland. 'The trawler didn't go down here, but they rowed to this point and then abandoned whatever plan they had,' Gaar said, looking around at the hills and rock faces on their side of Admiralty Inlet.

'But where are they and why'd they stop here?'

'I'm workin' on it,' Gaar replied, 'well, Kiqaloq is a far walk from here, and I'm sure it's got to be where they're heading—it's the *only* place around these parts. *But*, I'm positive that well beyond that point a couple of miles further north, it flattens out a bit. They knew that—they're navigators and they've travelled this inlet hundreds of times, I'm sure.'

'So, *why* they stopped here's a mystery—or just stupid.'

'I think the former. They wouldn't want to have to traverse these roundabout ridges and valleys.'

'Fine. So, let's get in the boat and do what you just said.'

Gaar looked closely around the boat and spotted some blood and large paw prints which seemed rather large for a wolf, leading inland.

'Blood,' Gaar uttered.

'That Sammy guy probably shot himself in the foot,' Max said, looking closer at the life boat. 'And look! A bullet hole in the side of the boat—never shoot the life boat—a cardinal rule of survival.'

'Maybe they were frightened by something in the water—at first,' Gaar replied, 'look at these paw prints. It looks like their was a scuffle here. Let's follow them and see where they lead.'

'Are you mental?! Let's *get* in the boat and ... Gaar?' he yelled out, as Gaar started to walk east along the tracks of the crew and the wolf. 'Are you forgetting that there's somewhere we've got to be—and soon?! Look!' Max shouted as he reluctantly parted from the security of the life boat and trailed after Gaar. He desperately pointed down at the trampled path, more for his own benefit than Gaar's, who at this time had his back turned and was moving up a hill side.

'There's more than just footprints!' Max screeched, 'There's blood and *huge* paw prints! Where there's paws, there's jaws! I'm casting off without you then—I'm going!!' He stopped in his tracks and folded his arms across his chest. He turned his body sideways as though he was actually going to swing around and head back to the boat. Teetering with uncertainty, he realized that Gaar wasn't going to turn back, let alone acknowledge his threats. Max abandoned the bluff and tore after Gaar before he lost sight of him.

Max joined Gaar near the crest of the hill, all out of breath from the ascent, and hung on to Gaar for some stability. He was relieved to have a breather. Gaar stopped and raised his hand for Max to stop and be quiet.

'What is it?' Max huffed, as the light snow-fall criss-crossed his face.

'Do you hear something?'

'Only my heart in my ears,' Max replied.

Gaar squinted his eyes and tilted his head slightly to decipher the source of the disturbance he thought he heard. With a determined look upwards, he pressed forward to the crest of the hill. He was sure there was a commotion nearby, and was proved right as they walked up over the top.

Max ducked immediately to his knees, as the two looked down on to the scene below.

In a fevered skirmish with a band of deranged wolves, Sammy rolled around on the snow in a feeble defence, kicking and lashing out with his arms, as he was snapped at and bitten without mercy. He backed himself into a little hovel under a ledge where atop lay the body of Captain Moses, with his throat ripped out and his life-blood spilling down on the brutal pack below.

Sammy's muffled yelps were lost in the snarling and ravaging of the vicious onslaught. A few yards away lay Jacob, the poet helmsman from the Akwanaque, lifeless and torn up in a churned up, blood-soaked mound of snow. Gaar started to move down the slope to the basin of terror, but was grabbed by Max who was terrified with the carnage.

'Gaar! Get down! There's nothing we can do for him!'

Gaar knocked Max's tight grip from his body, which was instantly re-fastened to his fur in desperation.

'*I* can do something—you told him about the gold didn't you?!' Gaar stated.

'Yeah, I *mentioned* it to him.'

'You only *touched* on the subject,' Gaar replied, breaking Max's grasp again, 'that big one's *Jag*, and the score's to be settled now!'

'Gaar!!' Max cried out as Gaar marched intently down the slope. Jag reared his grotesque heads from the voracious huddle around Sammy. Max's heart skipped a beat seeing the demonic monster which stepped back and lowered its heads, stalking Gaar as he neared.

'It—it's got *two heads*!!' Max screamed, as he began to pursue Gaar down the slope, but stopped, not wanting to get into the soup himself. His eyes bulged out of their sockets and his mouth dropped, fearing the worst for Gaar who was defenseless without even a trace of a weapon, and on an insane suicide mission.

Sammy's bursts of despair and terror, instilled a primal fear and hopelessness in him, knowing he was undoubtedly next for a slow painful shredding at the jaws of the ravenous predators. With Gaar torn to bits, he would be alone to face the cruel dissonant music of the wild. Trembling with the fear of the inevitable, and just as he was about to give in to the impetus to run fast for his life—to the rowboat if he could make it; the impossible happened. Gaar became a polar bear.

Max was dumbstruck. He violently rubbed his hands into his face. Peering down again, he cringed as the huge two-headed wolf leapt up at the polar bear with bloodied fangs and claws. The brazen affront was foiled as the bear reared up on its hind legs and shook Jag's clamped jaws from the bite he'd managed near his neck. The other wolves backed away from Sammy and dispersed, as Gaar again stood on his hind legs and ambled forward towards Jag.

Max spotted the Anknonquatok doll laying in the snow where Gaar had made the transformation, and made haste for it, knowing it was important to Gaar. He had heard Gaar speak of his familiars, and now finding himself bolting for the Anknonquatok, realized there was no turning back, as the dispersed wolves took a keen interest in him and re-grouped to trot with lowered heads, towards him.

Gaar swiped Jag with a tremendous blow of his large clawed paw and sent him flailing to the ground, where Jag tumbled unconscious. Gaar moved to Jag and leaned down on his body with his two immense front paws, attempting to crush the life out of the grotesque two-headed anomaly.

Max found himself surrounded by the wolves. As they started to nip their frightened prey, he fell and began to tumble down the short slope. The wolves tore at him, some tumbling with him in the shower of snow which was churned up as they plowed downwards toward the basin. Amidst the snarls and the snapping of intent jaws, Max yelped out with both panic and injury, causing Gaar to turn his broad head in the direction of the fracas.

The bear left its savage task, stepping off Jag and ambling over to Max to save him from the ferocious attack.

Max had ground to a halt near the bottom of the slope. In his random swishing vision, he caught a fleeting glimpse of his own blood on his hands. He again raised his hands to defend his face. In the flurry, a wolf caught hold of his left hand and bit clean through, tugging away greedily. It stared boldly into Max's terror filled eyes, with neither reverence nor insult.

Blood streaked down from his head now, and dribbled into his eyes. In the urgent thrashing struggle to avoid the incessant snapping of the wolves, he caught sight of the Anknonquatok a few feet from himself. The clamped jaw tore a portion from his hand and broke free. Max yelped in agony, then sacrificed his defensive posture, opening up his curled body and leaping for the doll. The wolves tore into his outstretched body.

He felt the piercing ache of a fang puncturing his leg. With a trembling right hand, he snatched the doll up and attempted to curl up again. As he folded his extremities in, and tightened himself into a ball of defence, the wolves reeled back with cowering whines, reacting to the aura of the Anknonquatok clutched in his hand.

The wolves fanned outwards to the perimeter of some invisible barrier, reluctant to breech the zone.

Gaar arrived swaggering high on his massive hind legs, bellowing a fearsome growl. Recognizing that Max was safe for the moment, Gaar came down onto his four paws, and swung back around to finish off his business with Jag.

Max slowly lowered his arms but remained in shock as he watched the wolves circle the site, staying out of Gaar's path, but interested in getting back to Sammy who lay watching in silent shock. Jag had regained consciousness, and as he staggered to his paws, he cast a savage glare on Sammy, and stalked his helpless prey.

Suddenly, the added head began to growl at the red-eyed counterpart, and in a split second there was a ferocious altercation between them. Fangs collided with fangs, and the wolf's body was thrashing around in front of Sammy who lay paralyzed in silence, witnessing the spectacle.

Jag abruptly began to transform back into his human form, but the transformation came to a halt at his midsection, leaving his lower half in bestial form. Sammy's eyes opened wide in astonishment at the bizarre and unearthly occurrence. Jag in his realization that Sammy could identify him, snapped off a long icicle which had formed from the dripping blood of Captain Moses' body, and fiercely rammed the icicle through Sammy's chest. Jag then swirled his head around in the midst of a chant and transmuted fully back into the deviant creature.

With agonizing groans, Sammy collapsed completely from the blow. Jag experienced a nip and a growl from his counterpart, and dashed from the immediate vicinity, as Gaar neared. Sammy looked up in a daze and stared at Gaar who briefly sniffed at him as he hovered.

Jag made his way into the pack of loosely congregated

wolves and mingled amongst them. Suddenly, he bolted off into the tundra in the direction the remaining crew members had made their escape in. The other wolves followed in a mad scurry.

Max limped cautiously toward Gaar and Sammy, holding the doll close to himself, and burying his wounded hand in his right armpit. His white fur clothing was soiled with blood, which made him think twice about getting too close to Gaar in case some animal instinct would prevail. He instead walked over to Jacob's dead body and began attempting to strip bits of material from his clothing for a bandage to apply to his dreadfully torn hand.

When Max looked back, he saw Gaar standing there in his human form. Moving from Jacob's body with scavenged material in hand, he approached Gaar who was attending Sammy. Max's face contorted as he looked on at Sammy's wretched wounds. As Gaar turned from Sammy, Max handed him the Anknonquatok doll.

'You were brave, Max,' Gaar said approvingly.

'You were a bear, Gaar,' Max replied flatly, 'Is there anything else I should know ... or is that about the extent of it?'

'Your hand is injured, you want me to wrap it with that?'

'If you don't mind. There's a radio and a bag over there that the crew left behind—don't think they'll be needing it now.'

'Can you feel your hand?' Gaar asked, as he wrapped Max's injured hand.'

'A bit,' Max answered.

'You're in shock ... just don't look at it,' he said, as he tied a knot in the bandage and pulled the soiled fur down over it.

'He's a *demon*! Two heads! How—?'

'Max, there's different rules in this arena ...'

'I don't think I'll ever be ready—to understand. And *I* thought wolves were afraid of people,' Max announced with frustration, as he peered down again at Sammy's injuries.

Gaar took the excess material which Max held in his good hand and began to wrap Sammy's wounds wherever manageable. 'Jag has somehow coerced a gathering of wolves into unnatural behavior—now they're manhunters.'

Sammy was barely conscious and had his eyes closed as Gaar attended him. 'If Sammy survives,' Gaar said, 'we've got Jag. He witnessed the transmutation—*but*, he's suffering from shock, and his testimony at the tribunal may be in our disfavour.'

'Poor guy's in pieces ... *we* witnessed it. Gaar, I've got a bad feeling about this place—'

'I wonder why that is,' Gaar remarked.

'Can we get out of here?' Max said with a frown, as he egged up closer to Gaar, and stared around the snowy basin.

'Can you give me a foot to breathe?'

'Sorry,' Max replied, 'I got so used to being chained to you, now I feel vulnerable without the link.' Max stepped back from his companion, as Gaar inspected the icicle dagger in Sammy's chest.

'If I take this out, he may bleed to death—but if we don't reach a doctor soon, the icicle will melt from his body heat ... then *no more plug*.'

'No more evidence, no prints, and no weapon. Only the word of a fugitive and his lawyer,' Max said in frustration, 'can we go?'

'On the other hand, he may come out of shock and say it was *me*—the cursed one. Sank his boat, and killed his crew.'

'*I'll* vouch for you,' Max offered with confidence.

'I'm sure that'll fix everything. Let's get to the rowboat. I'll get Sammy, if you grab the radio and the bag—with your good hand.'

§

At the water's edge, where the rowboat lay abandoned on the ice collar off shore, Gaar and Max lifted Sammy into the Akwanaque lifeboat. Max sat down in the boat and huddled with Sammy, as Gaar sat on the seat plank and grabbed the hinged oars. Pushing off into the slushy water, Gaar resolutely paddled out towards the middle of the channel where the going was easier.

'How long do you think we have before the tribunal? I wonder what time it is—hey, what about that bullet?' Max babbled. Feeling the ache of his hand injury, he was desperate for distraction.

Gaar rowed feverishly, pondering the state of things, emitting only grunts as he worked at the strenuous task with a tight jaw and a frown.

'Well,' Gaar said, on his forward movement, as he leaned towards Max, then thrust himself back into the stroke, 'it's late morning, I think. I'd say we have about ...' he continued between strokes, '... eight hours to reach Nanisivik.'

'Not at this rate,' Max shouted, as Gaar leaned back, 'this is a really big island—practically a continent!'

'Root through the crew's bag,' Gaar huffed at Max.

'Think there's a motor inside?'

'Max, I must see my father!' Gaar announced as he leaned forward.

'But ... what about—?' Max enquired, indicating Sammy, and then raising his hand in baffled confusion.

'Briefly! There may be a doctor in the village!'

'But, shouldn't we try to row straight up the channel to Nanisivik?!' Gaar pulled in the oars and closed his eyes.

'What is it?' Max said with concern, dropping a map which he'd just pulled from the bag. 'Gaar?!' Max shouted as he leaned forward.

Gaar mumbled incoherently, grabbing hold of the Anknonquatok which was strung around his neck.

Max tapped Gaar's leg. 'Is it the bullet in your shoulder?!'

Gaar removed the doll from around his neck. He looked down and picked up the map. Gaar rubbed the small figure around the map in the proximity of where they floated idle in the water. He stood as the doll began to heat up in his hand. He reached down into the crew's survival bag and rooted until he found what he expected—a rope.

Gaar tied an end of the narrow-guage rope around the doll. Securing the knot, he stepped over the two huddled invalids, and made his way to the bow. There, he lowered the doll into the frigid water which began to boil and bubble in the immediate area of the immersed doll. He secured the other end to an iron loop at the bow. Making his way back to his seat, he looked down at Max who was confounded by Gaar's silence and the unusual rigging he undertook with the Anknonquatok.

'Hang on,' Gaar warned.

Max was jolted, as the boat began to move forward. He looked out over the bow. The line was stretched taught. Something just below the water was towing them.

'What *kinda* fish took *that* bait?!' Max shouted with awe and amazement. 'Just don't turn into a bear in the boat!' Max excitedly shouted, amused by the speed at which they were travelling. He looked at Gaar with a smile, downplaying his fear and concern over these occurrences which he had no understanding of, nor any control over.

'You're a shaman, then—right?'

'I believe so. Don't be afraid, Max,' Gaar said with concern for the man who looked back at him, as though he was afraid for his life. 'Max—*relax*.'

'You said yourself I wasn't ready for it—and you're right,' Max admitted with a deadpan look, uncovering his injured hand to see what all the pain was about.

'Max, don't look,' Gaar said gently.

Max took a deep breath, and stopped his investigation into the extent of his damaged hand. The blood had now frozen on the bandages. 'I know, I just won't be able to take up banjo, right? Can you or the doll, or your *familiars*, fix Sammy?'

'I'm not sure,' Gaar replied, as the biting wind swept across his face. The snow had stopped falling, but the twilight hung like a heavy intermission curtain; the precursor to the lengthy darkness which lay ahead.

Gaar looked around and wondered where he'd be in the months ahead, and what he'd be doing—feeling the sadness now of being alone. He thought of his father and wondered whether it would be a cold meeting—perhaps the last quick acknowledgement of his instability in the world. He managed a warm smile for Max.

'My shoulder feels a bit better.'

'I was wondering,' Max replied, shivering in the bottom of the boat with Sammy, who bore the icicle dagger like a melting candle now. It was a sign that there was life, but more a sign of a diminishing wick which would drown the flame and snuff itself out with a quiet wisp. He wore the melted ice like a congealed red bib, and was now unconscious in Max's arms.

'This is all very new to me,' Gaar said loudly to Max, 'and I'm on kind-of *auto-pilot*, y'know—in a way.'

'I guess everything runs its course,' Max offered ambiguously, raising his shoulders in a puzzled way.

thirty-four

ON A U.S. INTERSTATE, the newlywed comedy team of Frank and Nancy barreled down the bright sunny highway on their way to their Florida honeymoon in their gift car, compliments of Roblaw. Frank pulled out a cigarette and depressed the car lighter.

' "Snuggly-time Scenic Valley Motel and Iguana Emporium"—like to see them fit that on a business card,' Frank said to Nancy, looking at her and flashing his eyes, '... more like "Smugglers Den"—home of the ten most-wanted. Remind me to call that TV show, when we reach a gas station.'

'Yeah,' she added, 'another minute, and those punks would have been cruising in our car. Smooth move on your part—ya great lug,' she squeaked, lifting her shoulders and mugging a dippy house-wife. She giggled factitiously and covered her mouth.

'You callin' me a dip-shit screw head? I deserve better than that for saving the car!'

'I know you do, you carp lovin', ceramic-dog-with-ash-tray-head and clock-eyes buying, horses arse!' she replied, stroking what little hair he had left.

'*That's* more like it. Y'know, I hope those guys leave jail with size-ten butt-holes!'

'Frank, I don't think they go up to ten.'

'Well, *whatever* the record is, I hope they top it. Say, look! There's over five hundred miles on the car.'

'Oh, yippee—so what's the big deal?'

'So, we've got to open her up—let her have a stretch. *Sports car y'know*,' he said, mimicking Roblaw. Frank put his foot down on the accelerator, pushing it down until it was stopped by the floor. The car sped up at his request and after it passed one-hundred MPH, a beeping sound—much like a door-ajar car bell, sounded out.

'I think the ciggy lighter is ready ... or something,' Frank said.

'*I'll* get it, honey-bunny. You just watch the road. Frank ... there's some turns coming up, so slow down a bit!' she requested, taking the lighter from its socket in the dash, and lifting it to the unlit cigarette hanging out of Frank's mouth.

The cigarette dropped from his lips as he gripped the steering wheel like he was putting her on. His eyes widened.

'*Frank*,' she warned.

'I *can't*—!'.

'I know, you're hooked on speed—Frank, *cool it*, will ya?'

'*There's no brakes*!' he screamed, as he furiously pumped the brake pedal. 'The accelerator! *It's STUCK*!' He was petrified. Nancy knew now, he wasn't putting her on. His eyes bulged and his jaw became rock-solid. He made swift desperate snatches at a glut of dash and transmission controls. Nothing intervened.

'*Fraaank*!' she pleaded, sitting up in her seat and bracing herself. She propped her arm against the dashboard, pushing back hard with terrified stiffness. Her legs locked as she pushed herself back in her seat, succumbing to the fear which froze her. The beautiful scenery outside swished past and turned into a blur of confusion.

'DO *SOMETHING*!' she screeched, holding herself back from interfering physically with his frantic steering. In desperation, she unlatched her seat-belt, and dove down under his side, grasping for the accelerator pedal. She couldn't free it. It was jammed and locked, but not on the carpet or anything obvious.

She emerged sobbing and destitute, throwing herself back into her seat, petrified with the uncontrolable speed. Her body vibrated with tension. She cocked her head aimlessly around, darting her alarmed glare from Frank's useless efforts, out towards the unwelcome road ahead. From her frustratingly powerless position, she was mesmerized and just stared at Frank as he steered in a frenzy. Frank whined in a tearful fit.

The incessant beeping taunted them, as the road ahead opened up to hilly terrain below the elevated highway—it was more like flying at that point.

Losing whatever composure she had managed to hang on to, she began to flail her arms, shrieking and randomly lashing out as she went to pieces.

The car madly approached a tight curve in the road. It was sign-posted as twenty-five MPH.

From the opposite direction, an on-coming car in the next lane lazily turned the curve. The uncontrolable runaway nearly clipped it, speeding straight for a meagre barrier on the outside curb. It railed a steep drop below.

thirty-five

BEHIND AN ANIMAL-SKIN drying-frame next to a small white house on blocks, a minor disturbance was underway. Adjacent to it, on the main thoroughfare of Kiqaloq, a dog stood barking at the lurking unwelcome guest, thrashing about and knocking against the fur-laden frame. The dog shut its yap, and began to stalk the intruder.

Out from behind the contraption walked Jag in his human form, with the ice-man swaying on his back. The dog lowered its head and skulked away as Jag neared it. He took up the snow laden roadway, making his way to the village moderator's house.

Further west, at Moffet Inlet—which broke east from the main channel of Admiralty Inlet, his men were undoubtedly waiting to ambush the fugitives who would arrive by water, aboard the Akwanaque trawler.

Coming to a house, with a small satellite dish perched on

the peak of the roof of the one storey box, Jag paused and assessed the modest hovel. It boasted a small sign near the door which relayed the designation: *moderator*, hand rendered in faded black paint. Jag noticed Agaluq's snowmobile parked at the rear of the house, and nodded his head approvingly, knowing he was inside monitoring the moderator's radio.

Their presence there was to be kept secret, giving them the advantage of surprise, when the time came to apprehend the fugitives—or the fugitive and his lawyer. To Jag, there was no distinguishing one from the other. *Shoot first*, crept into his mind.

He climbed the few short wooden steps, and knocked at the plain white door. Waiting impatiently for an answer to his knocks, Jag surveyed the meagre village, which was nestled in the middle of nowhere, and was as plain and desolate as only an Inuit could bear. The identical houses had snowmobiles, discarded household items, and miscellaneous snow-covered junk sprinkled around them. Most chimneys were fluting out the smoke of cooking or baking, which heated the houses adequately, but never comfortably.

The moderator's door cracked open and Jag squinted at the smell of booze, as the dim lighting from within cast a scant glow on his face.

thirty-six

LOUISE WAS FIT to be tied as she listened furious with disgust to the outrageous tape from her answering machine, being played back in Pat's car stereo. Pat drove with one hand. She held Louise's hand with the other. It squeezed unintentionally with such wrath, that Pat had to break the grip and retrieve her hand before Louise broke it.

Although Louise still felt the traces of her anesthesia, she was far from feeling sedated, and lashed out by smashing Pat's dash board in fits of outrage.

'Can you step on it?!' Louise irritably uttered, holding back her fury, not wanting to vent her wrath on her friend Pat. Louise stopped the tape, and angrily punched the rewind button.

'I'm speeding already. We'll be there soon,' Pat whispered.

'Not soon enough ... if it was him—if he could be ... so diabolical ... so wicked and cruel to me ... I—' Louise stammered, then burst out crying, and covered her face with her hands while stamping the floor of the car with both feet very rapidly. Pat stroked her hair.

'If Gaar was right ... what am I—' Louise sobbed, gulping her breath, and rubbing her eyes.

They began to slow down. A flag-man stepped out with a sign requesting traffic to stop. A cement truck pulled out into their lane of the two way street, and maneuvered into position in order to accommodate a sidewalk repair. The truck began to ooze wet cement into a hole. As the cement cascaded down the slide from the rotating barrel of the truck, Louise smashed her fist down on the dash again.

'Hurry up! I wish they'd—Pat, go around!' Louise yelled.

'I can't, there's on-coming traffic!'

Louise leaned into Pat's side and peered at the interspersed trickles of on-coming traffic. She sat back in her seat and stewed angrily. Pat began to turn the wheels into the on-coming lane, but abandoned chance after chance as cars turned into the on-coming lane from the nearby intersection. The cement truck gushed away and it appeared they would be held up for quite a few more minutes. Pat eagerly stayed on guard for a safe chance.

Louise leaned over again to get Pat's relatively unobstructed view. As Pat teetered in light of a slim opening in the congested on-coming traffic, Louise lifted her left leg over the transmission hump and shoved her wayward left foot down on top of Pat's cautious foot which was perched lightly on the gas pedal. Louise sent them barreling into the on-coming lane.

Pat shrieked as she haphazardly steered her way through the corridor, and then swerved around a car which came through the intersection to enter her errant lane. The intersection control lights turned against their favour, but Louise pressed harder on the pedal, and the two flew through on the red. Louise withdrew her foot. Pat was a wreck.

'Louise!—You could'a killed us!! What kind of stunt was that!? Don't ever do that to me again, *please*,' she laughed nervously, contradicting the frown she bore whilst gripping the wheel tightly. Louise had a fixed look on her face.

§

Louise angrily stormed through the Roblaw mansion's front door. Pat followed timidly behind her. Lola the maid, dashed across the foyer hallway buttoning up her blouse. Pat intuitively hung back in the foyer as Louise marched into the large living room and found her mother confronting her father about his tete-et-tete. She held a black studded mask in her hands—his.

There was a heavy silence in the air, broken only when the two realized Louise was standing in the doorway. As they glanced over, Louise launched into her father.

'Father!? What in God's name have you done?! I want *the truth*!'

'It's alright, sweetheart,' Louise's demure mother began, 'we'll pull through this ... I've forgiven him for his—*indiscretion*,' she announced with a timeless glance to the floor, as though the floor were her confidant, readily absorbing her inability to petition her wayward husband.

'Mother ... you don't know the *half* of it!' Louise barked, inadvertantly demoting her mother's rank another unfortunate notch.

Her mother walked toward her, stretching her arms out for a hug. As Louise distractedly hugged her mother, she glared with steely ire at her father. He fidgeted and squirmed in embarrassment having been caught red-handed after his wife had come home early from a cancelled appointment. To have Louise arrive was doubly inopportune, in light of the personal nature of the matter.

'I have fired the maid,' her mother announced candidly, pleasing the floor no end.

Louise stepped away from her mother and approached her father. '*This* has really fuelled my fire!' Louise shrieked. She stomped over to the entertainment centre against the far wall, dug out the tape, inserted it into the casette deck and pushed "play". She turned up the volume very loud, as both her mother and father looked quizzically at their daughter, wondering about her actions.

'Princess—' her father began, only to bite his tongue as he heard the voice of Nancy the comedienne imitating Louise's voice. Hearing the context of the conversation between the impersonator and Gaar, he feigned confusion at what he was listening to.

'Well!?' Louise shouted, as she stared at her father, watching his every facial movement, and catching his eye here and there. As the tape played on, Louise's mother covered her mouth in horror at what she was hearing. Louise watched her father like a hawk, and detected the tell-tale signs of deception, as he writhed with guilt, betraying his guise.

'It was you, wasn't it!? WASN'T IT?!!' she screamed at the top of her lungs, marching at him with venomous scorn. 'You're holding a spare key as a back-up for me! *You* had someone call me from the pharmacy!' she belted out with glaring eyes, detecting his alarm. 'It *was* you!'

'I—' he stammered, as Louise circled him.

'You're disgusting! I *loved* you, worshipped you—trusted you!!' she berated him, waving her arms and bursting into sobs. She regrouped herself to lash further at the perpetrator of the scheme.

'You orchestrated the destruction of my marriage!' she shouted, pointing at the speakers which blasted out the betrayal with poignant clarity as she paused behind his back. 'My *child*! *Gaar's* and my baby! I'm not your daughter—I'm a *possession*!'

She swiftly moved in front of him and faced him directly. In an incongruous motion, she slowly lifted his chin with her hand and looked him square in the eyes.

'Well, my baby—is very much *alive*,' she said with a gruff whisper.

The tears began to flow down her cheeks. Roblaw reached out to her with a trembling hand, almost with remorse for his actions, but more in an unspoken request for understanding. Louise could read his feeble veneer and saw the pathetic gesture as no act of contrition. Greed still motivated the man.

'Where is he?! WHERE?!' she demanded.

'... Nanisivik,' he mumbled, 'on assignment.'

'What?! Did you convince him to take a permanent position up there, thinking you had split us apart with your deception?! What did you do?!!'

Roblaw remained tight-lipped.

'Gaar was *so* right about you!' she growled.

Louise slapped his face, and turned her back on him, moving to her mother who was in shock with the revelations. 'Mum, are you up to speed with this—are you okay?'

Her mother took a step forward. 'Philip ... is this *true*? Philip!'

Roblaw looked at his daughter, and buried himself. 'Princess, it ... *it was for the best*—you've got to believe ...' he squeaked.

Louise walked to the fireplace and drew a fire-poker from the base of the mantle, waving it as she approached him.

'I believe *another word*, and I'll crown you!! Oh, *father*! The curtain's come down on this dark play of yours. I'm moving off your stinking gilded stage. I wish it hadn't taken the plaster to come crashing down on my head to see I was betrayed! I was warned, *but I wouldn't listen*. My eyes are wide open now—and the sight of you sickens me!!'

She turned her back on him and looked lovingly at her mother. 'Mum, will you come away with us from this place? For your sake and mine—Pat's here with me. *Please*?' she begged.

She walked with her mother out into the foyer, where Roblaw's luggage sat in waiting for his excursion to the IAR. Louise leaned over the luggage and plucked the airline ticket from under the handle where it was placed.

'Going somewhere—besides HELL?!' she shouted loudly, her voice echoing in the marbled foyer as she stormed back into the expansive living room and swooped in on her father. 'If I ever see your face again ... I'll send you some where where this'll come in very handy,' she sternly decreed, shoving the fire-poker vehemently into his gut.

Releasing the poker to fall stoutly to the floor, she stuffed the airline ticket in her pocket as she turned and walked out. Her mother stepped out of the closet with her coat in hand, and leaving the closet door gaping, Pat, Louise and her mother walked out the front door, slamming it behind them.

Roblaw put his hand to his forehead and grimaced. Lola came down the stairs with her suitcase in hand and headed for the door. He looked up and dashed into the foyer after her. She brushed him off and pushed through his outstretched hand. He bounded after her and grabbed her by her pony-tail, knocking her off kilter and causing her to drop her suitcase.

'It's all your fault!' he shouted desperately, 'you can't just leave—it's not that easy!'

Lola struggled. She managed to break his hold, and in an eye-to-eye showdown, she kneed him square in the crotch. He fell to his knees, breathless.

'Just watch me!' she taunted, picking up her suitcase. She walked through the front door leaving it ajar behind her. The cold October wind blew in on him, as he crumpled into a ball of excruciating pain on the hard marbled floor. No comfort was to be found in this floor again.

§

Louise passed successfully through an iris scan and a metal-detector security frame at the airport. Gathering the metallic odds and ends from a small basket handed back to her, she looked back and waved at her mother and Pat who saw her off with hopes for success on her rescue mission.

Smiling through the odd tear, she walked past a group of RCMP officers and headed for the departure lounge, where the flight was announced on the PA system. She had never been to the Arctic, but was eager to find Gaar and would do whatever she had to in order to get him back in her life. Come hell or high water, she would save their marriage.

She felt freedom and reveled in her anticipation of leaping into Gaar's arms, admitting her father's wickedness, begging his forgiveness and smothering him with tender kisses. Love's fine grace would be theirs again.

Showing her ticket and credentials to a man standing at the designated departure gate, she walked down the ramp and disappeared.

thirty-seven

THE BOUND DOLL SPIRIT, in the form of a Narwhal, skimmed the surface of the frigid water as it propelled the rowboat at a fast clip through the open centre of the channel. Gaar observed the point of land which jutted out into the waterway not far off now on the east side of Admiralty Inlet. It was there, that a relatively undemanding trek across the frozen tundra led to Kiqaloq.

He looked down at Max who was either dozing off or tuning out, and reached for the radio which was under his leg. Max became reasonably alert as Gaar tried to pry the cover off the radio to transmit a message.

'Max, can you remove the cover?' he said, as he stretched the hand mike from the unit. 'See if you can zero in on a band.' Max twisted the dial slightly, and Gaar gave it a shot.

'Breaker?! Come in Kiqaloq,' Gaar announced, 'Come in, over.' They listened for a reply and waited in vain— nothing happened. Max twisted the dial ever-so slightly again, and Gaar made another attempt. 'Breaker! Come in Kiqaloq, Come in Kiqaloq, over.' As they frowned again at the irritating silence, a voice suddenly emitted from the radio speaker in reply to Gaar's transmission.

'This is Kiqaloq moderator ... go ahead ...' an Inuit man replied, sounding sluggish of mind and of mouth.

'This is Gaar Injugarjuk, moderator—do you copy?'

'Copy that, Injugarjuk, what are ... your coordinates? Over.'

Gaar looked around, then replied as he looked down at Max, who was appearing to waste away. 'North up Admiralty, ten minutes from Ikaluvik Bay, en route to Kiqaloq. My party needs urgent medical attention—is there a doctor in the region? Over.'

There was a delay, then the moderator came back. 'That's affirmative ... Gaar. What is your ETA? Over.'

'ETA, two hours. Moderator, our presence at a high-council meeting in Nanisivik is imperative, this evening. Please have the doctor and transportation waiting to shuttle us there—is that possible? Over.'

'Affirmative ... copy.'

'Moderator, if anything should happen to us ... there is a crucial affidavit in a journal at the old whaling station at Itoqek Inlet that the council should have, and the Canadian authorities should see— copy? Over.'

'Copy, Gaar. ETA two hours, Ikaluvik Bay—affidavit at Itoqek Inlet. Over and out.'

Gaar hooked the hand-piece back on the radio and sat back, keeping an eye on both Sammy and Max. He reached to his chest for the Anknonquatok and not finding it, realized it was in the water. He rubbed at his ribs, feeling a pain. He *was* bitten by Jag there, but that was not what ailed him—it was something else, something worse than a bite.

thirty-eight

AT THE HALF-DRUNKEN moderator's house, Jag patted Isaac on the back for his assistance over the radio. Isaac scratched his bald head and stared at the ice-man on Jag's back but remained silent in his respect for the shaman and his mission. Jag and Agaluq walked out of Isaac's house and shut the door behind themselves.

Outside, the men walked to the rear of the house, where Agaluq mounted his snowmobile.

'When you meet with Triq and Kiratek at Ikaluvik Bay,' Jag whispered into Agaluq's hood, 'let them know of Brunhilde Hamilton's disappearance and that Gaar and the other man are with the fugitive. They may try and ambush you if you're not on your toes, so, shoot first—we formulate the reason later. Traitors are best dead at our feet, than alive at our throats.'

Agaluq started his vehicle and zipped off immediately with a nod to Jag. Jag walked back onto the main trail of the community and then off in the direction he entered the village from, intent on tying up some loose ends.

It was now around one in the afternoon. The twilight

stretched its presence through the great dome which at this latitude near the pole, churned with magnetism and reacted to solar activity with the greatest of eloquence in the dance of the northern lights. In the all-or-nothing six month day or night split, customary for the region, the high north was in a flux. The short-lived twilight was about the only fleeting period which went in and out of season like a mayfly. The houses never changed, the people hardly changed, the population rarely fluctuated, and the tales remained the same. How the stories were absorbed and reflected on, may have been the only aspect that moved like the Aurora Borealis.

§

Tunningham arrived on the back of a snowmobile, and was let off his ride with only a vague wave of a hand toward the Kiqaloq supply store. Handing his taxi driver some money, he stepped away from the vehicle as it zoomed off north, back in the direction of Nanisivik. He was left standing in the all but deserted village, with nothing but his parka and his black briefcase in hand.

Beyond him, in a flat ice-field between two houses, two boys played the "snake-slide" game. The lads took turns slinging a harpoon-like stick in fissured gullies in the ice, thrusting and measuring the potency of their pitching—laughing and hooting at their achievements.

Tunningham turned up-village and wandered along the main path, looking from side to side to distinguish the supply store from the rest of the white structures against their white background. He stopped and stared as a commotion flowed towards him.

A dog team trotted into Kiqaloq—without a navigator. It was the stray sled which gorged on Brunhilde. Girly caught his attention, as she exited a house nearby. Seeing the sled team mushing without a driver, she jogged down to the wide thoroughfare to intercept the team as it passed. As the snow-bearded dogs passed her with only a nonchalant glance from them, she ran alongside the pack, and as the navigator's post crept up beside her, she leapt on. Tunningham watched in admiration as she took hold of the reins and brought the team to a halt very near him. Girly walked to the lead dog and patted it on the head. Taking its harness, she led the team to a tie-down pole nearby, and began to secure them for a temporary layover. Tunningham approached her.

'An impressive job, miss. Odd to see a team without a driver,' he said, stating the obvious. 'I wonder if you could help me? I'm trying to find—'

Girly stood back from the dogs, lifting her index finger and stalling the questions. 'Excuse me—please. You can see I have my hands full at the moment, and it's very important I deal with this immediately,' she interjected, in a panicked way, 'could you call the moderator for me? Have him meet me here with the dogs, *please*. Tell him ... I have the team that killed that woman.'

Tunningham stepped back from the team and scrunched up his face. 'What woman?! *This* team—?'

'Look, it's a long story,' she sighed, sucking her lip to the side of her pretty face, 'perhaps you could mind these dogs while *I* fetch the moderator?'

Tunningham leaned into the harness webbing and scrutinized the branding insignia. 'These harness markings bear the 3R stamp!' he said, pointing down to the tethering. 'I'm an envoy of the Canadian Government, investigating the travesty at the Kabloona camp—'

'Yes,' she said abruptly, 'I know about it ... my sister was killed there, Friday.' Girly took a breath and pondered for a moment. 'She was an engineer apprentice and from what I hear, the lax security on *your* country's behalf probably cost her her life! It's a damn shame that the dregs from your system should choke the life from ours,' she said sternly, lashing out at him for being representative of the bureaucracy.

She pointed her finger at him, then thought better of venting her spleen on the messenger, and bit her lip.

'I'm truly sorry for your loss, miss,' he offered, looking down for a moment, 'I'm trying to get to the bottom of this, myself. There'll be a royal commission into the matter.'

'Royal commissions don't bring back the dead—they just toy with the living. A royal-pain-in-the-butt is all that ever comes of such things.'

Tunningham understood her anger and frustration, but wouldn't dare verbalize it. 'I want to make a difference,' he began again, striving for trust, 'I think I can help, but I need your cooperation—please.'

Girly relented and let go of her atypical posture which she felt could be an impediment to a constructive resolution of the matter.

'How can you help to *stop* making us victims, then?' she said flatly.

'For two days, I've been lobbying to bring some experts up to extract the trapped miners. They're prisoners—not friends of mine, but they're *people*. I've managed to get hold of some mining rescue experts from Canada who'll be in Nanisivik by tonight with the equipment to rescue the trapped victims in the mine. Is it incongruous for a politician to care? A little trust wouldn't hurt. So, if you *would* please, help me—before you get the moderator.' There was a silence. ' Were you a witness to this woman's death?'

'Kinda,' she replied, 'I mean, I saw the woman—she tried to strangle me! Then the dogs lit into her. What does she have to do with Kabloona?'

'She allegedly murdered a few people, then escaped.'

Girly felt her neck, which still bore the marks of the botched strangling. 'I see.'

'Was *anyone with her*? A lot rides on this—was there a *man* with her?'

Girly shook her head.

'No?' he asked with concern. 'Does the moderator have a radio?'

'Yeah. Say, do you have any proof of who you are? I already gave my name to some men a ways-out, asking questions, saying they were the law.'

Tunningham's eyes flared. 'Really? Who?'

'I don't know,' she replied, rubbing her head, 'a strange one—'

'... with a corpse strapped to his back,' he said, finishing her thought. '*Najagneq*, the superintendent of Kabloona.'

'*Jag*,' she said, ' ... of *course*, the superintendent. Matawi talked of him in her letters. He's a shaman. Not from these parts. Look, are you gonna prove who you are?'

'Oh yes,' Tunningham said, as he cracked open his briefcase and produced his credentials. 'See? Government of Canada—foreign affairs. So,' he said as he closed up his briefcase, 'are the dogs secure here?'

'I better take 'em to the sheds just down the way over there—to be safe. It'll just take a minute,' she uttered, undoing the harness from the tie-down post.

'Okay,' Tunningham replied, 'then we'll get to the moderator and his radio.'

'I hope this doesn't take too long, I've got a commitment at the store that I don't want to be too late for.'

'At the *store*? I want to go there,' Tunningham said eagerly.

'It's important to me—cultural aerobics. The moderator's house is over there,' she said, pointing across and down the hard-packed snow roadway.

Girly took the lead dog's collar and jogged with the team over to a public shed area. Tunningham stood and waited for her, watching as she secured the dogs.

Finishing her task, she made her way quickly back to Tunningham who got into step with her, matching her brisk pace to the moderator's house.

'Just what is it you do for your government, exactly?' Girly asked, turning her hood his way as they walked.

'It's a long story for such a short walk—diplomatic stuff,' he replied through the funnel of his hood as he watched his step along the undulating ground. 'You live here?'

'Originally from Tuktoyaktuk.'

'You're a long way from there,' Tunningham replied.

'You could say I'm a Northerner domiciling in the east and hailing from the west.'

'That's a mouthful,' laughed Tunningham.

'I get around,' she continued, 'my *calling* you might say. I'm visiting Kiqaloq for a couple of days. It's my job, *visiting*. House-calls. I spent a lot of years in these parts, and here.'

'Are you a doctor?' Tunningham enquired.

'A *cultural* doctor, maybe,' she replied, as they neared the moderator's house. 'I hope he's in.'

Girly climbed the steps, with Tunningham waiting close behind her. She knocked at the door. After a few moments of nothing, she knocked again and called out for him.

'Isaac! ISAAC?!' she shouted, turning the handle of the door. She had a sneaking suspicion that Isaac was in.

Abandoning the locked front door, she brushed by Tunningham as she descended the steps and walked over to a window through which she peered into the oil-lamp lit front room. Her suspicions were confirmed, as she looked in on Isaac, who was sitting on the floor against a couch of-sorts, apparently drunk and asleep. In his hands was clasped a half empty liquor bottle, and nearby—strewn all around him, was the community's weekly mail on the floor.

Tunningham moved from the steps to take a peek at what was captivating her. He stopped next to her and had a gander. A glare of familiarity registered in his eyes. 'Isaac, you said, right?'

'Jiminy! Stone drunk. Yeah, that's right,' she replied, '*pillar of the community*! Mayor and mailman. No wonder he locked the door—should'a closed the blinds. Well,' she said, breaking from the window and facing Tunningham, 'try later. I've got to get to my appointment, good luck with your mission, I've gotta run.'

'But wait!' he blurted, 'I'd like to get to the supply store myself, and if you would please, let me know where I can contact you,' he said, as they ambled along toward the store. 'You're an important facet to the investigation into Kabloona—y'know, the *woman* you bumped into on the tundra.'

'*Bumped into*!' she laughed, 'we can talk further at the store, after. I'll escort you … but—' she paused, not wanting to hurt his feelings, 'you're a *stranger*. A WASP, the briefcase … envoy of the pillaging past.'

'A walking symbol, huh?'

'A kind of … "just add water" type, I'm sorry to say. It's not your fault … just … please hold your tongue, and don't schmooze unless I'm with you, okay?'

'Alright,' he replied, nodding his head, 'I'll play it your way. The store is where the storyteller lives and works, right?'

'Yup. Is that what brought you here? Business or acquaintance?'

'An associate of mine—part of my envoy, it's his father, and I've come to pay my respects,' Tunningham said as he lost sight of Girly through his hood, and turned around to see her cemented in her steps.

Girly shook in rousing emotion. 'Gaar?!' she screamed

with exuberence. 'Gaar is *here*?! Where is he?!' She ran up to Tunningham and looked up into his hood.

'You know Gaar?'

'*Do I know Gaar*! We were great friends as kids!' She looked down for a moment and pondered with reticence. 'His father ... may not want to—there is a great rift between them,' she said, looking about nervously, '*don't* bring it up— *let me*. Where is Gaar?'

'I heard the old man's not well ... Gaar's with our tracker on the tundra. He wanted to come here, but he may have to go straight to Nanisivik this afternoon.'

'Uh huh,' she replied, as they again picked up the pace for the store. 'Well, you heard right. Gaar's father is not well— he's been like a father to me. *Don't* upset him. Let me handle this.'

thirty-nine

IN THE GATHERING at the Kiqaloq supply store, Girly and another woman faced each other in a kneeling position, breathing fast and furiously into each other's faces in a hypnotic repetitive tonal exchange. Staring into each other's eyes as others watched with rapture, they alternated their monotoned huffs in a ceremonial venting which corralled the spirit of those present, and electrified the room.

Tunningham looked on with interest, but all the same, was a stranger in a strange place. He had previously heard one of Abram's stories and was impressed by the exchange between the teller and the told.

The women finished their "breathing-song" with laughs of approval from the friends who had gathered, and Girly rose, walking with a bright beautiful smile over to Gaar's father who hugged her with fatherly pride. Turning back into the affair of thirty or so neighbours squatting on the floor and on boxes, Girly began to sing an Inuit song in her native tongue. This whipped up the congregation of men, women and children, fuelling all into a clap and sing-along.

A thought struck Girly, and she stepped aside of the merrymaking to approach a young man who stood at the wall clapping along with the song.

'Saul, it's good to see you again,' she said, hugging the young lad.

'Nice to see *you*,' he replied.

'Would you do me a great big favour?'

'I'll do my best.'

'There's a dog-team at the sheds ... would you be able to go and feed them? I saw some food in the locker there. I just didn't have time and I know that they've been starved. Please?' she asked, as the youth replied with a smile and a nod. 'Oh, ... don't get friendly with them, and keep your guard up—they mauled somebody earlier, so be careful. Thanks so much, Saul,' she said with a smile, turning back to her obligations with the celebrations at hand.

Tunningham left his perch at a window sill and approached Abram. Girly caught a glimpse of the exchange as Tunningham introduced himself to Gaar's father. A frown crossed her face which was cast aside as she was drawn back into the proceedings and swept along in the joviality. She darted an occasional disapproving glance at Tunningham, as he unabashedly mingled in defiance of her request.

forty

THE GROTESQUE, TWO-HEADED wolf tumbled and violently crashed into the weathered bear rifle-trap outside the old whaling station shack at Itoqek Inlet. The two heads ravenously snarled and bit at each other, as the massive body they shared aimlessly flipped and turned in a violent struggle with itself.

The secondary head with the turquoise eyes, clamped its jaws across the snout of the red-eyed one, and opened a gash below one of its eyes.

Suddenly, the wolf began transmuting. After a moment, Jag was standing there, feeling the gash and rubbing the blood from his cheek. In a fit, Jag marched to the shack and furiously kicked open the shack's fragile door.

With careless abandon, he angrily tore the ice-man from his back and thrust it upon the decrepit counter top, where he began to reprimand the corpse in his native tongue. In fits and bounds, he upbraided the mummy, violently striking out at it with shrieks of denouncement.

Having vented his wrath, he frantically began to search for the journal which held the affidavit, accidentally kicking the mound of remaining ashes from the fire which Max had fashioned on the floor. Getting down on his knees, Jag spied the floor for any signs of the journal. He checked under several elevated cabinets and rooted behind some piles of junk, becoming more and more frustrated with the search. Reaching under the base of the counter top, he finally put his eager hands on it.

Pulling out the journal, and gloating over the discovery, Jag opened the book and fingered through the pages until he came to the fresh entry. He tore out the page and tossed the journal over his shoulder.

Moving to the doorway, he held up the page in the dim twilight and with a cursory glance at the affidavit to confirm its contents, he crumpled up the page into a ball. Something occurred to him, and he uncurled the document, this time reading the contents with more care.

The final portion about Roblaw was enlightening. He tore away the bottom of the page with Max and Gaar's signature knowing with delight, he would use it against the industrialist to crush the inroads he had made in the Arctic at the expense of its inhabitants.

Stuffing the bottom half of the document in his parka, he took the remaining rumpled wad of yellowed paper and strode over to the perched ice-man and crammed the ball into the stiffened mouth of the gangly corpse.

Reaching beneath his caribou parka, he withdrew a small pouch which hung around his neck and opened it. Jag sprinkled something on the ice-man, and paced around the shack chanting and dusting the room with his mysterious mixture. Coming back around to the ice-man, he mumbled an incantation and was passionately swept up into a shamanistic trance, in which he evoked the ire of his spirit helpers.

Instantaneously, the ice-man burst into flames while Jag

was in the midst of his sorcery. The trail of his sprinklings ignited around the tinder shack. As the flames rose, malevolent shadows were cast in the wake of the fire. Jag slowly bowed out of the rickety hut.

Standing in the doorway of the burgeoning inferno, Jag looked up into the twilight sky and sang out his dissonant chant, petitioning his spirit helpers and familiars alike.

The red-eyed wolf, black as the coming darkness and free of its uncooperative companion which was now engulfed in flames, bolted from the doorway, and disappeared into the tundra.

§

In the waters through the middle of Admiralty Inlet channel, something was terribly wrong. Gaar was taken by surprise as the lifeboat slowed and the whale which towed them began to thrash about violently in the frigid water. Max was awakened from his sluggish delirium and became suddenly alert to the fact that something was happening. The whale went down and the fastened bow of the boat suddenly began to tip down—fast.

'Gaar! What—?!' Max screeched as he quickly rose to his feet, long before his stiffened body was ready for the action. He tumbled backwards as the bow began to submerge.

'Get something to cut the line!' Gaar shouted, as he also tumbled to the front of the plunging boat.

'My foot is caught! My foot is stuck, Gaar!!' Max pleaded

helplessly, looking back at his bent knee which was folded over the edge of the bench seat, with Sammy's unconscious body collapsed against it.

In a second, the boat was under water, and as Max looked to Gaar for help with a terrified expression and a desperate reach, he went down. Gaar grabbed his outstretched hand and snatching a breath, dove after Max. Sammy's unconscious body floated face down on the surface.

The ripples of commotion on the surface smoothed out, in keeping with the desolate stillness and peace which all things bowed-to in the quiet secret of the Arctic.

Max broke the still surface, gasping for air. He struggled to tread water in his desperate reprieve. Blue from cold, and as good as a mile to shore, he was tortured by the thought of his prolonged inevitable death—a death he wouldn't be fit to cheat this time. Gaar emerged from the dark deep with a gasp and a flutter of arms on the surface of the water. Max stared at Gaar despondently.

'You'll be alright if you listen to me, Max ...' Gaar said, coughing water from his mouth, 'will you trust me?'

'I'm not with the program anymore,' Max whispered out with a shiver, as his head bobbed slightly above water, 'what's left when you can hardly feel your body? Except to damn Roblaw to hell!'

'Max, pull Sammy towards you. Max! Try and hold yourself together! Reach to Sammy and pluck out one of his eyes, and hand it to me!'

'You're *insane*—' Max replied, scoffing with a trembling voice.

'Max, if you want to survive, do it! I can save you both!' Gaar announced. 'I can't do it for you! You've got to engineer this!'

'Alright, you goddamn sonofabitch—here!!' Max cried, violently molesting Sammy's head, and with squeaks of disgust and frustration, snatched the left eye from Sammy's face with his good hand and threw it at Gaar, who fumbled with the catch, but managed to grasp the stringy eye-ball.

'Now, one of yours!'

'Never! No!!'

Gaar floated up beside Max and placed his hand lightly on his head. 'Max, It'll be a new life for you both. I need you to be brave! You've got nothing to lose now; there'll be no pain. Do it for me.'

Max cringed in doubt, shivering the last bits of strength from his body. 'Where's your *friend*?!' he groaned, almost in tears.

'Something's gone wrong, and the doll can't help us. My familiars will assist us—but I need your willing help. *Pass me an eye*, and you'll see there's new life for you.' Gaar shivered and looked up to the sky. 'The bear is coming to pick up the pieces ... so *help yourself*. Give me the right one.'

Max let out a primal scream and in a fit of despair, plucked his right eye out and thrust out his hand with a gurgle of horrified disgust. Opening up his clenched fist, there was the eye which Gaar promptly relieved him of.

Gaar held the eye-balls, one in each fist, and began to chant. As Gaar's face began to change, he placed the eyes in his mouth and looked up into the twilight sky. Max fainted, dropping his exhausted head face-first in the water.

The bear corralled both Max and Sammy with his immense paws, drawing them both close in front of him in the water. Gaar promptly bit down on Max's head with urgent purpose.

forty-one

IN THE HUBBUB of the modest festivities at the supply store, Tunningham spoke confidentially with Gaar's father. Abram's face dropped when Tunningham said something which upset him. The old man weakened considerably on the spot, appearing to almost collapse with apprehension. He declined to talk further with Tunningham as he made his way from the man towards his room at the back.

Girly followed the confused glares of some folk who witnessed the sudden debilitation of Abram. Seeing the telltale results of Tunningham's loose lips, she bolted across the room to assist the old man. Girly flashed a glare of contempt in Tunningham's direction, as she braced Gaar's father, helping him into the back of the store where he lived.

Girly looked back at the concern of the staring crowd. With a worried smile, she nodded at the woman who had joined her in the "breathing-song". With an enticing swirl of her forearm, the woman got the message of Girly's animated gesture and led the proceedings into another sing-along. Girly lifted a lit oil-lamp from a ledge, and continued with Abram to the back.

Girly opened a door as the two of them passed through into the back where Abram lived. She assisted him into his bedroom–living quarters, which split off from the narrow hallway leading to his kitchen-washing area.

As he silently crumpled down onto his bed, Girly stroked his head lovingly. Leaving him to his thoughts, she stood upright. She didn't want to broach the sensitive topic at this point. Placing the oil-lamp on a simple chest of drawers, she dimmed it and walked back to him. Holding his chest in pain, he lifted his shaking hand towards a shelf, which she attentively moved to and surveyed.

'The pouch,' he said feebly.

Girly came across some medications in plastic vials on the shelf with a trace of dust on the surface of the caps. Briefly inspecting the labels of the vials for their contents and dates, she came to the conclusion that he had been neglecting to take his medications based on the label's dosage instructions and date.

Obliging his request, she reached for the small velvet pouch with its tiny delicate draw bands and retrieved it for him. His bed-living room was chock full of carvings, tacked-up feathers and an animal-skin mask which was fastened to the wall.

Girly stepped around some of the over-flow stock from the store and sat on the edge of the bed next to him. As he reclined, he clasped the small pouch with both hands over his chest and looked at her with gratitude. He couldn't conceal the anxiety which tormented him. His eyes darted aimlessly in confusion. He looked away from Girly, staring vacantly out a frosted window into the somber sky.

'Gaar ... is *here*,' he said in a thin whisper, betraying his embarrassment and shame.

'I know,' she replied, stroking his hair. 'Abram, you've been neglecting to take your medications. That's not good,' she said in a kind and caring way, devoid of any trace of a scolding tone, although she disapproved of his neglect.

Girly got up from the side of the bed and went into his kitchen. Moments later she returned with a damp cloth. She dabbed his perspiring forehead. She kissed him on the head and rose. 'Don't worry, everything will ... be fine,' she whispered as she walked to the door and gingerly disappeared from the room.

§

The bear trotted with an ambling stride along the frosted tundra. There was compromise in his steps, as his left shoulder impeded his gait and caused him pain as he trekked. Obliged to host the imbedded bullet, Gaar trod onwards, nearing the village of Kiqaloq, hastening the overdue confrontation with his own blood—his father.

With the community in sight now, Gaar slowed to a stop and surveyed the area. Confident the vicinity was clear and he was alone, he began to turn in a circle. With his paws close together, he squatted slightly and began to defecate. Looking up to the Aurora Borealis and huffing out great wafts of steam from his nostrils, he stepped forward.

There, lying amongst the bear droppings was a naked man, writhing in the soiled snow. Gaar, in his human form, approached and hovered over the man who looked up at Gaar with both confusion and joy on his face.

Kneeling beside him, Gaar took handfuls of snow and wiped him down. Undoing the sinew bindings of his furs, Gaar took two small pieces of fur and bound them on the man's feet. Standing up together, Gaar sheltered the shivering man under his cloak, and the two walked toward Kiqaloq.

forty-two

EMERGING WITH SUDDEN splashes from the frosty water of Admiralty Inlet, was the gold-faced giant. With furs drenched and draining buckets-worth of scalding cold water, the doll-spirit leapt up onto an ice-flow and moved swiftly for the land mass with assertive wide steps.

Reaching the shore, it paused and turned its carved bone face, to the south. It tilted its head upwards, mysteriously contemplating the sky.

With a powerful leap into the air, the doll-spirit metamorphosed into a peregrine falcon and flew upwards, letting out a screech as it swam through the air in a south-easterly direction. Flying high above the shoreline, above the tall hills and snow covered peaks, the falcon cut through the air.

Finally, the bird plunged steeply, zeroing in on a mound of smouldering ashes below. With a hovering flutter, it touched down on the toppled frame of the rifle-beartrap and perched itself there, looking on at the smoking remnants of the old whaling shack. The wind gusted and ruffled its feathers, but the falcon held tight with its sharp talons, perching like a sentry keeping watch over some secret amongst the ashes.

Suddenly lifting itself from its watch with a few powerful flaps, it landed at the periphery of the ashes and strutted about in the ash littered snow, darting its head at something of interest in the ruins.

With a brisk flap of its wings, it transmuted back into the gold-faced hulk, and trod into the smouldering remnants of the charcoaled wood. Locating the spot where the ice-man corpse was incinerated, the doll-spirit knelt down and corralled the ashes. Cupping its golden hands, it lifted a brimming handful and wiped the cinders into its expressionless face.

Standing slowly and backing away from the brief ceremony, the doll-spirit detected Jag's wolf tracks, and began to follow the impressions in the snow, stepping stiffly into each paw print for eight paces. With another powerful leap into the air, the spirit had embarked once again as the falcon—on a sacred mission.

forty-three

OUTSIDE, ON THE STEPS of the supply store, Gaar paused for a moment with his new companion huddled under his furs with him.

'Please,' Gaar said to the man, 'don't talk to anyone other than polite responses when spoken to, alright?' The unusually handsome fellow nodded his cooperation. The man was more Inuit than white, his curly hair being the most apparent giveaway of his Jewish side. As the man was about to speak, Gaar raised his hand. 'I know, I know,' Gaar said, 'we'll have a long chat soon about what happened to you, and who you are *now*. It must be very unusual to feel you have two pasts—the memories and all, but you're an *individual*, so try and streamline ... your thoughts. Be calm, and *relax*. Your name can be ...'

'Aaron,' the man said, looking around and nodding his head slowly with an approving shiver, 'Aaron.'

Inside the store, Girly meandered through the bobbing participants in the sing-song and approached the young man whom she asked a favour of earlier.

'Saul, I need you to do something *very* important,' she said excitedly to the attentive youth, 'go to the moderator's house. If his door is locked, kick it in! I'll take responsibility. I need you to get on his radio and call Nanisivik for a shaman and a medical doctor to come here immediately! Abram is very sick—maybe dying ... tell them he has a history of heart attacks and high blood pressure ... and he's been neglecting his medication—'

'Gotcha,' Saul replied, grabbing his coat and then running for the door.

As he reached for the door handle, the door swiftly opened inwards, cracking Saul in the forehead. He reeled back holding his head as Gaar and Aaron entered the store. With a quick glance at the unusual duo huddled under the one cloak, Saul realized from their flat expressions that they hadn't known they rudely smacked the door into his head, and dismissed the altercation as an accident.

He squeezed by the two slow-moving strangers, and made haste out the door.

Girly was oblivious to the newcomers, and had returned to the back of the store to attend Abram. The singing continued, with only the occasional three-second stare darted their way as they moved up the side of the gathering. Tunningham spotted Gaar and quick-stepped over to him with a surprised look on his face.

'Gaar! Thank God!' Tunningham blurted. Aaron uncomfortably writhed in his conspicuousness. Tunningham and others looked on at him as though he were a charity case. 'This *isn't* Max, is it? No, I've seen pictures and—so, did you find Max?! I thought the worst had happened, not having heard from you.'

Gaar looked up at some blankets on a shelf, to cover Aaron. 'You can stop worrying now, I'm here. Tunningham, pass me a blanket—nevermind,' he said, looking up at the wall next to him which had a display parka tacked to the wall. Gaar tugged the parka off the wall and handed it to Aaron.

'Here,' Gaar said, 'and grab a pair of boots from that lower shelf, there.' He closed his fur cloak and bound it around himself, free now from sharing his furs. Aaron quickly wrapped himself in the parka and slipped on a pair of insulated trousers from the supply store shelves.

When the song finished, Gaar walked further into the room and smiled at the gathering who for the most part looked his way in curiosity. 'Hello, everyone! I'm Gaar Injugarjuk, and that man is my friend Aaron, and he is Tunningham from the Canadian government,' he announced. Heads turned to each other. Whispers of Gaar's name could be heard.

A few words of greeting emanated from the gathering.

'Please, continue with your wonderful songs—perhaps I shall start one,' Gaar said proudly, as he looked around at the expectant faces, and began to sing out a very old Inuit song. Some of the older folks in the crowd picked up on his selection, and after a brief verse and chorus, he bowed out, leaving the momentum going and the gathering singing away.

Tunningham held Gaar's arm and looked into his face with concern. 'Where's McGregor and Max?!'

'Later,' Gaar replied, looking over at Aaron who was now slipping into some boots, 'will you see that the store gets paid for these items—I seem to have misplaced my charge card. I've got to go to the back and see my father—he's there, right?'

'Yes, he's back there ... he's not well at the moment.'

'Excuse me,' Gaar said, as he walked towards the back of the store.

Aaron walked to the edge of the gathering and looked on with keen interest. Tunningham scrunched up his nose and sniffed at the air after Aaron passed by him. Something stunk but he couldn't figure out where it stemmed from. He surreptitiously lifted his feet one by one and checked the underside of his boots.

Gaar stood silent and unnoticed in the doorway of his father's bed-living space. He looked on as his father lay resting with his eyes closed on his small bed, grasping the tiny dark velvet pouch to his chest.

Girly came up behind Gaar, returning from the adjoining kitchen with another damp cloth and a glass of water in her hand.

'Excuse me,' she said gently, 'he needs to rest. I've called for a doctor.' Gaar turned to her to get a look at his father's care-giver. Girly nearly dropped the glass of water at the sight of him. 'Gaar? Gaar!!' she delightfully announced, swishing water from the glass to the floor as she half-hugged him.

'Hello,' he replied in a somber whisper. 'I'd like to be alone with my father for a while, if you don't mind. May I?'

'Of *course*,' she replied congenially, 'do you remember me, Gaar? It's *Girly*—we played as children ...'

'I remember, Girly,' Gaar said warmly, returning her sincere affection with a sad smile.

'Well, I'll leave you two alone—it's long overdue,' she added with a nod. She reluctantly turned away from him and sauntered back into the gathering, glancing back with a longing in her eyes as she was immersed in the skylarking once again.

Gaar entered the room and shut the door quietly. He looked about the room in reminiscence and found that it hadn't changed much in the twenty-odd years since he'd left with his mother to be schooled in Canada.

His father however had failed very much from his memory of him. He was eager but afraid to break the funeral-like silence of the dimly-lit room. Gaar was startled as his reclined father opened his eyes and stared with alarm at his son who loomed near his bed.

Gaar was filled with apprehension as his father lowered his eyes in shame and turned his head slowly in retreat, looking away from Gaar and staring blankly at the frosted window. He clasped the little pouch tightly with both hands. Gaar felt the same awkward embarrassment which his father displayed. He saw the uneasiness in his father's trembling hands, and felt that he hadn't access to words which would bridge their silence.

'You've come,' Abram said in a feeble whisper, rife with anxiety.

'Yes, father,' Gaar replied in a half voice, happy to have started, but confused where to take it. He had so many things to tell him and many cobwebbed questions which needed dusting; but he felt dumbstruck. He didn't want to plead, neither did he want to suggest there was any blame to wear. The ensuing silence tortured him, but he wasn't there to dawdle and now that the moment had come, he was going to see it through. He wouldn't be satisfied until they had resolved the problem or crashed and burned in the attempt.

'The storyteller's son has a little story to tell,' Gaar piped up, 'a little boy—the end,' he said, and after a few moments of silence, he sighed. 'I guess I better keep my day job, huh? I'd never fill your shoes, but ... I wish you'd invite me to try 'em on ...' Gaar whispered, rubbing his nose and standing there with a quivering lip. 'I don't know who or what has estranged us,' he said with building conviction, 'but, I want it to end here and now! Father?'

'You have heeded your calling. I sense you've become ...

your grandfather's shadow,' Abram uttered with ominous overtones.

'Yes. Unprepared, I have been initiated—I exist in two realities now, and I've been filled with his spirit and taken up with my familiars. Will you say my name?'

'I ... killed my father—you must know that.'

'Where'd you get that from?!' Gaar asked, stepping forward and looming at the edge of the bed.

'I've suffered with illness ... these ... decades of silence. Now—' he said, rustling nervously, and gripping the pouch tightly, 'you have come to vent his wrath. It has been my premonition, as the century turned, that all that has been taken will be reclaimed in blood ... by the hunger of divine providence.'

Gaar swiftly moved to the foot of the bed to try and catch his father's eye. 'It's *not true!*' he shouted, 'there's retribution to be paid, *but not by you!* ... Father,' he said, tempering his voice down to a gentle, endearing level, 'call my name—'

'A little boy ... I pushed him over the cliff—at play ... my misdoing ...' he babbled, reciting his confession in a daze. I couldn't remember the spot for the police!'

'Stop it!' Gaar decreed, 'that's *false*. The blackbird—a rival dark-shaman ... Solomon Arluqinaqoosik, can you remember this?' he said, trying to break his father's fixation of guilt, 'the blackbird clipped him at the cliff, throwing him off balance as he meditated at the precipice. I've been witness to a first-hand account!' Gaar pleaded, pacing in frustration at the foot of the bed. 'Call my name—say it, and all's well!'

'It's all my fault ...' Abram went on in his painful delirium, '*I killed my father,*' he sobbed.

Gaar was swept into a fit, seeing his father ailing and drowning in front of him in a river of remorse; refusing to accept a saving hand.

With an excruciating moan, Gaar lashed out with the

madness of the impediment, flailing his arms randomly and striking at objects around the room like a trapped animal.

The singing which leaked through the door from the gathering out front had ended, and some women were now engaging in a "breathing-song". It fuelled the berserk spasms driving the pent-up insanity which was now unleashed in Gaar. Gaar was going off like a strip of fire-crackers, rolling at the walls and grunting with blind fury. He expelled one complete passionate breath of despair and ire in his wake.

'Have pity! Take the curse from my family!' Abram shouted, taking a locket from the velvet pouch and extending it with a trembling hand in Gaar's direction. His head cowered away from the wrathful display of what he saw as an avenging angel.

Gaar tore wildly at the seams in the wood planked wall, then turned and slid to the floor, collapsing from exhaustion into a heap at the foot of the bed, and falling victim to gulps of silent tears. He looked on with welled up eyes at the out-stretched hand of his father, who had his head turned away in fearful shame, trembling as he offered up the locket from his thin knobby fingers. Gaar reached for it, and as his father's hand retracted, he slowly opened the heart-shaped locket and was spellbound. There inside, adhered to the curves of the heart-shaped lid was a very old photo of Gaar at five years-old, his mother and his father, in a blaze of smiles. In the hinged base was a lovely portrait of his mother. Gaar's mouth quivered, and he snapped the locket shut. Rising to his feet, he took a deep breath.

'Father, I have been to the tree. I've walked its branches, and I have come to know many things of innocence and freedom, and of bondage and betrayal— both mingling in the halo which divides brilliance and darkness. Give me your hand now,' he commanded, 'and be shown then the *difference*.'

Abram reached out his quivering hand obediently, and dared only now to turn his head and look Gaar in the eye, to face the inevitable. He felt the grasp of Gaar's hand. The lamp began to flicker. As he came face to face with Gaar, he looked into the turquoise eyes of the bear, and was frozen; not with fear, but *frozen solid*.

There was a worried knock at the door, and after a few moments, Girly peered in with a look of grave concern, having heard the ruckus. Her face dropped in abrupt shock. She reeled back in fear, unfit to scream. With instinct, she swiftly yanked the door closed.

After a moment, she peeked in again and looked on in stunned disbelief. The entire room was frozen over. Every item and surface in the room was crystalized; and there, adjacent to the slim bed was a huge frozen polar bear standing on its hind quarters with its paw extended and Abram in a frozen reclined pose, reaching and touching the beast's under-paw.

With a breathless shiver, she slowly closed the door with a dumbfounded glaze over her face.

Girly drifted back towards the gathering in a daze. Pausing at the store's counter top, she looked out over the neighbourhood crowd which had now engaged in pockets of conversation. The group was spread about, sitting on boxes and leaning against walls.

Girly turned her head to notice Tunningham talking with Aaron. Observing the two strangers, she watched as Tunningham's face suddenly fell in response to something Aaron had said. He recklessly leapt out of his seat, knocking over the box he was sitting on. Aaron looked over at Girly who stood watching the exchange. The peculiar aura about Aaron puzzled her, and she wandered his way still reflecting on her experience in the back room.

This stranger, who appeared no friend of Tunningham's—who had now walked away flabbergasted, must have arrived with Gaar. She held out her hand in greeting as she reached him, and the two sat down. Girly slowly gathered herself.

§

Although he hadn't needed to kick the door in, as Girly suggested, Saul eagerly waited for Isaac to get off his fat ass and relay the urgent message to Nanisivik for him. Isaac had insisted on operating the radio himself, and Saul not being the pushy type, obliged the sizable drunkard.

'So,' Isaac said, with a know-it-all attitude and downplaying his inebriation, 'you say that ... two strangers sharing a fur cloak ... crashed the party ... and gave you that goose egg, huh?'

'You asked me how it happened,' Saul blurted with building anxiety, 'not quite as dramatic as you're summing it up—look, can you radio that message to Nanisivik, or will you let me do it? It's urgent!'

'Don't ... get smart with me boy, I'm the *mayor* of dis community. Show some respect ...' he said, getting up with a sour look towards Saul, and waddling to the back room where his radio was set up.

Saul rolled his eyes up to the ceiling, and shook his head in disgust. He wouldn't dare go breathing down his neck in the next room. He sat and waited for confirmation that the message got through. He could hear Isaac speaking in a hushed mumble, and without suspicion, sat rubbing the bump which had raised on his forehead.

After a couple of minutes, Isaac emerged from the back room and stood leaning on the door jamb. Saul turned in his rickety chair suddenly noticing he was standing in the doorway. Getting up with his hand glued on the bump, he looked quizzically at Isaac.

'Did you get through—and someone's on the way?'

'Everything'll be taken care of,' Isaac muttered.

'*Who* should I tell Girly, is coming?'

'Najagneq—the greatest shaman of the land, is coming to help,' he replied.

'*Najagneq*,' Saul said with awe.

'That's right—the one and only. I know him personally,' Isaac bragged.

'Wow. What about a doctor? There is a doctor coming, right?'

'Now get out, 'n don't give me no sass. There's no waiting room in *this* city-hall,' Isaac scolded.

'But, Girly said—'

'Old Joshua has a first aid kit and ... a medicine book. That's doctor enough for now, until we can reach one ... so, go get him,' Isaac decreed. A frown crept over his face in reaction to the doubt which registered on Saul. 'Well?'

Saul meekly moved toward the door, unhappy with the extent of the arrangements. Casting his reservations aside, he resigned himself to the fact that help was on the way—as Isaac had promised, and with no choice now but to heed Isaac's suggestion for interim medical help from Old Joshua.

He set his focus on fetching the man. With no love lost between himself and the "mayor", he bolted out the door without further ado.

Isaac pryed himself from his leaning post and reached behind the door of the back room, pulling out a rifle. He staggered towards the front door, and lifted his parka from a wall hook, setting the rifle against the wall while he put it on. Twice he lunged for the rifle to balance it as it teetered and began to fall as he clumsily fumbled with his coat.

Just as he was stepping through the door, something occurred to him and he turned back and shuffled through to the back room, where he noisily rooted through a junk drawer.

Coming from the back room with a pair of open handcuffs in his grasp, he made his way again to the front door, dropped the cuffs into his coat pocket and slipped out the door crashing to his fat bottomside on the step.

forty-four

THE THICK HUMID DARKNESS reeked of stale death. A couple of very faint cap-lamps swayed slowly at the wall of rubble which had given up some of its mass; but in having thinned out the outer later of loosely packed debris, they had revealed more heavily fortified sections of the mine blockage.

Eamonn lifted himself off a rock which he was sitting on, and flicked on the feeble beam of light from his cap-lamp. Only an occasional moan from the darkness broke the silence now. Everyone who laboured at the wicked mound moved almost in slow motion, weakly toiling at any dwindling opportunities. Headway had come practically to a standstill. The stout hearted merely went through the motions of picking away at their massive opponent.

There were no more energetic grunts, no more fights, less and less urine to drink (as the group had abstained from conserving expended urine for the first two days), nothing to talk about and less to hope for.

Eamonn's zest had now diminished and left him feeling like a discarded shell of what he was only three days ago. Now on their fourth agonizing day, it seemed more like forty days that they'd been trapped. Disappointment ate away at him, rapidly draining the sea of hope on which he sailed, and threatening to leave him high and dry on a cracked bed of salt.

One of his best workers, Williams, had had a critical accident. His leg was crushed from toe to hip by a concrete slab which was jostled loose when another chunk was being pryed. There were far more bodies dead and on the sidelines near death, than there were at the struggle to dig themselves out.

At this point, if they suddenly *did* miraculously break through, and if the shaft ladder which ran to the surface was undamaged and accessible, a fifteen hundred foot vertical climb was nothing to look forward to; and who was to say what they'd expect to find on the surface.

What kept running through Eamonn's mind was the absence of a rescue effort. A sign as simple as someone tapping on the blockage. The only sense he could make of the lack of activity on the other side of the mound, was that there was some kind of catastrophe up top; that, combined with bad weather conditions.

It had come to the point now, that even the taunts of the rotten apples in the group had ceased. This was a big change even from a day prior when Ribald and Thomason had taunted him for hours with their threats of death, revenge and cannibalism. These had eventually fizzled out and remained as idle musings of the damned. For all Eamonn knew now, those two could have died in a corner and been eaten themselves, judging from the peace and quiet that had prevailed for what seemed the longest time.

'Müeller,' someone called from the seldom used ramp which led up to the thousand-foot level, where exploration had ceased a couple of months prior. 'Müeller!'

'Yeah,' he replied, grateful to be called for any reason whatsoever, and now recognizing the French Canadian accent of the nominated "doctor", Barclay, the woman who had twisted her ankle when the whole mess began.

'Look what we found,' she boasted with a shortness of breath, 'and it's not "Arnie Saknussen" from dat James Mason centre-o'-de-Earth movie with de Swedish duck, it's *powder*! De next level, she's blocked, but here—scraps!'

Eamonn carefully tread their way, zeroing-in on their pathetic cap-lamps. As he neared Barclay with a male inmate companion at her side, he saw both of them in the dim exposure, each bearing a twenty-five kilogram sack of ANFO blasting powder on their shoulders. The discovery was a godsend. Eamonn was energized with new hope and vigour; perhaps enough to climb a fifteen-hundred foot stretch of ladder with one of the injured slung over his shoulder if he was given the chance.

'Well, doctor,' he said, drumming up both praise and comradery for the two, 'it's time for some long overdue surgery! Did you see anything else up there, like tape fuses with detonator caps by chance? This stuff won't ignite with a match—so it's a "water, water, everywhere ..." scenario without a detonator—useless.'

'Y'mean like dis?' she said confidently, holding out her hand and showing Eamonn the small diameter cord which looked like a six foot skipping rope with a copper end.

'That'd be it, doc,' he replied with renewed interest, as he took the tape fuse and the heavy sack of blasting powder from her and walked toward the stubborn mound with it.

'We've gotta contain the blast,' he said as they neared the blockage.

They reached the barricade. He and the other inmate

placed the sacks on the ground as others gathered around to listen in on the scheme. Ribald appeared from the shadows un-dead after all, looking on with doubt at what seemed to be afoot.

'It's useless for fucksakes,' Ribald interjected with a hoarse voice, 'it'll just bring more rubble down on that heap,' he hissed as the four faint cap-lamps swung his way to illuminate him.

'Says who?' Eamonn retaliated, 'if you look above it, you can see it's all come down. There's just solid rock-face left, and these two sacks ain't gonna budge that business. It's as plain as the broken nose on your freakin' face ...'

'My nose ain't—' Ribald began to state, then held his tongue, wary of the gist and what was coming next.

'Now!' Eamonn began with a spark, 'we're going to pack these sacks in the hollow we've managed in the middle here—then stack all that heavy material on top of them, to contain it'

'Yer all fuckin' dolts,' Ribald scoffed, then spit on a sack of blasting powder and turned away, walking back into the shadows.

'Don't come runnin' to me when you run outta piss you shit-head!' Eamonn barked, then turned back to the men who were there to pitch in. 'Right, let's get to it,' he said, tucking the sacks into the hollow in the midsection of the mound.

Barclay stepped out of the shadows and into the action, holding out some very thin wire she'd also found but forgot to produce. 'Y'need dis stuff, too?' she asked, as her hand was suddenly lit up with the glances of the curious.

'Perfect! *Igniter cord*! You're just a walking hardware store' he replied with a wide grin, taking the thin strip of wire from her and laying it and the tape-fuse on a flat rock beside the hollow. Picking up a pointed piece of wood from the littered floor, he punctured one of the sacks of ANFO and inserted the copper-capped end of the tape-fuse into the hole. He fed the tail over the shelved hollow and onto the flat rock where he'd laid out the igniter cord.

'Now, let's pack these blasting sacks tightly with the heaviest materials we can manage,' he said, taking an end of a large chunk of concrete and waiting for a counterpart for the other end. One of the inmates took the other end and the slab was maneuvered into position.

After a short time, the charges were tightly packed with rubble. Eamonn joined the igniter cord to the tail of the tape fuse by crimping the ends together crudely, using a rock as a tool. The labour intensive exercise was now fulfilled, and the time for detonation was near. The inmates illuminated each other in eager anticipation of the offensive.

'Before we blow this,' Eamonn announced loudly, with an exhausted but inspired voice, 'we've got to move everyone from this area way back into that tunnel, for safety. Let's pull together and clear the area.'

The cap-lamps of those standing, illuminated the perimeter of the walled cavern as they turned to assess the scope of the job at hand. The dim spotty lighting was diffused by the dust as they marched inwards to assist the injured. It shed light on the gruesome extent to which the dire circumstances had taken their toll. Although the seventy-odd certified corpses had been carted away into a tunnel days before, it was obvious that some survivors who appeared slouched over in sleep, were in fact dead. At Barclay's last head count, prior to her eight-hour venture up to the thousand-foot level, there were twenty-eight living. Of the twenty-eight, seventeen had injuries of varying degrees and eleven had either helped or just sulked.

Fourteen injured inmates were assisted into the cross-drift tunnel. Eamonn warned everyone of the blast concussion which would jostle them in a few minutes, then left the tunnel to ignite the fuse.

Reaching for his parka, he rooted through the pockets for his matches, but found them gone—as well as a stub of a cigar. Carefully going through his coat again to be sure, and certain now that the items were stolen, he stormed back to the cross-drift tunnel where the group was huddled.

'Alright, listen up!' he shouted, as the group went silent except for the coughs of the sick, 'I had matches and a cigar in my coat—and they're *gone*! If you want to get out of here, whoever took them, give them back *now*!' No one owned up to the theft. Eamonn looked at the sullen faces, illuminating each and every one of them as he marched slowly along the wall. When he came to Thomason and Ribald he could see the guilt on their faces and he knew he'd found the culprits.

'I thought I smelled the darkest of the four humors in this tunnel,' he growled, 'hand them over, *shit-heels*—or do I have to tear you apart to find 'em?' The promise of his fiery wrath, burned holes through the two inmates who were more at home in the shadows.

Thomason looked at Ribald, who dug into his pocket and produced the matchbook. Eamonn snatched the matches from him.

'The cigar?' he said with boiling anger, 'well?!'

'We ate it,' Ribald said with righteous indignation.

'You were next,' Thomason hissed, 'so consider yourself lucky if we get freed by your cockamamy plan, Müeller.'

Eamonn suddenly felt the dampness of the matchbook in his hand and sidelined his fury to inspect the matches. Shedding the light of his fading cap-lamp down on the matchbook, he saw blood smeared over the cover, and upon opening the matchbook up, he found the remaining few pathetic matches crumbling and damp from blood and moisture.

He purposely allowed the matchbook to drop from his hand to his feet. As Ribald and Thomason looked down, Eamonn grabbed their heads and smashed them together with such force, that he knocked the two out cold. They collapsed to the floor of the tunnel.

'Would anybody care to eat these two before they wake up, 'cause now, we ain't going—' Eamonn paused for a moment as he suddenly figured out a way to possibly ignite the cord to the tape fuse without matches.

'Can we start eating them, then?' a male voice called out from the darkness, ''cause, if it looks like we're gonna die forgotten ... it might as well be on a full stomach—and they'd be so fresh and juicy.'

'Hang on a minute,' Eamonn asked, 'I've got an idea. If I'm not back in two minutes, start without me.' he said, as he marched out of the stinking "toilet tunnel" as they had termed it, and headed up and around towards the blast site at the rubble mound.

Reaching the mound in the pitch black with only his very faint cap-lamp, felt to him much like being underwater in a dirty river. As he stumbled forward over the littered floor of the cavern, the adversary mound which had almost won the battle, loomed over him like an arrogant Goliath. He smiled mischievously knowing it hadn't got the best of him yet.

Feeling suddenly lucky with this absolute last ditch strategy, he was sure that he would soon be making the fifteen hundred foot climb up the ladder. He began to ball-up the thin ignitor cord wire which was coated with a gritty and flammable surface.

The strategy was based on a story told to him by a technician long ago, who said he'd ignited the sensitive wire once by doing just so, and striking the dense ball of wire with a wrench. It was going to work—no two-ways about it, and as he lifted a heavy rock from the floor, he greedily licked his lips and held the rock above his head preparing for the thrust.

With all his might, he smashed the rock onto the dense ball of wire. Nothing happened.

Trembling with doubt, he set the rock above his head again to give it a second shot. As he desperately aimed for the core of the ball, his cap-lamp fizzled to nothing and went dead on him. In a fit of frustration he slammed the rock down with tremendous anger, and in a flash, the igniter cord sparked into action from the blow. The cavern was suddenly lit with the glittering fuse which burned away like a hand held sparkler on the fourth of July.

Eamonn's knees went weak on him and he felt slightly inebriated having completed the task. The tape fuse would now take about six minutes to burn itself to the detonator cap. He could almost feel the rungs of the ladder in his hand; and the snow! How he'd love to eat, play, and make angels in it! If death was to come to him, he preferred the thought of perishing up top in the struggle to reach a settlement, rather than in the dank, stinking belly of the mine.

By the light of the effervescent sparkling of the igniter cord, he began to make his way back to take cover in the cross-drift tunnel with the rest of the crew. As he made his way down the dark tunnel towards the one cap-lamp that he used as a beacon, he heard a commotion at the huddled group.

Reaching the inmates, he looked on with curiosity. When the light of the only lit hard-hat flittered across some faces, he was sobered out of his delirium. Around their chewing mouths, dribbles of blood could be seen. The reality struck him like a ton of bricks.

They had begun to consume Ribald and Thomason.

An overwhelming sense of horror invaded his senses. He had off-handedly invited the cannibalism and inadvertently failed to return to the group in the time-span he'd indicated. They had taken him literally and acted on his wayward suggestion. He was the architect of the madness, at the helm of a ship of desperate fools. Loath to acknowledge the crime, he denied his guilt and shouted out a warning.

'Any second, that load's gonna blow! Sit down and brace yourselves—cover your ears until I say different!'

The group huddled against the wall heeding his instructions, and waited—and waited.

After what seemed an eternity, Eamonn stood up and paced over to the inmate bearing a lit cap-lamp. Stretching his wrist under the light, he looked at his watch and was confident that something had gone wrong. He alone would be the one to venture to the blast site and investigate.

'How many here have lamps that work?! Hello!' he yelled, moving along the huddled line and tapping everyone's shoulder, for them to uncover their ears. 'Anyone with a working lamp, turn it on now!'

Six lights were flicked on, all of them pathetically dim. He walked to the brightest of the scant demonstrations and extended his hand. 'I need your cap-lamp,' he said curtly, 'not your hard-hat, just the lamp.' He exchanged lamps with what appeared to be a man.

'What went wrong?' asked Barclay, coming up next to him.

'I don't know. I'm gonna check,' he said, suddenly reeling back from her with disgust, seeing traces of wiped blood on her face. 'Barclay—not you ... you're supposed to be—'

'I'm resigning my post as doc. It's every man for demselves now,' she replied without remorse, then walked back into the shadows.

Eamonn took her biting words to heart. If he couldn't rectify the problem which stalled the blast, then he would go off on his own somewhere to wait for death in privacy. The thought of eating one of those inmates repulsed him. He began to feel like a maggot. As he marched with a frenzied anger—which built with each step forward, he sensed his spirit teetering on the diving board of oblivion.

Reaching what he now considered the *demon*, he checked for the tape fuse which was now just an ash trail, burnt down below the tightly packed covering of rocks they'd piled against the ANFO sacks in the hollow.

Pulling madly at a few rocks which tumbled down the mound as he extracted them, he spied through a tiny crack, and saw that the fuse had burned down to less than an inch from the copper blasting cap and had fizzled out. It was damaged somehow. Whether it was internally damaged prior to their use of it, or if someone had carelessly handled it or bashed it with a rock, made no matter.

With a blank expression, he retired his ambition, knowing there was no way to ignite the blasting cap at this point. He sullenly dragged himself to a corner of the cavern, where he collapsed into a heap. He shut his lamp off.

forty-five

FRESHLY BAKED BREADS were being passed around the supply store. All indulged in the pot-luck offerings that several of the neighbours had provided. Tunningham's patience had run out. He put on his parka and approached Girly, who was uneasily intrigued by Aaron's fantastic story.

Tunningham burst into the midst of their conversation. He cast a wary eye on Aaron who had alluded to his ambiguous identity, and interrupted with urgent purpose.

'Excuse me; Girly, where is Gaar?! We've got to leave, it's almost five PM' he said, turning a glance toward Aaron, 'sir, I don't know *who* you are—or what kind of fool you're playing me for, but I'd appreciate it if you—and yourself, Girly, would come along with us to Nanisivik for the tribunal. Please? I'll go see if Gaar is in the back,' he said, turning away and quick-stepping his way to the back.

Girly grinned, not one to get in the way of *official* business. She watched as Tunningham stepped through the doorway into the back. A few moments later, Tunningham staggered out flabbergasted. He barely braced himself on a wall and attempted to steady his breath. Utter shock thwarted his attempts to compose himself. His disorientation amused Girly, having been witness to the back-room experience herself first hand; but, she being more suited to the mystical reality, dealt with the phantasm in a spiritual sense, and now accepted the episode with delight.

There was an abrupt opening of the front door. All heads turned as Isaac, the drunken moderator, burst through the door, slamming it closed behind himself.

'Where's Gaar and his companion?!' he demanded, holding the rifle as though it would steady his teetering.

An elderly Inuit man leaned forward from his wooden-box seat and waved his hand to brush off the interruption. 'Oh *relax*, Curly! Sit down and have some bread—it'll soak up all your troubles.'

'Where are they?' Isaac sternly blurted again.

'Gaar isn't here,' the old man said, 'say, can I borrow your sled, tomorrow?'

Isaac stewed silently for a moment and looked around. 'Look, I'm here on official business—I'm *on duty*, okay?' he said, looking back at the wrinkled old man.

'Doesn't look like you're here to deliver the mail.'

'Where's the man who arrived with Gaar? Look here, this is *the mayor* speaking—'

'And we don't even see the draw-cord—*how* does he do it?' the old man quipped.

A silence gripped the occupants of the store, as Tunningham staggered from the back, still dealing with what he thought he saw in the bedroom.

Isaac moved forward towards Tunningham. 'Fee-fie-fo-fum, I smell the stink o' the old-government's bum.'

'We should have *more* poetry readings by our esteemed

mayor. You're a better artist than mailman, Isaac,' the old man taunted, as Isaac stopped in front of Tunningham and pressed his rifle across his chest—to steady himself.

'You're under ... house arrest.' Isaac announced to Tunningham, who wasn't quite cognizant yet of what was happening around him. Girly rose from her seat and confronted Isaac.

'What's the charge?' she asked, putting her hands on her waist.

'It's an *internal matter*,' he replied, looking down at her.

'I think it's mental,' said the old man from the midst of the gathering.

Isaac grabbed Tunningham's wrist as he clumsily set the butt of his rifle on the floor and balanced it against his chest while producing the set of handcuffs from his pocket. Tunningham tugged his wrist back towards himself.

Isaac wavered. 'Obstruction of justice—see?' Isaac blurted, as he managed to clamp and lock a handcuff around Tunningham's wrist.

'Get *real*,' Girly shouted, poking the man.

'Just how many masters are you serving, Curly?' asked the old man.

Isaac steadied himself with the rifle. Standing upright and blowing himself up like a peacock, he dragged the amply stunned Tunningham past the service counter and toward the back rooms. Aaron grabbed his new coat and put it on, as Tunningham came to his senses and fought the arrest.

Finding Abram's bedroom door closed, Isaac grabbed Tunningham by the lapel and fiercely shook the reluctance out of him. He put his ear close to the door and then pushed it open.

He was immediately bedazzled by the spectacle which was rapidly thawing out. In a reflex reaction to seeing the bear, he raised his rifle to shoot the animal. His intention was thwarted by Aaron, who leapt on his back in a surprise attack, causing the rifle to discharge into the ceiling.

Falling backwards into the hallway on top of Aaron, Isaac wriggled to his knees, and struck Aaron in the face with the butt of his rifle. Grabbing the open swinging wristlet which hung from Tunningham's forearm, he locked the vacant cuff on Aaron's wrist. Girly dashed back with a large soapstone carving in her hands and struck Isaac on the head with it, knocking him out cold and sending him to the floor like a sack of potatoes.

Aaron frantically searched the body of Isaac for the keys to his re-occurring nightmare. Girly's attention was caught by the headlights of snowmobiles which began to shine through the windows. She was aware of the danger which was approaching. Turning around and dashing for the rear bedroom, she slammed into Gaar who was emerging with his father from the back.

'Gaar! They're coming for you!' she shrieked. Gaar calmly stepped over Isaac's body and looked at Tunningham and Aaron, who was still rooting through Isaac's pockets for the miniature keys.

'Aaron! Forget it—you two are married until we get to Nanisivik. Let's go!' Gaar decreed, 'Tunningham, are you with us?'

Girly stepped forward. 'He saw ... you.'

'Ah,' Gaar replied with a nod.

'Go out the back kitchen window!' Girly suggested, 'and take my snowmobile. The keys are in the ignition. I'll see you later!'

'Everyone!' Gaar shouted, addressing the gathering, 'pretend we're still here, and that you're hiding us somewhere. Thanks!' he said, turning and bumping into his father who he quickly hugged and made for the kitchen window with Tunningham and Aaron in tow.

'*Tunningham*,' Aaron said to himself as they dashed to the

kitchen. The "Max" part of him recognized the name from somewhere, though he had never met the man before. With that thought, he realized he was being pulled head-first through the window.

Outside at the front of the store, Jag's troupe pulled up and jumped off their snowmobiles leaving their motors idling, and made a dash for the door. In an abrasive barrage, the men stormed through the door.

Once inside, Kiratek shut the door, and the henchmen stood staring at the tight-lipped people at the gathering.

'Where are they?!' Triq yelled out, but was met only with cold shoulders as a collective reply to his rude and rowdy greeting. The congregation stared at Triq, who still looked a sight with his scabbed-over face and yellowed bruises from Brunhilde's attack. Girly moved close to Abram and put her arm protectively around the old man. Agaluq and Kiratek began to move through the store, checking faces and possible hiding spots as they made their way towards the back of the store.

The wrinkled old man sat forward on his box and addressed Triq. 'Are you here for some beauty supplies? Don't worry there's plenty of inventory. Abram will see you get all you need,' he boldly said with a smile, as a small round of giggles followed, to Triq's chagrin. 'And there's plenty of wet blankets; Isaac back there for instance,' he announced, as Agaluq and Kiratek came upon Isaac unconscious on the floor in the hall, 'he's as wet as wet can be ...'

Meanwhile, outside on a large hill overlooking the community of Kiqaloq, the black wolf looked down with its penetrating red eyes. The discipled band of wolves loitered behind him. In the distance, he saw the snowmobile, with three riders, and recognized Gaar at the helm.

Like a shot, Jag was barreling down the slope with the

wolf band following behind like an infantry. With Jag in the lead, they raced off, hot on the trail of Gaar's flight toward Nanisivik.

High in the air and cloaked by the twilight blanket, was the Anknonquatok in the form of the peregrine falcon. It coasted through the sky above Gaar and the others on the speeding snowmobile. The falcon screeched out, hailing the anointed one, but to no avail as the drone of the snowmobile's engine deafened the riders.

At the rear exterior of the supply store, Triq, Agaluq and Kiratek inspected the discarded storm window and smattering of footprints below the kitchen window frame. Sight-lining the trails of the fleeing snowmobile, Triq sucked his lip, pulled out a hunting knife and scurried along the side of the building, weaving in and out of a few parked snowmobiles.

'They've fled for Nanisivik!' Triq yelled. 'If they make it, all our efforts have been in vain, and their accomplishment will be an insult to our murdered brothers and sisters!' The trio marched to their vehicles.

'Let's get going, fast,' Triq announced, as they got on their idling snowmobiles, 'we'll take the eastern corridor, it'll take us to Nanisivik faster and they'll never know we're on their tails! Let's go!!' Triq yelled, pointing out the alternative route to his men. They zipped off, cross-cutting the main avenue. The three of them headed into the back hills, with the urgent whines of their vehicles diminishing as they disappeared.

Inside the store, Gaar's father held Girly's hand and compellingly looked into her face. 'Girly, we must get to Nanisivik to support Gaar at the tribunal!'

'Agreed!' she replied, then stared at him with concern, 'but are you fit for the journey?'

'I'm fit, and tuned!'

'Alright, if you insist,' she said, turning to the crowd. 'Does anybody have a sound snowmobile that's trip-worthy to get to Nanisivik?' she desperately asked of the energetically chatting congregation. They became quiet.

'You can use mine!' a young man excitedly replied, happily raising his hand. He along with the group, were seduced by the commotion and mysterious chase. He grabbed his parka, eager to see Girly and Abram catch up with the friendly fugitives.

Girly and Gaar's father bundled up for the trek. As they were ready to dash out the door, she scurried to Isaac, who was still unconscious on the floor at the rear hallway of the store. She intently searched for the keys to the handcuffs which Aaron and Tunningham shared. In a tiny pocket of his vest, she found them.

Making their way quickly to the assortment of snowmobiles outside, the young man escorted Girly and Abram to his vehicle. Some well-wishers joined them outside, while others remained inside the store, looking on and waving farewell to them from nearby windows.

Girly mounted the young man's snowmobile and attempted to start the craft, but to no avail. Another man mounted his snowmobile to save-the-day, but was likewise confounded. Looking down at the engine, he immediately figured out the problem.

'The spark-plug cable's been cut! Damn those hooligans!' he shouted, as the young man checked his engine, finding his machine identically vandalized. Girly jumped off his snowmobile and brooded.

'The sheds!' she blurted out, 'there's a sled team there!

Saul's fed them by now and they'd make the trip in no time!'
Girly and Abram raced toward the sheds.

At the southern edge of Kiqaloq, Saul bounded out of Old
Joshua's house. While Old Joshua hurried down the steps
from his front door with the first-aid kit and his medical
book in hand, a thought struck Saul.

'The *dogs*,' Saul said to himself. The ablebodied old man
collided with Saul as he stood cemented in his tracks.

'What's the matter with you, Saul?' Old Joshua asked him
as their snorkeled hoods met, 'first you run like a hare, then
you idle like a post—I thought this was an emergency.'

'Joshua,' Saul said, touching his arm with urgency, 'please
get to the store as fast as you can. I've got an important
errand that I almost forgot, *again*. See you in a bit!' Saul
dashed off for the north end of the community, as Old
Joshua shook his head, and shuffled his way in the direction
of the store.

Saul arrived at the vacant sheds, grabbing for a post to
steady himself from the sprint. His eyes bulged to see that
there was no dog-team to be found. He stood perplexed,
huffing with exhaustion. He knew that Girly wouldn't have
sent him on a wild-goose chase. He looked down and saw
footprints and fresh sled tracks leading from the shed, and
figured that perhaps the owner of the team had reclaimed
the property.

Walking up the roadway, past the sheds came one of the
men whose snowmobile had been sabotaged by Triq. As he
passed, he cast a glance over at Saul who was hugging a post
for support while he pondered the situation. He was ready
now to run back to the store to talk to Girly. The man

paused in thought, then walked up from the road, approaching Saul with a wave of his hand.

'Saul,' the robust man said, pulling his hood back and rubbing his light moustache, 'y'know that old clunker you got tarped at the side of the house? Think y'could spare its spark-plug cables?'

'Sure, but can you tell me—there was a dog-team here?'

'Girly's gone with it, and Abram,' he replied.

'They feed 'em?'

'Dunno.'

'They comin' back soon?'

'Rushed off to Nanisivik.'

'Yikes,' Saul muttered to himself.

forty-six

OVER AN UNDULATING area of drifted snow mounds and hazardous rock outcrops, Gaar maneuvered Girly's hearty snowmobile at a reduced speed, to manage the course. On the back, Aaron and Tunningham faced each other on the seat, in order to accommodate their bound wrists.

'I think the timing couldn't be better,' Tunningham shouted out to Aaron through their facing hoods.

'I'm gonna see that Roblaw goes down big time,' Aaron boasted loudly to Tunningham, whose face suddenly caved-in with a frown, at his declaration.

'What do you mean?!' Tunningham shouted over the whine of the struggling snowmobile's engine.

'I've got the evidence up here,' he shouted proudly, pointing at his temple, 'secret ledgers, names, accounts—he'll rot behind bars! And now that ... *I'm not Max anymore*,' he shouted with glee, 'I can't be tried for something Aaron didn't commit!'

Confusion was rampant on Tunningham's face. 'What ... ?' he replied, still shedding the hallucinatory experience at the store from his mind, and now having to deal with this man's claim of once being Max.

Sudden bumps and shakes took the trio by surprise, as the vehicle tread over questionable terrain.

'Aaron!' Gaar shouted over his shoulder, 'tell Tunningham to hang on!' Gaar shouted, as he took the snowmobile up the side of a small hill to circumvent the rough trail.

'Hang on!' Aaron shouted to Tunningham, and the man held tight, being on the back of the snowmobile and at most risk of falling off the craft. '*Tunningham* ...,' Aaron said to himself, as Tunningham leaned forward, wary that Aaron had said his name, watching Aaron's face as he stared knowingly at him. 'Tunningham! Now I know where I know your name from!' Aaron announced loudly, then bit his lip, realizing he may have put his foot in his mouth.

'Where would that be?!' Tunningham asked suspiciously. He was becoming anxious, realizing that if this strange fellow had the goods on Roblaw, "the goods" would inevitably fall in his lap. He was covertly up to his ears in criminal activities, beginning with influence peddling and ending in accessory to murder. Although it didn't look like him—this man *was* Max. McGregor had fudged the job.

'Um ... do you belong to a bridge club in Ottawa?' Aaron asked, doing a bad job of playing dumb. Tunningham saw through it immediately. He reacted as many an unfortunate man tempered by greed and faltering in desperation would; a man with his back to the wall and everything to lose:—he reached into his parka and pulled out a pistol.

Aaron was dumbstruck seeing the weapon which was levelled in his direction. Looking up from the gun to the frantic glare of Tunningham, he flailed his left arm at the gun to sweep it away from his guts. In the ensuing struggle, Aaron managed to grab Tunningham's gun hand and the wrestling match was in high throttle.

Gaar was aware of the commotion behind his back and began to slow down to investigate the skirmish. When the pistol discharged into the sky, Gaar ducked his head and momentarily lost control of the snowmobile. At that moment, Gaar heard another ear-splitting concussion of the gun's blast and felt a bullet penetrate his back. The shock of the realization, numbed his body and mind, and he slumped over on the instrument panel of the snowmobile. Reaching blindly for the brake handle, he squeezed the lever, and when the vehicle slowed to a crawl, he collapsed over the side and fell from the craft, leaving the thrashing men to their business.

Laying on his back on the icy ground and looking into the heavens, Gaar saw the falcon circling high overhead and heard its screech. Deliriously recalling the Anknonquatok, he began to mumble a chant.

Aaron and Tunningham tumbled over the side of the idling snowmobile, still grappling for the gun. The weapon popped out of Tunningham's hand as they both hit the ground with a dull thump. A reckless scramble to retrieve the pistol, followed. Aaron repeatedly slugged Tunningham in the face in a desperate frenzy, bloodying his nose, which allowed him to crawl for the gun. Once in hand, Aaron— who was well aware now of Gaar's injuries, swung the pistol in front of Tunningham's face, ready to deliver the man's just deserts.

As Aaron began to vengefully squeeze the trigger, something smashed into him with a demonic snarl, knocking him over. The gun went off, hitting the gas tank of the snowmobile, causing an immediate explosion, and setting his arm and hood—as well as a wolf, on fire.

A sudden swarm of deranged wolves ferociously snapped their jaws at the two, but to Aaron, his flaming arm and head took precedence over the ruckus which was primarily focussed on Tunningham. After frantically extinguishing himself, he realized he no longer had the gun in his hand, and that a wolf was lunging for his face. Putting his arm up to protect himself, the wolf ripped at his arm, and another tore at his hood.

With petrified shrieks, Aaron squirmed amidst the stale smell of wild fur, the almost generic whiffs of carnivorous breath, teamed with the razored jaws which he remembered only too well. It was a nightmare, shattered only by the heavenly sound of an ally.

Huffing and groaning with sonorous threats, Gaar moved near Aaron, scaring off the fiendish onslaught momentarily, as he simultaneously fought off the black wolf, in the whirl-wind attack.

The pack of six agitated wolves abandoned Aaron and Tunningham, only to disperse and fan out in a small cluster around Gaar, standing on his hind quarters and ready for battle. Tunningham reeled with pain over his shredded arms and legs, and suffered a tremendous gash over his eye which bled profusely.

The bear lunged forward to throttle a wolf which nipped at him in league with Jag, who had managed to take a chunk or two out of Gaar when he was caught off guard.

The entire pack joined with Jag, to focus on the fearsome downing of the polar bear. The pack attacked Gaar from all sides, forming a skirt which encircled him and mobbed him ruthlessly. Aaron could only look on helplessly, as he franti-cally searched for the elusive gun with the aid of the flickering light from the burning vehicle.

Letting out an ominous screech, the falcon landed in the foreground, and was instantaneously transformed into the gold-faced Goliath, who burst forward into the ghastly scene, tossing wolves off Gaar with incredible strength and purpose.

Jag bit hard into Gaar's throat, unaware of the Anknonquatok which came up from behind and grabbed Jag by the scruff of the neck. The other wolves skulked away, disbanding like ripples from a splash, in retreat from the formidable aura and abilities of their opponent.

They bolted off, hearing the large black wolf yelp in anguished pain. Jag was forced to release his jaws from Gaar's neck, as the figure clenched its debilitating grip even tighter around Jag's neck. The Anknonquatok lifted Jag into the air, dangling him like an animated pendulum from its fist.

Jag lashed violently in its grasp, throwing the Anknonquatok off balance and into the carriage of the adjacent flaming snowmobile. The Goliath held its squirming quarry with an iron-clad grip, and mechanically rose from the oil-burning skeleton of the snowmobile, clasping the large black wolf tightly in its blazing arms.

With tremendous strides, the Anknonquatok hastened its departure, containing Jag who snarled desperately in the crushing vise of its arms. Jag began to yelp as the engine oil, smeared over the furs of the Anknonquatok, began to burn. It ran off into the twilight tundra in a south easterly direction with Jag in its grips. Gaar bolted after the Anknonquatok, the bear's massive head and neck bobbing passionately to gain forward momentum in his stride. Although disabled and frightfully gashed, the bear held its own, and disappeared into the shadowed white landscape.

'Gaar!' Aaron cried out feebly after the bear. His idle plea steamed into the air like a wasted breath. He glared at Tunningham who was writhing in pain, and viciously leapt on top of him, gripping his neck with all the strength he had left. With aching, desperate squeaks of fury, he began to strangle the man, giving in to his full primal tendencies.

The dog sled team suddenly appeared, with Girly at the helm, and Abram on the sled in front of her. Noticing the smouldering snowmobile, her spirits sunk. She steered the team over to the grappling duo, and urgently pulled up near the two, leaping off to separate the men.

'Aaron! Stop it!' she cried out, trying to cleave him from his dark purpose. 'Where's Gaar?! Where is he?!'

'This *bastard* shot him!' Aaron replied, breaking his grip on Tunningham's neck.

Tunningham gasped for breath, appearing fit to die from his wounds without any extra help.

'A fierce black wolf and a band of rogue bitches attacked us!' Aaron wailed. 'It was Jag! Gaar overcame him with help from his grandfather's charm! They went off that way!' he yelled, pointing off to the pass which opened up into the interior. Girly ran to Gaar's father and hugged him.

'Gaar is in good hands,' Abram said calmly, stroking Girly's head.

The dog team began to lap at the bloodied snow. Tunningham spotted his pistol in the churned up snow under the snow mobile. He lunged for the gun with his bloodied hand and startled the dogs, who became very interested in the sudden motion and the gaping wounds all over the man.

In a split second, the dogs were all over him, taking their savage fill in a frenzy of snapping jaws which tore at him. The gun fell out of his fingers, as he shrieked. Girly and Abram ran to the skirmish, to separate what they thought was a dog fight.

Seeing the dogs voraciously fighting over a piece of Tunningham, Girly's repulsion was overshadowed by her concern for Aaron who was petrified and striving to get as far back from the ravaging as possible.

Aaron cringed at the screams of Tunningham, fearing the snapping jaws would work their way to him. He knew that they were as sharp as the fangs of the wolves, and brought about the same result—only their breath was worse.

As he stretched himself away to the limit the handcuffs

would allow him, Girly urgently scrounged through her pockets for the tiny handcuff keys. Abram snatched up a bat from the sled to attempt to heel the dogs.

'Girly! Girly!!' Aaron cried out, seeing Abram trying to intercede in the melee. Girly was struck with shock, observing Abram bravely but foolishly approaching the scuffle. He'd have to jump in with both feet and bash the dogs on the necks with the club to break up the fracas.

'Abram! *Don't get near them—please!*' she begged of him. He honoured her request, and stepped back. 'Saul, Saul, *Saul*,' she chanted with anger, painfully aware the dog's hadn't been fed as she had asked.

She fumbled for the tiny keys in her pocket and upon finding them, lurched in to unlock Aaron's bracelet. A nearby dog snapped blindly at her face, but was caught up in the main focus of the sloshing fury once more, and lost interest in her actions. Girly became frustrated with the keys. She frantically twisted key after key in the lock. Neither seemed to be the mate of the handcuff's lock.

'*Isaac* ...' she uttered in a panic, scolding the man in his absence, thinking that perhaps these were keys for a trunk or something.

The same dog which nipped at her before, snapped at her again, only this time caught her and opened a gash on her ear. As she fell back from the strike, the wristlet opened and Aaron went flying backwards.

Tunningham went deathly silent. It was horrifically obvious that the dogs had sent him on his final journey, and were now content, gnawing on the luggage he had left behind.

After a few minutes, the dogs had settled down. Girly assisted Abram and Aaron into the sled.

'Was Gaar hurt terribly?' Girly nervously asked Aaron as he settled into the sled.

'I couldn't tell ... but he was *shot* by that—you saw me let go of his neck, and he was still alive, right?'

'Don't worry, I'll vouch for you,' she replied, 'the dogs finished him off—and there was nothing we could do for him. He would have died of his wounds anyway,' she said, placating his fears over the responsibility of his death.

'Jag's responsible for this ... and Tunningham's responsible if Gaar—'

'Where was he shot?!'

'I dunno, he fell off the snowmobile and I was facing the opposite direction. Your ear's bleeding,' he said, pointing.

'It's nothing,' she replied, drawing her hood up and over her head, 'You don't know where Gaar went.'

'Towards the pass; but you can go three directions once through, so who knows ...' he said, lifting his hand, the same way Max used to gesture when at a loss for words, 'Gaar's golden-faced friend without the eyes, carried Jag off. Had him locked tight in its hands—the wolf, that is.'

'Let's continue our journey to Nanisivik—the tribunal,' Abram suggested, meeting with approving nods from Girly and Aaron. 'He'll know where to find us.'

'The tribunal's at what time?' Girly asked Aaron.

'Eight, I think, but I'm not wearing a watch. I'm weaning myself off anything that wraps around my wrist,' he replied flatly.

'Well, let's get out of here,' she said, taking the whip at the navigator's post, and snapping it with a loud crack. The dogs were roused and ready for action. Seeing a tangled harness, which had two dogs skipping in and out of the twisted loops, Girly dashed from her post to straighten out the meshed bridle gear.

'Careful,' warned Aaron.

Girly approached slowly, recognizing satisfaction in the faces of the ice-bearded dogs, sporting reddish burred-up balls of ice which were formed on their whiskers. She carefully straightened out the twisted harness, and made her way back to her post at the back of the sled.

'Gonna have to wean *them* off *people*,' she said with a morose glance over at the remains of Tunningham.

'All the back stabber deserves is a shoe box, anyway,' Aaron angrily stated, lashing out at the memory of the bureaucrat. 'He's food for thought—fox, bear, wolf, or whatever wants to pick 'm clean!'

'Aaron!' Girly shouted with a disappointed tone, 'spite doesn't become you.'

'I don't know what's become of me, frankly,' he said with a starchy grimace, then drew his hood over his head. Abram and Girly shared a brief glance over that thought.

Girly "mushed" the team, and they were off.

forty-seven

WITH TREMENDOUS SPEED and agility, the Anknonquatok approached the main gate at Kabloona, shoving open the sliding fence with a sacred quest at hand and an unceremonious delivery in arm.

It swiftly passed the charred remains of the structures which were once the out-buildings of the mining camp. The doll-spirit figure moved rapidly towards the collapsed head-frame of the mine shaft, navigating by celestial forces, and propelled by mysterious powers which sought atonement.

With its fur and cloaking scorched from the flames, the doll-spirit clasped the black wolf in its arms, confining the singed beast in its inhospitable cradle.

Jag's blood red eyes beamed with a desperate fury, clinging meanly to life with his fur burned down to matted webs. The one thing Jag could manage, was the occasional snarl of vengeful discontent, which he growled out angrily but impotently, in light of his situation. Jag was livid in his frustration. He was especially irked by his inability to transmute in the tight quarters.

Passing an expedition tent which had been set up as a field command post at the perimeter of the head-frame, the golden faced Goliath bounded up the incline which led to the head-frame and began to tear into the wreckage to gain access to the shaft.

A member of the six man advance rescue party, emerged from the tent with a rifle and flashlight in hand, to investigate the commotion outside; thinking it may have been the arrival of the expert team and their equipment, or more stray wildlife rummaging amongst the ruins.

Most of the surface victims' bodies had been transported to Nanisivik earlier in the day, but Kabloona still seemed to reverberate with the horrors which had occurred on the fateful Friday past.

Some of the advance rescue team felt that the camp was haunted. Their hands were tied, due to the extent of the carnage. Their lack of ability and equipment to help any mine survivors, made matters worse.

The stocky figure bundled himself up in his parka, and surveyed the area as best he could from a standing vantage point on which he swiveled his body like a periscope.

Knowing it wasn't the expert team, and seeing the main gate slid back, he wandered up the incline to establish the make, model and size of the intruder. They hadn't had many intruders since late Saturday, after they'd come to the conclusion that closing the main gate was a sensible deterrent to wildlife. This was a sound concept, unless an animal was trapped *inside* the expansive compound prior to the practice. In this case, the gate had recently been slid open.

The man stealthily checked around, wary of what might be a polar bear which had manipulated the gate open. The man kept his finger on the trigger of his rifle in the event of a sudden confrontation.

Getting close to the decimated head-frame structure, the man inspected the source of the ruckus, and caught site of the thrashing Anknonquatok in the beam of his flashlight. It also reflected back Jag's large penetrating eyes which peered outwards from under the arm of the doll spirit.

The man was struck with fear, and dashed back to the tent to rouse his team.

In a few moments, four of the six men quietly stalked the intruder. They crept-up on the head-frame with their rifles leading, not knowing what it was that was making all the racket inside the dark cavernous heap of the collapsed structure.

Then they saw it. Their four flashlights joining force to illuminate the sizable human-like figure. They looked on at it with awe. It was unconcerned with their presence. The wicked eyes of the black wolf struck terror in them, and a couple of them looked away in fear of its mesmerizing glare.

Ripping up the last piece of concrete which barred access to the shaft, the disheveled Anknonquatok teetered on the ledge which framed the gaping blackness of the deep shaft below. Lifting its hand, it rubbed at the residue of ash on its face, the traces of the spiritual dust of its incinerated master.

As the two remaining men energetically joined the awestruck hunting party, the doll-spirit suddenly burst into flames before their eyes. Shading their eyes from the spontaneous flare of light, the men stood motionless and dumbfounded by the ghost which was flaming like a torch.

Jag yelped in anguish as the Anknonquatok stepped over the edge of the precipice and dropped from sight into the fifteen-hundred-foot deep shaft.

'I told ya this place was haunted! I told ya!!' the man who had first spotted the Anknonquatok shouted. 'Someone should go look,' he added. All six men looked at each other with frightened expressions, obviously unwilling to peek down the shaft after the flaming apparition.

Eamonn lay quiet and still in the pitch black of the main cavern. The moans of the injured, echoing from the cross-drift tunnel, made the darkness almost unbearable, breaking the haunting silence the way it did. An overwhelming exhaustion enticed him to surrender to sleep. He was on the brink of it, as much as the starvation which compelled him to put something in his mouth; but, the thought of eating repulsed him, and the concept of sleeping only to wake up again *there*, was a hideous notion. He would deny himself these compulsions until death put a stop to all his physical woes.

He suddenly realized his eyes were open as rivulets of bright light emanated from the mound. The flowing veins which seemed to create a halo around some of the rocks caused him to burst out with a delirious giggle of disbelief.

He got up from the floor, and moved closer to gawk at the peculiar sight. He sobered up with a realization that the brilliant orange light radiating from the snaking veins, was actually the glow of *molten gold*! An angel wasn't going to appear, unless he stood there longer. The molten gold flowed gloriously in and around the hollow which housed the sacks of ANFO and the *detonator*!

With every ounce of energy that was his to expend, he bolted from the barricade to take cover. Aimlessly tripping over soft and hard obstacles, he strived to reach the cross-drift tunnel. Before he knew it, he was there. One tiny fire-fly of a light glowed from the hard hat of an inmate.

'Cover your ears!!' he yelled out, as he tripped and belly-flopped on to the hard rock floor at the feet of his cave-dwelling neighbours. His hands went swiftly to his ears.

forty-eight

THE BOEING TOUCHED down on the landing strip at Nanisivik airport. It was eight-fifteen PM.

Leaping from the short portable staircase which was snugged-up against the plane, Louise dashed across the icy, brightly lit runway to the terminal buildings.

A solitary cargo vehicle passed her. Its driver gawked at the silly looking woman who aimlessly propelled herself across the runway with the technique of a first time ice-skater. Her modest autumn overcoat didn't offer much protection from the penetrating cold. It was merely a fleeting inconvenience. Her overriding concern was to clear customs and find Gaar.

She was aware of her balance though, which was compromised by her short-heeled pumps. They had her slipping and tripping her way towards the most important looking of the two small central buildings which were skirted by a few utilitarian airplane hangars.

Entering the terminal building with only her purse dangling from her arm, she jogged through a doorway and approached a man who sat behind a counter, wearing a simple grey uniform with a colourful badge on his shoulder.

His eye caught her frantic approach and he looked up from his book to greet her.

'Welcome to the IAR,' he said cheerfully, 'are you here on business or pleasure?'

'I came to find my husband!' she replied breathlessly, handing him the regular assortment of documentation, which he perused, stamped and handed back to her.

'I guess that's business-like pleasure ... staying long?' he enquired.

'As long as it takes,' she replied with an exasperated gasp of air to settle herself.

'You can get a parka in town—and maybe some proper shoes. It can get ... cold?'

'Yes,' she said abruptly, 'where can I find the Canadian consulate?'

'Well, there's no consulate here. That's in Iqaluit, but there's an ambassador here who's on trade business, and he'd be over at the community center where there's a big meeting happening.'

'That's where I want to go, then. Do you have any maps for sale?' She asked politely but with impatience.

The man pointed to a set of doors. 'Go through there, and you'll see a red jeep—it's a taxi. Jeremiah'll take you there.'

'Thanks!' she said, as she turned and quickly made her way to the doors.

§

Jeremiah's cherry-red jeep sped into the community center's crowded parking lot and swung around a line of snowmobiles and pick-up trucks, pulling up with the passen-

ger-side door of the car facing the front steps of the building. Louise jumped out of the vehicle, dug into her purse
and handed the man some money, then swiftly ran up the
short steps where she stepped around a group of smoking
teenagers, and entered the building.

Once inside, Louise followed the scrap-paper signs which
directed visitors to the meeting hall. She could hear a voice
speaking over a PA system. She made her way through some
doors which led her to the gymnasium meeting hall.

As she entered the hall, she stepped to the side of the
doorway to orient herself. She didn't know the topic of the
meeting, and felt that perhaps she was in the wrong place
and wasting valuable time.

Looking around the Inuit crowd of around three-hun-
dred, she tried to spot Gaar. He would likely have been
sitting at a table adjacent to the head table, where several
serious looking Inuit men both elderly and middle-aged
presided over the meeting. Gaar was nowhere to be seen.

The chair of the meeting was George Tookaluktassie, the
bright and humorous elder who attended Roblaw's emissaries three days prior. George spoke earnestly into his
microphone, addressing the 3R presence in the Republic,
and the physical and aesthetic effects that were part and
parcel of the foreign influence.

Louise had the feeling someone was staring at her, and
looked to her left. On the far side of the doors against a wall,
she saw three men who stared at her with unpolite curiosity.
The three gawking men were Triq, Agaluq and Kiratek. The
trio suddenly abandoned their interest in Louise and huddled themselves, hotly discussing something on their own
agenda, oblivious to the cultural and environmental dissertation being given by George.

Louise nervously scoured the meeting hall for the
Canadian envoy which the customs officer had mentioned
would be at the meeting.

Moving up along the perimeter of the hall, she spotted a WASP looking man sitting off to the side of the officiating table. Discreetly approaching the man, she slowly and unobtrusively tapped him on the arm and got his attention.

'Excuse me, please,' Louise said, crouching at his side and whispering under the projected voice of George. 'Can you help me? I'm trying to locate my husband who's a lawyer for Roblaw Inc. His name is Gaar Injugarjuk—is he here?'

The man suddenly became very interested having recognized the names she mentioned. 'My name is Barker—Canadian trade ambassador,' he whispered back and shook her hand, 'I'm waiting for our foreign affairs representative to arrive—with Gaar, I hope. Neither are here, and I'm getting a bit worried ...'

'Yes, but do you know where my husband *is*?' she interjected with grave concern.

'I heard earlier that your husband was with another Roblaw employee who went off into the tundra trying to locate an alleged fugitive, to provide testimony in this meeting.'

'What?!' she replied, confused about the affair which was news to her.

'You know about the Kabloona disaster—don't you?'

'No, I don't know anything of the sort,' she said with a frustrated groan, 'please! I just want to find Gaar!'

'I was told by Oliver Tunningham—who I'm waiting for, that your husband left early yesterday morning to assist tracking ... the *witness*,' he said, recognizing that Louise appeared unstable and prone to hysterics. He wouldn't dare mention that the witness was an alleged murderer. 'He should be arriving with the man I'm waiting on ... and—'

'And?!' she begged, teeming with mixed emotions.

' ... and there's been no news.'

George finished addressing the public assembly. In the lull, Barker decided to officially petition for a postponement of the tribunal and any discussions on the future of 3R, or at the very least, to request a recess before launching into the official business. Barker looked at Louise next to him as he stood up from his seat.

'Excuse me for a moment, please,' he said, making his way to the council table for a confidential word with the committee. Louise stood up and followed him to the edge of the table. George covered his microphone and raised his head at the swift approach of Barker.

Through the doors of the hall came Girly, Abram and Aaron. A few heads turned at their arrival, but most notably, Jag's group. Girly looked at the men with contempt for the vandalism of the snowmobiles which they were undoubtedly responsible for. Triq and his men played coy. They made their way to the exit doors. The trio boldly brushed against the new arrivals and left the meeting to wait outside for Jag who would certainly arrive with the carcass of the fugitive. The doors swung closed and the group urgently made their way up the center aisle toward the officiating table. Occasional faces in the chattering audience turned in their direction, being absorbed with the building suspense of the interruptions which were stalling the meeting.

At the officiating table, Barker was filling the heads of the presiding elders with bureaucratic hogwash.

'So, are you, or are you not prepared to defend the Canadian government's position on the 3R affair?' George asked Barker. Simon, Matthew and the other elders leaned toward the Canadian official for his reply.

'Again, I am *not* prepared! Envoy Tunningham is *absent*, as well as our legal council, Gaar Injugarjuk,' Barker replied with frustration.

The panel of elders leaned back in their chairs and shared a few confidential words. George returned back to reply to Barker.

'I have no choice but to proceed in their absence,' he said, as he looked at Louise who seemed lost, 'Madam? Are you with the contingent?'

'I'm Gaar Injugarjuk's wife. Philip Roblaw is my father,' she replied. Barker was caught by surprise, having not gotten her name.

'Are you prepared to defend your father's stake in this affair?' George plainly asked of Louise.

'I wouldn't waste my breath defending his interests,' she stated. Barker nudged her, disapproving of her stark animosity, given this was a *business* matter.

George and the other elders shared an enlightening glance. Returning his attention to her and studying her face, George nodded in reflection. 'Words to consider, coming from his own flesh and blood.'

Barker couldn't believe his ears, and darted his head between the two. He put his hand on the table and leaned toward George. 'May we *please* have a postponement until a later date, when we *will* be prepared to defend our stake?' he pleaded.

'Sir,' George said, 'this tribunal has been arranged at great lengths to gather *all* affected parties. The *least* your people could do, is *show up*! There will be no postponement. Part of your delegation?' George asked, as Girly, Aaron and Abram arrived at the table. George suddenly realized that his old friend Abram was among the group. '*Hello Abram*. Is Gaar with you?'

'Hello,' Abram said with a warm smile and a handshake over the table, 'I'm afraid he is not,' he replied with a wafer thin voice and a shake of his head. He lifted his hand indicating his entourage. 'This is Girly, and Aaron. Maxwell, the alleged fugitive, is *dead*, as well as Tunningham. Nature can be harsh and cruel.'

'Where is Gaar?!' Louise pleaded.

'Are you ... Gaar's wife?' Girly asked.

'Yes, I'm carrying his child!' she replied defensively, then turned aggressive in the face of all the strangers, 'where ... is ... Gaar?!' she demanded.

'I am Gaar's father,' Abram said gently, outstretching his hand, and receiving a polite but anxious handshake from her. 'Please be calm, Gaar will be here soon. He's been injured, I'm afraid—'

'WHAT?!' Louise shrieked, as Girly touched her arm in a comforting gesture. A dramatic breath was drawn by the assembly behind them who were now very curious about the goings-on at the presiding table. Louise lifted her trembling hands to her face and immediately sank her expression into her cupped palms.

'What do you mean, Tunningham is dead?' Barker asked with disbelief.

'What part of *dead*, confuses you,' Girly replied to the bureaucrat, 'I'll draw you a map and you can arrange to collect his ... body—and by the way, *he's* responsible for shooting Gaar. He was on the *take*.'

'*Shot*,' Louïse sobbed, and collapsed into Girly's arms.

Aaron lowered his head in sympathy, then looked out at the assembly and felt very self-conscious, as though he were in a theater play without any lines and without any direction with the audience staring up at the performance. How he wished Gaar were there to bring the curtain down. He turned his head back into the thick of it.

'Gaar is strong, though,' Girly said to Louise, then looked up at the elders. 'He wandered off into the tundra with his familiars—'

'*What*?!' Louise blurted, 'what's all this gibberish?!'

'They assisted him in battle with the illegitimate one— Najagneq,' Girly stated to the council.

'Najagneq is a shaman of *merit*,' Simon said, looking to the other elders for confirmation.

'If there is redeeming merit for him *in death*,' Girly scoffed, '—the spirits have taken him back into the night. He was the *black wolf*! Responsible for many wicked deeds, no matter what his intention.'

'*It*, is so,' Abram reaffirmed.

'I witnessed it with my own eyes!' Aaron said, glad to finally be involved with the significant details brought before the council.

'These details will be corroborated by Gaar?' Matthew the elder, enquired.

'Yes,' replied Abram. 'He will not come to serve the interests of Roblaw, but only to tell you the story as it has unfolded. The *truth* will be laid bare for all to see. Gaar is a venerable shaman, and will appear before us in honour, having rid us of the disgrace.'

'Very well, Abram,' George said with a nod to the man, 'would you please put your account on paper with Kiloonik in your presence?' he continued, looking along the table and indicating Kiloonik the elder, 'All three of you sign the sworn affidavit for our records, please.'

Barker shook his head and angrily stormed back to his seat. Louise put her trembling hand across her mouth, and her eyes welled up with tears. Abram, Aaron and Girly— who took Louise by the arm, all moved away from the council table and sat down off to the side. The high council turned in their chairs and engaged in conversation off-microphone. After a few moments, the elders resumed their positions at the table and George Tookaluktassie leaned forward into his microphone to address the assembly.

'Since there is no one prepared to defend the Canadian position in its application for renewal of the 3R program, it is certain that in light of the sadly unfortunate events at Kabloona, that this issue will be closed and renewal of the bilateral treaty will be forfeited,' George announced, scanning the hall, as a dull murmur swept through the room. 'We will take discussions on the situation, as a matter of course, keeping in mind that this is not a case for a referendum or a public vote, but is of the opinion of the council, comprised of regional council heads, who reflect a unanimous consensus. This forms the basis of our official decision on the matter. In other words, *it's toast*, my friends.'

Simon leaned over to George and whispered something to him. George nodded and leaned into his microphone.

'Now, we shall take a fifteen-minute break for coffee and some lovely baked goods compliments of the Nanisivik Women's Collective. It's all out in the hall, and so are the washrooms. We will reconvene in fifteen minutes,' George deemed, then slammed down his gavel to make it official.

A young man suddenly burst through the main doors and dashed halfway up the center aisle. 'The miners have been freed! The miners have been *freed*!!' he yelled out, spinning in a circle and shaking his hands above his head.

A modest round of applause and a few whistles acknowledged the news, amidst the mass exodus for the coffee and snacks. Conversation became heavy in the air.

Up near the council table, Louise leapt up and frantically waved her arms and stamped her feet. 'Will someone help me find Gaar?! Please?! *Help me*—!'

Girly rushed to Louise's side and clasped her in a hug. 'Let's get her outside for some air—fast,' she suggested, escorting Louise along the wall.

Outside the community center, Gaar, in his human form, staggered up toward the front steps in a mortally wounded state. His throat and neck were darkened with the dried blood of the lethal bites which Jag had inflicted. This, coupled with the mid-section gunshot wound, were the two strokes which had all but finished him off.

He weakly climbed the steps, eager for medical attention and the comforts of justice, both of which were likely available inside amongst the assembly.

Jag's cronies, looming at the top of the steps, recognized Gaar and immediately moved down to greet him.

Intercepting Gaar on the steps, Triq blocked his passage, as Kiratek and Agaluq pryed his hands from the railing.

'Jag would like to have a few words with you ... if you don't mind waiting,' Triq said scornfully.

'Jag ... is dead,' Gaar replied in a gruff whisper, 'divine intervention,' he added, all the while being held by his arms by the other two men, and wavering on his feet.

Triq automatically hit Gaar in the stomach, causing him to fall backwards down the steps, as the others released their support of him after Triq's blow.

'What nonsense—*traitor*!' Triq hissed, jumping from the steps and kicking Gaar in the gut as he lay on the icy ground. 'To even *breathe* such conspiracy against the hope of our people!' Triq yelled with a scowl, launching another stiff kick into Gaar, this time at his head, 'you goddamn *half-breed*, no-good boot-licking lawyer!' he bellowed, denouncing Gaar and putting the boots to him now, with frenzied kicks.

Agaluq and Kiratek began to mercilessly jab at Gaar with the butts of their rifles. 'This'll warm you up for Jag!' Kiratek wailed.

Agaluq, seeing Gaar had had enough, quit hitting him, and put his arm up to Kiratek to stop his thrusts.

From within the community center, a woman emerged with a cigarette in her hand. She looked on with abhorrence as Triq continued with the unrelenting blows to Gaar. Agaluq and Kiratek took Gaar by the arms and legs and lifted him away from Triq. They began to cart Gaar off towards the parking lot to avoid prying eyes.

The woman let out such a tremendous scream that the men tripped up and dropped Gaar on the spot. Fear gripped Triq like a snapped rat-trap. He was caught with his pants down as more people streamed out of the doors for cigarettes, all of them getting caught up with the commotion and the woman's incessant screams.

Girly, Louise, Abram and Aaron slipped out en masse, and were affronted with the uproar which was taking place below, near the parking lot.

Triq and his comrades began to skulk away into the shadows, leaving Gaar writhing on the frosted ground.

Louise's eyes and mouth popped open in painful recognition as Gaar turned in an agonizing curl towards the doors. '*Gaar*!?—GAAR!' she choked out as she bounded down the steps and dashed over to him, falling to her knees at his side, overcome with anxious tears seeing her love grasping for precious life.

Cradling his bloodied head, she wept as he whispered loving words into her ear. She mumbled to him and he reached out and touched her tummy, as Aaron and several men ran into the background to apprehend the culprits whom had already started their snowmobiles in an attempt to flee.

A crowd began forming around Gaar and Louise as they hugged on the icy ground. Little heed was passed as Triq and his men were roughly escorted by the scruffs of their necks towards the community centre.

The crowd spread back quickly with a rush of fear, as Louise fainted. There in her lap lay the polar bear's head, its immense war-torn body stretched out beside her, and with one last heave—silence.

Girly approached Louise's limp body, as the crowd looked on with awe. She knelt and lifted Louise's head into her bosom and looked down lovingly at the magnificent head in Louise's lap, the bear's deep dark eyes reflecting the triumph of the quest—but sad, in its expired and extinguished feat.

Tears flooded Girly's eyes as the reality sunk in. The heroic wounds bore witness to the struggle. Its thick pink tongue hung lifelessly over his bloodied and noble fangs.

Girly felt Abram's comforting hand touch her shoulder.

forty-nine

'WHAT DO YOU MEAN you *left* the meeting?!' Roblaw roared into the receiver of the phone in his home office, 'I don't care if Tunningham didn't show up! You're paid to look out for my interests—you asshole! Where was McGregor?! ... There was another idiot there ... "Barker"—did he get a postponement?'

Roblaw stewed as Mac Tighearnain, Roblaw's "secret witness", explained the goings-on at the tribunal, giving him a blow-by-blow account of the meeting.

'Listen, what the *fuck* am I paying you big bucks for? I'm going to charter an executive jet for Nanisivik, and I'll see you at seven AM, sharp! Meet me at the airport. I'm not going to take this incompetent bullshit!' he screamed, slamming down the receiver.

In a fit of rage, he swept the telephone off the desk and into a wall where it crashed and fell down beside the desk.

Roblaw heard a peculiar noise, somewhat like a deep growl. Knowing he was alone in the house, he pulled open a drawer in his desk and withdrew a loaded pistol. He turned off the desk lamp and slowly reached over and flicked off the fish-tank light. He idled in the shadows with only residual light streaming vaguely in from the hallway. Roblaw stood perfectly still and quiet, to listen for movement. The fish-tank bubbled away in the darkness.

He looked cautiously around his large shadowed office, gripping the pistol nervously. Slipping some documents into his open briefcase, he closed the lid and snapped it locked. The growling noise came again, and seemed very close.

'Who's there?! I've got a gun and I'll use it!!' he shouted.

Perturbed by the presence of an intruder who somehow got in without setting off his security alarm, he clenched his jaw. Angry with himself for trashing his desk phone, he grabbed his briefcase and cautiously stepped across the polar bear rug towards the door. He paused, hearing the gurgling throaty growl, which seemed to emanate from somewhere between him and the door. He saw nothing in his shadowed path.

'Whoever you are—*you're dead*!' he threatened, firing a shot into the far wall as a dire warning to whoever was stalking him.

Feeling a false sense of security, having used the firearm, he edged toward the door of his home office. In a bitter suddenness, he dropped his briefcase in a panic-stricken state, shrieking deliriously in pain and disbelief.

Something bone-crushing clamped around his left ankle. In erratic terror, he aimlessly fired shots at his ghostly assailant—hitting himself one time in the foot as he aimed for the bear's head.

Across the street from Roblaw's mansion, a woman pulled off the road and drove her car up onto a short private driveway which stopped-short at a closed ornate gate. The woman got out of her Mercedes and pushed a button to speak into a two-way intercom connected to a monstrous mansion, hidden from the street by a perimeter of tightly packed trees and a high concrete fence.

Hearing what she thought were gunshots, she looked across the street at the Roblaw mansion, and witnessed the fiery flashes of the gun, suddenly illuminating the silhouette of Roblaw as he staggered past a window.

The woman leapt into her car and punched 911 into her cell-phone.

Roblaw tore himself free of the bloodied jaws, only to slip on his own blood. He crashed to the floor.

As he opened his eyes, he was mortified to find the bear's head breathing into his face. With a swift lunge, the bear's fangs bit into his neck. Realizing the pistol was still in his grasp, he plunged it into the side of the bear's head and desperately pulled the trigger several times. The chambers were empty. He beat the bear's head with the pistol, but to no avail. A gurgling, throaty growl deafened him.

He glared vengefully into the eyes of the bear and he saw Gaar.

The last thing he heard was the snap of his own neck.

A sudden influx of police cruisers and a SWAT van pulled up onto the Roblaw mansion driveway. Like a well-oiled machine, the task force streamed out of the back of the van and swarmed around the house with assault rifles firmly grasped and ready for action. The police held back a few curious neighbours at the street, and as an ambulance pulled up to join the contingent, some detectives and the SWAT commander, sought out the 911 caller. The woman stepped forward and a huddle ensued.

Finding all the exterior doors and windows secured, a SWAT sergeant cloaked with bullet proof body armour, emerged stealthily from the side of the mansion and conferred with some sharpshooters and detectives at the driveway perimeter.

In the flurry of the flashing cruiser lights, the area was cordoned off by uniformed police who taped-off the area. Taking cover behind the SWAT van, the commander lifted a mobile telephone and dialed a number provided by a neighbour who was eager to assist.

Inside the mansion, telephones rang in every corner of the house. The main marbled foyer, reverberated with the extended ringing, which went on for a couple of minutes. As abruptly as it began, the ringing went dead. Before the house had absorbed the final ring, the front door was broken down. The security alarm screamed out.

Prowling carefully through the front door, came the SWAT team, with their rifles up and ready for a confrontation. They slowly scoured the main floor, leading with extension mirrors to peer safely around corners.

Cautiously entering Roblaw's office, the SWAT team came upon the crime scene. Using walkie-talkies they relayed their find, and within a few minutes, the force had secured the mansion.

As a thorough search continued around the interior and exterior of the mansion, two detectives in overcoats, stepped into Roblaw's office and began to root around, careful not to disturb the scene. The remaining SWAT team members stepped out of the room, and began to chatter in low hushed tones as they walked through the marbled foyer. Someone finally silenced the alarm.

A police photographer and finger print expert entered the office and began their duties. The two detectives approached

Roblaw's body and stooped over the obscure situation, with the bloodied fangs of the bear rug still buried in the man's neck.

'Y'know,' the shorter of the two detectives said to the other, 'I hate to state the obvious, but this man appears to have been mauled by *a bear rug*.'

'I can feel the ulcer already,' the taller one replied, feeling his stomach, '... and look,' he said, pointing with his pencil, 'he was shooting the damn thing! *This* is too weird.'

'Why, whatever do you mean?' his counterpart replied sarcastically, as the two stood back and allowed the photographer to take shots of the body. 'Too bad the fish can't talk. Let's flip a coin. Loser's gotta write this one up and have lovely detailed chats with our forensic chums.'

'*And* face the press with a straight face?—Let this not be a homicide ... let this not be a homicide,' the tall detective chanted looking up to the ceiling.

The short pudgy detective drew a coin from his pocket. 'Heads or tails?'

The taller detective took a deep breath. 'Tails—definitely tails.'

fifty

ON AN ARCTIC summer meadow, a cute little boy of four, kicked a ball around with Abram, his grandfather. With a swift eager kick, the kid sent the ball flying through the bright blue sky. The ball descended and the boy covered his mouth with both hands. The ball landed almost in the lap of his mother who sat nearby on a blanket chatting with Girly and his grandmother. As the ball bounced off into the blossomed tundra, the ladies turned with surprise and burst out laughing seeing the worried antics of the child.

Relieved, and exploding with gleeful fun, little David chased off with his grandfather to race for the rolling ball. Reaching the ball at the same time, David, who very much resembled Gaar, wrestled playfully with his grandfather. They both ended up rolling around the blossoms with great frolic. The little fellow climbed on top of Abram's chest and was delightfully amused as Abram, laying with his back on the ground, lifted him into the air and suspended him there.

As Abram smiled upwards at David, he saw a peregrine

falcon hovering high overhead. With a proud screech from the bird circling in the sky, Abram lowered the boy and pointed up at the spectacular sight. David looked up with wonder. Abram propped himself up on his elbows. It was time for a story.